THIS edition, issued in 1954, is
for members of The Companion
Book Club, 8 Long Acre, London,
W.C.2, from which address particulars of membership may be
obtained. The book is published by
arrangement with the original
publishers, Victor Gollancz Ltd.

THE HOUSE OF MOREYS

"A blessed companion is a book"—JERROLD

THE HOUSE
OF MOREYS

*

PHYLLIS BENTLEY

THE COMPANION BOOK CLUB
LONDON

CONTENTS

BOOK ONE: WALTER

CHAPTER I

MY CHILDREN have often asked me to write down for them some account of the strange events, the twists and turns of fate, which shadowed the house of Moreys for so many years, and how it happened that my coming to Moreydale was the beginning of the withdrawal of that shadow. Now that my darling husband is gone, Catharine married, Richard (for I look on him as a son) grown into a noted physician and Edward become one of the principal factory masters of Yorkshire, my children do not need me as they used; time hangs heavy on my hands, and I may well employ it in making this record. Besides, it may lighten my heart, which is so heavy, continually sojourning in the grave with my husband, if I am often writing his name and telling of his wilful generous charm, which brought such great sorrows upon him, yet at length much happiness.

At first I found it hard to know where to begin.

"At the beginning, Mother!" cries Catharine quickly with her ringing laugh, her dark blue eyes—so like my husband's my heart turns over to see them—dancing and sparkling.

"But then, where is the beginning?" says Edward in his quiet courteous tones. "The beginning for Mother was when she first came to Moreydale. She can only tell what happened before, as it was told to her."

"It will be dull told like that," cries Catharine, pouting.

"I do not agree. There will be suspense and mystery. Besides, it will be truthful," says Edward. "She was not alive when those old things happened; she cannot pretend to have witnessed them."

"Edward, you are a dull old stick. You should have been the girl and I the boy."

"What would your husband say to that, my dear?"

7

At this Catharine laughs, blushes, tosses her fair head and runs from the room. She is a wild young thing, and I sometimes wonder, with anxious yearning love, what the future will hold for her. God grant no new shadow clouds her life! Her sweet merry face and restless slender body, her gay laughter and swift imperious frowns, her quick impulses, always acted on hastily and with all her strength whether for good or ill, are very dear to me—and to her brothers, though I can see that Richard is sometimes vexed and perplexed by her wild ways, so much less serious than his own. But he forgives her, as I can also clearly see, for her likeness to someone he loved well. It is true that she strongly resembles her father both in looks and disposition, while Edward's quieter and steadier—though I think no less resolute—nature is more like my own.

I will take Edward's advice, in any case, for it agrees with my own feeling; I can only tell the Moreys story as its strange mystery unfolded itself to my view.

CHAPTER II

IN THE February of 1809, then, in the twentieth year of my age, I journeyed north from London to Annotsfield in Yorkshire. I guess that I looked a sad little figure enough, for I had just buried my dearly loved father—my mother I lost before I was a year old, from fever, so I was now alone in the world.

My father, Walter Moreys by name, had left me under circumstances the most wretched, for he died a debtor in that prison called the Fleet. Looked at from one aspect, our whole life together was indeed one long struggle against adversity, but from another point of view we were singularly happy together. My father was a man who loved learning, and a true gentleman, kind and considerate to all around unless some would-be book-buyer cast scorn on one of his literary champions, when he flew into a rage. In his early days, when working for the London bookseller whose youngest daughter he presently married and whose business he later carried on, he had had the honour of meeting Miss Fanny Burney, the famous author of *Evelina,* and her father, Dr. Burney the music-master, who took a kindly interest in the country lad. He knew Mr. Boswell too, and Davy Garrick the actor, and poor Noll Goldsmith; nay, my father had once sold a book to the great Dr. Johnson himself! Now that these great men, Dr. Johnson and his friends, were dead or parted, my father often shook his head mournfully over the decay in literature. My father had married late in life a woman very much younger than himself; he was forty when I was born, and had but little notion of bringing up a child, talking to me as if I was a grown woman as soon almost as I could speak, and teaching me to read when I was barely four years old. I loved him dearly and strove my best to please him and was proud when he stroked my head and told me I could write as well as the great Miss Burney herself. At night when some of his book-loving friends came in to smoke a pipe with him and talk of books he was very happy; and crouched in a corner by his knee, on a little worn footstool which was mine by custom, I was very happy too.

In person my father was tall and stooped and dark. The Moreys, he used to tell me, were all tall, dark, burly men; but he himself was always thin and harassed looking, for he was a man of one great grief. I will not call it a grievance, for he was not so petty-minded as to pity himself; it was rather a kind of sad astonishment, a perplexed and sorrowing wonder that human beings should so ill-treat each other. He was nearly always pressed for money, for he was so soft-hearted he could not pass a beggar without a gift, and any scholar or poet had only to come to him with a tale of ill luck for him to defer the payment of their account, or even, what was worse, buy the tattered, dreary quartos from their shelves for a few shillings so they could get bread. But this was not his sorrow, for until the last few terrible years of his life this lack of money did not greatly trouble him; and I of course admired him in everything he did and thought it right; we laughed over our little difficulties and economies together. But all his life through, suddenly at times a cloud would come over his face, his forehead would twist into a frown, his eyes take on a look of questioning anguish, and he would tell me yet once again how his half-brother, John Moreys, had thrown him out of Moreydale.

It was a strange story, puzzling and unexplainable because so sudden and causeless. For one morning when Walter was in his sixteenth year, as he lay peacefully asleep in bed one of John's serving-men came to him and shook his shoulder to wake him, then in a frightened whisper, with his eyes very wide, said:

"Master says take this and be gone."

At the same time he put into Walter's hand a bag which later proved to hold twenty pounds in gold. Walter, astonished, half asleep and not believing his ears, stammered what and why, and when the man repeated the command, thinking a jest was being put on him, threw back the bedclothes and made to see his brother. But the old man, with a look of fear, held him back and implored him not to seek the master but to leave the house at once or the consequences might be dreadful. Walter was only a lad after all and subject to his brother's authority, and being but half awake and quite disconcerted, before he had gathered his wits he found himself dressed and out of the house, Wool Royd as it was called, and the serving-man—or perhaps it was a journeyman weaver; yes, I think that was the old man's employment—was urging him over the bridge and up the lane and out of Moreydale. The bag of money swinging in Walter's hand as he walked crackled as if there were a paper within, so Walter untied it and looked in and sure enough a piece of paper was there on which was scrawled *Walter go and do not return if you value your life John Moreys.*

Utterly dumbfounded, Walter belaboured the man with questions, but he knew nothing of the matter save John Moreys' furious orders and could answer none of them; so at an uneven pace—Walter sometimes hurrying on in a rage to get away from his tyrannous brother and sometimes standing still with the idiocy of the thing—the two at length came to the town of Annotsfield. Here the old man, evidently obeying his master's instructions, urged Walter to take a coach to London, skilfully exciting him about the fine sights it was said could be seen there. And so my father found himself a lad alone in London, without family or friends or provision except the twenty pounds, which, though a good sum, if I know my father's easy, generous habit, would not long be left in his pocket.

When he came to his senses a little he wrote letters to his brother, and indeed for many years he wrote home to Yorkshire every Christmas, but never received any reply save once some eight years after he left, when he had a note in a strange hand informing him that a son, Charles, had been born to John Moreys and his wife Caroline. My father, as his nature was, hoped some reconciliation was intended when he saw this, but his master (my grandfather later) was wiser and told him it was meant to show him John Moreys had an heir and there would be no inheritance for Walter from Moreydale. Walter had never thought of any inheritance coming to him from Moreydale, so this did not trouble him; moreover by this time, after some earlier hardships and struggles, he was happy in London, enjoying the books and the talk and the bustle of the great metropolis, and did not wish to return to Yorkshire; even his wish for a reconciliation with his brother grew fainter with the years. But what he passionately desired to the last moment of his life was an explanation of his banishment. Why had his brother turned so suddenly, so inexplicably, against him?

"Why? Why, Eleanor?" he said, pacing the room, his hands beneath his coat tails, his fine Roman head thrust forward. "What wrong had I done him? None! Eleanor, I swear to you, none! I was a lad of sixteen, and he was already married—to a most beautiful and gentle wife. Our father and mother were dead and the house was his, but we had always been good friends. I was apprenticed to him and learning the cloth trade; he taught me carefully and well."

Here my father would sometimes break off and explain to me the mysteries of this strange uncouth trade, as it seemed to me then, carried on in the dark wild Yorkshire hills. As I grew older I learned to lead him on in talk about this trade so as to keep him as long as possible away from thoughts of his brother John. He told me how they prepared the wool—I did not then understand the words he used as I do now—and spun it and wove it and carried the cloth

11

down the long folding hills to market in Annotsfield; how cloth had been shown there on the walls of the churchyard for many hundred years, but in that year when he was sixteen—and alas, here we were back at the old trouble again —a fine building was erected, a Cloth Hall, in which the cloth could be more comfortably marketed. There was to be a procession for the opening of the Hall, with speeches and fireworks, and boy-like the young Walter wished very much to see all this fun. The other apprentices and journey-men weavers employed by his brother, with the maidservants about the house, were all going down to the town, and as John Moreys had taken a stall in the new building, Walter assumed his brother and he would likewise attend the cere-mony. But then there came talk of who should stay in the house with Caroline, John Moreys' ailing wife. The poor woman had twice had miscarriages and had now lain upstairs abed for several months. She was a very sweet, kind, mild woman, said my father; in education above John, being a surgeon of Annotsfield's daughter; gentle in manner and quiet of speech, and very fair of hair and complexion. She was always good to her husband's young half-brother, not rebuking him overmuch when he tore his clothes or came late to meals, and seeing that he had that plenty of meat which means so much to a lad while he is growing. When therefore this question arose of who should stay with Caroline and it seemed to Walter that it was canvassed some-what too peevishly, as if she were a drag on the amusements of the others, he was very sorry, for he feared that her feelings, which were always very tender and delicate, would be hurt.

"I shall stay at home with my wife," said John Moreys shortly, a scowl on his dark face.

"There's no need," said one of the maids who stood by. "I can stay with the mistress."

She did not sound as if she wished to stay, and Walter, sorry for his sister-in-law, with his usual impetuous generosity cried out quickly that he would stay with Lina, so both his brother and the maid could go to Annotsfield.

"You daft young devil!" shouted his brother. "You'll do as you're told. Be off!"

Walter of course did not like being called a daft young

devil. But the Moreys were all somewhat given to such out-
bursts of temper, being full-blooded self-willed men, and
Walter was used to sharp words now and again from his
brother, if he were caught reading at the loom, instead of
weaving, and the like; so he just skipped out of his brother's
sight and presently went off down to Annotsfield and enjoyed
the events of the day there, without troubling himself too
much about John's anger. Staying to see the fireworks, he
walked the long lanes up to Moreydale in the dark, and
getting home very late thought himself wiser to creep off to
bed at once without seeking out his brother. Then the next
morning came the old journeyman with the money, and
Walter found himself homeless.

"Somehow I must have vexed him beyond bearing," said
my father to me. "But why? Why, Eleanor? Over such a
trivial matter? Could he really cast his brother away for
such a trifling disagreement? Again, I was only trying to
secure his pleasure. If only I could remember exactly what
I said to him! But even so—why? Why, Eleanor?"

I could only sigh and shake my head; I could not find the
answers. But two thoughts grew up in my mind. One was that
for some reason my father's kindness, too good and simple for
the harsh world, had lost him his home, and this was like my
father and would happen to him again often; and the second
thought was an angry dislike, a hot contempt, for those bar-
barous, rough, cruel, ignorant, hateful men, John Moreys
and all other such men in the cloth trade up in Yorkshire,
who did not admire and understand my father.

In the last few years of my father's life, when our troubles
pressed more and more heavily upon us, these thoughts grew
ever stronger in my mind. Somehow my father became debtor
for some money he had promised for a friend, on the one
hand, and on the other, he was in some way—for I do not
pretend to understand the matter wholly—responsible to my
mother's family for some moneys of theirs they said he had
had from the shop of my grandfather. (This I do know, that
whoever cheated, it was not my father.) Then our store of
books had become cluttered with old learned quartos which
people would not buy, and because of these other troubles
about money my father was not able to print fresh books for

sale. At last the shop and the books had to be sold and we lived for a little while in a garret lodging on what small moneys they brought, but my mother's relations—nieces and nephews chiefly—were even then not satisfied and sent my father to the Fleet in the end for what he owed them. During this time he dwelt more and more on Moreydale and Wool Royd and John Moreys and his wife Lina. His poor face grew thin and wild, his hair very white and scanty, his eyes seemed to start out of his head like a hare's, as he paced anxiously up and down, in our garret at first and afterwards in his wretched lodgings in the Fleet, talking, talking, talking about Moreydale and his brother. Why, Eleanor? Why, why? Did he resent my argument against his commands? Did he think it disobedience? Did he think my offering to stay at home made his thought of leaving Lina seem careless and selfish? Why? Why? Eleanor, why?

For my own part, I wondered whether perhaps, long ago in their childhood, some preference of their father's for Walter above John had sown the seed of anger and jealousy in John Moreys' heart. Such things have been known to happen between sons of different mothers, and surely Walter must have been a child far more lovable than John. But when I questioned my father, he could remember no such happening. Besides, John had been a good and loving brother to him until that fatal morning.

As the weeks went by and my father still stayed in the Fleet, with no hope of coming thence, I began to see that he was ill and growing weaker, and that this old mystery was preying on his mind. His hand in mine—for I went into the prison to him every morning—was now always hot and parched and quivering, the blood leaping beneath the dried skin as he harped continually on Moreydale. So at last I urged him to write plainly to his brother and demand an explanation of the old quarrel. After so many years, surely no rancour, no venom, could be left in his brother's mind against him. He seized on this suggestion with great eagerness, but when I brought pen and ink and paper, ready to write, as I had often done, to his dictation, he put me off with too many excuses, and I saw he wished to write the letter himself privately. Next day he was copying it, but still did not show it me, and the day after he had despatched it by the hands of the turnkey.

By the time, two weeks later, a reply came, my father's health was very much worse. He lay in bed always, and for several days had eaten nothing. He was much respected in the prison, and many kind services were performed for him and for me by the other prisoners. Even the turnkey—a sour, brutal fellow enough—seemed pleased to be able to bring him this long-looked-for Yorkshire letter.

"Read it, read it, Eleanor!" cried my father, his cheek flushed, his eyes glittering.

I took it in my hand and just for a moment my young hopes soared and bright visions smiled on me. Perhaps my father and my uncle could be reconciled, perhaps the letter had a warm, friendy tone! Perhaps it would announce my uncle's coming, and soon he would be here, would pay the debt and rescue us and set us up in some pretty little cottage and my father would get well again and we should all be happy together. So my hand trembled as I unfolded the letter. It was written in a neat, firm, workmanlike hand, very clear to read through with a few spelling mistakes, and the very firmness and neatness of the writing seemed to make the words harder and more hurtful, for indeed it appeared to me then of all letters I ever read the most unkind and ungracious. I have always kept it, and copy it here.

Wool Royd, 25th January 1809.

Sir,

I have yours of the 10th instant it as been delivered to me as my father Mr. John Moreys died fifteen years ago. My mother you send your respects to died when I was born. I ave no knowledge of the matter you mention. Had always understood from my father you ran away to sea. Good riddance he said you would never have made a clothier. Am sorry to learn one of my name is in prison for debt it is bad for my credit if you will let me ave a note of the sum I may help you but make no promiss if you are ill unlikely recover seems useless to throw good money after bad as we say here. Trade is bad here because of the war and will never be right till we beat the French soundly. My father built a big fulling mill by the Morey beck and I ave made it bigger but happen you have forgot what fulling is. As regards your daughter Eleanor she is my cousin I suppose. We are so many in this household now one more will make little difference if she wishes to come to Wool Royd after your death she may but happen you are mistaken and will live long. Let her take the CLOTHIER coach to Leeds and the HIGH FLYER thence to Annotsfield and one of my nephews will meet her at George Inn there. Tell her to lay the account of the coaches to me I will speak them about it next market day.

I am Sir

CHARLES MOREYS

Everything in this letter seemed to stab at my heart. It was clear from it that my father knew he was dying and had said so in his letter. Then the mercenary selfishness of grieving for our trouble only because it damaged this Charles Moreys' credit, and the cruelty of telling my father on his deathbed that his brother was glad to be rid of him! To think of losing my dear father soon, as evidently Cousin Charles expected, and of going to live with such rough, unfeeling, unmannerly people as the Yorkshire Moreys now proved themselves to be, for the letter confirmed all my previous ill views of them —to think of such wretchedness was suddenly more than I could bear, and I found myself sobbing with all my heart.

"Nay, Eleanor, nay!" said my father tenderly, stretching out his trembling hands to draw my head down to his shoulder. "Nay, child! It's no use to weep. What does my brother say?"

To my astonishment, when he read the letter, though he exclaimed mournfully over his brother's death with their quarrel unexplained, he took the rest of it without hurt and even smiled over some portions.

"The husk of the Yorkshire folk is rough but the kernel is sweet," he said. "Your cousin conceals his real kindness by a jesting manner."

"I see no jest," I cried, still choked with angry tears.

"You must learn to like the Yorkshire folk, Eleanor," said

16

my father very soberly: "for you must go to Moreydale."

"No! No!"

"Yes, my dear. There is no one here to care for you."

"You, Father," I wept, clinging about him.

"I shall not long be here, my dear little Eleanor," said my poor father. "When I am gone, you must go home, go to Moreydale."

I tried to believe that it was all nothing and soon he would be well again, but as I leaned against him I could feel his poor heart racing and pausing and guessed that life could not long continue on such terms. Sure enough by the next afternoon the fever had heightened so that he did not know me, but threw his arms about wildly and spoke of rocks and bracken and heather and told me to be quiet so that he might hear the larks singing and the stream tumbling below; he held his face up as though to feel the wind on his cheek, and smiled so sweetly that it almost broke my heart. At dusk—for I obtained permission to stay with him—he fell suddenly into a doze, with his eyes closed, breathing raucously, and continued in that way all through the long night. In the morning just when the light came his breathing quietened, so that for a moment I thought he was better and my hopes rose; but then I heard each breath he drew come fainter and fainter, and suddenly his dear hand in mine, always before so loving, warm and sentient, changed in my grasp to a mere lump of unfeeling flesh, and he sighed once long and fluttering, and was gone.

In story-books there is always a break at such dreadful moments, but in life there is no break and one must live through them. But in life, too, there is kindness from others to help these moments pass, and one of the other prisoners having heard me weeping, he summoned the turnkey, who brought a woman to me and in his surly way did me many services. Indeed I had more help and comfort from the prisoners and turnkeys than from my kinsfolk, and I shall never forget how I cried out in a great storm of anger against my mother's eldest nephew (a mean-looking middle-aged man with a thin line for a mouth and very knuckly hands, though dressed genteelly), because I thought he wished to spend little on my father's funeral.

"Do you wish him to be buried like a pauper?" I cried in a fury.

He gave me strong assurances to the contrary and in fact he buried my poor father's remains very decently; but I felt that this was done more to support his own credit than for my father's sake—just as with Charles Moreys, though this London cousin did not speak out his motive as bluntly as the Yorkshireman.

The days I spent with my mother's relations were so unspeakably wretched, my cousins made me feel so wholly unwanted, an object of such reluctant charity, that I was glad at last to show them Charles Moreys' letter and say that my father wished me to act on it. Their faces brightened so at this that I felt sick at heart, and urged my eldest cousin to write to Moreydale immediately, and book a place in the coach for me without waiting for the answer. I begged him urgently, for the sake of his own pride if not for mine, to pay for my place in the coach and not leave it entirely to the charity of my Moreys cousins. He looked down his nose and said he would do so.

"You would not object to travel outside, I suppose, cousin?" said he.

"Certainly I should not object," I replied composedly.

The weather was very cold and my cloak was worn and besides I thought I should make a mean appearance not very creditable to my mother's family, arriving on an outside place, but none of these things mattered now that I had lost my father. I had no money of my own above a few shillings, and could not ask any more favours.

However, when my cousin conveyed me to the inn where the coach started, I found that I had an inside place after all. This cheered me and sweetened my leave-taking with my cousin, and so, very early on a mild February morning, I left London.

BOOK TWO: ELEANOR

CHAPTER I

THROUGHOUT the journey my spirits veered like a weather-cock on a gusty day.

Sometimes I felt lively and happy. To have escaped from my low mean cousins, by whose doing my father died in the Fleet, was a true relief, nor could I help rejoicing in the fresh sweet breeze with its promise of spring, after the foul stale air of the prison. To be riding along the roads and seeing villages and towns, with churches and great houses and thatched cottages and children playing and dogs barking and so on, was very agreeable; I was set out on an adventure after all, and as young girls will I dreamed of some fairy prince who would board the coach and take me away to happiness with him in a palace. Then I thought of my father and grieved. But yet his troubles had been so great of late and his gentle heart had suffered such anguish from them that I could not but be glad in a way that he was escaped from the trials of this life and safe at rest. Again, for all my twenty years, I had never travelled alone by coach before, and I could not but be a little nervous and anxious at times. At first I disliked very much riding in a coach called the *Clothier,* which seemed to me a low trading kind of name, so that I felt sorry when people in the streets stopped to look at us. But I soon found that this was a new post-coach, which rolled along very swiftly; we were to be driven by four differ-ent coachmen so that there should be no delay, and to be only one night out between Leeds and London. Then when we first drew up at an inn and the passengers went in and ordered breakfast, I hung back, diffident and uncertain. But a man in a striped waistcoat who seemed to have charge of the coach places called out my name and when I answered came up to me and behind his hand told me: "Your break-fast is paid, miss." It was so at all the inns; a new sensation for me, of ease and even luxury. But sometimes again my heart was very heavy, when I savoured my loneliness. At the inns, husbands and wives met with a kiss and a loving word and went off arm in arm, parties of friends had supper and joked together. I was alone and should always be so; there was none to care for me. I felt as though all eyes were upon me, that I looked odd and strange as I sat alone and silent, yet if anyone spoke to me I shrank back, shy and afraid. Still, after a time I grew used to the coach and the inns, and held my head up and felt more at ease and even began to converse a little with the passengers, who were very kind to me, so that my heart quite sank when we came to a busy, smoky, noisy town and were told that it was Leeds.

I did not know where to look for the *High Flyer* coach to Annotsfield, and almost lost it by this ignorance, running hither and thither in anxiety and asking questions of strangers in an agitated flurry I deplored but could not restrain. The coach was already started down the yard when at last I found it and the ostler had to shout to bring it back; then when at last I climbed in, almost weeping, the places were full, all the passengers except myself being men. They made way for me kindly enough, but their uncouth language and rough manners were very frightening to a stranger. However, at last I reached Annotsfield and found myself waiting in the George Inn, with my trunk at my side. The George was not then so grand a place as it is now, but still it was bustling enough, with serving-men and maids hurrying back and forth, and many guests, all men. It was market day in Annotsfield, I learned, and indeed the talk I heard—in loud rough voices—was all of trading; money and yards and colours and merchants' names and bankruptcies and bargains. I did not like to thrust myself on the public notice by calling for any refreshment, so although I was faint with fatigue and cold, I sat motionless on a very uncomfortable chair, with my eyes down so that they should not meet any other person's. I felt so wretched, both at my present situation and the prospect of meeting my Moreys relations, that I had to bite my lips to keep back my tears. After a time my heart grew so desolate that I could no longer maintain my composure; my eyes brimmed and overflowed.

"Who are you waiting for, love?" said a voice in my ear.

Terrified, I looked up to see an elderly man, very respectably dressed, with a glossy beaver in his hand, looking down at me with a kind and friendly expression.

"Don't cry now, love," he went on; "I don't mean you no harm. Tell me who it is and I'll try and find him for you."

"Mr. Charles Moreys," I whispered.

"Moreys o' Wool Royd, eh?" he said. "What are you going there for, love? 'Tisn't just the best place for a young lady to go to, if you understand me."

"He is my cousin," I said, trembling.

"Cousin?"

"My father and his father were brothers."

"Oh, well, that's different," said my friend more cheerfully. "If he's a real cousin. Couldn't be a nicer fellow than Charles Moreys, if it weren't for his misfortunes. I never heard John Moreys had a brother, though."

"My father's name was Walter Moreys."

"Oh, the half-brother that ran away to sea. Well, I'll go out and see if I can find someone to take you up to Moreydale. Don't you stir from here, now."

He left the inn. I dried my eyes, but hardly knew whether to feel more affrighted or comforted. That the Yorkshire Moreys should have misfortunes was an idea so strange that I did not know how to receive it; to me they had always seemed models of selfish wealth and arrogance. I could now see my friend pushing his way towards me through the crowded entrance; a young man followed him. My heart beat faster with dread and expectation.

"This here's Mr. Morey's nephew, Jacob. You'll be all right now, love," said my kind friend, and with a wave of his beaver he left me.

You who have known Jacob in his happy years will be astonished by the description I must now give of him at the age of twenty-one; but I speak truthfully. He was of good height and well made, but slouched as he stood, and there was a general air of slovenliness and neglect about his person. His neckcloth was dirty, his gaiters splashed, his waistcoat spotted; his ungloved hands were grimy, and blue with cold. A swarthy skin, large dark eyes, a blunt nose, a shock of untidy black hair and a full crimson mouth which he kept open, displeased my fastidious taste, for though I am so fair myself and attraction is supposed to go by opposites, I have never much cared for very dark-complexioned people.

Still I cannot say that Jacob's appearance altogether displeased me. There was an honest, simple look about him, and his manner to me, though unpolished, was not impertinent.

"We didn't know you was coming today, d'you see," he said. "Uncle would have sent the gig if he'd known. As it is, there's only the waggon."

"I am sorry to incommode you, Mr. Moreys," I began.

"My name's not Moreys. It's Lee," said Jacob shortly. "You can call me Jacob if you've a mind," he added in a kinder tone.

To this ingenuous invitation I naturally made no reply.

"Well, shall we get started, then?" said Jacob. He picked up my trunk, swinging it carelessly in his large hand as if it were weightless, and led the way out to the square. In a few moments I was settled at his side on the box of a waggon with *CHAS. MOREYS, Wool Royd Mills* painted on its rear, and began the last stage of my journey to Moreydale through the February twilight.

To me this journey was very wretched. From the enormous sacks heaped in the long waggon behind me rose a most repulsive oily smell. The two big brown horses—I was to know and love them later as Bess (the shaft horse) and Moll, but now they seemed great, clumsy, ugly beasts—stumped stolidly along, their heavy heads with coarse yellow manes sawing up and down as they climbed, for our road wound continually upwards. The landscape we traversed was singularly dreary. We seemed to go forward until our way was blocked by a hill, then winding round it found ourselves in another ascending valley faced by yet another hill—indeed hills rolled away, rising out of each other, in every direction; grim, wild and colourless. On either side rose steep fields of rough grass enclosed by sombre walls. Spring had warmed the air in London but winter still lingered here; snow streaked the folds of the hills and mouldered in forlorn grey heaps in the angles of the walls and by the roadside. Now we turned into a narrower road and entered a region of dank grey mist. Sometimes this mist lay still and sullen, then round a turn in the hills we found it blowing swiftly across our path in long swirling wreaths and scarves—I hardly knew whether it struck more chill and sinister on my heart when still and brooding, or in this ghostly motion. The lane grew very rough; steep, rutted and stony; an occasional sharp crackle and jar told that one of the ironshod wheels of the waggon had crushed a patch of ice. Here and there tussocks of long grass, bleached as I learned later by the winter storms, sprawled in long, pale, smooth strands, for all the world like the hair of a drowned woman. The cold was bitter. In spite of myself—for I wished to make no complaints—I shivered suddenly and drew my thin cloak more closely round me.

"Are you starved, eh?" shouted Jacob in a loud friendly tone, bending towards me.

"No, I'm not hungry, thank you. Only cold," said I, striving to sound cheerful.

You will laugh at this, knowing that *starved* is the Yorkshire expression for *very cold*, but I was ignorant of it and so was surprised when Jacob seemed taken aback by my reply and fell silent. However, he drew the long whip from its holder beside him and flicked the nearer horse; it shook its head in protesting acknowledgment but did not mend its pace.

"You can sit back there among the wool, if you've a mind," said Jacob after a while. "It'd happen be warmer."

The very thought of being surrounded by those odorous sacks made me feel faint and ill; I refused the offer as politely as I was able.

"Eh, Uncle Charles is going to be mad when he sees you!" exclaimed Jacob, laughing.

My heart sank. But I thought it better to face this frankly and asked him: "Why?"

"He thought you'd be a decent middle-aged body, like, somebody of his own age, who'd teach Tessie and help in the house."

"I shall be very willing to earn my bread by doing both," I replied quickly, for my pride was touched. "It is no disadvantage to be young and strong, I think, in either."

"Will you teach me too? Figures, and such like?"

"Certainly, as far as I am able."

Jacob gave a kind of grunt which I took to express satisfaction. I was glad even of this small comfort, for in truth I felt very desolate. That I had been sent for under a misapprehension and should be a disappointment and quite unwelcome, made me wretched, and for a moment I thought I should weep again as I had done in Annotsfield. But I turned my face away from Jacob, and bit my lip and clenched my hands, driving the nails into my palms and I rebuked myself for my lack of courage and told myself that from being so continually with my father I was quite learned and very well able to teach children.

"How is it you're so young, then, seeing my grandfather and your father were brothers? You don't look any older nor me, scarcely, Miss Eleanor."

"I am nearly twenty. My father married late in life. When he was young," I said with some bitterness, "he had not sufficient prosperity to marry."

"Well, Uncle Charles will be mad," repeated Jacob. "You're such a bit of a thing. But happen he'll get over it. It's best to keep out of his way when he's mad," he advised me seriously. "Joah'll be glad, though."

I felt too disheartened to pursue the subject.

"Joah's my brother," explained Jacob as an afterthought.

The road was now more level and occasionally a few buildings loomed through the mist; it seemed we approached a village. I asked Jacob if it was so; he hesitated but said "Aye," and told me the place was called Booth hereabouts. Presently he pointed with his whip at a cluster of buildings, dimly visible as a patch of deeper darkness in the falling dusk.

"Upper Hey," he said.

"Friends of yours live there, perhaps?" I suggested.

"Aye. Mary Greaves. I want us to be wed, but her mother's against it."

"Perhaps she'll change her mind," I encouraged him, for his rough country voice held real sorrow.

"Happen. But she thinks us a wild strange lot, at Wool Royd."

At this moment the horses began to descend a hillside; the lane was steep, winding and narrow. Jacob tightened the reins and put on the brake and seemed too much occupied with his driving to continue to talk, and I was glad of it, for I needed encouragement too much myself to be able to give it to another. The waggon swung round a bend in the lane and a medley of sights and sounds suddenly rose on my attention: a solid lighted building with a high square chimney at one end; a heavy bang and thud which came with curious regularity; the gleam and splash of water.

"Here's the mill. Hold tight," said Jacob.

He took off the brake, shouted and flicked both horses sharply. It was clearly an accustomed signal, for the animals suddenly set off full tilt down the lane, their clumsy haunches bouncing. I could scarcely repress a cry of fear as in the light from the mill windows I saw water ahead of us. Jacob drove straight into the stream. The hoofs of the horses splashed, the waggon rocked, the wheels thundered; cold drops stung my face, my bonnet fell back, my shabby reticule slipped from my hand; I stooped to retrieve it and was almost shaken off into the water. This time I cried aloud and Jacob seized my arm with his left hand and hauled me back to safety.

"Water-splash," he shouted in my ear. "Quicker than going round by the bridge, d'you see."

The horses ran strongly uphill for a few yards, turned to the right past a big round pond and drew up in the mill yard. Jacob jumped down and shouted; doors opened, figures came out and began to help him unload the heavy sacks from the waggon. In the patches of light and shadow (for it was now quite dark, the night had fallen) these men looked uncouth and misshapen, and their loud rough voices uttered a barbarian tongue I could not understand a word of. I did not know whether to climb down from the waggon or stay where I was; the wheel looked high and I was afraid of falling. The horses from time to time raised a huge hoof and brought it down impatiently, striking sparks from the paved courtyards. One of the men, a fellow in a yellow striped waistcoat and corduroy breeches, now came up and began to unharness; in despair I stood up and called out for Jacob. He came running and with a sheepish grin admitted he had forgotten me; he held up his arms and I was obliged to trust myself to them, which was very disagreeable to me because of his slovenliness and the smell of wool which hung about him.

"I'd best take you straight up to Wool Royd," he said,

picking up my trunk and making towards a lane which led up the hill opposite to that we had descended.

At this moment a ringing voice cried: "Jacob!"

Jacob halted at once and looked perplexed and even somewhat frightened.

"That's Uncle Charles. Happen I'd better—still—well—I don't know," he stammered, looking first at the mill and then at the hillside.

The voice called: "Jacob!" again on a note of anger; Jacob dropped my trunk as though he had been stung and made off towards the mill door hurriedly.

"Go straight up this lane—the house stands on the left—you can't miss it—it's only a moment," he called back to me over his shoulder.

Thus left alone, I climbed the steep lane slowly. I call it a lane, but indeed to me it seemed more like the bed of a stream, for water trickled down beneath its coat of ice, soaking my thin shoes if I trod too heavily; I had to step from side to side on the rough stones to avoid it. At last on my left I saw a paved way and a house with light in its upper windows. Faint with fatigue and anxiety, I made my way beside the long low building. The broad shaft of light streaming down from the windows above showed me a stone porch; I entered, and stood at last before the doorway of the Moreys' house, Wool Royd.

CHAPTER II

IT WAS very dark. I removed my gloves and groped over the jamb for the bell-handle, but the stone was harsh and gritty so that I shrank from it. Then I passed my hands over the great door, but I could find no knocker, only a kind of flat iron bar which seemed to be the latch, for it moved upwards as I touched it. I rapped on the door with my knuckles, but the sound was feeble and I was not surprised that those within did not hear me, for they were shouting and laughing in loud rude voices. The laughter had a coarse, cruel, jeering note and I remembered with a sinking heart the various reports I had heard of my Moreys cousins—a wild strange lot, whose house was not a good place for a young lady. Just for a moment as I stood there in the dark before this inhospitable door, with that hateful laughter ringing in my ears, my courage failed me. I sank down on the stone bench within the porch and covering my face with my hands I sobbed aloud and wished I were lying dead beside my father. Then suddenly through the laughter came a scream of pain; a cry long, shrill and piercing. I listened for a moment, not believing my ears; the cry came again—it was a cry of a child, a child in helpless anguish.

I sprang to my feet and fumbled urgently for the latch and raised it and pushed with all my strength and the heavy door swung open; not waiting to close it behind me, bruising myself on a table holding a lighted lamp I ran up the stairs and flew towards the lighted chamber. The door stood open and I saw the three by the table as if they were held within the frame of a picture.

Even in that first moment of anger I could not but think how handsome they all were, though two of the faces bore the print of evil. Poor little Dick, with his golden hair tumbled and dank on his head, his fair face flushed with pain, his blue eyes wide, his mouth open and distorted, was as sweet and lovely a child as I had ever seen and my heart ached for him. Joah, who stood over him twisting his arm, was so like Jacob that he must surely be his brother, yet there was all the difference in the world between them. Each had the thick black hair, the large black eyes, the crimson mouth, the burly body; but while Jacob was a slovenly good-natured lout, Joah was a handsome overdressed devil. His hair was pomaded and he wore rings on his fingers and a great gaudy pin in his neckcloth; his features were all sharper than Jacob's, he was shorter but more in command of his muscles. Those huge shoulders and thick hands must hold immense strength—a strength he was employing at the moment to give pain to a child half his size. Tessie's beauty at that time—she was fourteen—was somewhat dimmed by her dirty outmoded gown, very much frilled and torn and of a bright rose colour, so that it looked tawdry, and not even cut with a short waist. But with her long dark curls and flashing eyes and the rich colour in her cheeks, she was without doubt a beauty. She stood at Dick's other hand, laughing and making faces at him and (I'm afraid I must say) pinching him.

"Say it! Go on, say it!" cried Tessie, thrusting her face into Dick's. "You're not my brother! Go on, say it!"

"I won't," wept poor Dick faintly, holding down his head.

"Oh yes, you will," said Joah, laughing. "Won't he, Tessie?"

He tightened his grasp of Dick's arm and began to bend it backwards.

"Let the child alone!" I cried in a fury, bounding forward. "Leave him alone! How dare you! Don't hurt him!"

They all looked at me: Dick, poor child, with a pathetic yearning hope; Tessie, I am glad to say, rather shamefaced. Joahs' expression, at first sneering and defiant, changed, as his glance fell on me, to an impertinent leer; he looked me up and down and smiled hatefully.

"What will you give me to stop, eh?" he said.

"Release the child's arm at once," I commanded.

"Who are you to give us orders?" cried Tessie, tossing her head.

"I am your cousin, Eleanor Moreys."

"You mean you're Father's cousin."

"A very pretty cousin," said Joah smoothly.

"Let the child go," I repeated.

"I shan't learn lessons from you. You're too young," said Tessie, hopping from one foot to the other and staring at me with a scornful smile.

Joah laughed and gave Dick's arm a twist. The child uttered a wild helpless cry of pain and I struck Joah hard across the face with the glove I was carrying. He gave a shout of fury and sprang at me, his face crimson.

"Hit her, Joah!" cried Tessie, dancing.

"No, no!" screamed Dick.

"I'll teach you to strike me, Miss!" shouted Joah.

"Don't dare to lay a finger on me," I said firmly, gazing straight into his eyes; I was terrified but did not intend him to know it.

What would have happened then I do not like to think, but at that moment the house door downstairs closed with a loud bang. The three persons before me were at once frozen into listening immobility. A footstep sounded.

"It's Father," whispered Tessie. Joah nodded.

The tableau before me dissolved and formed into quite a different picture. Now there were three pleasant agreeable young people talking together.

"What's to do up there?" cried a ringing voice. "I could hear you shouting almost down in the mill yard."

"Nothing, Father," said Tessie.

"Just a game, Uncle Charles," said Joah smoothly. He gave Dick a violent shove in the ribs and whispered fiercely to him: "Say something."

Dick opened his mouth and tried to speak but no sound came out of it. Joah scowled at him menacingly.

"Come down here, all on you," called the voice below.

Tessie and Joah exchanged glances; they were obviously frightened. Tessie smoothed her hair, Joah gave a sharp tug back and front at Dick's jacket and jerked at his neck-frill.

"Coming, Uncle Charles," he called. "You go first, Tessie."

"I won't. Let Dick go first."

Joah shoved Dick forward so roughly that the child stumbled. But without a word of protest he gathered himself up and went forward—-it filled my heart with indignation to see him, for it meant that he was used to this bullying, had resigned himself to it. The look of bewildered fear in his childish eyes, the tears undried on his soft young cheek, the way his mouth turned down at the corners, made me burn with anger; I rejoiced I had struck Joah and wished I had struck harder. I stood aside to let the others pass and then followed them. They crept down the stairs cowed and silent; I held up my head proudly.

"Crying again, Dick?" said a voice distastefully.

I looked over Tessie's shoulder and saw Charles Moreys, leaning in a careless attitude against his house door and swaying a little on his feet, for (as I learned later) he had been to market and had drunk too much, as his habit was at that time. Having heard him called *Uncle* and *Father*, I had expected him to be in the fifties, and was astonished to see a man so young; but swiftly calculating as I stood, from when my father left Moreydale and so on, I concluded, rightly as it proved, that he was about thirty-five years of age. He was without doubt the handsomest man I have ever seen, extremely tall and extremely fair, with straight-cut features of classic beauty, though at the moment his lean face was flushed and his blue eyes red-rimmed from over-indulgence in liquor. But even so those eyes, with their long fair lashes, were wonderfully handsome; a clear warm azure with a black iris, so that they always seemed shrewd and impish and merry, reckless and cynical and scornful. His fine mouth was twisted and his forehead lined as though from some deep canker of unhappiness. After the slovenly and outlandish dress I had seen since coming to Yorkshire, it was a pleasure to look at a man so modishly and elegantly clad as Charles; his stock and shirt-frill were freshly white, his blue coat well-fitting, his grey waistcoat spotless and his boots most excellently polished. Moreover, you can say what you like, Edward, but the dress of those days displayed a man's figure to more advantage than that of modern times; the broad shoulders, the slender hips, the well-turned leg, were more noticeable in skirted coats and long tight breeches and top-boots than in today's shapeless garments. As I stood and looked at Charles Moreys two opposed feelings rose and battled in my heart. I was afraid, and wished to go away at once and leave these hateful Moreys, and at the same time I felt a throbbing interest, as if I were at a play, and longed for the action to continue.

Tessie ran down to her father and threw herself on his neck and caressed him, but it seemed to me all false, a factitious assumed affection, and from the tone in which he said: "Well, Theresa!" I guessed that deep in his heart he knew that as well as I did.

"Crying, Dick? What are you crying for this time?" repeated Charles.

His voice angered me on Dick's behalf, for it was contemptuous, so while Tessie said in a falsely pitying tone: "Poor Dick, he's always such a cry-baby," I stepped forward. Charles Moreys' eyes lighted upon me and widened in surprise, and then he deliberately widened them further in order to tease me. He smiled too, and said:

"Well, well, well! Am I to understand that you are Miss Eleanor Moreys, my new cousin?"

"I am Eleanor Moreys," I said. In spite of myself my voice was nervous and uncertain.

"How is it you are so young, my dear?" said Charles Moreys, carelessly kind. "Remember, Joah," he went on without waiting for my reply: "Eleanor is more your aunt than your cousin."

"Am I to call her Aunt, sir?" demanded Joah, sneering.

"No I think Cousin Eleanor will suffice. But don't forget the true relationship."

"Oh, if we begin on relationships at Wool Royd we shall find ourselves in a pother," said Joah insolently.

"Silence, sir!" shouted Charles. The flush on his face deepened and he struck the door behind him an angry blow with his fist, so that it shook loudly and we all started. "It ill becomes your father's son to make such a reference. Tessie, have you shown your cousin her room?"

"No, I thought that was Adah's business," said Tessie pertly.

"Do it now," said Charles. His tone was ominous, and Tessie at once obeyed, skipping nimbly out of his reach. "Is supper nearly ready?"

"I don't know, Father," said Tessie, running up the stairs.

"What a house I have to be sure!" said Charles Moreys bitterly. "It is pleasant to return to after a hard day's work."

Tessie tossed her head and ran on rapidly. Taking a candle from the room I had seen before which she told me they still called the nursery, she showed me into a small apartment next door with a row of mullioned windows. From the arrangement of the windows it seemed probable that the nursery and my room had been joined into one apartment at one time, and wishing to be friendly, for I must win Tessie to better ways, I asked her if this was the case. She seemed affronted, tossed her head and would not reply, but Dick, who came in timidly bearing a jug of hot water for my use, told me that it was so; in the time of his great-grandfather Wool Royd had been a clothier's house where cloth was made, and the long room now divided had been the loom-chamber.

"*Your* great-grandfather! You haven't got a great-grand-father," jeered Tessie.

"Yes, I have," shrilled Dick.

"We don't use that old common name Wool Royd now, anyhow," went on Tessie. "We call the house Laverock Hall. The mill is Wool Royd."

A thump and crash at the door now announced the arrival of Jacob with my trunk. It was quite a pleasure to see his honest stupid (as I then thought) face; he placed my trunk where I wished and had the courtesy to ask if there were anything I wanted, then withdrew and took the others with him. The room was solidly furnished with good mahogany, and though not clean, not as dirty as I had feared; I washed and changed my dress for a clean muslin and brushed my hair and was ready to go down when a great clanging bell summoned me to supper.

The Wool Royd dining-room I found to be a fine large apartment, handsomely furnished with a huge oval mahogany table and elegant-shaped chairs with curving legs and claw feet, to match. (Both chairs and table however were sadly in need of polish, and the table was most unpleasingly scratched and stained.) On either side of the hearth hung portraits: one of a dark-haired full-blooded young man with his hair tied in a queue in the style of the last century, and a very fair and beautiful young woman in a blue gown, with a ringlet lying on her neck, to match. To one who had seen London paintings as I had, the portraits did not appear great works of art, but I judged they were good likenesses for all that, for the dark young man, who I supposed was John Moreys, my father's half-brother, had quite a look of my father in his face (though lacking his refined intelligence and spirit), while his lovely young wife Caroline had clearly bequeathed her aquiline features and fair complexion to her son Charles and through him to little Dick. I had time to see all this and to note an old oak settle standing at right-angles by the fire and to wonder at the great roaring blaze which leapt up the chimney, bigger than any fire I had ever seen in London, because for some minutes no supper appeared, and, no one venturing to speak because Charles Moreys was silent, we all sat mute and embarrassed, trying to avoid each other's eyes. At length Charles Moreys lost patience, and shouted "Adah!" in a loud imperious tone which yet, unlike those of

32

Joah and Jacob, showed little trace of the heavy Yorkshire accent. A door in the wall beyond the settle, which led direct to the kitchen, opened, and a huge smoking dish of mutton was brought in.

What shall I say of the first meal I ate under Charles Moreys' roof? The food was good enough, and though too rich and savoury for my taste not ill-cooked. But it was wretchedly served by Adah, who proved to be a bent old crone in half a dozen filthy petticoats, whose large dark eyes flashed strangely as she handed round victuals in themselves commonplace enough. Her hands were brown claws, the finger-nails long and dirty; her greasy black hair, dressed in some old-fashioned style I had never seen in London, hung about her neck in snaky locks. The thought of eating food she had cooked was repulsive to me; moreover the dishes were dirty. Some of these dishes were of fine china, others of coarsest earthenware, and there was the same variation in quality with the glass and silver. I marvelled that a man so cleanly and elegant in his person as Charles Moreys could put up with this slovenly service, until I noticed that what was set in front of him was always of the best quality. Tessie sat on her father's right hand, Joah on his left; I faced Charles at the end of the fine long table, with Jacob beaming on my right beside his brother, and poor Dick cowering at my left. This arrangement suited me very well; I should not have liked to sit next to Joah or Tessie. Charles Moreys and Joah drank heavily of wine, Jacob in moderation; I refused it and it was not offered to the two younger children. Charles Moreys served the meat himself, helping us all with a lavish hand. All the children ate in an unmannerly style; even Dick, to my disappointment, held the tarnished silver mug from which he drank with his dirty little forefinger crooked over the rim so that it dipped into the milk within. I could not eat much, from the strangeness of my situation and the dirt of the dishes; my cousin perceived this but out of kindness did not press me. We ate in silence at first, Charles not speaking and the others seeming not to venture, but at last he said to me with his careless courtesy:

"I hope you had a pleasant journey from London, cousin."

I was about to reply that the *Clothier's* performance had

been admirable, when Tessie blurted rudely:

"Did you come inside or outside?"

"Inside, of course," said Charles Moreys.

I perceived it was he, and not my mother's relations, who had paid for my coach place and my dinners. Ashamed of my error on this point, I could not prevent myself from blushing as I replied that my comfort on the journey had been cared for most handsomely. He seemed pleased and amused, though more by my blushes than my thanks, I feared.

"Jacob here didn't soak you in the beck, then?" said Charles.

"No—only a drop or two fell on me," said I, remembering from my father's talk that the beck meant the stream.

"The jolt nearly shook her off, though," grinned Jacob.

"You'll be shaking wool off into the beck one of these days, Jacob," said his uncle in the slurred utterance of the slightly drunken: "coming through the splash at the pace you do. And then I shall have something to say you won't like, my lad."

"No, Uncle," agreed Jacob.

I was rather surprise by the excessive meekness, not to say fear, with which the nephews and children of Charles Moreys behaved to him, for though I too felt that he was in some way formidable, he had hitherto behaved with perfect gentility. Moreover as his voice was very agreeable and he spoke with less of a Yorkshire turn than anyone I had heard since coming to Annotsfield, I regarded him as more civilised than the rest. Now I was to learn my error. The crone Adah was mumbling and stumbling round the table with some dishes for another course when suddenly Charles Moreys shouted at the top of his voice:

"This plate is dirty!"

He sprang up, plate in hand, and threw it furiously at Adah. All of a sudden the room was in an uproar; the plate skimming through the air caught Adah at the waist, then fell crashing to the ground; Tessie screamed, Joah gave a loud nervous guffaw, and Adah cried out in a voice of surprising depth and strength:

"A curse on you, Charles Moreys, for striking an old faithful servant!"

34

"A curse on you for serving me in this filthy disorder!" shouted Charles. (I could not help surmising that he had noticed my shrinking from the slovenly appointments of the table and felt disgraced before his guest, and I was sorry.) "You think you can do as you like because I have no wife, no wife, no wife."

His voice, which had been very loud and angry, decreased almost to a whisper on these repetitions, and all the noise fell from the room as suddenly as it had risen. The children cowered dumb and motionless as if terrified, and even Adah did not move. I gazed at my cousin in horrified alarm; his face was white and distorted as if with pain, and God knew what his eyes, fixed in a stare of anguish, saw before him. Then Adah gave a slight cackle of laughter and Charles seemed to come to himself. He glanced round the table, and no doubt reading fear on every face and disliking what he saw, cried out in a tone of angry revulsion:

"Get out of my sight, the lot of you! Get out! Get out!"

The children sprang from their chairs and rushed from the room, leaving their meat half eaten on the table. I was unwilling to take part in this undignified scramble, but Dick pulled my sleeve and I found myself scurrying with the rest. We all ran upstairs together; in the confusion and the dark I seized the handle of a door I thought belonging to the nursery, but it would not turn, and Tessie pulled me away, whispering in affright: "Not there! Not there!" We all found ourselves jostling each other breathless in the nursery door; in the light of the lamp they all looked pale and afraid.

"You must never go into that room," said Tessie to me in the least unkind tone I had yet heard her use. "It's locked. Adah goes in to clean it once a month."

I thought it best to make no comment on all these strange matters, but asked if we could not have some coal put on the dying fire. Jacob, who seemed glad to take orders from some-one in command, built up a grand blaze, so that the old room began to look more cheerful. Joah, after jingling the money in his pockets uncertainly for awhile, to my great relief departed, muttering something about the Pack Horse, which I rightly assumed to be the name of an inn. Without asking me to sit down, Tessie planted herself in an arm-chair right before the fire, but the child looked so pale from the fright and shock that I did not hold this lack of manners against her. Instead I drew up a chair for myself and thankfully stretched out my hands to the blaze.

"Where is Dick?" I said, looking round.

A white little face peered out at me from a corner between a large cupboard and the wall.

"He thinks Joah won't see him if he sits there," said Tessie scornfully.

"Come to the fire, Dick," I said, holding out my hand.

Dick at first hung back, but when I repeated my command he stole out timidly, with faltering steps, and soon crouched beside me and put his hand in mine. This small hand, fine and slender and very white, was cold as ice; I chafed it; the child's frightened eyes gazed up at me gratefully.

"I am a little confused as to who you all are," I said, trying to make easy conversation. "You, Jacob, are Joah's younger brother, I suppose, and you are both Mr. Charles Moreys' nephews."

"Half-nephews," corrected Tessie, tossing her head.

"That's right. We're the sons of Uncle Charles's half-brother," agreed Jacob. He seemed to speak with some reluctance, so I said cheerfully:

"My father, Walter Moreys, was half-brother to your grandfather."

"There are always half-brothers in the Moreys family," said Adah, who had come in unperceived. "And they're always trouble-makers."

"My father was not a trouble-maker," I said, quietly but with some anger.

"That's as may be," said Adah grimly.

She gave me a most strangely baleful look; if I had not known she had no cause to hate me, I should have thought it a look of hate. She had brought a tray and a teapot, both fine silver but much tarnished, with teacups and saucers, fine china again but not of a set.

"And Dick and Tessie are brother and sister and Mr. Charles Moreys' children," I concluded cheerfully, beginning to pour out the tea.

"Dick is not my brother," cried Tessie.

"Yes, I am," said Dick in a faint but stubborn tone.

"Hush up! Hush up! And be off to bed all of you as soon as you can," commanded Adah. "Don't disturb the master with your squabblings tonight or you'll regret it."

"Is he drinking, Adah?" enquired Tessie.

"Yes, my gorgeous," said Adah fondly. "He'll drink himself to death soon if he goes on at this rate."

There was a kind of gruesome relish in her tone which I strongly resented.

"But why do you allow it? Tessie, why don't you go down and sit with your father? Or you, Jacob? If he had cheerful society, perhaps he would not——" I could not finish my sentence; the impropriety of discussing such matters with Charles Moreys' children struck me as too strong.

"Go down yourself," said Tessie rudely.

"No! Do as you're bid and go to bed," said Adah, her dark eyes flashing.

"He likes to be alone when he's like this," apologised Jacob.

"Adah! Adah!" shouted Charles Moreys hoarsely from the room below.

Adah, again bidding us with an angry scowl hold our noise and go to bed, stumbled swiftly from the room.

Suddenly, what with my grief and the suspense and anxiety, my two days' journey from London, the wretched wait at Annotsfield, the long cold drive through the swirling fog, the watersplash and the strange scenes and situation I had found at Wool Royd, I was so tired that I could not hold up my head.

"Yes, let us go to bed," I murmured.

"Joah isn't in yet," objected Tessie.

"Joah must fend for himself," I said.

"Adah'll let him in," said Jacob.

I took Dick's gentle little face between my hands and kissed him tenderly and he clung to me, then, conquering some repugnance, I kissed Tessie's carmine cheek, at which she looked much surprised but not altogether displeased. Below stairs Charles Moreys now began to sing in the raucous tuneless fashion of the drunk and Tessie was frightened again and made no further objection to retiring and soon, to my great relief, I lay in bed for my first night at Wool Royd. The noise of the beck and Charles Moreys' singing was so loud in my ears at first that I thought I should never be able to rest, but presently they mingled together and formed a lullaby and I slept.

CHAPTER III

I WAS woken by the heavy thudding noise I had heard from the mill the night before. The beck still sounded and there was a great rushing of wind among trees. I went to the window and looked out; the mist had gone and the dawn was cold and clear.

To you, Edward and Catharine, the situation of Wool Royd is deeply familiar, part of your earliest childhood memories; to you therefore it seems most ordinary and natural. But to me it was all strange and I had never seen anything like it before. The house, with other single houses in the distance, seemed to stand on a green shelf of land; the hill sloped sharply upwards behind the house (to the moor, as I afterwards knew) and sharply downwards in front of it to the tumbling stream. Beside this stream, the Morey beck, stood the mill, with a huge water-wheel at its side and a great pond, partly fringed by big bushes, above, and a chimney twice the height of any house-chimney I had seen, and stables and a small house (the miller's) across the yard. A stone bridge crossed the beck and beyond rose a steep hillside, part thickly wooded, part covered with that rough long grass I had seen in my journey from Annotsfield the night before. But what made the scene so especially strange to me was that beyond this hill there seemed to rise another hill, and then another; in all directions they rolled, dark or bright according as they turned towards or against the morning light, with shadowy valleys between. Here and there I could see a lane, just a few yards of it as it wound round the shoulder of a hill and caught the light. Perhaps because this had been my father's birthplace, or perhaps for some other reason, I rejoiced in the wild romantic nature of the landscape; my spirits suddenly rose and I felt that I was embarked upon an adventure and would not return to my old quiet life in London even if I could. I dressed quickly, eager to continue the story, and went downstairs just as the big house-bell sounded.

The table was ill served, as on the night before. Dirty plates and cups stood by three places, and Dick, who was waiting alone in the cold cheerless room, explained that his father and Joah and Jacob had eaten their meal and gone to the mill. Old Adah, grumbling and muttering, brought in three plates of oatmeal porridge and slapped them down before Dick and myself and Tessie's empty place. I gave her a pleasant good-morning; she muttered something unintelligible and flounced back into the kitchen, which was reached, as I said, directly from the dining-room by a swinging door. No sooner was her bent but massive figure out of sight than Dick softly rose and, tiptoeing, changed Tessie's plate of porridge with his own.

"That is not good manners, Dick," I said. But then I paused confused, for after all I had no right to reprove him.

He looked at me anxiously; his white frightened little face, with the dark lines beneath his eyes—blue like his father's and pretty enough though not of the same charm—moved me to pity. I laid my hand over his cold thin little paw impulsively and patted it and said: "Never mind." At this moment Tessie came flouncing in. Her hair was too obviously unbrushed and her face unwashed, and she wore the same dirty and unmodish dress as on the night before, yet even so the child was darkly beautiful. With a baleful glance at Dick and no word to me, she sat herself down in her place and began to spoon up her porridge, but soon pushed it away, crying that it was not fit for pigs to eat.

"I'll have yours, Dick," she said, and made a snatch at it.

But this I really could not suffer; I spoke sharply to Tessie and bade her fetch more porridge from the kitchen if she wanted it.

"Why should I do as you say? Your father was bankrupt and died in prison," said Tessie, tossing her curls.

"And if he did it was not his fault," said I hotly. "Your grandfather treated my father most unfairly."

"What did he do to him?"

39

"He turned him out of his house and deprived him of his rightful patrimony."

"What's a patrimony?" enquired Dick.

I explained, and was pleased to see that my hot answer had somewhat taken Tessie aback. Adah came in with a great plenty of eggs and Tessie berated her about the porridge, but when she had gone the child said in a more friendly tone:

"Shall you teach us, then, like the others?"

"What others?" said I.

Dick and Tessie tumbled over each other in their eagerness to tell me of their former governesses, who seemed certainly to have been many and ill-fated. If old, they had "got across" with Adah or had their lives plagued out, said Dick, by Tessie; if young, said Tessie, Joah had been caught by their father making love to them—or perhaps it was the other way round, said she, her laughter pealing loud. (She had a way of throwing back her head and opening her mouth so that one saw her crimson throat, which I found very distasteful.) I began to understand the unfavourable remark on Wool Royd of the elderly gentleman in Annotsfield, and felt troubled; moreover that a young girl like Tessie should know of such matters, much more speak of them, struck me as quite horrible. It seemed to me that I was clearly called to try to remedy this state of affairs if I could do so, and so when we had finished our meal I asked the children to show me their lesson books.

They scampered up into the nursery, where I was glad to see a big bright fire burning, and showed me a most lamentable collection of cracked slates and dog-eared primers. I enquired into the state of their educational accomplishments and finding them most woefully ignorant began to instruct them in the elements of spelling and arithmetic. The novelty of this, both for them and for me, for I had never attempted such a task before, kept us all happy and interested for a while, but presently things began to go wrong between Dick and his sister. Dick, though two years younger, was much quicker of apprehension than Tessie, and to make up her backwardness she began looking over his shoulder to copy what was on his slate. This so angered Dick that he smudged his sums rather than that she should see them. She called him mean and struck his arm aside so that his pencil fell and broke; he wailed and called her cheat and in a moment they were at fisticuffs, and all my commands would not stop them. It pained me to see how Dick was afraid of his sister and shrank from her blows and wept, yet I could hardly urge him to strike harder at a girl. The sun, having now got round so as to top the opposing hill, struck through the windows and came to my aid; I cried that we should go out and they should show me Wool Royd and Booth and Upper Hey and so on, and the notion pleased Tessie and she ran off for her cloak and bonnet. Dick, left behind, sat down at the table and laid his head on his arms and sobbed in a most heartrending manner so that I simply could not bear it; I sat down beside him and put my arms round him and drew his head to my breast and wiped his eyes and kissed his cheek and in general comforted him as I had done my dolls as a child and my father in his last illness, and thinking of that I too began to cry and my tears fell on Dick's neck and he looked up and asked what was the matter. I told him I was thinking of my father whom I had lost.

"Did you love your father very much?" asked Dick.

I told him yes.

"So do I," said Dick in a whisper, and he buried his face in my breast again after this confidence.

I bade him take courage and dry his eyes and come out with Tessie and me, as the air would do him good, and soon the three of us were scrambling down the lane towards the mill. I own it was a relief to me to be out of the house, for there was something lonely and sinister in the air of it. There was a pleasant soft breeze and the day seemed spring-like. A man came walking up the lane with hand on hip and arm akimbo, carrying a dripping piece of cloth over his shoulder, and another passed down on horseback carrying a dry piece over his saddle. To accommodate this he rode at the rear of his horse in a decidedly ludicrous fashion, and the greetings of both men were unintelligibly Yorkshire, but they looked homely and friendly, and I was frankly glad to see some company other than Moreys, though of an indifferent kind. The children, too, seemed more cheerful now that they were out in the world. Tessie was in a good humour, pointing out distant houses to me and telling me their names and their inhabitants, Dick warned me where to walk to avoid the trickles of water and told me the names of the becks and the hills. I climbed the sloping grassy bank at the side of the lane and turned to look up the stream at the beautiful, steep, rocky, wooded glen—a clough, I suppose you would call it—and stood a moment enjoying the landscape.

When I turned back Dick and Tessie were both out of sight, I supposed round the bend of the lane. I hurried forward. There sure enough was Dick, just vanishing through the mill doorway. I imagined that Tessie was in front of him (though in this I was mistaken) and followed them to the edge of the mill yard. Here I paused, for I hardly liked to enter the mill without Charles Moreys' express invitation and hesitated to thrust myself on his notice. While I stood there doubtful I heard my name called from above and looking up saw Dick standing at an open doorway in the third storey, laughing and waving to me. I was alarmed and cried out, for their seemed no barrier to prevent him falling, but Jacob, who had come out of the mill unnoticed and stood beside me, laughed and said there was no danger. A great hook and huge chains attached to a rope suddenly came down as it seemed to me out of the sky, really over a wheel above the high doorway.

"Dick likes to play with the crane," said Jacob comfortably.

"What is the hook for?" I asked to conceal my alarm, for the great thing's descent had been so swift I thought it was falling.

"To take sacks of wool up," explained Jacob. "Uncle says you can come in and see the mill if you've a mind," he added.

I have always felt that if only, that first morning, Charles Moreys had conducted me round the mill instead of Jacob, I should have understood the cloth trade. But Jacob's statements were always muddled unless he could put them down in an arithmetical way, and his explanations that morning were no exception to this rule. He showed me the scribbling and carding and slubbing-machines, where the rough wool was teased into a soft white sheet and then stretched and twisted into soft thick threads, and then took me to see the fulling-stocks, the great wooden hammers which fell upon the cloth and beat its threads together; but how the threads had become woven into cloth he did not mention, and it was years before I understood that the two processes carried on at Wool Royd were at the beginning and the end of cloth manufacture, the clothiers performing the middle part, the weaving, for themselves in their own homes. (My husband has had many a laugh at my ignorance and confusion, but it was not to be remedied, and he presently gave up the attempt, merely joking about it from time to time.) All I gathered then was that in the room where the carders stood the air seemed full of flying fluffy wool, so that my throat tickled and I coughed, that beside each slubbing-machine stood a man and a small child helping him, that the man in charge of the big fulling-stocks was called Dan Dennett, and that it was their heavy thuds I had heard from the lane and the house the night before. Jacob also took me out by the stream and showed me the mill dam, over which the water ran very noisily, and the big round pond where the water was stored. From the pond down to the stream stretched a very steep rough bank of grass and rocks, fifteen or sixteen feet in depth at the near end, with a very narrow path at the top running along between pond and stream; Jacob, laughing, urged me along this path. I did not much enjoy it, as I was afraid I should fall either into the deep pond or down the bank into the rocky stream below; however, I tried not to show my fear. Then Jacob showed me the great water-wheel at the side of the mill, its huge spokes slowly turning, and then brought me into the mill again to see the new steam engine which drove the machines when the water in the pond was too low to turn the water-wheel. He described this steam engine with such enthusiasm that it was quite touching, but in terms quite incomprehensible to me, so that I was hard put to it to show a decently encouraging interest such as he deserved. At long last he finished with this engine, and then he opened a door and invited me to step inside, but such a blast of heat came out that I stepped back instead.

"Dryhouse," said Jacob, laughing.

Over all lay such a sour and heavy smell that I was glad when Charles Moreys' ringing voice called: "Jacob!" and Jacob hurriedly pushed me through a door into his uncle's counting-house. Here everything was clean and polished, with papers lying about and a silver inkhorn on the great desk; the smell was diminished and the noise less overwhelming. But I had hardly time to feel relieved before the door behind me closed and I felt an oppression of spirits at being left alone with Charles Moreys.

He was not now flushed and drunk, but looked cold and hard and haggard, the lines on his forehead and the twist of his mouth which I had observed the previous night being very noticeable. He placed a chair for me with a kind of impatient courtesy, and himself stood leaning against the edge of his desk with his arms folded, looking down at me appraisingly. His eyes roved over my person and I felt he missed no detail of my shabby cloak and mended gloves. I clasped my hands tightly in my lap and held my head high and tried to look unmindful of his gaze, but my cheeks burned. He now asked me whether I had seen what I wanted in the mill. I noticed that just as he had changed from his handsome market clothes of last night into a plain coat, gaiters and striped waistcoat, so his speech was turned from the genteel into that of the rough Yorkshire business man. In reply to his question I stammered something about the flying wool—the wheel—the children with the slubbers. I used this word *slubbers* simply because it was so strange to me it had stuck in my memory when Jacob used it, and I was taken aback by the effect it seemed to have on Charles Moreys.

"Them slubbers!" he exclaimed with angry vehemence. "Unreasonable dogs! I've more trouble wi' them daft devils than with all the rest put together!"

I suppose he saw that I was unused to hearing such language, for he added: "Good workmen, though," on a kinder note, which he spoiled by a cynical grin.

"Well now," he resumed with a business-like air, "do you think you can settle down and like Wool Royd, then?"

"For my father's sake," I said, "since it was his home, I will try."

"Ah, your father. What like of a man was he, then?"

"The kindest and best," said I. I spoke with emphasis and raised my eyes and looked full into his face.

"Oh? I'd fancied him something like Joah's father, my half-brother, you know."

"Like Joah!" I cried revolted. "He did not resemble anything whatever to do with Joah!"

"No? I'd fancied him as a rogue, d'you see?"

"No!"

"If not that, then, I suppose he was a weakling."

I rose. "If you insult my father's memory, sir, I will leave your presence and your house."

"Nay, don't fly off at half-cock. How can I know what your father was like if you don't tell me? If he wasn't a rogue and wasn't a fool, how did he come to die in the Fleet, eh?"

I strove to speak but my throat was choked and I could not utter. Charles Moreys looked at me sideways, shrewdly.

"Your mother's folk cheated him, happen?"

I bowed my head.

"There you are, you see. If I'd sent money, they'd have got their claws into it—it wouldn't have done *you* any good. Of course, if I'd known you were so young and minikin, I'd happen have acted differently."

"If I could understand your meaning, sir, I should doubtless be able to give you a proper answer," said I.

"Oh, the word has a pretty, silly little meaning, much like you yourself, cousin," returned Charles Moreys carelessly.

"The small in stature are not necessarily small in spirit," said I, deeply mortified. "If you are not prepared to treat me with proper respect, Mr. Moreys, I will leave at once."

"And where will you go, you silly child?" said he with contempt.

"No matter. I will not stay anywhere to be insulted!" I cried, and I looked at him with all my anger in my eyes.

"I see you've some of the Moreys spirit, for all you're so fair and small," said Charles Moreys in a kinder tone. "Come, cousin! You mustn't take it amiss if we don't turn our compliments as neatly here as in London. Sit down." He put a hand on my shoulder and compelled me into the chair; indeed between resentment at his rudeness and a sense of

45

wretched dependence upon his will I trembled so that I could hardly stand. "Now if you'll settle down here and teach the children and try to bring some comfort and order to the house you can make your home at Wool Royd and welcome. I can't say fairer nor that."

I began to say: "I will try, sir," but was interrupted.

"But let me warn you, don't play the fool with Joah."

This was too much. "I wish to have nothing whatever to do with Joah!" I cried.

"I'm glad to hear it. Keep away from Joah, or as we say in these parts, you'll rue. And Jacob now, he's fixed himself with a girl already."

"At Upper Hey," I said coldly, glad to show I was aware of the state of Jacob's affections.

"Aye, Mary Greaves. Jacob's a decent good lad and his figuring's good if it were writ so you could read it. Why don't you fancy Joah, then?"

"He bullies the younger children," I said.

There was a pause.

"Let me once catch him at it, that's all," said Charles.

The words were spoken in such a quiet level tone that I looked up at my cousin in some disgust at his apparently calm acceptance of cruelty. But his quiet had been due not to lack of feeling but to feeling repressed, for his cheek was pale with anger and his blue eyes blazed. (His fair complexion made his moods very visible in his face at all times, as I presently discovered.)

"If I know I am supported by your authority," I began.

"Well—that depends on how you frame, you see," Charles Moreys interrupted me roughly. "You'd best try your hand at it all for a month or two and we'll see how you make out. But if you get across with the children or make up to the lads, out you go like all the rest, Moreys or no Moreys."

"I have no male relative but yourself to resent insults on my behalf, Mr. Moreys," I said, quivering with rage. "So if you——"

"Oh, nonsense," said he impatiently. "Don't be so touchy, cousin. Have some sense. I'm only advising you for your own good. You'll never get on in Yorkshire if you rear up at a word like that."

What I should have said to this I do not know, for my anger at his insults was hot and yet I saw some sense in what he said. But at that moment one of the workmen put his head in at the door and with a backward jerk of his thumb summoned my cousin.

"We'en getten a mix-up wi' some wool, mester," he said.

Charles Moreys sprang up at once and went into the mill.

He left the counting-house door open and I could not but gather something of what followed. It seemed that Jacob had confused two packs of wool belonging to two different customers—the one of white, the other coloured. They had been put on the carding engine together and emerged inextricably blended. I could not hear all that Charles Moreys said, but such of his rebuke as I distinguished was blistering.

"You daft young fool—your head's always in the clouds over a girl who's too much sense to take you—you don't earn your keep—you must get your mother to keep you, for by God I'm tired of it."

This was all so painful that I stepped quietly to the door, thinking to slip away so as not to witness Jacob's humiliation. But it was impossible, for the eyes of all were turned towards me. The large room looked like a scene on a stage, with the workmen clustered round the walls, Jacob in the centre hanging his head and Charles Moreys just in front of me berating him. What surprised me was on the one hand that the men did not show much sympathy in their looks for Jacob, and on the other that Joah, who stood at the back and seemed to be trying to conceal himself from his uncle, appeared genuinely troubled.

"Well, I suppose I shall have to sort it out myself," said Charles at length, dropping into a kinder tone. "But I'm ill vexed with you, Jacob. You must mend your ways and think on more—get Miss here to teach you to figure so as I can read it—nay, if you could read it yourself it'd be something. At present you're no use to God or man—or woman either," he concluded, suddenly laughing heartily. The men all laughed loudly with him, so that I shrank. "Come on, then, come on!" continued Charles Moreys, pushing Jacob cheerfully out of the way and approaching the machine. "We've got to get this wool sorted out if we can manage it. Dick!

47

Take Miss Eleanor home. This young lady's my cousin," he added to the men: "Miss Eleanor Moreys."

They nodded their heads and I bowed, though with some disquiet because of the odd looks they gave me.

"Dick! Where is that child?" said Charles Moreys.

He strode out into the yard, and I was glad enough to follow him. Dick was standing at the open garret door, as before, a workman at his side; the great hook was going upwards slowly.

"Put that safety-chain across! And come down, Dick," said Charles Moreys. His voice was harsh and cold, and had none of the undercurrent of affection he had used to Jacob. "Come down quickly."

For answer Dick drew in the hook and seized it; the workman, laughing, pulled on a rope he held in his hand which I suppose released some brake on the crane, for the hook ran down into the yard as before, only that now the child came down swinging with it. I cried out in alarm, and Charles Moreys too cried out:

"You daft young devil!"

This time his voice was kinder, and he went forward to the boy and took him by the waist as he neared the ground so that he could release the hook the sooner. Dick gave a happy smile at this and a colour came into his pale cheek and he looked up at his father gratefully. But if he expected a kind word or even a rebuke he got neither; his father put him down on his feet and turned away and went into the mill in silence.

It was only then that I remembered Tessie.

"Dick, where is your sister?"

"She felt sick and went home," replied Dick calmly.

I exclaimed at this, feeling guilty for my neglect of her, and began to hurry up the lane. Dick, kicking stones at my side and whistling, glanced at me once or twice as if to speak, then seemed to decide against it. At length he said—and it was amusing how his childish pipe took on a sardonic tone like his father's:

"Adah will take care of her."

You who know the story will understand the significance of all this, but at that time I was quite blind to it.

48

CHAPTER IV

WITH great difficulty and struggle, so that every day seemed a battlefield and I was unspeakably thankful when night came to bring me a respite, I contrived gradually to introduce some order and decency into Wool Royd.

I could not give orders to Adah, for she would have rejected them outright with contumely; all I could do was to delve myself into the many closets and drawers, and into a store-room there was above the cowshed, and bring out fresh china and glass and linen and silver, and set them on the table and in the rooms with my own hands. There was a great store of all kinds of handsome household stuff hidden away, some of it moth-eaten and mouldering—which I caused Jacob to have burned for me at the mill—but some needing only laundering and mending and polishing to restore it to use. Adah grumbled and muttered but did not actually forbid me when I set irons in the kitchen fire to heat or asked for needles or mops. At first she obstructed my efforts when she could do so without too much trouble, but when she saw that I did not call on her to help me—for indeed with seven of us to feed she had plenty to do—she let that slide and tacitly allowed me to do as I wished, merely scoffing and sneering and withholding all help and encouraging Tessie to do the same. I could see she enjoyed seeing me perform menial tasks, but I did not mind, I did not consider honest labour for another's good beneath me. Jacob gave me help whenever I asked it; he did not see my need without being asked, but he was truly eager to have Wool Royd set to rights, so as to show Miss Greaves that he was a proper suitor for her hand. Dick, poor mite, of course helped me all he could and tried to aid in everything, so that he had to be restrained from carrying weights too heavy for him; I had won his love from the first by defending him against Joah, and always retained it. So that with regard to the arrangements of the household, I had some success quite early. It was not too long before Charles Moreys, looking round the supper table, to which I had at last contrived to give an appearance suitable to a gentleman's house, remarked: "Well, come! This looks better."

They all looked in my direction to see what I should say, turning upon me four pairs of dark eyes—including Adah's, which were very fierce—and two pairs of blue, Dick's adoring as always, and my Cousin Charles's, sardonic as always too. Not wishing to give Charles Moreys the satisfaction of thinking I liked his praise I said nothing, and as it chanced this pleased Adah, for it seemed to give her a share in the credit, so that she was slightly less difficult for some time thereafter. What was also very helpful, Charles Moreys now turned to his daughter and asked:

"I suppose you help your Cousin Eleanor in the house, Tessie?"

"Yes, Father," said Tessie glibly.

It was a flat lie, and she knew we all knew it; being only a child after all, though a naughty one, the warm colour rushed up into her face and she looked the picture of guilt. Her father gave her a most piercing and bitter look, his mouth twisted as it was in his worst moments, and said in those quiet smooth tones which with him were always ominous:

"You are very like your mother, Theresa."

There was a long silence; everyone round the table sat very quiet and looked down at the plates, seeming not to dare to move; until at last Charles Moreys touched his glass as a sign to Adah, who at once filled it, and the meal moved on.

After that Tessie was very industrious in the house for a few days, and even after a week or two could still be coaxed occasionally into helping to wash china or dust a room. *A propos* of this: one day when I was suggesting to Adah that the big bell which hung on a high rod in the hall beside the front door should be polished, she grumbled that she had no time just then—the Master had ordered the locked room to be cleaned, she said, and given her the key; it was always cleaned once a month and that was the appointed day. Partly from simple goodwill, partly from the idea that the locked room must be in an ill condition if it had received only Adah's ministrations—for like many women who are good cooks she was a poor cleaner—I said:

"Would you like me to help you with the room, Adah?"

She screamed out: "No!" with her eyes blazing. "Nobody shall touch Mrs. Moreys' room but me."

"If the room belonged to Tessie's mother," I said mildly, "perhaps Tessie would like to help you."

"No! No! No!" screamed Adah.

I was astonished by her vehemence, which seemed uncalled for, but of course I bade her do just as she pleased. Tessie seemed troubled yet relieved, I thought; she was quite pale and subdued all that day. Later in the morning as I passed along the landing the door of the locked room stood open. I caught a glimpse of some drapery rather crudely pink, curtains perhaps or cushions, before I hastily averted my eyes. Because I made no more trouble about the room, Adah asked Charles Moreys to send up a man from the mill with a ladder, to clean the bell. (Its rope was renewed at the same time.)

By such small clashes and courtesies and persistences, as I say, I gradually put the house into a better order. If that had been all, my life at Wool Royd would have been easy; but it was only one thread, and that the least important, in a tangled skein.

I felt I should never win the children's confidence, and indeed should not deserve it, if I went continually running to Charles Moreys about their peccadilloes and bringing down his dreaded anger upon their heads. So in the first few weeks I made no approach to him at all, though God knows I sometimes longed quite feverishly for the sound of his step in the hall at night and the clang of the door behind him, since the moment he entered the house, all other voices were hushed, and quarrels sank to rest. When he was out of the house, and especially on days when he was absent from the mill on business, there was such turbulence and difficulty in Wool Royd as drove me at times almost to my wits' end; a hundred times I had to bite my lips and clench my hands to keep back my tears—I dared not yield to wretchedness and weep, for my authority would have been lost for ever at any sign of such weakness.

To begin with, Adah was quite unlike any other maid-servant I had known. A stern, stormy, passionate nature still persisted in her bowed frame; there were relics of beauty in her large features, her abundant black hair, her fierce black eyes. She muttered to herself when angry in a language I did not understand, but in general spoke a purer English than any of the household save Charles Moreys. After a time I learned the reason for this. Once when Tessie was indulging, as I am afraid she often did, in coarse local expressions quite unsuited to her childish lips, I strove to put some shame into her by remarking that Adah spoke in a less Yorkshire way than Tessie.

"Adah isn't Yorkshire, silly," jeered Tessie.

"Oh? Where does she come from, then?" said I.

"She's a gipsy," put in little Dick.

"I'm telling Cousin Eleanor, not you," shouted Tessie, driving her elbow so sharply into her brother's ribs that he gasped with pain. "Adah's a gipsy. We don't know where she comes from, she was here at Wool Royd before Father was born."

This served to explain too why Adah's whole life seemed to be spent at Wool Royd; she never left the house, visited no friends, never relieved us of her presence. Adah always favoured Joah and Tessie, was indifferent but not unkind to Jacob and bitterly hostile to Dick. I found, for instance, that Dick's unpleasing mode of holding his silver mug at table, with his forefinger dipping into the liquid within, was adopted because the mug, which had no handle, was too fat for his small fingers to clasp safely; indeed he had difficulty, even so, in lifting it at all. I therefore asked Adah to give him another drinking-vessel, but this she would never consent to do.

"That's his christening cup," she said with her harsh cackle whenever I attempted a remonstrance. "Mrs. Dennett gave it him, it has the letters of his name drawn on, they say. Let him be a little gentleman and drink from his own silver cup."

From this determination she would not stir, so poor Dick had to continue crooking his forefinger. In the same way, Dick was always given the broken chair, the scorched linen, the smallest and least pleasing portion of food. Why this should be so I could not think, for the child was always pleasant and well-mannered to Adah, whereas Tessie was rude and exacting; but so it was. I combated it as well as I could, but after a time I saw that I could do nothing, for

52

Adah hated Dick; I therefore simply waited for an instance of ill-treatment bad enough to report to Charles Moreys. Once when angered on Dick's behalf because he had been soaked and bruised by a bucket of water set as a booby trap above his bedroom door, I threatened to tell my cousin; but to my alarm Joah, Tessie and Adah, who had all had a hand in the trap and stood round enjoying Dick's discomfiture, burst into raucous laughter, quite throwing themselves about in their mirth.

Poor little Dick! As I said, I had won his confidence from the first; he clung to me and loved me, and his love was a consolation and a joy to me. But it was a sorrow too, because I was in such continual anxiety on his account. He was such a delicate little boy; often cowardly, often crying, often ill. I sat up many nights with him, laying cold cloths on his hot damp forehead, holding his hand in mine and feeling the quick irregular pulse jump in his wrist, nursing his fair little head against my breast after a bout of sickness or weeping. One night as we sat thus with my arms about him, in the dark early hours of the morning, everyone asleep, the house being very still except for the wind rushing through the trees and moaning down the chimneys, I gently stroked his hair—he had been very sick—and put a soft kiss on his flushed cheek. He turned and clung to me so convulsively that I was startled.

"Nobody kissed me for years before you came," he whispered.

"Why, Dick!" I said pityingly. I wondered then how long the poor child had been motherless. "When did you lose your mother, Dick?"

"The day I was born," he said. For a moment he was silent, then he seemed to make up his mind, and putting his hand inside his nightshirt he drew out a locket which hung on a chain round his neck, and opened it. "This is my mother," he whispered.

He held it towards the candle, and I saw the miniature of a young and pretty woman. It was a sweet, innocent, childish and—for I must be honest—rather simple and ingenuous face. Her hair was soft and dark, her cheek had that lovely rose flush one sometimes saw on Tessie's. The mind behind that face would not, I thought, find itself very easy with that of Charles Moreys; I imagined her saying sweet silly nothings which he would wither with a blast of sarcasm.

"Isn't she pretty, Cousin Eleanor?"

"*Very* pretty. Dick, what was her name?"

"Rose."

"That's very pretty too."

"Nobody knows I still have this locket," said Dick. He turned it and opened the other side. I had been wrong, I thought, about Rose's chance of happiness with her husband, for the Charles Moreys pictured there, so fair and young and handsome, had the same sweet ingenuous air as his pretty wife. "You won't tell anyone I have it? They might take it away."

"How did you get it, Dick?"

"It was round my neck when they found me."

"Found you?"

"In the mill pond."

"But——"

"You won't tell anyone I have it?"

"No."

"Not Adah, or Joah, or Tessie? Or even Jacob?"

"No. Jacob wouldn't take it from you, though, Dick."

"No. But he might tell about it without meaning to," said Dick seriously.

I sighed and hugged the child closer, sad that he had learned this shrewdness in the painful school of adversity; for it was true: Jacob was invincibly simple.

Jacob was the easiest person in the house from my point of view; yet even he caused me uneasiness—never by opposition but only because I felt such sympathy with him. I instructed him, every evening when his mill work was over, in writing and figuring, so I had plenty of opportunity to become acquainted with his character. He made good progress in his studies, for he had a quick mind enough when it was properly directed, only that usually it was overlaid with thoughts of his Mary or some calculation he was engaged in about the improvement of the steam engine. He was clumsy in writing and made terrible blots until I had the notion of asking Dick to sharpen his pens. Dick, like his father, was always neat and skilful in his actions, and between us we subdued Jacob's sprawling calligraphy into something like a readable hand. I was always glad to see Dick and Jacob friendly together. Dick, poor child, sorely needed a friend, with everyone's hand against him, but poor Jacob was made almost equally wretched by his conflicting loyalties. He adored his uncle Charles, and felt for Joah an unquestioning brotherly love. But at Upper Hey, he told me, Charles Moreys was regarded as a drunkard, Joah as a profligate, and Wool Royd as a house no decent modest girl would set her foot in. I myself did not feel that Jacob's plight was quite as bad as he feared, for from one or two slight references I had gathered that Mr. Greaves, a clothier by trade, was one of Charles Moreys' steadiest customers. I also took leave to wonder sometimes whether Mary Greaves was worth all the anguished love Jacob spent on her. But he was sure of it; Mary, he said, loved him and Mr. Greaves favoured his suit, it was only Mrs. Greaves who held Wool Royd in such disfavour; but alas! Mrs. Greaves was the most powerful person in the household. I took the liberty of hinting to Jacob that Mrs. Greaves might look on his suit more favourably if he bought himself a new coat and kept his linen cleaner. He was quite astonished, poor lad, but thanked me heartily and took my advice at once. The two brothers earned wages at the mill, both having passed out of their seven years' apprenticeship, so Jacob had money at his command. He had his hair dressed next market day and bought himself a good blue coat and a most sumptuous waistcoat of dove-grey cashmere embroidered in purple silk. It was a little too modish, perhaps, for a young clothier of Wool Royd, and I saw Charles Moreys' glance light on it at supper with a satiric gleam; however he said nothing and Jacob went out to visit the Greaves wearing the waistcoat and came back very happy. Next Sunday morning he appeared in it again and announced he was bound to attend the Scape Scar chapel nearby favoured by the Greaves; but—Charles Moreys being abed after a night's drinking—Joah teased his brother so unmercifully about the waistcoat's splendours, saying the minister would be too dazzled to read the gospel and so on, that Jacob in a torment rushed upstairs and tore off the dove-grey, and then, ashamed of his old shabby waistcoat, did not attend chapel at all, thereby earning himself a bad mark from Mrs. Greaves, I was sure. He was so desperately hurt about the waistcoat that I urged him to buy a plainer one for simpler occasions, next market day; but it seemed he had spent all he had on the grey and could not raise the price. Dick and I were very sorry but having no money could not help him, though for his sake we disliked Joah more than ever if that were possible.

Joah of course was the great difficulty of life at Wool Royd. After what I had said to Charles Moreys in the mill about his bullying ways, I think Cousin Charles had given Joah a strong command on the subject, for he no longer indulged in open ill-treatment of Dick, at least not until an occasion of which I shall speak later. But he glared balefully at the child so that Dick cowered, snapped his fingers loudly in front of his face while he was eating so that Dick was startled and dropped his spoon, threatened him with various torments which he described in hateful detail, played tricks on him and in general made the child's life a misery without actually employing physical force against him. To me Joah behaved with a jeering, sneering, over-done politeness which sickened me, the more so because I was not quite sure what it covered. At times I thought he hated me and had never forgiven me for the blow I had struck him on the day I arrived; at other times he seemed to press up to me, to lay his fingers on my arm, to gaze into my eyes, as if he thought I was one of those loose women whom, Jacob in his simplicity informed me, Joah visited from time to time in Annotsfield. If Joah had known how much I loathed his dirty finger-nails and greasy hair, his loud voice and bullying ways, he would certainly have hated me entirely, in return; but I was in some doubt how to treat Joah, because of his influence on Tessie.

There were times when I thought some matrimonial project had already been settled for Joah and Tessie, cousins —or half-cousins was it?—as they were. For Joah continually flattered Tessie about her beauty, using a frankness and particularity of comment which might just have been allowable had they been betrothed, and Tessie behaved to Joah as she might possibly have been permitted to do if that were the case, though even so her conduct would have been somewhat too forward. Whatever she was doing, when Joah entered the room she desisted from it; if we were at lessons, she left a sum in the middle and went with a flounce of her skirt to sit beside him; if she were sewing, she threw down her work without even waiting to fasten her needle. She listened avidly to all he said, her full mouth slightly gaping, her eyes glowing with laughter and delight. She copied his rough phrases—rude enough from him, quite shocking from her—and his rough manners; she quoted his opinion on all occasions, and recalled with tremendous gusto his triumphs with gun or rod. (When the mill was not busy, Joah and Jacob fished sometimes in the dam or in the river Ire, of which the Morey beck was a tributary, and shot in the autumn months on the moor above.) There were times when Tessie's selfishness and rudeness and vulgarity vexed me so much I thought that Joah was a fitting husband for her; but then again, looking at her childish face gaping in ignorant wonder, I felt compassion for her and wondered where my duty lay. Ought I to mention the matter to her father? But if it were settled, it was not my concern; if it were not, perhaps the mention of it would put it into his head, which I was loth to do. She was only fourteen yet, after all; I hesitated, in much perplexity.

But oh, the struggles I had with Tessie! She would not wash, she would not mend her clothes, she would not brush her hair; she slapped and scolded Dick even when the child was pale and sick with headache; she took the best of everything for herself as if it were her due and we ought to be grateful to her for doing so. She lied; in such simple games as we played together she cheated; she was a coward too, screaming and running and clutching at my skirt when on our walks we met a barking dog or a hissing goose. All this I could have forgiven—as for the dog and the goose, I feared them too—if only she had shown some warmth of heart, some affection for anyone besides Joah. I learned by chance from Dick that Tessie was supposed to run downstairs and greet her father each evening as he came from the mill. To a lonely and embittered man, as Charles Moreys seemed to be, I could well understand that such a greeting would mean very much; a child's soft arms round one's neck, a child's kiss on one's cheek, a gladness of welcome in a child's eyes because you have come—all these warm the heart and make life worth living. I therefore tried to ensure that Tessie should be washed and brushed, tidy and in a good humour, and listening for her father's step, about the time he usually came each evening from the mill. But Tessie would not trouble to fall in with this plan. She would sit over a book or a game till it was too late, or refuse to tidy herself, or when she heard the door open would yawn and stretch and say: "*You* go down, Dick!" (At first I thought this a good suggestion and tried to persuade Dick to adopt it, but he wept and was distressed and I saw that Tessie meant to mock him, so though I did not understand why it should not be good, I desisted from it.) But I must make here a qualification, though one not in Tessie's favour. On the market days (which she knew), or when Charles Moreys returned on horseback instead of afoot and had therefore probably been to Annotsfield, Tessie rushed down to him willingly enough, for on such occasions he sometimes brought her some small present, a ribbon or handkerchief or even a pair of gloves. I strove to bring home to her how mercenary this behaviour was, but she thought it natural and saw no shame in it and stared when I pointed out how it must wound her father. Indeed though her emotions were turbulent enough if she was any way thwarted, Tessie seemed to have no feeling for anybody but herself. Joah brought her a kitten once which Dan Dennett at the mill had sent up to Wool Royd from a litter. At first Tessie raved about its black-and-white beauty—for it was indeed a sweet playful little thing—and would not come to her lessons for playing with it by the hearth. But soon she forgot to feed it. Then Dick took on its care. This passed unnoticed by Tessie until once the kitten showed a preference for Dick, by leaping to Dick's lap when she had called it. She leaned forward and slapped it cruelly. At this Dick fired up and slapped her hand and we had a bout of fisticuffs most distressing to witness. I had to call Jacob from his book to separate the brother and sister.

On the other hand, poor Tessie had never received any religious teaching and did not even know the Commandments until I taught them to her, much less the Catechism, so perhaps it was hardly fair to expect much in the way of good principle from her. The Wool Royd household seemed not to attend church or chapel on Sundays. A week or two after the waistcoat episode I begged Jacob—partly for his own sake, partly for Tessie's—to take Tessie to Scape Scar chapel with him, and proposed to accompany them myself; for not knowing where a church of the kind I was accustomed to, or indeed any kind, was to be found in this wild neighbourhood, I had not attended Divine Service since I came to Yorkshire and was much troubled by this lapse. Although with reluctance, Jacob agreed. Then Dick was ill that morning and I could not leave him and did not even see Jacob and Tessie go, though I heard their voices as they left the house. When they returned they were flushed and sullen and would not speak to each other.

"Summat gone wrong between you two?" jeered Joah as we sat at the dinner table.

"I'll never take Tessie anywhere again!" flashed Jacob.

Such temper was so unusual from the mild good-humoured Jacob that we were all astonished, and Tessie burst into tears and sobbed in a way that, if one believed she had a heart, one would have called heartbroken.

"What's to do, Tessie love?" said Charles Moreys, more kindly than usual. "Didn't you behave well enough for Jacob's grand friends, eh?"

"She wouldn't stand up and kneel at the right times!" cried poor Jacob.

At this Charles Moreys and Joah burst into a roar of laughter.

"I hate you! I hate you! I hate you!" screamed Tessie.

She leaped up from her chair and hurled herself at me round the table, and kneeling beside me buried her face in my breast. Her grief was so genuine that I was quite amazed and did not know what to say or do, but by instinct my arms closed about her, as they would about any crying child.

"Don't cry, Tessie dear. You'll know better next time."

"No, I won't. I know now. I did it on purpose," cried Tessie fiercely, striking at me with her fists.

"But why, Tessie?"

"Those hateful Greaves—the way they looked at me. I

59

thought I'd give them something to look at. It doesn't matter for you."

"I don't know what you mean," I said, perplexed.

"Your father's bankrupt—it doesn't matter for you."

"Theresa!" thundered Charles Moreys.

"Well, Father, it doesn't. She's poor. It doesn't matter what Eleanor looks like. But we're rich. Those hateful Greaves!"

Then I understood the cause of her humiliation. I blamed myself for not having thought of it before, but as she truly said, I was so used to poverty that it had not occurred to me; I had thought of cleanliness rather than of appearance.

"I think Tessie means that she needs new dresses if her appearance is to support her station," I said.

"Why the devil didn't she say so before, then?" demanded Charles Moreys, flushing angrily. "And why didn't you? What are you here for, eh? Write all down that she needs and it shall be bought in Annotsfield."

Tessie let out a whoop of joy at this and sprang up from her knees, snapping her fingers and laughing, while Adah gave me an astonished look, as if she could not believe her ears, and cried out too. For my part I felt vexed and affronted, and raising my voice to carry above the noise Tessie was making, I said coldly:

"And for Dick too?"

"And for Dick too," replied Charles Moreys in his driest tone.

During the next few days I turned over all Tessie's pitiful garments and caused Jacob to do the same with Dick's and made a list which came midway between what Tessie wanted and what I thought absolutely necessary to be bought for them.

The difficulty then was to decide on an appropriate moment for offering the list of cloth and cambric and muslin, shawls and stockings and shoes, to Charles Moreys. Although this was never mentioned between us, we all felt it would be wise to present it when he was in a good humour. But when this would be, was doubtful. He went early to the mill, so that he could not be approached in the morning; when he came to the house during the day his mind was on wool and coal and the iniquities of his slubbers and he was apt to be short-tempered. No man likes to be interrupted at meal-times by household matters, so it seemed unwise to proffer the list while he sat at table. After supper was clearly the best time, but a day must be chosen—alas that this had to be considered!—when he was not drunk. On market days he came home partly drunk and continued the process after supper, on days when he rode to Annotsfield to obtain some sort of Government rebate on the soap used at the mill, it was the same. Then, he sometimes went out at night to meetings of master mill-owners similar to himself, or went to the play in Annotsfield, or to drink at the Booth inn; at other times the mill ran late being very busy, or "throng" as Jacob called it, with work. Altogether it was most difficult to know when to catch him. Tessie was growing impatient, nay she had long since grown so, and even Dick remarked sardonically one night that we had better ring the big bell in the middle of the morning—that would bring his father back double quick, from the mill. This bell—I have mentioned it before—was a great thing which hung high in the hall by the front door, with a thick rope and tassel hanging beside; it was rung to summon Charles and Joah and Jacob from the mill for meals, for if you opened the door and pulled the rope sharply, the peal could be heard right down by the stream. We all laughed together, I must admit, at the thought of summoning Charles Moreys thus to give him a list of children's clothes.

"Can't you see his face?" spluttered Jacob.

"Can't you hear his oaths?" laughed Tessie.

"Tessie, Tessie!" I reproved her.

Her coarseness of speech was always a grief to me, though with Joah—and I must say too at times her father—as her model, she could hardly be blamed for it. I could not but smile, however, if rather sadly, at the picture of Charles Moreys' fury if summoned from his mill for such a cause. So we were all merry together when he passed by the nursery door and looked in on us.

"What's the joke?" he said.

We hardly knew what to reply to this. Dick's smile left his face and he cowered; Tessie giggled and tossed her curls; Jacob smiled with his usual candid and surprised air but said nothing. I bit my lip and bent over my mending but had an uncomfortable conviction that a dimple I had in my left cheek was showing itself. (Hardly a dimple, however, for a dimple sounds as though the cheek it dints is plump, and my face was always very slender; a small crease, perhaps, which appeared when I was amused.) Charles Moreys stood leaning against the door-frame, striking his whip against his boot and gazing down at us. He looked handsome, masterful and cynical as always and was a little the worse for liquor, but not much; enough to warm his cheek and perhaps even take the chill off his heart. At all events, he spoke quite kindly and even smiled at us.

"Well—laugh then. Laugh while you can. I wish I'd laughed more while I had the heart for it."

He turned away and made off down the stairs.

"Oh, cousin!" I cried, bethinking myself and running after him, "can I show you the list for Tessie and Dick?"

"Not tonight, cousin," said he. "I am already late."

We heard the great front door slam behind him.

Tessie was so much vexed by my loss of this opportunity to present the list, and I myself was so much vexed by my own cowardice in the matter, that I made up my mind to proffer it the very next night that Charles Moreys was at home, be his temper good or bad. As it happened, this chance occurred a couple of days after. Jacob came in beaming—for, good fellow that he was, he was as keenly interested in the children's clothes as if they had been for himself, and bore no malice against Tessie for her bad chapel behaviour—to tell me that his uncle had given orders that they should work at home, posting the mill books, that night. It seemed that the quarterly mill Pay Day approached. The accounts were all to be made up in the books and notes written out of the sums owed to Wool Royd, which Joah and Jacob were then to deliver to the customers, with an invitation to attend at the Pack Horse inn in Booth, one evening the following week. It was the local practice to offer refreshments to the customers as they paid their accounts. Jacob, who never said anything disrespectful about his uncle, nevertheless made it clear to me that when Charles Moreys made up his mill accounts he was always quite perfectly sober.

"But would it not be better to wait till after the Pay Day?" I suggested—partly because this seemed reasonable, but partly also because now that the time was near I dreaded to take the list to Charles Moreys lest there should be some explosion of anger from him. "When the money has come in, will not your uncle feel richer and more inclined to buy?"

Jacob shook his head. "Nay—Pay Days are nearly always disappointing. Sometimes we don't get above a third or even a sixth of what's our due. But when the notes are being made out, d'you see, the sums owed us look large and we feel hopeful like." Seeing me still hesitate, he added: "Uncle Charles is a rich man, Cousin Eleanor, you don't need to be troubled."

Joah was fortunately out that night, and supper passed off quietly with us all on our best behaviour. Tessie indeed overdid her politeness, so that her father glanced at her shrewdly, but Dick began to talk about some birds which it appeared had that day returned to Moreydale after a winter absence and Charles Moreys was interested and asked questions about them, so that all went off well. Immediately after supper Jacob and his uncle spread out their books and papers on the dining-room table. I waited upstairs a little while, until I heard Adah take in a cup of tea for them, then with the list in my hand I went down and opened the door and walked timidly into the room. Jacob at once slipped out, which I had not bargained for, and I was left standing at my cousin's elbow like a school-girl, his fair head just at my hand. He hummed slightly to himself as he added figures and when he began to write a letter I despaired of his noticing me and was obliged to cough. He started and looked round.

"I beg your pardon, Cousin Eleanor," he said then kindly. "I'm so busy writing sharp dunning letters, I didn't see you. These Iredale clothiers are devils to bleed."

He saw my distress at his language and laughed.

"Well, come, sit down. What's to do? Tessie and Dick quarrelling again? Jacob languishing? Adah saucy? Or is it Joah, eh?" At this last notion he frowned.

"No—I have just brought you the note of the children's needs, cousin," I said, proffering the paper.

He took it in his strong well-shaped hands—always very fair and clean, in spite of his work in the mill—and read it through.

"Why, it is not unreasonable," he said. "Jacob shall take you and the children down to Annotsfield tomorrow in the gig and you can make the purchases yourself. I'll give you a note to a couple of shopmen, and they can send the accounts to me." I thanked him, much relieved.

"I see there's nothing noted here of your own requirements, Cousin Eleanor."

I was silent and I felt my colour heighten.

"Too proud, eh? Well, consult my pride a little also, cousin. I like all Moreys to go well clad."

"You did not trouble yourself about my father's wants, I believe, sir," said I very quickly, for I was angry.

"What was the use, when he told me he was to die within a week? Buy yourself a nice warm cloak, or pelisse or mantle or whatever you call them. Scarlet for Tessie, blue for you."

"The spring is here and I do not need a warm cloak."

"Nay, cousin, you don't know our Yorkshire weather. No warm cloak for March? Do as I say or you'll feel the weight of my displeasure. If you catch cold you'll be a burden on the house."

There was a pause. I was strongly vexed, yet there was some sense in what he said. I stretched out my hand for the list, but he did not give it to me; he folded it and tapped it against the table.

"The house is beginning to look better, but it's not right yet," said he.

"There is too much to do for Adah alone," I said.

"And Tessie of course never lifts a finger."

"She is beginning to learn," said I, unable truthfully to say more.

"It's awkward, you see, cousin," said Charles Moreys, leaning back so that he tilted his chair and speaking in a friendly tone. "I'd be glad enough to get in another servant to help Adah, but it's awkward. If they're old Adah quarrels with them, and if they're young Joah goes after them."

"Could you not impress Joah with a sense of the wickedness of such conduct?" said I severely.

Charles Moreys laughed, then shrugged his shoulders. "He inherits it, you see—he can't help it. Gets it from his father. My half-brother James that was. That was," he repeated musingly.

"I do not consider the excuse valid, sir," said I, very stiff.

"Very likely not, Cousin Eleanor," said Charles Moreys, laughing in his most bitter and cynical style. "But you are not a man, d'you see. And now be off, while I write some more notes for these dishonest, dirty, altogether devilish Iredale clothiers, be damned to 'em."

I fled from his language, but having to struggle with the door a little because Jacob was returning and held it from the other side, I faced round towards the table for a moment and found my cousin glancing at me sideways with a very merry look in his blue eyes. It was really very difficult to know how to take my cousin Charles Moreys.

The next day, as had been promised, Jacob drove us down to Annotsfield. It was a wild, cold, dark morning, with a strong wind which continually lashed us with pelting hail and sleet—even the horse's mane blew in the wind and its haunches grew black with damp. Tessie had of course chosen to sit beside Jacob in the place of honour, but when the hail came she found it so exposed that she cried out for me to change with her. This put me in a quandary; I dared not leave Dick and Tessie alone together by going forward myself and dared not send the delicate boy forward into the battle of the elements. So I called Tessie to come back and sit with us and we all three crouched close together beneath a shawl, and I must say Tessie was less forward than usual from the adventure of it, and for once we were all happy together.

In Annotsfield the icy rain was sweeping through the streets and the shops were empty, so that we received much attention and were able to make advantageous purchases. The notes Charles Moreys had given me for the shopmen authorised expenditure on a generous scale—I had never before had so much money to lay out—and it was a great enjoyment to fit the children up so lavishly. I had been afraid that Tessie would be difficult and wish to buy taste-less and crudely fashioned things, but, poor child, she was quite struck dumb by the town and the shops, which it seems it was years since she had visited, and so she took my word in everything. Indeed I was much struck by the appearance of Tessie and Dick now I had them against this background, so familiar to me, of a town; they looked so handsome and yet so uncouth that my heart quite ached for them. They trembled and their eyes were as wide as saucers, when we entered the first shop. Dick's frailness seemed more noticeable here and the commiserating looks the shop people gave him alarmed me; I had the uneasy impression too that he looked more ill than when I had first seen him. However he was not sick at all and seemed to stand the fatigue of the day surprisingly well.

The pelisses, with bonnets to match, were bought as Charles Moreys had ordered; my own a soft quiet grey which matched my eyes, Tessie's a rich crimson. This last was a most enormous price, being made, so they told us, of cloth costing forty shillings a yard! But it suited the child well and she greatly desired it, and after all the daughter of a man whose wealth came from cloth ought to wear good cloth—or so at least I promised myself to tell Charles Moreys if he should grumble. Dick was measured for a jacket and some ankle-length nankeen breeches which were to be brought home next market-day, and we bought shoes and bonnets, gloves and linen and muslin, and met Jacob at the appointed time by the George Inn with some of our packages carried there by the shopmen, and drove off home in high feather with parcels heaped around us, laughing and chattering. Jacob also was in a very good humour because he had met Mr. Greaves in the town and learned that next week there was to be a party at Upper Hey to which we were all invited. I made up my mind that Tessie should have a clear muslin frock by that time, such as was then the proper wear for all young ladies; necessity had given me some skill with the needle and I began to plan how to cut out her dress, and we discussed whether it should have blue ribbon or pink, for a girdle.

The storm had cleared and the evening was fresh and bright with a golden sky in the west behind the hills towards which we were driving. Suddenly who should draw level with us but Charles Moreys on horseback, sitting very erect and cool and wearing his hat at a rakish angle. He touched his hat to us and was about to pass, but Tessie called out and we all waved to him. He appeared a trifle vexed and startled, but seemed to relent as he glanced at us, perhaps because we looked so cheerful together, and reining in his horse rode beside us for a little way, pointing out to us the Ire Bridge, just above which our own beck from Moreydale ran into the river, and telling me the names of the various hills, rolling out of each other as he said, "every which way." Then after a while, giving us a courteous bow, he touched his horse with his heel and rode on ahead of us. He certainly looked a very fine figure of a man on horseback and we all watched him admiringly, Dick especially craning his neck and even standing up in the gig to follow his progress.

Charles Moreys reached Wool Royd before us, of course, and came out of the dining-room as we entered the house and bade us show him our purchases. I felt anxious lest he should disapprove, but he made no criticisms, and when he came to the pelisses, which we had brought with us, he made Tessie put hers on and turn round and round to show it off to him. He approved its colour and felt the cloth between his fingers appraisingly. I had my sentence about the daughter of the man whose wealth came from cloth, at the end of my tongue, but it was not needed; he passed on to my grey coat, felt its stuff and nodded in silence.

The children were almost too tired to eat, and Dick fell asleep at the table, his fair head suddenly dropping forward. I took him upstairs and helped him into bed, and was much troubled by the sight of his thin little body, the ribs of which could be clearly seen—more clearly, I thought, than a week or two ago.

When I came down again, Adah had cleared away the supper; Joah was out, Charles Moreys and Jacob were busy with the mill books, and Tessie had gone to bed. The house seemed so quiet and peaceful that I took the opportunity to cut out Tessie's muslin gown on the round table in the nursery, then sat down to baste the long seams of the skirt.

"Not abed yet, cousin?" said a voice. I started. "It's time you stopped work. Jacob and I have given up for the night. I saw your light beneath the door."

"I should like to finish this seam," I said. I held it up to show him and there were only a few inches left to sew.

"Then why try your eyes by this poor candlelight? There are plenty of lamps about the house, surely," said Charles Moreys impatiently.

He flung away, returning in a moment or two with a fine large lamp—taken, I thought, from the drawing-room below; a place I had not yet been able to set to rights, which was therefore never used. He lighted the lamp and replaced the chimney, turned down the wick and when the flame steadied turned it up again, then set the lamp exactly where its light fell best across the muslin. All this he did in his usual neat and skilful way; his hands were most singularly deft and strong. Folding his arms, he leaned carelessly against the table and watched me as I sewed.

His silence, his gaze, his large masculine presence, the quiet of the house and the lateness of the hour, embarrassed me. I felt my colour rise and my fingers tremble. To break the spell I forced myself to speak.

"I hope you were not dissatisfied with the purchases today, cousin?"

"No, I was not dissatisfied. I noticed that Tessie's coat was some two or three times as costly as your own."

"How did you guess that, cousin?" I stammered, taken aback.

"By the feel of the cloth, child," said Charles Moreys impatiently. "The crimson had altogether a softer handle. If I couldn't judge the quality of wool by this time, I should be a poor tool in my trade, shouldn't I?"

"The crimson pelisse was certainly costly," I said in some dismay. "But the colour suited Tessie so well, and surely the daughter of a——"

"You mistake my meaning, Cousin Eleanor. I was not dissatisfied to find that you spent less on yourself than on Tessie. Many women would have done differently."

"You are mistaken, Cousin Charles," I said with as much dignity as I could muster. "Every woman does the best she can for children entrusted to her."

He laughed. "I believe you really think so," he said.

"Certainly I do."

"Well, at least you are one of those who can be trusted," said Charles Moreys. "Tell me, did you enjoy your excursion to Annotsfield?"

I told him we had all enjoyed it greatly, even Dick; who, though he was so sleepy, seemed really no worse for it. Having thus introduced Dick into the conversation, I went off to lay my fears for him before his father. Charles Moreys listened with a scowl.

"He is a wreckling and will never make a man," he said. "The sooner he goes, the better perhaps for him."

"How can you say such a thing, cousin!" I exclaimed indignantly. "He must be cared for and cured—perhaps we should send for a physician?"

He seemed unwilling to listen and tossed the subject from him impatiently, but I persisted, and at length he agreed to take the child to a doctor in Annotsfield.

"I would rather the doctor came here so that I myself could hear what he says about Dick," said I.

"You are devilishly persistent, Cousin Eleanor," said Charles Moreys.

"There is nothing devilish in caring for a sick child," I replied hotly.

"True," he admitted.

At this moment I came to the end of my seam and the clock in the hall downstairs struck twelve, simultaneously. I was horrified by the lateness of the hour and began to throw my things together hurriedly.

"Twelve! I have talked an hour without one recourse to the bottle," said Charles Moreys, laughing.

"It seems to me, Cousin Charles," said I, gathering up all my courage, "that if you can compel yourself to be sober when posting your mill books, you can compel yourself to be sober on other occasions."

"You are a prig, my dear," said Charles Moreys, laughing again.

I rose up—for my work was now all tidied—and faced him and lifted my eyes to his and said reproachfully:

"Why do you drink to such excess, cousin?"

The laughter died from his face, which turned harsh and brooding.

"The story is not fit for your pretty little ears, Cousin Eleanor," he said coldly. "Come! To bed, or you will not be able to open those agreeable eyes of yours in the morning."

In spite of this somewhat unfriendly termination to our conversation, I went to bed feeling happier than I had done since my coming to Wool Royd. Nay—happier than for some months or even years before my coming, for what with my poor father's illness and before that his misery about the debt and then in the Fleet, life had held nothing but sorrow for me for a long time. At Wool Royd I now felt useful, even wanted. And after all, my father had sent me here, it was his own home, I was in a manner native to it. Perhaps even this very room where I slept had been his, all those years ago. From this I fell to wondering about a matter I had not thought of for long enough, the mystery of his departure from Wool Royd, which had been effected, as I now reminded myself, by my Cousin Charles's father. Sometime I must ask my Cousin Charles about his father. The wind rushed through the trees and shook the windows, the beck gurgled noisily as it rolled headlong over the rocks and moss-grown stones and roared over the dam, but these seemed not strange but friendly sounds to me now; Wool Royd had become home to me.

CHAPTER V

BEFORE the party at Upper Hey, which was to shed such light for me on the Moreys' affairs, took place there occurred two incidents, both fraught with warning if only my eyes had been open then to see it.

The first was when the physician, Dr. Bradshaw—I learned afterwards he was the best in Annotsfield and certainly he took much trouble with the case—came to see Dick. He seemed puzzled by the child's condition, examined him most carefully from head to toe and finally concluded that he was under-nourished. He asked many particulars about the bouts of sickness to which Dick was subject, prescribed some medicine and ordered him to drink three pints of milk every day, which was to be set aside for him in pitchers in the morning with the cream on. I shall never forget the look which crossed Dick's face as this was said. The poor child was sitting up in bed with his nightgown huddled about his shoulders so that Dr. Bradshaw could listen to his heart and lungs, and his thin little body made a sad picture. As the milk was ordered, he gave me a strange look, a look of such despairing anguish that it quite broke my heart; I sat down beside him on the bed and drew his head to my breast and tried to comfort him.

"Don't you like milk, Dick dear?" I said.

"I don't like it in a pitcher like that," he whispered.

"Why not, my boy?" said the physician. As Dick did not answer, he continued to me: "Don't you keep cows here?"

"Oh, yes indeed," said I, for at the far end of the house was quite a large cowshed, and there was another in a field a little distance away, all the fields round the house belonging to Charles Moreys. I was alarmed when I met the big brown-and-white beasts in the yard, as we did sometimes, and Joah and Tessie were apt to jeer at me and tell me they would soon be turned out to pasture when the weather came warmer and then I should be frightened to walk through the fields.

"Wouldn't you like to go to the cowshed when they're milking and have a drink of the warm frothy milk in the bucket?" suggested Dr. Bradshaw.

To me this suggestion was repugnant, for to a townswoman the hind-quarters of the cows seemed very dirty and fouled with being indoors all winter and the less connection the milk I drank had with them the better I liked it. But small boys— or at least so I thought at the time—had odd wild notions, and I was not too much surprised when Dick seemed to brighten and after a moment whispered that yes, he would like it.

"But that's only two pints of milk a day," he said slyly. "One in the morning and one in the evening."

"Very well, let us say two pints, then," agreed the doctor, humouring him.

So we followed this prescription. Dick's health seemed to improve on it, though he ate little at other times. I tried once to persuade him to drink a third pint in the middle of the day, which could easily be set aside for him, but he scowled quite in his father's style and said "No!" so emphatically that I desisted.

The other incident occurred on the night of the Pay Day—which, as Jacob told me afterwards, was a very successful one. I had always rather dreaded this Pay Day, for I very much disliked to see Charles Moreys drunk and feared that on this occasion I should do so. Jacob, however, assured me that I should not, for his uncle never touched liquor when there was any business on hand. Still, I found myself unable to sleep that night till the men should return from the Pack Horse; I lay awake uneasily, and as it turned out it was well I did so. Shortly after midnight I heard the three of them coming up the lane. They were making a great deal of noise —or rather, as I found when they came nearer, a great deal of noise was being made by Joah. He was singing and shouting in a raucous voice, and apparently staggering, for I heard the sound of a fall and his uncle speaking to him impatiently. Even Jacob seemed to be what gentlemen—so mistakenly in my opinion—call *a little merry*, for he laughed in a silly hiccupping way at his brother's mishap. Eventually Jacob and Cousin Charles helped Joah into the house between them and half lifted, half dragged him up the stairs; then their voices receded; they were in fact in my cousin's room, sorting out the bills and notes and money which they had brought home with them from their customers. I let myself slip into drowsiness, relieved that nothing worse had happened.

Suddenly I became aware of a cold draught blowing over my face and stirring my hair. I raised myself and drew the bed-curtain aside and looked about the room, and there to my horror stood Joah in the open doorway. He held a candle aloft in one hand, and was swaying on his feet so uncertainly that the wax dripped to the floor and the flame sputtered. Joah's face was crimson, his mouth gaped and drooled, he laughed in a thick drunken way and his great black eyes leered at me. I was very much frightened.

"Go away, Joah," I said sternly.

Joah laughed but still stood there swaying.

"Go away at once."

He laughed again and suddenly lurched towards me.

"Cousin Charles!" I screamed, terrified. "Cousin! Cousin!"

Joah staggered forward and grasped at the bed-curtains to preserve his balance; they ripped from the pole and he fell on his knees heavily. At this moment Charles Moreys entered the room, walking swiftly; with a look of livid fury on his face he seized Joah by the collar of his coat and dragged him out of the room as a man might drag a dog by its collar. Even in that moment I could not but wonder at the strength he thus exerted, for Joah had a heavy burly figure. Charles Moreys seemed to throw his nephew down outside the room, then turning back on the threshold he said to me: "Tomorrow I will have a lock put on your door," and slammed the door behind him. He spoke with a cold disgust which I thought rather unfair, as after all I was not to be blamed for Joah's misbehaviour.

Next day I was troubled lest Joah should make an apology and troubled lest he should not; Charles Moreys perhaps saw this, for he called me back after breakfast, which the men ate with us for once, to tell me curtly that Joah, having been quite drunk, had no recollection of what had happened the night before and that it would be better not to remind him. I was thankful to have no further reference made to the matter, and most thankful that Tessie and Dick had been asleep and knew nothing of it, but I thought I saw in Adah's look a most unfortunate awareness. I found her in the after-noon leaning against the stairhead, watching the man whom Charles Moreys had sent from the mill to put locks on all the bedroom doors, and there was a scornful sneer on her grim face which displeased me greatly.

CHAPTER VI

THE UPPER HEY party began with a moment's happiness for me which was soon dimmed, then continued to grow darker until trouble filled my whole sky.

The happy moment came when I had dressed Tessie and Dick in their new clothes and sent them downstairs to their father. With their faces shining clean and their hair well brushed, and wearing everything new from head to toe, they looked a handsome pair and I was proud of them. Tessie was perhaps a trifle plump in her long muslin frock and Dick perhaps a trifle thin and pale, but these deficiencies would be remedied in a year or two, I hoped. Tessie ran down first, and bouncing up and down in the hall cried out: "Look at me! Look at me, Father!" Dick came behind shyly, but he smiled and held up his head more confidently than usual. Charles Moreys came out into the hall and was well pleased with them, I think, for he smiled; it gave me a tender happy feeling in my heart to see how like his smile was to Dick's. Then his glance lighted upon me and my happiness died, for anger gleamed in his eyes. I saw at once that he did not like my old brown sarsenet gown; he was vexed I had not provided myself with a new one, angered that I, a Moreys, should appear in public thus unhandsomely attired; he thought me either too proud or too silly to take advantage of his bounty and despised me either way. The truth was that I had not known of the party until we were returning from our Annotsfield shopping and so had not provided material for a gown for myself. Charles Moreys had not commanded it and I had not thought of it. Indeed even if I had done so, I should not have had time to make it up, having so much sewing to do for Dick and Tessie. However, I now saw how my lack of a new gown must look to my cousin, and hanging my head and colouring I said hurriedly:

"I suppose I shall not go to the party; I shall stay at home?"

"You must go," said Charles briefly, scowling.

To my surprise, it appeared he did not intend to go himself; he commanded Joah and Jacob to see that the lanterns they carried were in good condition, take thought for the comfort of the rest of us and bring Dick home if he grew too tired, then ushered us out of the door without a word about the children's dress. This, I must own, was a keen disappointment to me after all the trouble I had taken.

As it was only a short way by the mill lane to Upper Hey, we were to walk the distance. Joah and Tessie set off in advance, arm in arm and chattering and laughing, so that I was obliged to call out to Tessie to remind her to hold up her dress out of the mud. Dick ran off after them, but in a moment there was a cry and he came running back wailing and with tears in his eyes, holding out his hands, which were

74

thick in mud. Joah had pushed him roughly aside and he had only saved himself with difficulty from falling full-length in the lane. I sent him back to the house to wash, and Jacob and I stood waiting for him.

"Why does not your uncle accompany us, Jacob?" I asked to fill in the time.

"Uncle Charles and Mrs. Greaves are old enemies," replied Jacob crossly.

A sharp voice and a wail from within told me Dick had encountered his father, and Jacob meanwhile was so restless and impatient, being kept from his Mary, that between one and another of them my spirits sank very low and I found it not easy to keep from tears myself. However, at long last we reached the Upper Hey buildings where Mr. Greaves carried on the trade of clothier, and found light streaming from all the windows and a great noise of talk and laughing within.

I felt wretchedly shy at having to meet all these new people, especially as Jacob rushed away, to Mary I suppose, the moment we entered the house and Joah sidled off and joined a group of young men clustered round the door, so that Tessie and Dick and myself were left standing, not knowing which way to go and jostled continually by guests and servants passing by. As I did not know my hostess by sight and Tessie and Dick had fallen into one of their panic fits and were clinging to my arms almost senseless with fright, I found myself in a real difficulty. We were extricated, however, by Mr. Dan Dennett, the miller as he was called because he looked after the big wooden fulling-stocks at the mill. He was so spruced up that at first I did not recognise him, but luckily Dick trembled out his name. A short, square, wooden-faced man with tousled brown hair, very silent usually, I was inclined to trust him because I had noticed that when we passed by the mill yard—his neat little house stood at one side—he nodded his head in a kindly way and it was he who had sent the kitten up for the children. So I accepted gratefully when he offered to take us to our hostess.

I disliked Mrs. Greaves the moment I laid eyes on her. Not that she was a wrong-living woman or anything of that kind; she was thoroughly respectable and honest, I felt sure, a regular attender at chapel, a good wife and mother according to her lights, a notable housewife, hospitable and not unkind or bad-tempered or (except on one point, as I found later) malicious. It was just that she had a self-seeking way with her; she knew emphatically, to use a vulgar phrase, on which side her bread was buttered. She was modest and decent enough in all matters except those which concerned her family's advancement; but on that subject she could scarcely keep her coarseness in control. Any fine feeling or noble sentiment seemed to her "silly work", as the Yorkshire phrase goes, a childish and contemptible waste of time. A large solid woman, not ill-looking in a massive way, with somewhat scanty brown hair, big bold features and shrewd little eyes, she was very neatly dressed, her house was spotless and well equipped and the entertainment she offered was ample and well arranged. I say *her* house and entertainment, because I saw at once that Mr. Greaves counted for little in it; a friendly, foolish little man with large anxious eyes, whose manner of speaking was that often described as "with a plum in his mouth," he ran up to his wife continually for guidance —and I may add, always received it. Mr. Dennett introduced me: "Charles Moreys' cousin Miss Eleanor."

"Well, Tessie! Well, Dick!" said Mrs. Greaves in a hearty, Yorkshire, condescending tone, her eyes meanwhile taking in every detail of the children's clothes. "Very fine tonight, aren't you? By what right do you call cousins with Charles Moreys, Miss? Is it just a courtesy title, eh?"

Vexed and astonished, I replied rather coldly: "My father Walter Moreys was the half-brother of Mr. Charles's father."

"Ah! There's always half-brothers in the Moreys family," said Mrs. Greaves, shaking her head vigorously. "John and Walter, James and Charles, Dick and——" She looked at Dick and Tessie and checked herself. "And a bitter trial they are. I'm not minded our Mary shall start another set, I can tell you." She looked at me defiantly, but seeing that I had not the least idea what she was talking about, she became somewhat mollified. "Well, if you're Charles Moreys' real cousin, of course that's different."

"I hope I shall have the pleasure of meeting your daughter tonight, ma'am," I said. "I have heard so much—so much that is agreeable—about her."

Mrs. Greaves gave me a shrewd look. But what I had said was perfectly sincere, and her expression slightly softened.

"Mary! Mary love! Come here!" she called.

Mary threaded her way through the throng obediently. Mrs. Greaves gave a tug at her daughter's sash and tucked a curl in over her ear, then faced me with a look which asked: "There! What do you think of her?"

It was clear to me at once that the chief passion of Mrs. Greaves' life was Mary. Just as strongly as I had disliked Mrs. Greaves at first sight, I liked her daughter. She was not a great beauty or a great wit, but a good, comely, honest, sensible, brown-haired, brown-eyed girl, with a sort of robust kindness about her of which I could well understand the attraction for Jacob. She looked at me in a rather perplexed and appealing way, and at once I understood her situation and felt deeply for her. She loved Jacob dearly, but her mother was against him, and her mother ruled Upper Hey. At the same time, I read in Mary's bright eyes a determination to fight for Jacob, if only Jacob would live up to his best self and be worthy of the struggle. I made up my mind to help them both as far as ever I could, and I tried to show this in my smile. She smiled back at me and we were friends and have always remained so.

At this moment Mr. Greaves came hurrying up and with great goodwill and half a dozen unfinished plopping sentences swept Tessie and Dick away to join a game which the young people were arranging. Mrs. Greaves went off to her kitchen and took her daughter with her; left alone again, I withdrew quietly to the side of the room and seated myself on a long wooden settle. It is very uncomfortable and embarrassing to be alone and unknown amid a large party of people who are all familiar with each other; I tried to hold up my head and smile and look at ease, but was really much relieved when Dan Dennett came up again and presented me to his wife. She was a small, dark, birdlike woman with a rather shrivelled brown skin and very fine bright dark eyes; I thought her kindly and was glad when she seated herself beside me on the settle.

"What do you think about Mary and Jacob, then?" she said, smiling.

I was taken aback; it hardly seemed proper for me to discuss Jacob's affairs with a stranger.

"Our Jacob's told me how much you've done for him, teaching him and that," went on Mrs. Dennett.

Again I was disconcerted.

"Ah, I see," said Mrs. Dennett, smiling rather sadly. "I see how it is, like. Jacob hasn't said owt about me to you, has he? I'm his mother."

"His mother!" I exclaimed.

"Yes. I'm Joah and Jacob's mother," said Mrs. Dennett quietly. "Dan there is my second husband. I was James Lee's wife."

There seemed a world of suffering and sadness in her last few words. I looked at her in amazement, at a loss what to reply. The game had now begun and was proceeding very noisily; nobody took any notice of us and we were able to talk quietly together under cover of the surrounding din.

"James wasn't a good man," went on Mrs. Dennett with quiet dignity. "And it makes me worried, you see, about Joah and Jacob."

I could but feel that as regards Joah her anxieties were only too well founded, and doubtless she read this in my face, for she sighed, and continued: "Jacob is a good boy."

"He is indeed," said I, glad to be able to agree heartily.

"And devoted to Mary Greaves."

"And she to him, I believe," said I.

"Her father would do anything for Mary," said Mrs. Dennett. "But it's her mother, you see."

Just then Mrs. Greaves came bustling back. Evidently well satisfied with the state of her supper preparations, she sat down beside us, smoothed her dress, glanced us over shrewdly and began to turn politeness to advantage.

"I understand Wool Royd had a very good Pay Day this quarter," she said.

I said nothing, not thinking myself entitled to discuss my cousin's affairs, and Mrs. Dennett was also silent, but her husband, who had come up behind us puffing a long pipe, withdrew it from his mouth long enough to remark:

"Pretty fair."

"That mill is worth its weight in gold," exclaimed Mrs.

78

Greaves, her eyes quite gleaming at the thought. "If Joah and Jacob had half shares of *that* coming to them, now!"

"Well, they haven't," said Dan Dennett.

"More's the pity," said Mrs. Greaves sharply. "If everyone had their rights, now, things would be very different, wouldn't they?"

"Charles Moreys built most of the mill," said Dan Dennett.

"He built it out of his father's mill with what his father left him, I suppose," said Mrs. Greaves with asperity.

"James never had any claim to it," said Mrs. Dennett.

"You're altogether too good, Lucy," Mrs. Greaves told her.

"It's a good thing one of 'em was good," said Dan Dennett with his mild irony.

During these exchanges, which she had obviously embarked on for my benefit, Mrs. Greaves raked my face with her sharp eyes to see if she could learn anything from my expression, but perceiving that I was entirely ignorant of the matter in hand, she sniffed with disappointment and went off to some more rewarding gossip. Thinking over what she had said, both at our first meeting and just recently, through much bewilderment I thought I perceived her meaning: that Charles Moreys had inherited all his father's substance at the expense of James, his half-brother. Then I remembered what I had hitherto lost sight of, though I knew it: that the name of Jacob and Joah was Lee, not Moreys. They were six or seven years older, too, than Charles Moreys' children. I turned impetuously to Mrs. Dennett and asked her:

"Was your husband—Mr. Lee—older or younger than Mr. Charles Moreys?"

"Older."

"But how could he be older?" said I, puzzled, thinking of the ailing beautiful Caroline who had been John Moreys' wife. "And how could his name be Lee?" I added.

Mrs. Dennett glanced over her shoulder at her husband, who turned away and pretended to be unconcerned with us.

"It's not a thing to mention to a young lady like you," said Mrs. Dennett in her soft melancholy tones; "but James Lee was born on the wrong side of the blanket. He was a love-child of John Moreys."

"Good heavens! Who was his mother?"

"Oh, I don't know. Nobody knew. Well, James may have known, but he never told anyone, not even me. You see, for a long time Mrs. Moreys—Caroline was her name—had nothing but miscarriages and stillbirths. Seemed as though she never would bring a living child to birth. So her husband brought James Lee, a little toddling boy, to Wool Royd. Everyone knew he was John Moreys' son; John Moreys never denied it. Then when James was rising seven or eight, lo and behold Caroline had a live child, and died of it."

"And the child was Charles Moreys?"

"That's right. He was the legitimate heir, do you see, and put James's nose right out of joint, as the saying is. But don't let anyone ever tell you Charles Moreys behaved ill to James for he didn't. And after James's death, when Dan wanted to marry me but didn't want to take my children along with me, Charles promised to keep them and bring them up. That's how it all was, you see."

"And you left your two boys, your children?"

"Well, Dan couldn't never bear the sight of Joah and Jacob. They were always so like their father, and Dan always hated James Lee. Dan and I were courting, you see, before James Lee"—she hesitated and I read the whole sorry story—"forced me into marrying him."

"Oh, heavens!" I exclaimed. My cheeks were crimson; beneath the respectable, rather dull surface of this provincial party, I perceived black abysses yawn and smoke.

"It isn't the right thing to be talking about to a young lady like you, I know," said Mrs. Dennett again in her soft drone; "but as you're living at Wool Royd, Dan and me, we reckoned you'd better know what you're in the middle of. Dan and Jacob both speak well of you to me. Mrs. Greaves now, she thought at first you were no better than you should be."

"Upon my word!" I exclaimed in fury.

"But I daresay after tonight she'll think different," said Mrs. Dennett soothingly.

"Oh, this is unbearable! But tell me, Mrs. Dennett," I said, turning to her again: "since you know so much, do you know why John Moreys turned my father out of Wool Royd?"

"Nay, love, that would be before my time. Before I was born. But it would be something best left untold, I reckon. They have a dark history, the Moreys. Poor Charles Moreys has had a wretched life of it."

"Why?" said I.

"There are several ways of telling that story," replied James Lee's widow cautiously.

"Tell me one of them."

Mrs. Dennett considered but shook her head. "Nay— nobody knows the rights and wrongs of it but Charles Moreys. And perhaps not him, rightly."

I became sensible here that my demand had passed the bounds of discretion, that indeed our whole conversation was not such as my cousin, and my own view of what was proper, could approve. So it was a relief to me that supper was then announced and we all passed into another room. Dick, looking flushed and happy, came running to me, sat at my side and ate prodigiously of the good things Upper Hey offered; I was pleased to notice that Mary Greaves kept coming to him with some special dainty as if she had a warm corner in her heart for Jacob's cousin. Such was Dick's appetite, indeed, that I feared unhappy consequences, but he was not ill, and fell to dancing after supper with the rest, with much enjoyment. During this pursuit Tessie's voice was heard rather more loudly and more often than I could have wished for manners' sake, for she had taken dancing lessons, it seemed, at one time in Annotsfield and ordered the others about to comply with what she had been taught there. But she looked so happy and I must say so beautiful, with her dark eyes sparkling, her rich colour warm in her cheeks, her dark curls falling not ungracefully from their ribbon, that I smiled indulgently and thought she might be forgiven a litle childish exuberance. Not so Mrs. Greaves, who, as she passed about the room attending to her guests' comfort with Mary beside her carrying a huge jug of ale, paused once behind me to drop into my ear:

"What a little madam Tessie is! Don't you find her an awkward handful?"

"She is motherless," I said excusingly.

"Well—Joah will get his share back that way," said Mrs. Greaves, looking across the room to where Tessie, as I was sorry to see, was partnered for the fifth or sixth time by her cousin. "But there'll be nothing for Jacob."

"Mother!" exclaimed Mary in an angry whisper.

My heart was now sunk so low that I yearned beyond measure for the end of the merry-making. I could hardly hold my head up a moment longer. For the pattern of life at Wool Royd was, I thought, now made clear to me. There was a solid ground for Joah's habitual bad behaviour to Dick, his habitual flattery of Tessie. James Lee's sons— though I absolved Jacob from such evil envy—might well think themselves cheated of their inheritance by Charles Moreys and his children. Joah hated Dick for supplanting him, and meant to marry Tessie and as Mrs. Greaves said get his share of Wool Royd back that way. It did not escape my attention that James Lee had been born, if Mrs. Dennett's vague indications were correct, in the year that my father was driven from his home by John Moreys. Perhaps the two events were connected, though I could see no connection. What I saw—as I thought very clearly, though I was wrong there—and it made me wretched, was the danger of Joah Lee's presence to those I loved at Wool Royd.

CHAPTER VII

A STRANGE uneasy period for me now followed.

Outdoors the season was on the turn. The wind no longer howled cold and fierce down Moreydale, sweeping sleet or hail along in its icy blast, but blustered cheerfully with a milder rainy breath. The sky was high and pale blue, with cool white clouds swiftly sailing; the trees became misted with green buds, the soaked grass lifted its head and took on a fresher colour, the knobby roots of the bracken swelled and began to uncurl their fronds. So many larks sang their sweet songs *at heaven's gate,* as Shakespeare says, around us that I well understood why Wool Royd had once had the name of Laverock Hall though it was no longer used, Dick having explained to me that *laverock* was the Yorkshire name for this trilling bird. Presently lambs with charming black faces began to appear in the fields around. It was an endless pleasure to me to see their pretty gambols and even Tessie's heart seemed softened as we watched them, and she exclaimed that they were sweet. I had a great desire to touch one of their curly coats, so one day Dick caught and held a lamb for me—Dick had a good way with all animals, hir hands were firm yet gentle, so that they were not afraid of him and he did not hurt them. But alas this was a disappointment to me, for the fleece which looked so soft was harsh and oily to the touch. The Moreys and Lees all laughed at me (in their different ways) for my ignorance in this matter, and laughed again at the account Dick gave them of my anxieties over the straying of the lambs from their mothers' sides. It was an anguish to me to see a lamb which had lost its mother timidly approach ewe after ewe in search of her, only to be butted away. Its frightened bleats and the perturbed response of the mother from a distance, the difficulty they experienced in locating each other, seemed to me quite heartrending, and I longed to direct them, sometimes even calling and pointing to them over the wall, though I knew of course that that was foolish.

"Cousin Eleanor would like them to have coloured ribbons round their necks by which they could distinguish each other," suggested Jacob, laughing.

"Or bells tuned to the same note," said Dick.

"They *have* tuned bells; their voices are tuned bells," said Charles Moreys. "You must leave the sheep to manage their own affairs, cousin."

But he smiled and spoke kindly, so that the rebuke seemed uttered rather for my sake than the sheep's. It was the same on one soft sunny April morning when as I came down the lane with the children we were met by the cows from the shed, running full tilt out of the yard. I cried out in alarm and climbed the grassy banks at the side of the lane and Tessie climbed too and clung to me, and we stood there waiting for them to pass, but one cow stopped and gazed at us in a most baleful manner and would not go on till Dick gave its brown haunch a friendly slap. Charles Moreys chanced to be coming up from the mill at the time and he laughed to see us there but came up and offered his hand to me to help me down from the bank, which was certainly somewhat precipitous.

"A woman of your spirit should not fear a cow, cousin," said he, affecting to roll his eyes reprovingly.

"But why did it pause and stare at me so?"

"A cow has all the natural curiosity of a female."

I could not but laugh. "But why do they *run*, cousin?" said I. "I have never seen a cow running fast before."

"They are excited at being let out of the shed, eager to get into the fields for the first time after the winter months. I am sure, cousin," went on Charles Moreys gravely, "that you with your tender heart would not grudge the enjoyment of spring even to a cow."

"Why, no," said I, somewhat ashamed. "Certainly not. But——"

I was interrupted by a roar of laughter from Dick and Charles Moreys. I smiled; it was always a pleasure to me to see these two laugh, for when I first came to Wool Royd they had both seemed incapable of laughter, and if I were the cause of their merriment I was quite content.

In general, since the party at Upper Hey Charles Moreys seemed much milder and gentler in his manner to me. Though I rejoiced in this, I could not understand the reason for it. Sometimes I thought he had heard agreeable reports of Dick and Tessie at the party, sometimes I thought perhaps it was merely his satisfaction with the good Pay Day. Sometimes, again, I thought perhaps I had mistaken the nature of his glance at my old brown gown on the night of the party; perhaps he had not been angry with me after all. This supposition gained some strength when a week or two after the party Jacob came into the nursery carrying two large parcels, and with a grin dumped them down in front of me. When opened they proved to be lengths of soft blue crape and fine grey merino cloth. Tessie was excited, thinking them intended for her, but they were addressed to me and Jacob said they were a gift to me from Charles Moreys. This did not prevent Tessie asking her father at the supper table that night whether the blue crape might not be made up for her, since it was "too young" for Cousin Eleanor. Charles Moreys' scowl at this was something quite prodigious, even for him.

"No, Theresa," he said. (He always called poor Tessie by this name when he was displeased with her.) "The dress lengths are a present I am making on your behalf to your cousin, to show your gratitude for all she has done for you."

Poor Tessie, who had never thought of uttering a word of thanks to me for the sewing I had done for her—and why should she, poor child? I wished her rather to think of me as a member of the family than as a stranger who needed to be paid by thanks—poor Tessie for once looked quite taken aback, and I too stammered my thanks with more confusion than I wished.

"It is very good of you, cousin. I am very much obliged."

"Nowt o't'sort," returned Charles Moreys roughly, putting on his broadest Yorkshire.

"Tessie has nothing to thank me for."

"I'm the best judge of that," said Charles Moreys. "Now listen to me, all on you; those stuffs are for your Cousin Eleanor and don't let me see them used for anyone else, or there'll be trouble."

Dick clapped his hands softly together, the good-hearted Jacob grinned with pleasure. (Mrs. Greaves was turning a kinder eye on his suit lately and he was much encouraged.) But Joah's heavy face was like a thundercloud, and Adah's look was curiously menacing. That James Lee's eldest son should resent a gift to an outsider of any Wool Royd wealth, I might deplore but could now understand; but why Adah should dislike it was less obvious. Jealousy, I supposed; perhaps it was long since she herself had received a gift from her master. (Of what wages were paid her, I knew nothing.) It occurred to me that when opportunity arose I would suggest to Charles Moreys the present of a black silk gown.

But this scene was symbolic of the uncertainty and uneasiness of my life at this time. Out of doors, and in Charles Moreys' presence, all seemed springtime, gay and sunny; but as soon as he quitted Wool Royd, the house felt dark and sinister, with a most uncomfortable impression of watching behind doors and whispering in corners. Dick had a bad bout of sickness which puzzled the doctor. Joah was so savagely ill-humoured that at last even Tessie seemed afraid of him. Indeed one day about dinner time when I was in Dick's room I heard her cry: "No! No!" and come running out of the nursery, which I had seen Joah enter a moment ago. I went out quickly to the stairhead, and sure enough there was Tessie holding her wrist, her face flushed and tears in her eyes, and Joah beside her, glowering.

"If you cannot behave well to Tessie, Joah, I must report it to your uncle."

"I'm sorry," growled Joah. "I didn't meant to hurt you, Tessie. I wouldn't hurt you, Tessie! You know that, Tessie."

Tessie pouted and swung her foot, not ill-pleased, I thought, to hear this declaration from her cousin. To show his repentance was sincere, next market-day Joah brought her a pebble brooch, and after that they were very friendly indeed, giggling together in corners and encouraging each other to be rude to me. Twice I thought I almost caught them kissing, but could not be sure enough to speak of it, and they certainly held hands on the stairs, so that I grew more and more troubled about their association.

At last one day when I saw Joah openly encircle Tessie's bare arm with his huge dirty fingers, I felt the responsibility for the matter was no longer to be borne alone. I went into the kitchen and mentioned my uneasiness to Adah, speaking of the unwisdom of this increasing intimacy between the cousins.

"They are only young," said Adah in a smooth sugary tone, continuing to stir the contents of a small pan which stood on the kitchen fire.

"Tessie is now fifteen," I said. (She had recently had a birthday.) "Adah, do you think Mr. Moreys would approve if he knew? Ought I not to mention it to him?"

For a moment Adah's spoon stood still.

"Mr. Charles knows it already," she said then impatiently.

"Oh, indeed?" said I with relief. "If I thought that, if I thought he intended it, my mind would be easier. Yet no. Poor Tessie! She ought surely to see some other young men before——"

"Why should you come here and interfere?" said Adah

angrily. "What is done at Wool Royd is no concern of yours."

"My father," I began. "Walter Moreys——"

"If Walter Moreys had not interfered with things which didn't concern him, it would have been better for him," muttered Adah, stirring fiercely.

"Why, Adah! What do you mean? Do you know why John Moreys turned against my father? Did you know my father?" I cried, suddenly perceiving that from her age it might be so and wondering why I had not thought of it before.

Adah looked at me for a moment, her bushy eyebrows drawn together in a scowl; then she smoothed her face and resumed her sugary tone.

"Aye, I knew him," she said.

"What was he like as a boy?" I cried eagerly. "Why did his brother turn against him?"

"How should I know? Because he was a soft-hearted fool like yourself, I suppose," said Adah. "Always concerned with other folks' affairs rather than his own."

"He always remained of that disposition," I said sadly, remembering my father's kindness and seeing him as he lay, ill and wretched, in the prison.

"He did himself no good by it."

"He did others good, however," said I.

"Maybe. Maybe not," said Adah.

"But why did John Moreys turn him out? Tell me, Adah, tell me!" I urged. "He so longed to know the reason of his brother's unkindness. Tell me, pray!"

"I know nothing of it," said Adah crossly.

"The old weaver who brought my father the money and the message—is he still alive?"

"What, Thomas Greaves? Tom and Lucy Greaves' father? He wasn't all that old, mi duvel. But he didn't live long after; the worry of it finished him. Folk pestered him asking where Walter was, and he knew nothing to tell them. John Moreys was not the man to spread his affairs before a weaver."

"Tell me what *you* know," said I.

Adah was silent a moment, stirring the mess in the pan.

"I know nothing," she repeated emphatically at length. "But I will say that if Master Walter had minded his own business it might never have happened so."

"Is that a hint to me to mind mine?" said I, vexed.

"If the cap fits, wear it, my clever one. Mr. Charles won't thank you to interfere about Joah and Tessie."

"You think not?" I said, perplexed.

"I'm sure of it," replied Adah.

Distressed and uneasy, I left her. Strangely enough, perhaps, my heart was never more tender towards Tessie than at that moment. To think of that silly, selfish, ignorant, conceited child married to Joah, her wilful temper beaten down into fear, her pretty looks bullied into a wan and peevish sullenness, made my heart ache, and I determined to save her from such a fate if I could possibly do so. All that day I revolved the problem in my mind, and my resolution hardened at the supper table, for it seemed to me—and this was all part of the strange feeling I had that I was watched and spied upon—that Joah knew of my talk with Adah. He scowled at me with a sullen animosity in his eyes, his heavy face crimson; it even seemed to me that he and Adah exchanged meaningful glances

After supper Jacob went out as usual to Upper Hey, Joah to the village. When I had seen the children off to bed, I sat sewing alone in the nursery (or schoolroom as we now tried to call it) and presently I thought I saw what should be done. Tessie ought to be sent to school, I decided, to some boarding-school for young ladies in Leeds or Annots-field. There she could make friends and see her friends' brothers and have some chance of meeting an agreeable young man who could make her happy. She should not be sacrificed to the brutal Joah; I would fight the matter out with Charles Moreys, I would tell him sternly what I thought of such a project. The sins of the fathers might be visited upon the children by a far-seeing Providence, but he had no right to pay for his father's sins with his daughter's happiness. My heart burned within me as I thought of all this, and I decided to take the first step immediately by finding out the names of some suitable schools in the locality —I had seen some such advertised in the local newspaper. The house was very quiet and I thought Charles Moreys was probably out, but even if he were not, in my present mood I was ready to face him. Down I went therefore to the dining-room in search of the *Leeds Intelligencer.*

As soon as I opened the door I saw I had been mistaken. Charles Moreys sat lounging in front of the fire, a bottle of wine and a glass, both half-empty, on a small table beside him, and the sheets of the *Intelligencer,* much crumpled, in a heap on the floor. Charles Moreys was a very tall man, as I have said, and usually very vigorous and active, so that to see him lounging there, his long legs stretched idly towards the fire, his hands hanging listlessly over the arms of his chair, was unnatural and somehow distressing; there was something in his relaxed attitude, his bowed head, his unseeing stare, which looked painfully sad. At the sound of the door he roused himself and at sight of me at once adjusted the mask he wore in society.

"Ah! Cousin Eleanor!" said he in his ironic tone. "This is as great an honour as surprise."

He rose and bowing with a some exaggerated politeness, set a chair for me.

"I came only to fetch the *Leeds Intelligencer,*" said I coldly, not taking the chair.

"The *Intelligencer?* What can you want with that, cousin?" said Charles Moreys, nevertheless picking it from the floor and beginning to set it in order. "There is nothing in it at present but notices of bankruptcies and men selling their timber, the more fools they. Trade is bad, cousin, owing to this accursed war and the American embargo."

It did not seem a very propitious moment to open to him a matter which must involve him in additional expense, but I forced myself to begin:

"Yet you had a very good Pay Day, I understand."

"Give me a little credit, my dear Cousin Eleanor," said Charles Moreys, handing me the newspaper with an over-elaborate bow: "I may be a drunkard, but I am also a good business man."

Involuntarily I sighed and shook my head sadly.

"These preliminaries seem to suggest you want me to spend money on something, cousin," said Charles Moreys. "Come! Let me know the worst."

"I think it would be well for Tessie to go to a boarding-school," I blurted.

89

"Poor Tessie! Do you think she would be happy in a boarding-school?"

"Not at first," I admitted.

Charles Moreys laughed. "Your honesty must often obstruct your plans, cousin," he said. "But come, sit down and let us talk it over."

Some spark in his eye, some twist in his smile, warned me that he would think less well of me if I did so; it struck me suddenly that he might think I had made the school plan an excuse for seeking his company. This angered me. Accordingly I replied coldly that it would be better for me first to ascertain the names of some schools and write for their terms.

"Do not commit me to anything without consulting me," said he.

"That is not fair, cousin," said I hotly. "Nothing in my conduct has given you the right to make such an insinuation."

"Little spitfire!" said he, laughing. "How your grey eyes flash! Is that how they looked when you struck Joah in the face? Come, let us be friends; I apologise; sit down and talk to me."

"I think I must not do that, cousin," said I, troubled by his tone.

"Not even to keep me from drinking?" said Charles Moreys quietly.

I sighed and shook my head and went towards the door, but all very softly and slowly, for indeed I was reluctant to leave him. As he stood in the firelight he looked so handsome, so embittered and so ruined a man, like a tall fine tree secretly cankered, that I was truly sorry for him and longed to help him.

The next day all the uneasiness of this time came to a head.

CHAPTER VIII

It was peculiarly annoying, after the soft feelings I had experienced for Tessie the day before, to find her at her worst that morning. I had slept ill and longed for a walk in the fresh air but could not take it, for the weather had changed, the sky was dull and grey, the air damp and chill, so that it was not fit for Dick, who rose from his recent sick-bed for the first time that day, to go out, and I could not find it in my heart to leave him. Perhaps Tessie resented this care for Dick on my part; perhaps she disliked sharing with him my attention in the schoolroom, which had been all her own during his illness. Or perhaps—poor Tessie—it made her unhappy to be subjected once again to the humiliation of Dick's greater quickness in lessons. However hard I tried to minimise his mental superiority, it continually appeared, especially as he liked his books and worked hard at them, while Tessie was careless and idle; besides it was not fair to Dick to depreciate his talents, it was right to praise his achievements. Thus whether I should pity or rebuke Tessie that morning, I did not know, but I knew most assuredly that her behaviour was intolerable. She looked aside and hummed when I spoke of history and when called to attention made outrageous comments; she did not listen to my explanation of fractions and so could not do her sums but copied down Dick's answers; she threw the slates about and broke one, ran to the window on various trifling pretexts (seeing Joah cross the yard and the like), trod on the kitten's tail as she returned, which upset Dick greatly, and finally contrived during their writing lessons to ink the sleeve of my dress.

"Oh, Tessie!" I said reproachfully. "You really must be more careful."

"You did it on purpose, Tessie," said Dick angrily.

"I didn't."

"Yes, you did," persisted Dick. His pale face flushed, a pulse beat in the vein on his temple. He looked terribly frail this morning, leaning languidly in his chair, which I had lined with cushions; I dreaded the effect of these quarrels on him.

"Well, if I did, what does it matter? She can ask Father for another one," said Tessie coarsely.

"How dare you speak like that, Tessie?" I cried, deeply angered. "Apologise at once."

Tessie looked rather frightened and muttered something

which might be taken for an expression of regret, but without much conviction. It struck me that the child would not have thought of such an insult for herself; she had heard it said and was only repeating the coarse comments of others.

"Who has spoken of me to you in this way?" I said, still very swift and hot.

Tessie swung her foot and said nothing. I knew the answer to my own question; of course it was Joah. Whether it would be well to force this answer from her, on second thoughts I rather doubted; if she admitted it, I must take it up with Charles Moreys, since I could not suffer his nephew, a grown man, to insult me thus, and this might bring about a declaration of his intentions concerning Joah and Tessie which would bind the child in exactly the way I most deplored. So I let the matter drop for the moment and went to my room to apply water to the inkstain.

I was fortunate, the stain coming out quickly, and I returned almost at once to the schoolroom to hold the damp mark to the fire. My return was thus earlier than the children had expected, and I caught Tessie full in the act of cruelty. Laughing with savage glee, she was jerking the cushions one by one from her brother's chair, he with his thin weak hands striving vainly to prevent her. Just as I entered, she pulled at the top cushion so roughly that his head fell against the chair-back with a heavy thump. The child, long used to such tyrannies, exclaimed but feebly, but looked white and sick.

"Tessie," I said quietly, hurrying forward. "This is too much. I shall report this to your father. How can you be so unkind to your brother when he is ill?"

"He's not my brother!" shouted Tessie suddenly, losing her temper.

"Yes, I am," panted Dick. He pulled himself erect in his chair and repeated stubbornly: "I am your brother."

"No, you're not. He's just a bastard," said Tessie scornfully.

"Tessie!" I cried in horror. "Such a word should never be heard on the lips of a gentlewoman! It is not decent, it is not modest."

"It's true all the same. Bastard Richard, ha ha ha!" jeered Tessie, sticking her tongue out at her brother.

92

Dick burst into tears, and covering his face with his hands, sobbed bitterly.

I must own that I suffered. Indeed for a moment I felt as if cruel fingers were compressing my heart. So many strange items of behaviour at Wool Royd were explained by Tessie's statement that for a moment I did not doubt it. And so I suffered. It was no concern of mine, I told myself, that the handsome Charles Moreys should have had a mistress and a love-child, like his father before him, but yet I suffered.

"I know nothing of the matter," I said, trying to keep my voice from quivering; "but at least you have the same father, and should be kind to each other on that account."

"No, we haven't, cousin; how silly you are!" cried Tessie contemptuously. "We have the same mother, but not the same father. *My* father is Charles Moreys of Laverock Hall and Wool Royd, but Dick's father is the same as Joah's and Jacob's."

"He is not! He is not!" screamed Dick, striking his hand on the side of his chair.

I was so relieved that I laughed, for this was preposterous. "But Tessie, my dear," I said in a cheerful soothing tone, "that is nonsense. Dick resembles Cousin Charles most strongly—much more closely and strongly, in point of fact, than you do, Tessie."

With a cry of rage, Tessie threw herself upon me and beat at me with her fists. Her face contorted into a mask of fury, her lips drawn back from her strong white teeth, her eyes glaring, she did not spare her blows. Exclaiming: "Come, Tessie! Now, Tessie! I meant nothing but that you were truly brother and sister," I strove to put her aside without hurting her, for I could not raise my hand against a child. But I should have fared badly, for she struck with all her force and was now aiming at my face, had it not been for Dick, who, crying passionately: "Leave her alone! Leave her alone!" dragged himself up from his chair and seizing his pen jabbed it sharply into Tessie's wrist. He had not strength enough, fortunately, to make a deep penetration, but Tessie screamed at the pain and fell back; for the moment I was free; snatching Dick's hand I ran with him from the room and made for the stairs, for I heard the latch of the door rise and hoped that Charles Moreys was entering Wool Royd.

But alas, it was Joah. Dick and I stopped where we stood, halfway down the stairs. Tessie had followed us from the room and stood at the stairhead, Joah at the foot; we were caught between two enemies.

"What's to do?" said Joah, his eyes lighting with pleasure as he saw our discomfiture. "What's going on here, eh?"

"She's says Dick is Father's child and I'm not!" screamed Tessie.

"What!" shouted Joah, lunging forward. His face filled so suddenly with blood, it looked as if it would burst open. "Let me get at her!"

Dick, with an intrepid courage which I shall remember to my dying day, threw himself in front of me. Joah exclaimed with fury, and seizing the child by his wrist, whirled him round and threw him at arm's length down the staircase. There was an awful crack, and Dick lay on the floor of the hall, limp and unconscious.

"You have killed him!" I cried.

To do him justice Joah seemed dazed by what he had done; he stood there swaying on his feet as if stupefied, and made no attempt to assault or detain me as I rushed past him. I seized the bell-rope by the open door and pulled it wildly, madly. At this Adah hobbled out from the dining-room; she seemed to take in the situation at a glance, as though she had been listening to what went on from behind the door, as indeed perhaps she had.

"Get away, Joah! Get away before your uncle comes!" she urged, pulling at his sleeve. "Come out the back way! Through the kitchen! We'll say the boy fell and hurt himself. You say that too, Miss, mind," she said, turning to me warningly. "Joah! . . . Come!"

Joah semed unable to move, but stood stupidly staring down at Dick.

"Is he dead?" he muttered.

Adah moved towards Dick and made as if to bend over him.

"No!" I cried, on an impulse springing in front of her with outstretched arms. "Don't touch him!"

At this moment running footsteps were heard in the yard. Adah seized Joah's sleeve and began to drag him, staggering backwards, towards the dining-room. But before they had reached it Charles Moreys entered the house. Adah glided through the doorway, leaving Joah crouched against the wall, motionless.

"Dick is hurt—Joah threw him downstairs," I gasped. Now that help was at hand, I realised the full extent of my previous terror, and could hardly stand upright.

Charles Moreys turned and gazed at Joah, whose face, recently so crimson, had now turned livid with fear. Nor did I wonder, for my cousin's glance was terrible. With slow menacing steps he advanced on Joah, who cowered and put out his hands defensively; then, seizing his nephew by one wrist, Charles pulled him from the wall and performed with him exactly the action which Joah himself had recently inflicted. To see the heavy burly muscular Joah whirled helplessly across the hall gave me a fearful sense of Charles Moreys' strength; with a mere turn of his wrist, it seemed, my cousin threw this big young man out of the open doorway. Released from his uncle's grip, Joah flew backwards out of the porch, staggered helplessly and at length fell sprawling. Charles Moreys advanced to the door to follow him.

"No, no!" I cried, seizing my cousin's sleeve in my agitation: "don't kill him!"

"Why not?" said Charles Moreys, staring down at me. His blue eyes were really terrifying; I had never seen such rage in any look before.

"It might bring you into trouble," I stammered.

My cousin stared at me a moment longer, then smiled, albeit a trifle grimly.

"Thanks, little cousin," he said.

He stooped towards Dick and felt his pulse, then picked the child up with the utmost care and tenderness and carried him into the dining-room. Half fainting, I sank to the ground; I saw as through a veil Tessie's white frightened face bobbing for a moment at the stairhead, and Adah's bent form gliding out of the doorway towards Joah. Then Charles Moreys' voice sounded from the dining-room.

"Eleanor!"

He had never spoken to me before like this, without a prefix. I gathered my shaking limbs together, and went into the dining-room. He had laid Dick on a long oak bench which he had pulled out from the wall.

"Is he dead?" I queried, trembling.

"No, no. He's bruised his head and put out his shoulder," said Charles Moreys impatiently. "Where is Adah?"

"She went out of the house to Joah."

"You must do instead, then. Cut me a thick crust of bread."

I was astonished, but obeyed quickly; I ran into the kitchen and came back with the crust he had asked for. As I approached the oak bench I saw to my joy that Dick's blue eyes were open; he was conscious, though he looked infinitely pained and weary. I bent down and kissed him.

"Look, cousin," said Charles Moreys. "I am going to try to put his shoulder in again—it is a knack I learned in my youth. Hold his ankles thus, tightly, straight together, and do not flinch when he starts and winces. See, Dick," he went on in a very kind and gentle tone: "I am going to put your shoulder in and it will hurt you. When the pain comes, bite on this crust."

Gazing up at his father with a look of utter trust which was very touching, Dick meekly accepted the crust between his teeth.

It was all over in a moment and I can hardly describe it. Charles Moreys stood astride of the bench and took Dick's left arm and shoulder between his hands and suddenly jerked them; Dick gave a muffled cry of pain and (I think) fainted; I clung to his ankles as I had been bidden but then fainted too. When I came to myself I was in a chair with Charles Moreys' arm about me and he was offering me a drink of brandy.

"All over, cousin," said Charles Moreys cheerfully. "The shoulder's all right, I think. See! Dick's raising his arm."

It was so indeed, and the brave little boy even smiled at me, though wanly.

"Now you have both recovered, I will carry him up to bed," said Charles Moreys.

"Do not leave us—do not go back to the mill, cousin," I besought him.

"You will be quite safe—Joah shall not return. I will send him to—a relative—in Annotsfield," said my cousin, taking Dick up carefully in his arms.

The rest of the afternoon passed quietly. When Dick was settled in bed, and my cousin returned to the mill, I went in search of Tessie, whom I found trembling and cowering in her room. She dared not ask me to conceal her attack on me from her father, but her eyes, huge in her pale and frightened face, mutely implored it, and I did not wish to bring his anger on her if it could be managed otherwise. One glance of reproach I gave her, but no word; I bathed and bound up her wrist, then without any scolding gravely bade her to go to bed, brought her a Bible to read and a seam to sew, and locked her bedroom door. She was worn out, I think, by the emotions of the morning, for she made no objections to her punishment and fell very soon asleep— at least she was sound asleep when I looked in an hour later. Dr. Bradshaw, summoned by Jacob, pronounced that Dick's shoulder had been properly replaced and that the contusion on his head was not necessarily serious; he prescribed rest and quiet and left some sedative medicine, and after the child took a dose he drowsed peacefully. I sat at his bedside quiet and still, but I did not drowse, I was too much troubled by dark and disquieting thoughts.

It had become very clear to me that if Dick were dead or disinherited, and Tessie married Joah, all Charles Moreys' property would ultimately pass to Joah; Joah might think that through his illegitimate father he had more right to Wool Royd than Charles Moreys, and scheme to make it his own. But on that one word "scheme" I halted, perplexed. I could not imagine Joah scheming; he simply lacked the necessary intelligence. I could imagine him murdering Dick, or even murdering Charles Moreys; but to court Tessie for a far-off purpose, to teach Tessie by long innuendo to think her brother illegitimate, that seemed to me beyond Joah's power. If my suspicions were correct, why indeed did not Joah try to murder Charles Moreys? That he did not take this much easier course, for with his uncle out of the way

Dick and Tessie would be much easier to dispose of, seemed to prove that my suspicions were wrong. Yet no; there might be a reason for that too. Charles Moreys' careless mention of the bankruptcies which filled the papers might furnish me with the reason, for, in difficult times, there was no doubt that my cousin would guard the Moreys' wealth much more securely than Joah.

There were moments when this all seemed clear and probable to me, moments when it seemed obscure and wildly absurd. The house of Moreys, I thought, was doomed to tragic misunderstandings, witness the fate of my poor father. I revolved in my mind again that wretched story, and through John Moreys came again to Joah, the offspring of his illegitimate son. Backwards and forwards through the Moreys' story I wandered, till I came to myself at last with a start to hear china and silver jingling peacefully together as Adah set the supper table.

Supper was a silent meal. Only Charles Moreys, Jacob and I were present. My cousin, once he had enquired the surgeon's opinion, sat silent and moody, and neither Jacob —who was clearly distressed about his brother—nor I ventured to disturb him with much conversation. Only Adah appeared smoothly cheerful, indeed rather more affable and deferential than usual, as if in an attempt to soothe the household and restore its normal tone. I sent up a tray of food to Tessie, giving Adah the key of her room so that she might take it in to her, and told Adah to take also a pitcher of milk to Dick, bidding her however not to rouse the child if he were sleeping but let him lie.

When the meal was finished and Jacob had taken a stammered leave to go to Upper Hey, Charles Moreys said abruptly:

"I'll go up and see the child. Cousin, you had better come with me."

I was uncertain which child he meant and was much relieved when he led the way into Dick's little bedroom, which was, to speak truth, both cramped and ill-furnished. Charles Moreys looked about him distastefully as he entered, but made no comment. I had lighted a lamp and shaded it from Dick's eyes before I went down to supper;

the pitcher of milk stood untouched on the table by the lamp. My cousin picked it up casually, frowned and smelt it. "This milk is sour!" he exclaimed, looking at me reproachfully. I was too astonished to reply. Charles Moreys took the sleeping child's pulse, felt his delicate little ears, and with kind fingers stroked back the hair from his damp forehead.

"One sees that you are a surgeon's grandson," I said quietly.

"Aye—I would like to have studied medicine had I not been a clothier."

"Dick has the same feelings—he is skilful and tender with animals. He is like you in so many ways," said I, observing with a pleasurable warmth the two fair heads, the two handsome faces, the very hands, of father and son, so much alike.

"Nonsense!" exclaimed my cousin, colouring deeply. "You don't know what you are talking about—you are talking nonsense."

I was so astonished I simply gaped at him. "But, cousin," I began.

"You are in waters too deep for you, cousin. Withdraw before you are drowned in them," said Charles Moreys roughly. He put down the lamp and left the room with a hasty step.

I paused for a moment, then took my resolution, gathered my courage, and followed him. At the stairhead a thought struck me; I turned back to Dick's room, stole in and took up the pitcher of milk, then locked the door and brought pitcher and key away with me, slipping the key into my reticule.

When I entered the dining-room, Charles Moreys stood by the table, pouring a glass of wine.

"Cousin Eleanor," he said sternly, "last night you refused my invitation to sit with me. Tonight I do not invite you."

"Yet I must stay here," I said, crossing the room towards him.

"Why? To complain of Tessie? I hear from Adah she was rude to you. She is young, she is sufficiently punished by being sent to bed, you must forgive her."

"I have already forgiven what she did to me, but we are not allowed to forgive wrongs to other persons," I said, setting the pitcher of milk on the table.

"And whom, pray, has Tessie wronged?"

"Her brother."

Charles Moreys moved impatiently. "It is a pity you ever came to Wool Royd," he said.

I was deeply wounded. "That is very unkind, cousin," I said, striving to repress the tears which choked me. "I do not know what I have done to deserve such unkindness. I have tried to be of service."

"Do you suppose I have not seen that?" said Charles Moreys quickly in a different tone. "Do you imagine your unselfishness, your sweetness, your gentleness, your loving heart, have gone unobserved? It is for your own sake I say you would have done better to stay away from Wool Royd."

For a moment I was quite overwhelmed, then I gathered my courage and spoke steadily, looking up at him.

"Cousin Charles," I said, "something strange is happening in this house. If I am to help you, you must be frank with me, you must tell me——"

"Tell you what?"

"Everything about Dick's parentage."

"No! No!" he cried hoarsely. "You with your quiet eyes and your quiet soul, stay out of this sordid and hateful story."

He spoke as if in agony, and I was distressed to see the sweat start thickly on his forehead.

"I cannot help you unless I know the story."

"Do you want to help me, cousin?" said Charles Moreys in a jeering tone.

"Yes."

"Why? To what am I indebted for this interest?" said my cousin sardonically.

I could not find the true answer to that question (or perhaps I did not wish to) so I evaded it.

"I wish to help you, and Tessie and Dick and Jacob," I said.

"In spite of Tessie's bad behaviour to you, you wish her well?" said my cousin in a kinder tone.

"Yes. Cousin Charles," I said firmly, gathering my courage; "it is not right, believe me it is not right, to think of marrying Tessie to Joah."

His face flamed up in one of his sudden passions.

"What nonsense are you talking, you silly child?" he shouted angrily. "Tessie and Joah? Good God! Who ever suggested such an abominable idea?"

"Adah said you knew—Adah said you would not thank me to interfere," I faltered.

He strode across to the door leading to the kitchen, and shouting "Adah! Adah!" threw it wide.

Adah was revealed framed in the doorway. It seemed to me that my first glimpse of her showed her eyes gleaming, her face distorted, with rage, but I could not be sure, for the next moment she was smiling apologetically.

"So you're listening at the door, eh?" said Charles Moreys grimly. "Well, that makes it easier—you know what is going on."

"You must forgive an old servant who has served you all your life, Master Charles," said Adah in a whining, fawning voice. "Can I help being concerned in all that concerns you, sir?"

"Did you tell Miss Eleanor that I wished Miss Tessie to marry Joah?"

"No, no! How could she say so? How could you, Miss?"

"I did not—you said Mr. Moreys would not thank me to interfere," I protested.

"And that is true, indeed indeed it is true," whined Adah, shaking her head reproachfully. "What more likely than interference to throw them into each other's arms?"

There was so much truth in this that I was taken aback and began to believe I might really have mistaken her meaning. However, I managed to get out: "What then are your real wishes, cousin?"

"Tessie and Joah will marry only over my dead body," said Charles Moreys emphatically.

I shuddered.

"A goose walking over your grave, cousin?" said my cousin lightly, turning to take up his wine.

Or perhaps over yours, I thought but did not say.

"Very well, Adah—be off; you are excused for this time," went on Charles Moreys. "But don't let me catch you at the keyhole again."

Adah with a smile and a curtsy withdrew. As she closed the door she seemed to look beyond me to the table; I followed the direction of her glance and saw the forgotten pitcher of milk. My suspicions woke again and battled with my more rational powers; I stood there irresolute.

"Never mind, cousin," Charles Moreys adjured me. He drank down his wine and began to pour himself another glass. "Adah is an old servant and you must excuse her if she resents your intrusion into our family life. But you were right about Tessie and Joah. Such an alliance would be intolerable."

"Cousin Charles, I beg you to tell me the cause of the strange relationships in this house. Do you not see, if you leave me in ignorance, I shall continually make mistakes? Perhaps I shall even do harm," I faltered.

I was hurt and troubled, and I suppose my voice showed it—I know that as I looked at Charles Moreys my eyes swam with tears. He looked down at me consideringly and his expression softened, as I had seen happen earlier when he bent over Dick.

"Do not take it all so much to heart, my dear," he said kindly.

"I cannot see misery without wishing to relieve it."

"You have a heart as soft as velvet, cousin, that I know. But in this case the misery cannot be relieved."

"If only you would let me try," I said, and I believe I unknowingly clasped my hands in supplication.

"It would be an agony to tell—but yet perhaps also a relief," he muttered. "I have not spoken of it to anyone for nigh on a dozen years."

I said nothing, but continued to gaze at him imploringly.

"You will not enjoy it, cousin," said he.

"Enjoyment is not my object, Cousin Charles," said I.

He sighed.

"Well—sit down then and listen," he said.

BOOK THREE: CHARLES

CHAPTER I

I SHALL never forget the night on which Charles Moreys told me his story.

The day had been still and dreary, shrouded in dank clinging mist, but now as I sat waiting for my cousin to speak I heard the trees on the far side of the beck begin to moan and whisper and soon a few intermittent raindrops heavily splashed. As Charles Moreys talked, the wind gradually rose; sudden savage gusts which rattled the windows came ever more frequently and more strongly, till at length the gale swept with a continual wild angry roar down Moreydale, the house shook and heavy rain lashed pitilessly at the windows. Being half a Moreys, I have never feared storms of wind and since coming to Moreydale I had learned to love them, and this storm was certainly most fortunate; the tempest of noise drowned the murmur of our voices so that what we said could not be clearly overheard, and the fierce grandeur of the conflict imparted a kind of tragic beauty to the terrible story Charles Moreys had to tell.

"I don't rightly know where to begin," he said. "It began long before I saw Rosie. When I was a child, James—my half-brother—was always there, you see."

It was strange and sad to me, indeed it wrung my heart to see how Charles Moreys' face changed when he mentioned Rosie. The hard, assured, sardonic look dropped and he appeared quite pitifully young and helpless—I saw before me the young man's face I had seen in Dick's locket miniature. Moreover the sweat started thickly on his forehead whenever he spoke Rosie's name and his hand shook as he reached for his glass.

At first his words were disjointed and incoherent, and I cannot remember them very accurately. But I gained a picture, clear and poignant enough, of a small, fair, motherless boy, continually struggling against the dominance of a malevolent elder brother. Everyone at Wool Royd, house and mill, the boy Charles included, knew that James Lee was John Moreys' illegitimate son, who had been kept away from Wool Royd so as not to vex John Moreys' adored fair wife Caroline. Caroline died in childbirth, leaving her husband a legitimate son in Charles, and she was hardly cold in her grave before John Moreys left home for three days and returned bringing the swarthy eight-year-old James with him. The two boys, James and Charles, were brought up at Wool Royd together. But their father's temper towards them was harsh, moody and uncertain; at time John Moreys treated Charles like a prince, lavishing on him expensive gifts, ponies and riding-coats and handsome spurs and the like, and setting nurses and tutors and grooms to attend on him; at other times he made sarcastic remarks to Charles (and remarks to others aimed at Charles) about the nuisance he was to his brother.

"It seemed as if he couldn't make up his mind which of us to like best," said Charles Moreys sadly. "He could neither settle it nor leave it alone. Sometimes he quite gloated over my fair hair and blue eyes, which I had from my mother, and he would tell me I was his heir, the house and lands and the new mill should all be mine and I should be very wealthy and important. Next day perhaps he would take James between his knees and praise his dark curly hair and sallow cheeks, and say that all true Moreys were of dark complexion, and the pair of them would laugh together because my fair face, which shows every feeling, curse it, was crimson with mortification.

" 'He'll have to have Wool Royd because he's a Moreys, d'you see,' my father would say to James in a confidential tone; 'but I'll leave as much as ever I can to you, James, so don't fret, lad.'

"Then I would cry out in a fury: 'Let him have it all! Let him have it all! I don't want it'

"But then, you see, my father's face would sober and he would shake his head.

" 'Nay, Charles,' he would say, and there was pride and love and yet a kind of dislike in his voice, so that I didn't know which to choose between them; 'you're the heir. You're the one, lad. I look to you to bring the Moreys up in the world, d'you see. You've got the headpiece. It's a pity for poor James, but there it is; you're the right heir, he's only a love-child.'

"I don't know whether you can understand this, Eleanor," went on Charles Moreys, "but I grew to feel that my very existence was a wrong to my half-brother. It was an agony to me, it was indeed, to feel that my very life was an offence against justice. To be free of that feeling of guilt and obligation, I would have given anything. I loved Wool Royd, God knows, but I'd gladly have left it all and gone out into the world with nothing but what I stood up in. But, you see, on the other hand, I soon grew to see that what my father said was right about me having the best headpiece. James was good on the moor, you know; he was good at tracking birds to their nests and finding bilberries and climbing trees, and clever in his knowledge of wind and weather. But at his books or in the mill he was unteachable, not only rude and careless and idle but somehow stupid. If the Moreys' fortunes were left to him, it would be a bad day for Wool Royd. I felt that if I left Wool Royd and went off and made my own fortune, if I ran away to sea perhaps like my Uncle Walter, it would be happy for me but wrong, it would leave James in the lurch because he'd never be able to fend for himself. Sometimes, you know, when my father was in a good mood, he would say the same. I remember once when the new scribbling machines had just been put in and Father and I were standing side by side together after the men had gone home, admiring them, he spoke in that way.

"'Charles,' he said gravely, 'you must look after James, you know. He hasn't got your head—hasn't had your chances. He couldn't make a way for himself; you'll have to make one for him. It's hard on you—but then, it's hard on him.'

"I sighed and agreed. And that's what my childhood was, you see; I was never at ease, I was always torn between hatred and obligation to my brother.

"Perhaps you'll think I ought not to have hated him, Eleanor. But wait a minute. I hated James because everything in his nature went contrary to mine. He always wanted to hurt and kill things; I liked to save them, and keep them alive. There was an old bent woman in Booth village then

who lived alone, she had a hard job of it to totter down to
the beck with her bucket for water. James would wait till
she'd filled the bucket and was climbing the hill to go home,
then he would run round her mocking and jog her elbow
so that the water spilled. I was so mad at him once I took
the bucket and filled it and carried it home for her. Well
then, James told this tale to my father, jeering at his pretty
brother's pretty ways, and my father scolded me for stooping
to such menial offices. My father, you know, Eleanor, had a
view of the Moreys family so lofty as to be almost mad—
especially of me, whom he was set to make a gentleman. But
about James: he was a bully, a cruel bully, in everything
he did. He threw stones at every cat he saw; he struck a dog
once between the eyes; he pulled the wings off the fledgling
larks so that I hated him to find a nest; he put an overturned
bucket once over a frog and sat laughing at the hollow noise
the poor thing made leaping vainly against the sides of the
bucket. He couldn't pass a fly or a spider without wanting
to kill it or imprison it somehow, and if I set it free he
pushed and cuffed me. He was a bully to the Booth village
children too. He pulled the girls' hair and twisted their arms
so that they were afraid to pass him if he stood in their way;
he fought the boys and struck them so savagely that the
blood ran.

"So I hated him for all that, you see. And yet I couldn't
help feeling sorry for him all the time. I used to wonder
whether after all I should have been any better if I had been
the love-child, nameless and disinherited, instead of my
brother.

"Then another thing which made it worse for both of us
was that I was a very pretty child, always attractive to
women. My fair hair and rosy cheeks and blue eyes used to
send them silly; they crowded round me and stroked my
hair and kissed me and asked me questions in that fond
cooing tone which women use to pretty children. You do it
yourself, Eleanor, to Dick; you know you do; I've seen
you at it, so don't think I haven't. I couldn't help but enjoy
being petted—I always had an eye for a pretty woman and
I like women, I won't deny it. But I grew to dread seeing
that fond look in their eye, because they never looked at

James—or rather, they gave him one look and passed him by, when he was a child. He was swarthy, you see, and ill-mannered. My father took great pains over *my* manners, hiring tutors for me and so on; besides, I used to stay sometimes down in Annotsfield with my grandfather the surgeon, who was a very easy, affable-mannered man. What I used to think so unjust was this: my father took every means he could to make me speak well and behave well, and then he and James would jeer at me for doing so.

"James was eight years older than me, so at first we weren't very much together. I was in the nursery and the schoolroom while James was working in the mill, or supposed to be, apprenticed to my father. But presently I grew old enough to roam the moors under James's care. In point of fact, when we were on the moors together James and I were at our friendliest, for we both loved them. When we were tramping through the purple heather, or lying hidden in the deep green bracken, or climbing the rocks, or running homewards against a frosty winter wind which nearly took our faces off, then we were at ease together. But one day even this was spoiled. James, you see, being in his teens now and strong and burly, usually led the way for me to follow. We were climbing the high waterfall on the Morey beck. James got up first and stood watching me, feet astride and arms akimbo.

" 'Take care, Charles!' he cried, pointing. 'That stone's not safe.'

"I looked about me and asked: 'Which shall I try, then?'

"Without saying anything, James pointed to a rock that was covered with moss. I was surprised, because the rock being within reach of the spray of the waterfall, the moss was soaked with water, and damp moss is always slippery. However, I put my foot on it—and the next minute I was up to my neck in the pool below. James stood laughing at me and I was furious; I climbed up to him pretty quickly and seized his arm and said: 'You knew that moss would make me slip.'

"James's laughter died, and for a moment we glared at each other.

"Then James said: 'Well, what if I did?' and flung away.

"Half an hour later, on one of the moorland paths, we chanced to meet a woman, a villager from Booth. By this time, soaked to the skin as I was, I was shivering in the cold March gale.

" 'Been dipping thysen, love?' said the woman to me as we passed.

" 'He couldn't climb the fall, and fell in,' jeered James.

" 'Why'n't take child home, then?' said the woman, stopping. 'He'll catch cold, happen, if he stays lapped i' wet stuff.'

" 'He's enjoying himself out here,' said James haughtily.

" 'Nay, I reckon he isn't at that,' said the woman. 'He looks right starved to me. Thee come home, love,' she said to me. 'Come along o' me. Tha mun doff thi coit and breeks soon as tha gets into t'house.'

" 'Poor baby Charles!' mocked James. 'Got a skin like a girl and a spirit too.'

"Well, I thought it all over," said Charles Moreys, wrinkling his forehead. "I had to decide pretty quickly, you see. I was shivering, my teeth were chattering, and I longed to go home and change my clothes. But I hated the idea of seeming soft and cowardly in front of James—I knew I should never hear the last of it. But then I considered: James persuaded me to tread on the mossy stone because he wished me ill. So perhaps he wants me to stay soaked because he wishes me ill. I made up my mind there and then—I was only a child, you know, but I made up my mind—never to yield to James's wishes. So I went back with the woman to Wool Royd. I caught a cold, but nothing worse.

"Then the question came up, what was I to say to my father? He heard about my wet clothes from the tutor I had at that time, and scolded both James and me for not having the sense to come home at once after my fall into the water. While he raged on, calling us daft and gaumless, I sat looking away out of the window. But I knew James was watching me very anxiously. He was afraid I should tell tales of him to my father.

"But I didn't, you know. Partly I scorned to do it, I felt I couldn't like myself if I told tales. But partly also, I must say,

108

I felt it would be useless. I felt James and I had got to fight this out by ourselves. I made up my mind then, while Father raged on, that I must learn to be quicker and stronger and surer and cleverer in every way than James.

"I knew it would be dangerous. And by God, it was! Such a look James gave me when Father's harangue was over and he knew I didn't mean to tell on him—his eyes fairly gleamed with cruel triumph. After that day he took every opportunity to hurt me that he dared—short of actual fighting, you know, which my father would have found out and punished. But when two boys are playing together, there's a score of chances for one to hurt the other without appearing to have any hand in it. You can stick out your foot so that the other will trip over it, you can nudge him at the wrong moment as you stand together on a wall, you can let the branch fly back into his face as you pass through a wood, you can dare him to dangerous feats—and what boy can resist a dare, if he's any spirit? You can shove him while appearing to fall yourself—I remember James once nearly had me beneath the great wooden hammers of the fulling-stocks. All these tricks James played on me. But they didn't have the result he intended. I didn't get killed or maimed; I learned to jump, to run, to climb, to balance, aye and to see and plan, in order to save myself. I made up my mind never to show fear in front of James, always to laugh and pretend I didn't care for anything. But eight years is a good deal, you know, eight years makes a good deal of difference in boys' strength while they're growing. I don't know that I should have been able to hold out long enough against James, only that one day he went too far and his malice against me was discovered.

"Do you remember, the first day you were at Wool Royd, Eleanor, seeing Dick come down from the mill garret on the crane hook? Well, at the time I'm speaking of, that part of the mill was newly built and James had taught himself that trick: to swing by his hands from the hook and persuade one of the men to pull the rope and lower him to the ground —it was a showy trick and James was fond of showy tricks. Well, one day—it was market day and my father was away in Annotsfield—James had run up to the garret to do this trick and I had run after to watch him, when the mill bell rang for the men's afternoon drinking-time, and the man who was to have lowered James couldn't be prevailed on to stay, but went off to his drinking. It was a hot summer's day and all the men went out into the yard and sat with their backs against the wall, drinking the ale which had been fetched for them from the village. They shouted up jokingly at James as he stood in the crane doorway. James never enjoyed jokes against himself, and his face darkened with anger, so I offered to pull the rope for him.

" 'You haven't the strength,' he said contemptuously. 'But stay—how would *you* like to go down on the hook, Charles?"

"Of course I said I would like it very much; not that I really wished it, but it was a rule with me never to hang back when any dangerous feat was suggested.

"So James, grinning and chuckling, drew out the hook and held me up so that I could catch hold of it. (The very grasp of his hands on my body was cruel.) Then he pulled on the rope to release the brake, and I went dangling down through the air, hanging on to the hook. I must say I enjoyed it at first, and I kept my feet and knees together so as to look graceful. The men in the yard below laughed and applauded. Then suddenly with a jerk the hook stopped moving. James had put the brake on, you see, and there was I left dangling some twenty feet above the ground. Again, for a moment or two I enjoyed the trick; I kicked out my legs and swung myself backward and forward, showing off. Then my arms began to tire.

" 'Let me down now, James,' I cried.

"James laughed. Even yet, you know, after all that had passed between us, I was still credulous about him, I was surprised when he laughed and strained back my head to look up at him. Well, his eyes were flashing with cruel enjoyment, his face was crimson with glee. He leaned against the side of the doorway laughing, with his arms folded round the rope of the crane.

" 'Let me down or I shall fall, James,' I cried. To make my voice sound not afraid, I sang the words out in a kind of tune.

" 'Let the lad down!' cried some of the men below.

" 'Why? He's enjoying himself. Aren't you, Charles?' said James, mocking me.

"I said nothing and stayed quite still. The only way to bring James's tricks to an end was always to pretend not to mind them. If I began to kick or swing or call out frantically James would enjoy it and prolong the joke; the only thing to do was to hang on quietly so as to provide no entertainmen. So I hung on. But first my wrists began to ache, then my arms and then my shoulders, till I seemed to ache all over, and then—what was worse—my muscles began to twitch and quiver as if they meant to crack.

"Just at the moment when I felt I could hold on no longer and was wondering how best to drop, there came an angry shout from James and the sound of a scuffle above my head, and suddenly with a jerk the hook descended in a run and I found myself staggering on the ground. The stones of the yard felt like heaven, I can tell you. I looked up at the garret door and there I saw Tom Greaves—he was one of the apprentices at the mill at that time, you know. Tom had run up three flights of stairs and snatched the rope from James's grasp and let me down out of my predicament.

"Poor Tom!" said Charles Moreys reflectively. "He was the son of a Booth widow in poor circumstances, you know; his father had been one of my father's journeymen weavers in the old days. He was rather a simple lad at that time— well, he always has been simple, poor Tom, but he was specially so while he was in his teens. Plump and pink, with large staring eyes and his hair always on end, and not very skilful at his trade though only a few years from the end of his apprenticeship. The men were apt to make a butt of him. But you can guess what *I* thought of him, after this. I didn't want James to have the pleasure of knowing what a fright he'd given me, so I strolled quietly off then with my hands in my pockets, but I went straight up to Wool Royd and fetched a guinea piece my father had given me last birthday, and when the men had finished their drinking and were back at work I found Tom and quietly slipped it into his hand. But Tom, poor lad, was too foolish to keep a quiet tongue in his head. He was proud of his guinea and showed it to all the men, and of course they judged the size of my danger by the size of my gift. They fell to abusing James, James fell to abusing Tom, Tom fell to shaking his head and wailing: 'Eh, I was feared child'd be mashed on t'stones,' so that the whole mill rang with the story, and when my father came back from market he heard it all almost before he was dismounted.

"So that night at supper, my father, who had been very silent before, spoke out suddenly.

" 'Hearken, James,' he said. 'If Charles ever happens an accident in your company, you leave Wool Royd for ever that night.'

"James was very angry. For one thing, my tutor, and the serving-man we had then, and Adah, were all in the room so that he was humiliated before them, which I must say I thought unkind of my father. James protested, crying out: 'How can I help what the fond brat does?' and the like. But my father raised his hand for silence.

" 'I mean what I say now, James,' said he; 'and don't none of you ever forget it.'

"I must say," said Charles Moreys grimly, "that after that my life was decidedly less hazardous. Besides, after rating the tutor soundly for not taking better care of me, he dismissed him, and sent me instead to a school in Annotsfield. During the term I lived in Annotsfield with my grandfather the surgeon. I think James found life dull at Wool Royd without someone to tease; certainly he almost welcomed me when I came home for the holidays.

"And then, all of a sudden as it seemed, I was in my teens. I shot up to my full height and grew much taller than James, who was always burly rather than tall in figure. I was slimmer than him but I had a longer reach and a nimbler foot, and muscles of iron from long practice. If we'd fought now, which of us would have won was doubtful, and I didn't hesitate to let James see I knew it. In another year," concluded Charles Moreys with satisfaction, "it wasn't doubtful —I should have got the better of him. So, luckily for me, our battle of strength was won before I left school and came home to Wool Royd."

CHAPTER II

You may be sure, Edward and Catharine, that I did not hear all this in blank silence or with an unfeeling heart. I did not interrupt my cousin when his narrative flowed fast, merely letting my close attention, my eyes fixed on his face, speak my mute sympathy; but when he stumbled or hesitated or seemed perplexed, when he looked haggard and drawn and his eyes showed pain, I strove to ease his path by those small ejaculations which show the listener's feeling. Now that he paused and seemed reluctant to continue, I felt I might properly show the interest I felt, by asking some questions. So I said softly:

"Did not your father love your mother, do you think?"

"Yes, yes," said Charles Moreys. "He adored her. But he showed himself jealous, envious, almost resentful of her too, in what he said of her. She was much his superior in education and manners, or so I always understood."

"Yet he had an illegitimate child."

Charles Moreys shrugged.

"That is not as uncommon as might be wished, cousin," he said sardonically. "My father kept all knowledge of the matter from my mother. He kept James away from Wool Royd for her sake, till after her death."

"And James's mother?"

Charles Moreys shrugged again. "I suppose so," he said. "I knew nothing of her—I never heard her mentioned."

"It was a deep wrong," said I.

"Do I deny it?" said Charles Moreys angrily. "Was I not always sorry for James? Did I not always feel remorse for having damaged my brother's prospects?"

"It was not your fault, Cousin Charles," said I softly.

"I felt it all the same," said Charles Moreys.

"You had a wretched childhood, cousin," said I. "I burn with rage when I hear of James's persecution of you. And it is still here with us now; Joah and Dick are enacting it again in Wool Royd."

"No!" exclaimed Charles Moreys fiercely. "Nothing that Dick does is like me. That crying, cowardly, peevish child has nothing of me in him."

"But, cousin, the child is in continual fear; as you saw today, Joah continually hurts and torments him."

"Then let him harden his heart and his muscles and his nerves, and fight back as I did."

"The child is ailing and has no strength in his limbs. It is a matter about which I want to speak with you very seriously, cousin."

"You speak of little else," said Charles Moreys impatiently. "You know, cousin," he went on after a moment's hesitation, "when we were boys together, if James would have given up his cruel ways, I would gladly have been friends with him."

"You were too generous," I said. "I cannot so easily forgive him."

"Well," said Charles Moreys, "it was so. I was truly sorry for him and wished him well, if only he would have believed it. There were times, too, when I think James had a fondness for me. He liked to earn my admiration. But after such moments he always hardened again. For instance, after the crane business, he asked me quite kindly whether my wrists or my shoulders hurt most, and might perhaps have remained friendly, if my father had not humiliated him in front of the servants about it."

"Seeing that you know the dangers of the crane exploit so well, cousin," said I, "it seems to me that you have no right to accuse Dick of cowardice, since he performs it."

"There is no danger—none of the men would dare to leave Dick suspended," said Charles Moreys angrily.

"Joah might."

"Nonsense. The child knows the story of my hanging on the crane, and mimics me to gain my attention."

"Perhaps. But it needs courage all the same," I said. I felt sad at heart, for I remembered the child's telling me how much he loved his father. "Why do you dislike Dick so much, cousin?"

"You shall hear," said Charles Moreys grimly.

CHAPTER III

MY COUSIN seemed now more at ease. Having once made the effort to break his proud reserve and speak of his affairs, and finding from my comments that my sympathies were warmly engaged on his side, he probably felt it a relief, as we mostly do, to tell what was weighing on his heart. At any rate his speech grew less hesitant and his posture relaxed; he leaned back in his chair and stretched his long legs out to the fire and lounged thus, his fair head pressed back against the cushion so that I could see his long lashes gleaming in the firelight. With one of his fine sinewy hands he twirled the stem of his glass, the other dangled over his chair arm—except when at times the pain of the narration became too much for him, when he passed his hand heavily over his forehead.

"It was while I was in my teens, James being then in his twenties," said Charles Moreys, "that James began to get across with my father—that's a Yorkshire expression, cousin; but you can doubtless guess its meaning. It was at this time that my father began to be ill from the disease that really killed him a few years later; he suffered much from rheumatism or gout or whatever it was, and began to limp about with a stick and be very tetchy and irritable. His hair began to grey and his face to yellow, and his shoulders grew bowed. I remember I was quite astonished to see him look suddenly such an old man, for I think children always expect their parents to remain unchanged. We all suffered from his temper—Adah was the only one who could soothe him down—but James suffered the most, because, to be truthful, James most deserved it. James was by this time a drunkard, a gambler, a liar, a bully and a coward, and also continually went a-whoring; and he hadn't the sense to keep his sins out of our father's sight and restrict them to leisure hours, but let them sprawl all over Moreydale and interfere with his work at Wool Royd. He was never one for much work, in any case.

"For instance," continued Charles Moreys with a slight laugh, "once when he was down in Annotsfield with the waggon, bringing wool up to Wool Royd, he got so drunk he contrived to lose a whole pack on the way home. As ill luck would have it, this wool was not our own, but belonged to another clothier. You see, cousin, I know you Londoners don't rightly understand the cloth trade, but surely you'll have learned enough since you came here to know that partly we scribble other folks' wool for 'em, and partly we scribble wool of our own and sell it to the clothiers. In those days we were still clothiers ourselves as well, and wove some of our own wool up into cloth. Well, this wool belonged to a very particular clothier over in Iredale, a fiery sort of fellow, Oldroyd of Syke Mill, he knows his business well; there was no hope of putting him off with other wool, he'd know the wool he'd bought and you couldn't deceive him with any other.

"Well, here was James come home without this wool. How he'd lost it, goodness knew; he remembered loading it on the waggon down in Annotsfield, but nothing more; whether he'd loaded it ill so that it fell off, or whether he'd locked wheels with some other waggon on the way home and shook it off that way, or whether even he'd had a fight with somebody on the way home, he couldn't tell. He drove into the yard shouting and ranting, roaring drunk, with the horses all steamed up and the wool-packs tossing about, and there was this one missing. It was very fine quality wool and worth about fifty pounds; besides, we were like to lose Mr. Oldroyd's custom; nobody likes to think of his wool being dropped about in the lanes. We settled to have some handbills printed offering twenty pounds reward for the recovery of the wool, and I went down to Annotsfield that night to see about them and I stayed the night at my grandfather's; and as luck would have it as I was bringing the handbills home next day I saw some wool blowing about in a field just above where the Morey beck joins the river Ire, and I turned off up a steep side lane towards the field, and there was the pack lying split on its side in the lane and wool blowing over the countryside every which way. What James had been doing up that lane with the waggon goodness knows—but we could guess, you know; there would be some woman or other at the top of it.

"Well, the wool was all over the place, as I say; it took

Tom Greaves and me all of two days to gather it. Of course the tale spread all over the countryside and people came and watched us wool-gathering—Oldroyd himself came, and stood laughing and swearing at us. At that, when all was gathered we could see, we were nigh on a stone short. Well, that sort of silly work maddened my father. It hurt his credit and it made him look a fool, two things he very much disliked; besides, he took a real honest pride in his mill turning out good work. When he heard that Tom and I had become a sport for the neighbourhood, too, that maddened him further. On the second day he had himself driven down to us and stood up in the gig and shouted and waved his arms at us to come away and leave it, he'd rather pay Oldroyd for the wool than see me grubbing for it—he had such ideas, you see, about me being a gentleman. I pretended not to hear and went on picking wool out of the grass and heather, and Father had Tom Greaves running backwards and forwards between us with messages, poor Tom puffing and panting and getting more and more distressed as Father grew crosser and me more obstinate— for I saw no sense in leaving the job when it was so nearly over. James and Father had a real set-to over that business, and of course James hated me more than ever for finding the wool and gathering it, setting *his* mistake right as it were. I often think now, cousin, that if there had been in those days one thing which James did better than I, it might have saved us."

He paused, and put his hand to his head as if at some very painful recollection.

"But there was nothing, cousin?" said I.

"Not at that time. Presently there was. Oh yes, presently there was one thing he did very much better. But at that time, when once I was grown to my full strength, there was nothing in which he excelled me. But how could I help it? What could I do? Even when he was sober he was useless, to speak frankly, in the mill; he had no feeling for wool or cloth and took no interest in any part of the business except the pay. He was no good at figures or writing, either, and the men all came to hate him for his bullying ways."

"And did you try to stand between the men and

your brother, cousin?" I asked him, knowing the answer.

"Aye, when I could. But I wasn't always there—or quick enough when I was there," said Charles Moreys. "You saw Dan Dennett and Tom Greaves at the party at Upper Hey, didn't you, cousin?" he went on. "Well, at that time Dan and Tom were just coming to the end of their seven years' apprenticeship with my father. James always hated poor Tom Greaves because he let me down off the crane hook, you remember, and he lost no chance of knocking Tom about and shouting at him. Of course poor Tom was always rather foolish and not able to stand up for himself, though a good, friendly, warm-hearted lad enough; I've seen him break out crying under James's teasing, and James smile to see the tears rolling down Tom's plump pink cheeks. Dan and Tom, being of an age and apprenticed together, though not alike in their dispositions, were friends, chiefly perhaps on account of Tom's sister Lucy, that Dan's now married to."

"Mrs. Dennett is Tom Greaves' sister!" I exclaimed, surprised.

"Yes, yes," said Charles Moreys impatiently. "As things stand now, brother and sister married brother and sister— Tom Greaves and Lucy Greaves are married to Martha Dennett and Dan Dennett. Dan always had a fancy for Lucy Greaves—as for Tom and Martha, I don't feel so sure; I judge poor old Tom found himself pushed into it. But at that time things looked different. Dan's father was our miller at Wool Royd, in charge of the fulling-stocks, as Dan is now. To be a miller is a well-paying job, you see, because milling can spoil a piece of cloth entirely if it isn't done careful, and so the clothier usually brings his cloth to the mill himself and watches the milling done, and besides paying for it in the ordinary way he usually gives the miller a small fee—crosses his hand, you know—it's quite the usual thing, and allowed for in the arrangements you make with the miller. So Dan's father was nicely off, you see, while Lucy Greaves' mother was a poor widow, as I said before. Well, James often bullied Tom, and one day, being angered because Tom ventured to answer him back, he picked the lad up and carried him along, kicking and squealing, and dropped him in one of our lead-vats which was full of blue dye. Luckily it was cooling so he was not scalded, but he came up with his shirt and breeches all blue and the dye streaming down his face, looking very pitiful and blubbering. Dan Dennett ran up and helped him out of the vat and tore off his shirt and gave it a great shake, and the dye flew all over the yard and spattered James, who was standing nearby laughing at poor Tom, from head to foot with big blue splashes. The change in James's face from glee to fury as the dye struck him—he was always very dandified in a greasy sort of way—was really very funny," said Charles Moreys, laughing. "We all laughed and James rushed off in a rage to change his clothes, and from that time forward he hated Dan Dennett.

"Of course," said Charles Moreys, "Dan Dennett was a very different kind of lad from Tom. Dan was square-faced and sturdy, not very tall but strong and solid and very stubborn. James couldn't throw Dan about or frighten him as he did Tom Greaves. But he took other means to vex him. He used to stand beside the fulling-stocks when the clothiers were paying old Dennett, ask them how much they'd given the miller, tell them it was too much and that some of it ought to be paid to Mr. Moreys, and so on."

"You mean, cousin," said I, "he gave them the impression that the miller's fee was a wrong and an imposition?"

"That's right. Then one time for a couple of days he took all the fees the clothiers paid Dennett; the stocks were very throng just then and the sum was quite considerable. Old Dennett was a peaceable old chap who didn't want to make trouble, but Dan was angered and being as I say very stubborn and hating James anyway, he insisted on his father coming to my father and telling him about it. My father was furious that his son should so lower himself as to take the miller's money, and he had another set-to with James, shaking his stick and shouting at him. James didn't argue but stood silently lounging against the door in the counting-house with a sneer on his face, until my father said the money must be returned, when he cried out savagely that it was impossible, he no longer had it in his possession. He had lost it, of course, betting and gambling. London is not the only place, cousin, where you can find gambling dens and cock-fighting."

"A most loathsome, cruel, disgusting sport!" cried I hotly.

"As you say, cousin," said Charles Moreys. "I always hated it. I hated to see the fine glossy cocks with their feathers dabbled with blood and their eyes out, and most of all I hated to see the beaten cock with its spirit broken. But James loved it. And he loved dicing and drinking, and his women cost him, and so he borrowed money continually from me until one day I grew tired of it and offered to fight him for the guineas. Then he gnawed his lip and scowled and shrugged his shoulders and went off, for by that time I was more than a match for him. Being taller, you see," said Charles Moreys with satisfaction, "I had a longer reach and could hit him before he could get at me."

"But what happened about Mr. Dennett's money?" I asked.

"My father paid it back himself. But such things fretted him bitterly about James. It was the same over the wool-buying, too. It was my father's custom to ride off to Leicester-shire every year, wool-buying; there were a couple of farms there he always visited. Naturally he took James with him to teach him his business. But he soon stopped doing so and took me instead, for what with running after the daughter of one, and trying to fix up a crooked deal with the son of the other, James made a tremendous pother and neither farmer would have him on the place again. All this wounded my father, who whatever his private faults cared much for his business reputation, his credit. He grew sick of the sight of James and especially hated to see him about the mill, and so grew to rely on me, like, though I was still only a lad in my teens. He was fonder of me at that time than he had ever been before. James hated that, of course; he hated to come into the counting-house and see Father and me together, bent over the books or some wool that was wrong, or a letter. Father would look up and scowl and say something sharp and cold—for James always slept late and came to the mill dirty and dishevelled—and James would shout some insult or other and bang out of the room and we could hear him raging through the mill causing noise and confusion wherever he went. Poor Father! How he hated it! As his illness got more grip on him and his spirit drooped, he hated it more and more—to see James in the mill, I mean."

"*The gods are just,*" I murmured, "*and of our pleasant vices Make instruments to plague us.*"

"Aye!" exclaimed Charles Moreys with feeling. "That's very true. If it stopped there, it would be right enough. But it doesn't, you see, cousin. It goes on. The sins of the fathers are visited upon the children to the third and fourth generation."

"Only on those who hate God," said I. "He shews mercy to thousands that love Him and keep His commandments."

"I never hated God," objected Charles Moreys.

He looked so childishly resentful as he said this, had such a youthful air of grievance, like a boy falsely accused of breaking into a jam cupboard, that I could not but smile, though sadly, for in truth it was a wretched story.

"I wonder your father did not set James up in some other business," I said.

"He wished it," said Charles Moreys. "But James refused at first. He fancied himself as a Moreys of Moreydale and stayed in the mill to keep a grip on it. But after a time the men in the mill, who had stood in awe of him for his strength and his bullying, found out his cowardice and twitted him with it. Slubbers, you know, Cousin Eleanor," said Charles Moreys—"as I told you the first morning you came to Wool Royd—are always troublesome rascals. Full of temper. They're well paid, you see; skilful workmen; they can always get their price. So they think they can do as they like. They'll stay away from work a couple of days, drinking, whenever the fancy takes them, and if you say anything when they come back, they're off in a minute. Leave you at a word. You've got to be on top of slubbers or they're on top of you, and that's a fact. I," said Charles Moreys, smiling grimly, "am on top of mine—now. I had a job with them at first after Father died, I can tell you. But what I'm saying is this: slubbers are that kind of man, they're full of pluck and spirit and they scorn any show of the white feather."

"But surely, Cousin Charles," I said, "your half-brother was not so foolish as to ask you for money, and decline to fight you for it, in front of the slubbers, in the mill?"

"No, no—they found him out another way. It was one dark night—I don't remember the time of the year but it was dark at supper-time—and we three were sitting at the supper table when Dan Dennett came rushing in to tell us he thought the dryhouse was on fire, he could see a flickering light beneath the doorway. It was locked, you see, being full of wool. My father took the key out of his pocket—he was awkward about it because of his twisted rheumatic fingers—and threw the key down on the table and James snatched it up and we both ran off, with Dan Dennett following close behind. By the time we got down to the mill yard the flames were curling round the dryhouse door. We ran across the yard and suddenly James stopped dead, so that I almost fell over him; I gave him a sharp knock with my shoulder, I daresay, and the key fell out of his hand to the ground. I heard it ring on the stones, so I groped for it and found it and ran ahead—I was only a lad, you know, seventeen or so at that time, eager for adventure and excitement—and I unlocked the door and pulled it open without a thought of danger; I was astonished when the flames leaped out. However the fire hadn't got right hold as yet; and with Dan Dennett and me running with buckets of water from the mill pond we managed to keep it down while we got most of the wool out. But about three packs of wool were right ablaze, and the roof fell in and one of the walls fell down, and the whole dryhouse had to be pulled down and built again. It happened very unluckily, as I remember," mused Charles Moreys. "We had a deal of wet wool by us and the weather turned stormy and we couldn't get it dry. There wasn't another scribbling mill in Moreydale at that time—well, there isn't now; that's why we do so well, you see—and we didn't know how we should manage. However, my father bethought himself of asking Mr. Oldroyd over in Iredale, who by that time had built himself a small mill, whether we could dry some wool at his place. You remember Oldroyd, the clothier whose wool James lost? Well, I had the job of riding over to ask him the favour. I can't say I fancied it—he's a red-headed man, as fiery in his temper as his hair. But he took it well and dried quite a lot for us, till one day James got across him some way or other. James got across everybody after a time. However, by that time our new dryhouse was nearly built. Cost us nigh on two hundred pounds. But why am I telling you all this rigmarole about the dryhouse, cousin?"

"You were explaining how the men at the mill found out your half-brother's cowardice."

"Ah, yes! Well," said Charles Moreys, his face, which had been happy and animated, falling into its usual bitter lines: "I can't say I noticed it at the time. I was too busy throwing on water and pulling out wool to notice what James was doing, or whether he did anything at all. But Dan Dennett, being an enemy of James for more reasons than one, noticed it clear enough and told it all over Moreydale. James, a man grown, stood in the mill doorway doing nothing but shout a few instructions, Dan said, while a boy (that was me) ran into the flames and dragged the wool out. The first time I heard Dan say this I shut him up sharply, told him he was not to spread such a lying slander. He said it wasn't a slander.

" 'You tell me, Mr. Charles,' he said, 'what your brother did at the fire, and I'll tell the story same as you do.'

"Well, I didn't know what to say, you see, cousin, because I didn't remember James doing anything.

" 'You see, you can't,' said Dan, very bitter. 'Your brother's a man only when he's with women.'

"The scandal spread everywhere and when James came into the mill the men jeered at him, asking where the fire was and calling out: 'I daren't go in—send for my brother,' and so on, till James wouldn't show his face there. It was easier for Father and me without him, but of course he had more time on his hands for getting into trouble."

"I suppose Dan was thinking of Lucy Greaves?"

"Aye! That was it," said Charles Moreys, sighing. "Poor Dan! Poor Lucy! You know, cousin, some men are attractive to women, and some are not, although you may not think so."

"Why should I not think so?" said I, somewhat vexed.

"Because you're too young and minikin to know owt about it," said Charles Moreys roughly. "Dan is one who's never been attractive, not right attractive, to any woman. The Moreys men on the other hand seem to have a sort of devil in them which draws women like bees to a honey-pot."

He paused, and looked at me with a gleam in his eye, but this was not a matter on which I wished to make any pronouncement. After a moment he laughed.

"I've done a bit in that way myself," he said.

Remembering his portrait in Dick's locket, I did not doubt it. I saw him a young man handsome, gay and debonair; laughing and spirited. Besides, he had a caressing, affectionate manner with all things weaker than himself, when he chose to employ it; when he so chose he would indeed be quite irresistible.

"I always liked dancing, you see, cousin," went on Charles Moreys in a lively tone. "And—why should I deny it?—I like the company of women. They're such soft, pretty creatures. And the more helpless they are, the more I like to help them. I like to flatter them and make them happy and see their cheeks colour and their eyes brighten; I like to coax them into liking me and then to steal a kiss—yes, I was a great flirt in my time," he concluded cheerfully.

For some reason my heart burned at this, and I said rather crossly: "There was little difference in this, then, between you and your brother?"

"Nay! That's not fair, cousin," said Charles Moreys, his fair face flushing. "I flirted, he seduced. I stole a kiss, he stole their honour. Ask any of my old flames up and down Iredale and Moreydale," he went on in an injured tone. "Any of them will tell you."

"Why, then, has Mrs. Tom Greaves, Martha Dennett that was, such a low opinion of you?"

"Nay, I don't know," said Charles Moreys with a frown. "It wounds me very much that Tom and Martha have turned against me. God knows I've never done them anything but good, and Tom owes me a deal of money."

"Tom Greaves owes you money?" I exclaimed, surprised.

"Aye, a deal of money. Not that I make any claims on

that account," said Charles Moreys hastily. "But to pretend to stand between Jacob and Mary because of my ill deeds, I think is wicked."

"I agree with you heartily, cousin," said I with emphasis. "But how did Tom Greaves and Martha Dennett come to marry?"

I felt some real curiosity on this score, if Tom were the rather foolish, flustered lad my cousin had described, and Martha the shrewd, managing woman I had seen her.

"I reckon it began that day James threw Tom in the dye vat," said my cousin consideringly. "Poor Tom was all blue, you see, a pitiful sight, quite broken-hearted and blubbering. Martha came running out of the miller's house to fetch him in, just as Dan shook Tom's shirt and spattered my brother. She laughed—it was she who started us all laughing. Yes, she laughed and pointed at James and went on laughing, doubling herself up and laughing with a wide mouth, a loud jeering cackle such as you sometimes hear on the stage. Invented, like. Artificial. But I think she was really very angry. She took Tom's arm and drew him into the house and gave him clean clothes. Nay, the story goes," said Charles Moreys, laughing, "that she scrubbed him naked. If she had a mind to it she would, you know. A very determined woman always, was Martha Dennett. She took a fancy to Tom Greaves that day, or so they say, and never let go of him. Her father was against the match, Tom being so poorly situated, but that didn't trouble her. As for James, you can imagine how he liked being laughed at by Martha Dennett. What with Dan spattering him and Martha laughing at him, you can guess he hated the Dennetts. It's my belief he made up to Lucy Greaves partly to vex Dan Dennett. Or at least, he began to go after her seriously on that account. James was a man who leered at every woman he saw, thinking they were sure to fancy him, but he only went after them seriously if *he* fancied *them,* if you take my meaning."

"Had he ever fancied Martha Dennett?" I asked.

"Nay! Have some sense, cousin!" said Charles Moreys in a tone of disgust. "No Moreys could ever fancy Martha Dennett."

"Why not?" said I sharply.

"She was so abominably plain, my dear," said Charles Moreys. "Large-featured, dull-complexioned, and a most unconscionable shrew into the bargain."

"You are very arrogant, cousin," said I, for I disliked his tone about women.

"No," said Charles Moreys. "I was arrogant once, Cousin Eleanor; but all that was stripped from me twelve years ago."

"Lucy Greaves, then," said I in a sardonic tone, for I was still vexed, "had sufficient beauty to satisfy the fastidious taste of your half-brother?"

"Ah, you are angry, cousin," said Charles Moreys, laughing. "Your eyes sparkle when you are angry. Poor Lucy Greaves was never angry in her life. She was a soft, sweet, bright-eyed, gentle little creature, shy and timid and always giving comfits to children. A quick, even spinner, though. She was always kind to me; I was glad enough to have her for my sister. But that was the trouble with Lucy, you see; she couldn't say no to anybody, even my brother."

"Perhaps she loved him," I suggested.

"Nowt o't'sort," said Charles Moreys contemptuously. "She loved Dan Dennett but hadn't the spirit to stick to him. So up comes the widow Greaves one evening to Wool Royd in tears, with Tom behind her turning his hat round in his fingers, to say that Lucy was with child and was laying it to my brother. They were such a long time getting to the point, my father thought at first they were come to beg off paying for Tom's cloth milling—there was a Wool Royd Pay Day the following week and the notes had just been delivered."

"Tom's cloth?"

"Aye—he was out of his apprenticeship a while since and had got himself a loom and started weaving."

"Where did he get the money to buy himself a loom?"

"Well—I gave it him," said Charles Moreys crossly. "Listen, cousin," he went on, striking his hand against the arm of the chair. "When Tom Greaves braved James and let the crane hook down, he saved me from death, or from what would be as bad as death for me, and that is maiming.

If it hadn't been for Tom Greaves I might have lain in bed for years, a helpless cripple. Never to ride again, never to walk over the moors, always to be weak and dependent, with a limping leg—that's what Tom Greaves saved me from. So I gave him the loom then, and I put him into Upper Hey later, and if he owes me money now the fault is as much mine as his. I don't consider him under any obligation to me. I can't press him to give his Mary to Jacob. If he doesn't want his girl to marry James's son, I don't blame him; but to put it down to my account as Martha does is unfair—nay, it's cruel."

I did not know what to say, for both from what Jacob had told me and from what I myself had heard at Upper Hey, I knew that Mrs. Greaves fancied she had a grudge against Charles Moreys.

"If Jacob were a rich man she would forgo it, however," I said, rather thinking aloud than addressing my cousin.

"Aye! I don't doubt! But perhaps you'll tell me how to make Jacob a rich man, cousin?" cried Charles Moreys vehemently. "You know how heedless he is, how young and unawakened? If I leave anything to him, he spoils it."

"He has a good head for figures," I murmured.

"He's improving under your teaching, I agree," said Charles Moreys. "But he's a mile away from being able to earn his own living. If he weren't my nephew I wouldn't keep him at Wool Royd a minute. I do the best I can for him. And it wounds me, it hurts me," he went on, his voice falling, "to have Jacob turn against me."

"Surely he has not done that, cousin. Jacob is greatly attached to you."

"He used to be—when he was a child he was a nice little thing, you know, with pretty brown eyes and a soft heart, like his mother. He was almost my only consolation, Tessie being what we both know she is, cousin, hard-hearted and selfish and mercenary. Jacob was a nice boy, and I used to take him out with me, riding pillion down to Annotsfield on market day, and up on to the moors walking on Sunday; and I used to tell him things and talk to him. He was a kind, good, affectionate lad—I used to think his was the only true affection I had about me. Then when he came spluttering to me about his Mary, I encouraged him. I was sorry in a way, for she isn't much of a match; Tom won't be able to leave her a penny unless he changes his ways—and his hands and his head too, which isn't very likely. Mary isn't a beauty either. But she's a good, nice kind of girl, and if Jacob wants her, let him have her. That's what I said, and I promised Tom Greaves to set them up in a clothier's business. I should have to run the business for them, same as I run Tom's, but what of that, I'm used to running other people's businesses for no profit. And then Martha Greaves must needs turn against me and say she doesn't want her daughter to marry into my family, and Mary shan't set a foot in Wool Royd, and so on and so on. And Jacob takes her side and turns against me and seems to think it's all my fault that he can't marry his Mary. It wounds me, it hurts me," said Charles Moreys, striking the chair arm again violently. "Yes, after all I've done for the Greaves and for Jacob, it cuts me to the heart. I was pretty nearly desperate when you came, cousin, I can tell you."

"Cousin Charles," said I, looking at him very steadily: "pray continue your story. When I know all the shadows that lie on this house, we can try to clear them away together."

"How do you propose to clear away that particular shadow, eh?"

"I can find out what Mrs. Greaves' grudge against you is, and remove it."

"It will need more wisdom than lies in your young head to do that, cousin. However—where was I?"

"The widow Greaves has come to your father about Lucy."

"Oh, yes. Well, I was not in the room when she told him poor Lucy's trouble, for, as you can imagine, she had asked to speak to him privately. I was lounging in the window-seat here when I heard a heavy cry, a roar like an ageing bull. It was my father's voice, and he'd been looking so ill of late that I thought he'd had a fit or something of that kind, and ran quickly across the hall to the other room. The widow Greaves was weeping and Tom had his head down on his chest, and my father sat cramped up leaning over with his two hands on the top of his stick, looking as if a snake had bitten him. His face was livid, nay it was almost green, and somehow pinched and distorted; his mouth open, his eyes full of pain.

" 'Keep out of this, Charles,' he said when he saw me. 'Go away.'

" 'What's to do, Father?' said I.

" 'It's James and Lucy Greaves,' he said with bitter disgust. 'Oh, God, will it never end? I told you, Charles,' he said again, banging his stick on the floor: 'keep away. This is not your affair.'

"Just then I heard the door at the back of the house close. James had a habit of entering the house by that way when he came down off the moor, and I guessed it was him now. I thought if my father and he met while my father was in his first rage there would be an angry quarrel which would be bad for both, so I went out of the room and came into the kitchen. There sure enough was James, perched on the edge of the table, drinking one of Adah's odd brews that she used to give him to bring him round after his drinking bouts—she's a gipsy, you know, and skilful at herbal concoctions. The serving-man with his coat off sat by the hearth smoking a pipe.

" 'You'd best keep out of the house for a few hours, James,' said I. 'Till my father's anger towards you cools a little.'

" 'What have I done wrong this time?' said my brother.

" 'Mrs. Greaves says you have got Lucy with child,' I said, throwing it out thus brutally because I was so grieved for Tom's sake.

"Adah exclaimed reproachfully in her gipsy language, the serving-man was so startled he dropped his pipe, and even James had the grace to colour—darkly, after his fashion.

" 'And what is that to you, brother Charles?' he said, sneering.

" 'You might have told me I was to have a new sister,' I said.

" 'New sister be hanged,' said James, and with a coarseness which I will not inflict on you, Cousin Eleanor, he made it clear that he had no intention of marrying Lucy. Then he gulped down the rest of his drink and went out of the house. I followed him. Just as I closed the door behind us, we both heard a woman wailing and my father's voice raised in angry reprimand. James laughed, though to do him justice in a rather shamefaced fashion.

" 'You'd better go back and soothe them down, Charles,' he said.

" 'Shall I tell them you'll marry Lucy?'

" 'No!'

" 'James,' said I: 'I marvel that you mean to bring a child into the world to suffer in the same way you do.'

"James gave me a strange look.

" 'There are times, Charles, when I almost like you,' he said. Then he added hastily: 'But this is not one of them.'

"Be that as it may," continued Charles Moreys, "very soon after, James married Lucy. Whether my father insisted on the marriage—as he easily could, holding the purse-strings—or whether James had some feeling for the coming child on the lines I had suggested, I do not know. I reckon it was both, perhaps. Anyhow, they were married in plenty of time for Joah to be born in wedlock. That turned people's opinions round a bit in James's favour, naturally, but you can imagine what poor Dan Dennett thought of it. He left home and went away to work at a fulling mill in Iredale and didn't come back for long enough—not till after my brother's death, in fact. But my father bought Upper Hey for James and settled him there as a clothier, with four new looms and everything very handsome. At first it seemed as if James had really turned over a new leaf, as they say; he kept his journeymen weavers in good order and rode to market every Tuesday, and of course Lucy was very kind to the weavers and apprentices and they all liked her and worked well for her sake. But it didn't last long. James could never stick to one woman or one kind of work. Nay, he could never stick to any kind of work. He began to drink and gamble again and what was worse he let his weavers take to drinking and gambling too, till the cloth they turned out wasn't fit to sell. At last my father had to put

Tom Greaves in with James as a partner, to try to keep the business straight."

"But, Cousin Charles," I objected, "you said just now that when Tom Greaves was still apprenticed, he was not very skilful at the clothier's trade."

"True enough. But he'd learned some sense by then. Not much, of course; poor Tom will never set the Ire on fire. But at least he was honest, and not given to drink."

"I'm surprised he wished to be associated with your brother."

"Well, Martha wanted to be getting married, you see, and I reckon she pushed Tom into accepting the job, once my father had proposed it. Martha always knew which side her bread was buttered."

"And how did the marriage turn out, between Lucy and your brother?"

"Ah," said Charles Moreys with a look of pity, shaking his head. "Poor Lucy! You see, she was afraid of him. How often have I said to her: 'Lucy, you must stand up to him; Lucy, you mustn't show him fear.' If you showed fear with James, it was all up with you. You had to meet him eye for eye and word for word and blow for blow; you mustn't yield an inch or he'd be on top of you. Didn't I know it! But Lucy, she was afraid, she shrank and wept, and James enjoyed tormenting her. And then there was Joah, you see. I'm fond of children, you know, cousin, and I inclined to feel sorry for this child of my brother's—not wanted really by either parent, and with such a father to struggle with as James. I haven't lost that feeling for Joah, I'm still sorry for him and always shall be so. But from the time he began to walk, he was always a most detestable brat. A big, rough, coarse child, bullying and cruel; I've seen him strike his mother so hard as to leave bruises——"

"Oh no, Cousin Charles! Poor Lucy! No!"

"Aye, but I have. I told you the story was not fit for your agreeable ears, Cousin Eleanor. Yes, I've seen him strike her, and Lucy sitting there with a sad smile, not trying to command him, scarcely trying to turn aside his hands."

"But what did your brother say?"

"James was not there—he was rarely in his own house after the first year of married life."

"And what did *you* say, Cousin Charles?"

"Oh, I used to tell Joah my opinion of him in a quiet sarcastic way; he didn't like that. Or sometimes I'd lift him off his mother and hold him quite still for a minute, with his hands tight at his sides. Oddly enough he was rather fond of me—I used to take him apples and tops and such, you know, cousin; he was a child, after all. But between Joah and James, poor Lucy had a wretched life of it. Then Jacob was born and he was Lucy's consolation. A bonny friendly little lad, was Jacob; he took after his mother in disposition, you see, and partly in looks as well. He used to put his hand in mine and toddle round the mill with me. And then that damned woman, Martha Greaves, turns him against me! It's a shame, Cousin Eleanor, a cruel shame! I feel right down hurt about it. What have I ever done wrong to Jacob?"

"How did your father feel towards James's children?"

"He disliked both of them," said Charles Moreys soberly. "Yes! He could hardly bring himself to speak them kind. Joah he never could endure to have near him and it was no wonder, the child was so rough and noisy and rude. I used to try to bring Jacob to his notice—when Jacob was prattling, you know; children are very lovable, I always think, at that age—but it was useless. Father used to look down his nose at poor Jacob as if he were a piece of cockled cloth, and if the child called him grandpa he scowled and turned aside. Lucy didn't keep the lads very well looking, you know. Their clothes seemed always rather too bright and too tight, ill matching, with buttons off and poorly mended. She had no heart for the job, I expect, poor girl; besides, though Lucy has as kind a heart as you could wish for, she's not what you'd call a good manager. A bit too simple and easy-going. So though Joah and Jacob were well-grown healthy little rascals, they never looked as Father thought his grandsons ought. I used sometimes to think it was a good thing James was so much away, or he might have taken it ill, the way Father looked at his children. But happen he wouldn't have cared; he didn't take that much notice of his sons. I was sorry Father couldn't fancy Jacob, though, for Jacob was a grand little fellow. And now look at him! Turned against me! As though I haven't my plate heaped high enough with troubles without Jacob adding to the pile!"

CHAPTER IV

"I HAVE not yet learned these troubles, Cousin Charles," said I, as he did not go on.

"Do you suppose I don't know that?" said Charles Moreys savagely. "I tell you about these Greaves and Lees and Dennetts to put off the moment when I must come to my own wrongs."

A very strong gust of wind and rain striking the house with a great shriek at that moment, Charles Moreys rose and strode over to the windows. Standing with his arms outstretched, his hands resting each side of the frame, he gazed out at the streaming rain in moody silence. I thought it a good moment to replenish the fire, which was sinking low, but as the sounds of my movements reached his ears Charles Moreys turned back quickly and took the business out of my hands, kneeling by the hearth and piling the coal on lavishly after the Yorkshire fashion. The flames leaped up.

"But you are weeping, Eleanor!" exclaimed Charles Moreys.

I turned my head aside quickly, for in truth there were tears on my cheeks and I did not wish him to see them.

"You must not take it so much to heart, my dear. If you weep now, what will you do later? I warned you the story was a wretched one."

"The story is very sad," said I in a trembling tone. "But," I went on, changing the subject somewhat so as to fight down my tears, "there is matter about which I am grieved with you, cousin."

"Grieved with me?" said he, his look hardening. "I am sorry to hear that, cousin. Everyone else in the world seems to be grieved with me, but I had hoped for your indulgence. You, too, think I wronged my brother?"

"No, No!" I exclaimed with emphasis. "But how could you compare my dear father, Walter Moreys, with your hateful brother?"

"Walter Moreys?" said my cousin, frowning in perplexity. "Have I said anything of the kind tonight?"

"No, but in the mill—the first morning—in our first interview," said I, stumbling in my vehemence, "you asked what manner of man my father was, and said you had thought him like Joah's father, your brother. It was bad enough to compare my father to anyone of Joah's family," I cried hotly. "But now that I know what James Lee was, I think it was cruel of you, nay wicked, cousin! My father was the sweetest, the kindest, the best of men, fond of children and courteous to the old and weak, as you are, cousin." I stopped, astonished by my own conclusion.

"Nay, if Walter Moreys was like his daughter, I am ready to grant him all the virtues," said Charles Moreys, smiling kindly. "I just thought perhaps, with his running away to sea, he had made Moreydale too hot to hold him, d'you see, cousin."

"Your father drove him out of Wool Royd, giving no reason why he did so, and it was a lifelong anguish to him."

"Aye, I remember he mentioned it in his letter to me," said Charles Moreys thoughtfully. "Had he really no notion why my father dismissed him?"

"None whatever. Oh, if you had heard him time after time lamenting his ignorance of the reason to me, pacing up and down the room—and later up and down the prison. 'Why, why, Eleanor?' he would cry. 'I had done him no wrong. Why should he banish me from Wool Royd?' My father loved Wool Royd, Cousin Charles. His last words to me were that I should go home to Moreydale."

Here I was overcome by my various emotions, and fell to sobbing. Charles Moreys came and stood beside me and laid his hand kindly on my shoulder. At this I buried my face in my hands and wept all the more bitterly.

"We have not treated you well at Wool Royd, Cousin Eleanor," said Charles Moreys, putting back my hair from my face and touching my cheek with his fingers very gently. "We have not thought of your grief for your father, but only of our own need of you. My father, too, died when I was twenty," he added. "I know how forlorn one is left by the loss of even a not greatly beloved parent."

This recalled to me the real purpose of our conversation and I was ashamed to have interrupted Charles Moreys' sad history with my own griefs.

"Pray continue to tell me, cousin," I said, gulping down my tears and drying my eyes very vigorously with a handkerchief which he proffered me.

"Take a glass of wine first," said he, stepping to the table to pour it. "Or would you prefer we should break off the story here, Cousin Eleanor? It is too much for your nerves, perhaps—you are trembling."

"I wish to hear it all," said I more firmly. "Only, please never again compare my father with your half-brother."

"I will not, I promise you," said Charles Moreys, handing me the glass. "I have not filled it full, cousin, lest you should shake it over and spot your dress in your agitation."

This small but very real kindness had almost set me weeping again, for it was so like my father and my cousin. However I swallowed down my tears and looked up at Charles Moreys expectantly. He had poured some wine for himself and now stood, glass in hand, leaning against the mantelpiece. In the firelight his hair shone very golden, and his fine clear features, softened as they were just now by the sympathy my distress had roused in him, looked singularly handsome.

CHAPTER V

"YES, I was in my twentieth year when my father died, just as it has been with you, cousin," said Charles Moreys.

"I never loved my father as you loved yours, but with his advancing illness I felt much compassion for him. In my childhood he had been a big, burly, powerful, tyrannical man of whom everyone was afraid; to see him now shrivelled, stooping and hollow-cheeked, with his hair thinning and even his voice, which used to be so frightening, grown weak—to see him like that filled me with astonishment and pain. Then at the mill he forgot the names of things he had been familiar with all his life and was vexed with himself for forgetting; the men who had been with us for a long time knew his trouble and were kind to it, but the younger ones didn't understand and gaped at him when he tried to instruct them and forgot what he meant to say. Then he raged at them and they turned sullen, and I had to come round and soothe them down. It got to such a pitch of difficulty that I urged Adah to try to keep him at home as much as she could, and she tried to keep him in bed late and persuade him to rest in the afternoon. But she couldn't do much in that line, for he was miserable if a day went by without his coming to the mill—and it was his mill, after all. A very trying matter was that he took it into his head to have himself weighed on our scale-pans that we use to measure out the dyes. He was losing weight every week and it troubled him, so I told the men to do a little cheating with the weights and they grew quite skilful at deceiving him and kept his weight about the same each time, so that he was cheered and went off looking brighter.

"Well, one day I'd just helped him on to the scales and old Dennett was fiddling with the weights, when James came in. I hated the way James's eyes roved over Father at this time; you could see he was thinking how long it would be before he died—for James of course expected a substantial share of the Moreys wealth; my father had always promised it to him. Well, that afternoon James looked at Father in his usual gloating, sneering way, and old Dennett, who of course as you can guess hated James very heartily, was perhaps made a trifle nervous under his gaze, and he fidgeted clumsily with the weights so that James noticed it. Of course James was delighted to catch somebody out; he pointed at Dennett and shouted:

" 'What are you doing with that weight?'

"Everyone looked at Dennett and there he was, holding one of the weights up just off the scale, so that Father appeared to be weighing five pounds more that he really was. Of course all the men knew what Dennett was about and of course so did I and I have this cursed trick of colouring up very easily because of my fair complexion, so I suppose we all looked guilty and embarrassed. My father was no fool even if he was ageing, and he looked at us shrewdly and saw the whole thing, and naturally guessed that this wasn't the first time we'd cheated him. He gave me such a look! Angry and yet loving. Then without a word he slipped off the scales and stumped out of the mill, leaning on his stick. (It was a very fine ebony stick with a silver plate on, that I'd got for him from London.) We all watched him go, and I went to the door to follow him, but he heard my step and turned and waved me back, and went off not up the lane to the house, but towards the beck, towards the water-splash. It struck me he wished to be alone for a while till he'd recovered from the shock and disappointment of discovering he was losing weight steadily—besides, our having deceived him showed him we thought ill of it. It grieved me to have hurt him and I stood there wondering which would be best to do, to let him go alone or to follow him, when suddenly there came a splash and a cry, and there was poor Father floundering in the water; trying to stride over, he'd slipped and fallen. I ran across and took him under the armpits and pulled him out quickly, but he couldn't stand, his leg was broken.

"We carried him up to the house and put him to bed and I sent to Annotsfield for the surgeon. It was old Dr. Bradshaw—the father of the one who came to Dick the other day; the young one didn't set up practice with his father for another year or two. The surgeon set the leg, but from the first he didn't give us much hope about Father. He spoke to me and James about it, privately, downstairs, and said he feared Father wouldn't recover; his heart had been much weakened by his rheumatism and couldn't stand the strain of the fracture. I didn't believe Bradshaw. I thought he was old and fussy, or perhaps eager to gain credit for a wonderful cure by making out the patient to be very ill. James on the other hand believed him at once— I suppose the wish was father to the thought in both cases. But after Bradshaw had gone, when I went upstairs to see Father, then I believed him. Poor old Father could hardly speak; you could almost see the life ebbing away from him.

He fixed his eyes on me with a look of terrible anxiety, and said my name: 'Charles,' though in an imperfect slurring manner. I took his hand in mine and told him the surgeon said his leg had set well and he would be soon about again, but he didn't seem to hear, he still gazed up at me as if he wanted to say something but couldn't manage it.

"A thought struck me and I went downstairs and came into this room and lifted down the portrait of my mother from the wall—that one—and took it up and put it on a chair at the foot of the bed, and told Adah to hold it steady; and I raised my father up on my arm so that he could see the portrait. It was sad to see him then, for tears fairly spurted from his eyes. James had followed me up into the bedroom and my father looked from me to him, and then he spoke again. He said:

" 'Charles, what have I done to you?'

"At least, it was something like that; his utterance was so blurred that I could hardly make the words out. He didn't speak again, and was gone before morning.

"Don't weep, Cousin Eleanor," continued Charles Moreys grimly. "Keep your tears for me; I am going to need them."

"I cannot help but be sorry for the old man," I faltered. "He repented of his vice; with that we must credit him."

"Aye! But it is I who have had to pay for it," said Charles Moreys with deep feeling. "When I heard my father's will read by the attorney, my heart stood still with disappointment. I had guessed Father would not leave James a share in Wool Royd, but imagined he would bequeath him a large sum of money. Already I was casting round in my mind how best to raise the sum without crippling Wool Royd. To pay James off, to have nothing more to do with him and his affairs, would be such a happiness to me that I did not care how narrowly I stinted myself to achieve it. But my father had willed otherwise. He left James only five hundred pounds; all the rest of his estate was left in trust for me and my children, so that I drew a life interest only; in default of issue of my body, the money after my death was to go to found some almshouses in Annotsfield. Meanwhile I was instructed to take care of James. Those were the words: *I trust my son Charles to take all due care for James Lee.* Can you imagine anything, cousin," said Charles Moreys bitterly, "more hurtful, more unjust?"

CHAPTER VI

"BUT IT was a very clever will, Cousin Charles," said I. "It saved you."

"Saved me!" exclaimed Charles Moreys angrily. "It left James and his children at my mercy, and myself——"

"At the mercy of your own generosity. True," said I. "Nevertheless it saved your life. If you died, James lost all."

Charles Moreys frowned.

"Well, that is true of course," he said in a troubled tone. "I have seen it so myself, sometimes."

"I am sure your father saw it so. And," said I, gathering my courage: "it still saves you today. But once Joah has married Tessie, as he intends, I would not give a farthing for your life. Or for Dick's."

"You are wrong, my dear," said Charles Moreys. "You are allowing yourself to become overwrought by the violence of the storm. We are living in the year 1809, after all; we are not savages; there is a law in England. In any case, Joah has not the cunning for such a distant plan. Besides, he knows that his prosperity hangs on me. Nor would he dare any violence against me; he is afraid of me, I am the stronger. As for Dick, he is the instrument of my father's punishment. Tessie and Dick will halve the Moreys wealth between them—for the will gives all my children equal shares—and the old wrong will be righted, at my expense."

"You are talking riddles, Cousin Charles," said I impatiently. "Dick is a sweet, good, merry little boy—or would be, if he could get over his ill-health. And as to that——" I turned towards the pitcher of milk which stood at the far end of the table, but before I could speak what was in my mind about it, Charles Moreys interrupted me:

"But Dick is not my son," he said.

I was so stunned by this statement, to me utterly

unexpected and preposterous, that I stared at him for a moment speechless.

"But, Cousin Charles," I faltered then, "that is surely impossible! Dick resembles you so closely! In every way he is so like you!"

"Nonsense!" said Charles Moreys roughly.

"His complexion," I began.

"Children's eyes are often blue and their hair fair when they are young, but they do not stay so. Dick's hair will darken soon, no doubt."

"But in disposition——"

"Do not insult me by likening that peevish, mardy little coward to me."

"You are unjust, cousin," said I. "Whatever the story of Dick's birth, the child himself is most charming and lovable."

"His mother was charming and lovable too," said Charles Moreys. "Or so at least I thought. But you shall hear."

He threw himself down in his chair and with a very sneering and bitter look on his face resumed his story.

CHAPTER VII

"PERHAPS I should never have married Rosie," he said, "if my life after my father's death had been less dreary. But consider my situation. Imagine James's fury over my father's will. Imagine what the neighbourhood thought of the will. Yorkshire folk pride themselves on speaking their mind and they spoke their mind to me pretty freely. They all thought James was wronged by our father's will—and so indeed he was; but what could I do about it? All the suggestions I made to the attorney for giving James a settled income he continually rejected. It was clear to me that old Battye (the attorney) disliked James and had learned this dislike from my father and had rejoiced in laying the Moreys' property most carefully out of James's reach. But James naturally enough saw only the difference in Battye's manner when he spoke to me and when he spoke to him, and resented it.

James talked loudly about the unfair treatment he had received, all down Iredale and all over Annotsfield, till folk began to look askance at me when I rode in for market-day. But I could do nothing against it; I could hardly tie a placard round my neck saying how much I was paying over to James each week, or explaining that I knew nothing of my father's will till after his death. Besides, too much eagerness to excuse yourself always excites suspicion, so I just had to put up with it all in silence. But it was not agreeable to be greeted with looks of displeasure by all the folk I most cared for, and received with a wink and a smile by all the smooth-tongued rascals. I was an affectionate, open-hearted sort of lad in those days, and it hurt me sorely.

"There there was trouble at the mill, with those confounded slubbers.

"For a week or so after the funeral—where they were well treated, cousin; I gave them all suits of black and gloves and a very fine funeral breakfast—well, for a while after the funeral, as I say, they were very decorous and respectful. They they began to get out of hand—partly because I was only twenty, after all, and partly because they were genuinely disgusted on James's behalf. As you can imagine, James encouraged them. They began to come late, to leave early, to spend far too much time over their afternoon drinking. Being a soft-hearted sort of lad, as I said, I disliked to be always nagging at them and did not pull them up as sharp as I should, and presently the very pieceners—the children who help the slubbers, you know, cousin—began to make faces at my back and answer pertly when spoken to. Then the slubbers began to stay away for a day or two, whenever they had a mind. I'd nobody to help me, you see; old Dennett at the mill had got into a mumbling, muddled old man and seemed to think Dan's living away from home was all my fault, so he wouldn't interfere with the men. As for Tom Greaves, being in James's employ it wasn't easy for him to take my side.

"At last one day it all came to a head. I'd had complaints from some of the Iredale clothiers about the poor quality of our slubbings; they were uneven and—but it's no use going into all that with you, Cousin Eleanor; you don't understand a word of it; it's enough to say the clothiers had grumbled. I was greatly vexed, remembering how poor Father had always prided himself on the good quality of all Wool Royd work, and I went into the mill that afternoon to try to find out who was responsible for the bad work, in a mood just spoiling for a row. The slubbers all evaded my questions, pretending not to understand me and telling outrageous lies which they all laughed at, and I was crimson in the face and feeling badgered and furious, when in came Tom Greaves looking very hangdog.

" 'Well, what do you want, Tom?' said I sharply.

"Mr. James had sent him, he said—you know how he talks, as if he had a pebble in his mouth; you can't always make out what he says and I had to ask him to repeat it, which made the men snigger—Mr. James had sent him to make a complaint; an Annotsfield merchant had returned one of the Upper Hey pieces of cloth he had bought at market yesterday, saying it was not properly woven; the Upper Hey weaver said it was not his fault, the yarn was wrong, and the spinner said the poor yarn was not her fault, it was due to faulty slubbings. My men fell silent at this and looked somewhat shamefaced, for of course the slubbings were their work.

" 'Tell Mr. James I'll ride to Annotsfield with him at once, and see this merchant—the piece shall be replaced at my private cost,' I said to Tom.

" 'Now?' said Tom, with his eyes popping out of his head.

" 'Now,' said I.

" 'And that,' said I angrily, turning on the slubbers, 'that's the result of your bad work. I pay you good wages, you should do good work. It's not fair to do bad work for good wages.'

"Well, at this they all shouted and there was a regular turmoil. 'Fair!' they said. 'There's nothing fair at Wool Royd. What's fair about you having all and Mr. James nowt?' And so on. Some of them even shook their fists at me.

"It was one of those moments like when I fell in the beck and when I dangled on the crane. I felt I had to harden my heart and show no fear, or I was done for. I kept my hands stiff at my sides and my head up and waited for them to stop shouting, and after a while they grew tired of getting no answer from me, and fell silent. Then I spoke. But I felt as if I'd aged ten years during the last ten minutes, and this time I spoke in a very quiet, cool tone and tried to sound sarcastic.

" 'Considering I share everything Wool Royd earns equally with my half-brother,' I said, 'you aren't going the right road to help him.'

"They all gaped at me, and I turned my back on them and walked out of the mill and shut the door behind me very quietly. And I can't say I've had much trouble with them since," said Charles Moreys, laughing.

"However, at that time I didn't know what would happen. I brushed myself up and put on my very best clothes to go to Annotsfield, because I was so downhearted and sore and miserable that I felt I should never get through without something to help me. When I called at Upper Hey for James he wasn't ready and I had to dismount and go indoors to fetch him. He didn't seem inclined to come, and I had to make him. If only I'd left him alone! But the row with the men had got my spirit up and I felt I mustn't yield to anyone, so I took a very cold, lofty tone with James—considering he'd thought fit to humiliate me by sending Tom Greaves down to Wool Royd with a complaint, I said, he might at least take the trouble to accompany me when I tried to put the matter right. He scowled and swore and grumbled, but I stood there declining to sit down, and poor Lucy timidly got out his best coat—it was a handsome maroon coat and I think it helped to persuade him. It was little Jacob that clinched the matter, however. Jacob always wanted to be helpful, when he was a child; he had a soft heart like his mother and couldn't bear any kind of scolding or quarrel. He and Joah were playing in and out of the room while all this argument was going on. Joah didn't take any notice—but Jacob began to pause and listen and look troubled, and presently he exclaimed:

" 'Shall I go with Uncle Charles, Father?'

"James didn't answer; but you know how children are, they keep on asking a question till you answer them; Jacob went on saying: "Shall I go with Uncle Charles, Father?

143

Father, shall I go with Uncle Charles?' till James was sick of it, and suddenly shouted at Lucy to keep the damned child quiet, and rushed from the room and came back dressed in his market clothes, ready to go with me. In spite of his drinking habits he was still a handsome man enough if you like coarse colourings and flashing eyes, and he preened himself in front of the mirror and seemed to recover his temper, and we set off, with him in good spirits. But I felt very low. I thought then I'd never felt so low in my life before, and hoped I never should again. I was on a pinnacle compared with what came after.

"We came to Annotsfield without mishap and called on the merchant at his warehouse. Or rather merchants; two brothers, Whitacre by name, one of them a man about my father's age and the other a good deal older. I put on my very best air and apologised about the bad slubbings which had spoiled James's cloth they had bought, said Wool Royd had been a little disarranged the last month because of my father's death, but all was now running smoothly, they could rely on high quality from now onwards, and so on—though how I should be able to fulfil these promises, inwardly I very much doubted. I felt so desperate, I talked with particular conviction, and as I talked they relented a little from the cold surly reserve with which they'd first received us. They exchanged looks, then showed us some of the fine cloths which they bought to send abroad. I was always knowledgeable about cloth, you see, Cousin Eleanor, even in those days; my father hadn't neglected to teach me my trade in amongst all my book schooling. So the Whitacres gradually warmed up to me; and James having the sense for once to keep quiet and stay in the background, the good impression was not spoiled. Presently the younger Whitacre looked at his watch and then they exchanged meaning glances again. Of course I began at once to take my leave, but the younger Whitacre, after humming and hawing a bit, brought out an invitation.

"It was his daughter's birthday and he and Mrs. Whitacre were entertaining company that evening, and would be very glad if I and my brother would join them, and so on. I could read in his eye the thought that I was unmarried and comfortably lined—that's a Yorkshire expression for being well-to-do, cousin—and would make a very suitable partner for his daughter. The sight of his calculation sickened me but if I wanted to keep his custom for James I knew I had to accept his invite, and that after all was a calculation too. I made polite objections about our lack of the proper dress, and he as politely waived them, and presently James and I rode out with the brothers to the younger one's house, a handsome mansion enough, newly erected, a mile or so on the other side of Annotsfield.

"Miss Whitacre was a kind, bouncing, honest girl enough —I've often thought since how much better I'd have done to marry her; but at the time of course, being young and accustomed, I must confess, to being flattered and spoiled by women for my good looks, I rejected her as soon as I set eyes on her. She was all teeth and bosom, with fluttering ribbons and a gushing way of talk. I was always somewhat apprehensive when James was of the company; he had no idea how to behave in polite society, was apt to drink too much and come out with coarse remarks and oaths not fit for ladies' ears. To cover this up I talked a lot all through dinner and flirted mildly all round, admiring Mrs. Whitacre's cap and complimenting Miss Matilda on her curls. James, I could see, was drinking hard and beginning to sneer and working himself up for some sottish explosion; I felt more and more wretched and the more wretched I felt the livelier I talked. Then after dinner fifteen or twenty other guests came in, young folk and their parents, and Mrs. Whitacre led us into another room for dancing. There was a fine new piano there, and a harp, and Mr. Hervey, a music preceptor from Annotsfield, to play for us, with his daughter Rosie.

"Rosie. She was the loveliest girl. Soft dark curls, and soft satiny cheeks flushed like her name, and the most perfect round white arms and soft young bosom. For some reason, I don't know why, I dislike women's arms which start thin at the wrist and swell out fat towards the elbow. Rosie's arms were not like that; they were curving and slender, the same width all the way up so that I longed to span them. As she played the harp her hands and arms were really a dream of beauty. Then again, you see, the poor child looked unhappy. Mr. Hervey was a small, hunch-backed, Frenchified sort of man wearing an old-fashioned wig and shoes with large buckles, very polite and full of bows and fine phrases. But his features were sharp and his eyes were sharp and even his fingers seemed sharp and somehow snapping; if Rosie played a wrong note what a look he gave her! She played a good many wrong notes, poor child; she wasn't very clever, you know, my poor little Rosie! But lovely! Pretty—the prettiest thing you ever saw. Pretty in a very delicate, refined fashion. I have a very fastidious taste in women, Cousin Eleanor; I can't bear any line about them to be coarse or clumsy. Everything about Rosie pleased my taste at that time—I could have spanned her waist between my ten fingers. All her movements were so pretty too; soft and quick and delicate, like a kitten. I caught her eye once or twice as I danced with the bouncing Miss Whitacre and tried to throw into my look all the admiration I felt for her, and I had the satisfaction of seeing her delicate colour deepen. She looked away, then down at her harp with great attention, but the attention was pretended, not real, for she played a whole set of notes at random. She went wrong in the timing too, I think, for old Hervey scowled at her and banged the notes more loudly and emphatically as if to recall her to the beat. Poor Rosie gave him such a timid deprecating look, it made my heart turn over.

"A man has very strong protective feelings towards a young woman in distress, you know, cousin; at any rate a man like I am has such feelings—I'm a very affectionate warm-hearted sort of fellow, really, though you probably don't think so. With my life being as it was, you know, having no mother and no sister and my father and James and Joah being as they were, and being unable to show too much affection to poor Lucy lest it be misinterpreted, there was only Jacob, you might say, I could feel affection for, and after all there are limits to the love you can show to a nephew. In a word, I was starving I suppose for love, and especially for someone I could show love to, and my poor sweet Rosie looked so hapless and helpless, I longed to rescue her.

"Presently the music broke off, so that the guests might

have supper, and we all streamed away into another room. I took a glass of wine and had some chicken put on a plate and came back to the harp to give them to Rosie. As I approached across the room, I saw that she was looking more than ever unhappy and frightened, and when I rounded the piano I saw the cause—James was lounging in an armchair beside her. All the anger I had ever felt against James rose up hot within me and I put it all into the look I gave him. I halted deliberately, then took a strong step forward. I judge my aspect must have been quite menacing, for James got up hastily and crying:

" 'All right, all right, Charles! No offence intended,' in his thick drunkard's voice, he lounged away out of the room.

"Rosie gave me such an admiring, grateful look from her pretty eyes, I felt immensely proud of myself. I bowed and handed her the viands I had brought, and drew up a small table to place them on, and prepared to stand beside her and make agreeable conversation. Mr. Hervey however was looking very sour and peevish because I had brought him no supper, and Rosie proffered him hers. He refused, since manners demanded it, sharply but with reluctance, and it was plain I should have to go and fetch some more before I could talk to my pretty dear. I turned away, but was saved from the necessity of departure by Miss Whitacre, who entered the room at that moment, followed by a serving-man carrying an ample supper for the Herveys. Naturally she was astonished to see me, but as her glance moved from myself to Rosie she understood it all. A rather sad look came into her eyes, but she spoke most kindly to the musicians, and had the serving-man set out the supper very conveniently, and talked meanwhile to Mr. Hervey about music for the dances, giving me a chance to speak to Rosie. I told her my name and enquired for hers and where she lived and admired her playing and contrived to turn a compliment, clumsy enough no doubt but I was young, about her soft bright eyes. Then Miss Whitacre withdrew and, not to appear unmannerly, I had to escort her. But I had secured the means of pursuing the Herveys' acquaintance.

"A young man's courtship is much the same in any and every set of circumstances, I suppose," continued Charles

Moreys sardonically. "He calls to enquire if the young lady suffered fatigue on the occasion when he met her; he calls again with a nosegay; he calls with tickets for a theatre, concert or the like; he calls to bring new music, he calls to hear her play it; he calls once when he knows she will not be at home, in order to pay court and compliments to her parents. At one point or another in this series of calls, depending on the wealth and character of the household, he is invited to dinner. If the young lady and the young man belong to the same group of friends, they meet also at social gatherings—parties and dances, picnics, expeditions, church perhaps—and the dinner invitation comes sooner and means a little less. I met Rosie nowhere but at the Herveys' drab lodgings, and the dinner invitation was longer in coming but meant more when it arrived. Hervey with his cold, dry, formal manners was either a man of honour or a good imitation of one who saw where his daughter's advantage lay—I have never been able to decide which. A widower, he had nobody to whom to entrust Rosie's safety; he watched her himself very closely. I did not resent this; it was natural, I thought, to guard such a treasure with great care. I see now that he was suspicious of the intentions of a young man so much above their social rank as I was. How often have I sat with Rosie in the back parlour while Mr. Hervey gave a music lesson in the front, the folding-doors between the rooms being scrupulously left one yard open! The tinkling notes of scales and exercises and the sharp rebukes of Mr. Hervey to his pupils mingled with our love-making, which in such conditions had to be restrained and polite in manner. We made up for our forced reserve in speech by expressive glances. Not that I ever had a glance really ardent, really full of love, from Rosie; she was always timid, shy, uncertain.

"However I was about to tell you of my dinner engagement. Had I been less in love this might have checked my courtship. That the table appointments were poor and the service lacking in urbanity I could have borne without discomfort, knowing the Herveys' poverty, but even in my love-besotted state I perceived that Rosie had no notion how they could or should be bettered. Mr. Hervey knew their deficiencies and was vexed by them and tried to give Rosie sharp hints of how they might be remedied, but my poor little Rosie just stared at him in open-mouthed perplexity; she was simple, not quick in the uptake and—as I saw even then—a trifle lazy and slatternly. But my heart rushed to her defence, assuring me that when my dear girl was my wife all these minor defects would be rectified. How could she be neat, how could she be fastidious, in her household appointments, in such dreary poverty as Mr. Hervey's musical earnings condemned them to?

"I see you do not agree, Cousin Eleanor, with these excuses. Neither do I—now. But then, you see, I was in love. I saw her through rose-coloured spectacles, my pretty girl.

"There were not wanting warnings to me against the marriage. Mr. Whitacre, in a way I now think kindly meant but then resented, reminded me of Rosie's lack of genteel upbringing. I replied hotly that that was not Rosie's fault.

" 'Neither is a deformity or a squint,' said Mr. Whitacre shrewdly; 'but yet we do not gladly wed women with them.'

"His own daughter had just become affianced to an up-and-coming young clothier living near them, so I suppose he felt he could speak freely to me without being suspected of interested motives.

"Martha Greaves, too, had to have her say through Tom, urging that Miss Hervey was not only poor and ungenteel but feckless, and even Lucy did not seem to care for Rosie when I brought her out to tea at Upper Hey, as much as I had hoped. Lucy was troubled, I think, because Rosie was wearing a handsome hat with feathers, which she guilelessly admitted I had given her for the occasion—they were all the fashion at that time.

" 'You are so open-handed, so warm-hearted, Charles,' Lucy told me after Rosie's visit when I ran eagerly in to ask her what she thought. 'I want you to have someone very warm-hearted very sweet-like, for your wife.'

" 'Rosie is sweet,' I said.

" 'Yes,' agreed Lucy. 'But has she any strong feeling for you, Charles? She likes your presents and your pretty speeches, but does she care for *you*?' Seeing the vexation on my face at this, she added hastily in that soothing, appeasing tone of hers: 'I daresay she loves you as much as she can love anybody.'

"On the other hand, James for once was on my side. He thought Lucy's scruples ridiculous, and without praising Rosie too much to me—which would certainly have made me angry—contrived to indicate that he thought I was a lucky fellow to win her, that she would make a perfect mistress of Wool Royd. Adah, too, to my relief, fell quite in love with Rosie and declared herself very willing to serve her.

"Old Mr. Hervey brought the matter to a point. The next day when I called I found Rosie weeping and pouting—she was the prettiest thing in tears I have ever seen—with the hat spread on a table by her side. It seemed her father had told her it must be returned, he could not allow her to accept such a gift from a young man who was not affianced to her. So Rosie wept—stroking the feathers and smoothing out the pink ribbons with her pretty fingers. Of course I drew her to me, took her curly head on my shoulder, kissed her rose-petal cheek and swore she should keep the hat. When Mr. Hervey came back from the school where he gave weekly singing lessons I rose and made him my best bow and asked for the honour of Miss Hervey's hand in marriage, and Mr. Hervey with his cold ironical smile granted it to me.

"So we married. The wedding was a great affair, for which of course I paid. As the bells rang out in Annotsfield Parish Church I thought myself the happiest young man in England. Rosie looked lovely in her wedding gown—I had sent to Brussels for the lace—and when her little hand rested on my arm and we came down the aisle as man and wife, my heart melted in tenderness towards my darling bride. Besides, I felt so proud to be a married man like other men. My childhood and youth had been harsh and lonely, and because of James I had always felt different from other lads of my age, but now I was to have a wife and a home of my own and a mistress of that home, just like other men. I had had the best bedroom at Wool Royd refurnished for Rosie at a quite fantastic charge—Rosie chose the pink drapes and covers—she was fond of pink—I could deny her nothing when she pouted her rosebud mouth as for a kiss and said:

'Please, Charles.' Not that she was greedy, cousin; no, no, not greedy; just endlessly thirsty for pleasure and not clever enough to know that for pleasure, some price must always be paid.

"We married and took a wedding journey to Scarborough, which Rosie had heard was very fashionable, and then returned to live at Wool Royd."

CHAPTER VIII

"And were you happy? Rosie truly loved you, Cousin Charles?" I said softly, thinking with an ache in my heart of the sweet silly face I had seen in Dick's locket.

Charles Moreys grimaced. "What do you think of Tessie's power of loving, Cousin Eleanor?" he enquired sardonically. "She is very like her mother, you know."

"It is not as good as Dick's," I replied, as I thought with some skill, since Dick was Rosie's child as well as his sister.

"For God's sake leave Dick out!" shouted Charles Moreys. "Forgive me, cousin," he added in a quieter tone. "You will soon understand why to speak of Dick to me is to pour salt on a wound."

CHAPTER IX

"Well! There were some moments of sweetness, moments of rapture even," continued Charles Moreys. "That I will not deny. Rosie had much beauty of person. Though even there——" He broke off, and passed his handkerchief across his forehead, which was beaded with sweat. "Her face and arms were the most agreeable to the eye—her body though pretty enough had not that delicacy of grace—which rejoices a really fastidious fancy. But I should not speak of such things to you, cousin," said Charles Moreys hurriedly. "Her mind was untaught, or rather, as I found by degrees, not much capable of learning. She could not give her attention long to any but simple things. There was something very sweet in the way she would hang on my arm and look up at me with her rosy lips parted in wondering astonishment, while I explained to her the action of the water-wheel, or where to look for the lark, or the return of the lapwing. But she never heard me out; after a sentence or two her attention slipped, she turned her head away and looked at some other thing; sometimes she even interrupted me without knowing that she did so. 'What's that bird, Charles?' she would say, pointing perhaps to a rook which I had named already a hundred times to her, or: 'Look at that horrid Martha Greaves with a flower in her hat!' It was sweet and pretty and I had a great compassion and tenderness for her, but I found myself—if you can understand this—lonelier than ever. There was nobody to share my mind—and no hope, such as I had had before, of some day finding a wife to share it.

"Still, Rosie's dependence on me, her reliance on me to help her in every detail of her life, touched my heart. She was not a good housekeeper—but that was hardly her fault, as I told myself; the Herveys had lived in lodgings for years and she had no experience of managing a household. It is not agreeable to a man to come home and find everything at sixes and sevens, or to bring in friends and have to instruct his wife how to entertain them. Adah, though the soul of devotion, has not the capacity, as you have discovered, to run a gentleman's household. However, I engaged additional servants and instructed them myself as far as I was able, and we managed fairly well.

"It was during the months before Tessie's birth that the rift between us widened. Rosie took her pregnancy very peevishly. Though she was not sick as I have known some women to be, she resented any indisposition very crossly, and when with the passage of the months her figure thickened and her brilliant complexion dulled slightly, her indignation was quite prodigious. She did not want to have a child, seemed indeed never to have given a thought to such a possibility, and regarded motherhood as a piece of cruelty towards her. She quite turned against me and dis-liked me even to kiss her. Not having any parents to advise me, I was quite dumbfounded and perplexed and took what I now see to have been the wrong course of action; I continued to fondle her and make protestations of love when I should have left her to discover their value by their absence. However I thought all would be well once the child was born.

"It proved otherwise. Old Dr. Bradshaw assured me that the birth was in reality an easy one, but I suppose childbirth is never a very easy matter to a woman, especially when the child is the first. Rosie at any rate made a great to-do, screaming and accusing everyone of cruelty because we did not relieve her pain, and when Tessie was born she seemed positively to dislike her. Perhaps she was vexed because the child was a girl—though God knows I made her no reproaches on that score, nor indeed ever felt any. When Tessie was first put in her arms she turned away pettishly from her; she did not want to feed the child and made such a fuss over the matter that she lost the ability to do so. You can imagine that with all this Baby Tessie was not a very contented child; she always had a temper, and screamed and kicked continually. The nurse left in a flounce because Rosie was so petulant, and if it had not been for Adah, really I do not know whether we could have kept the child alive. For my part I loved the little thing very dearly, but being a man there was little I could do for her. She was a beautiful child always, and when she began to walk and talk, I thought there was nothing in the world like her.

"Strangely enough, as I thought at the time, it was my fondness for Tessie that seemed to bring Rosie back to me. She grew jealous of the attention I gave to the child, and would take her out of my arms if I held her up to look out of the window, or pack her off to bed if she was toddling about playing at ball with me. If I showed vexation at this, Rosie would try to soothe me, hanging about my neck and caressing me—I found this agreeable enough, being young and hot-blooded, and though I still felt sore and hurt with Rosie on Tessie's account, and sad that we seemed so far apart in understanding, I took the pleasure I could get and let the other go.

"Especially was this the case after I came back from my

wool-buying. You may remember I told you it was my father's custom to ride into Leicestershire and to the fairs to buy wool. In the year of Father's death, which was the year of my marriage, I left this wool-buying business to Tom Greaves, being busy with other matters; but Tom had not the feel for wool that my father had and his purchases didn't just please me, so ever since then I've gone myself. That September I'm speaking of, when Tessie was rising two, Rosie didn't seem much distressed when I left Wool Royd to ride to Leicestershire, she didn't shed a tear and had turned away from the door, after our farewell, before I reached the lane. But when I returned she acted different, she ran into my arms and wept and said she had been lonely without me, and she had Tessie all dressed up in silk and lace to greet me and had been teaching her to say a pretty speech to me, and Adah had cooked a special supper for me and so on. I was astonished by this unusual welcome and couldn't quite take it at its face value at first, but it seemed genuine enough and was certainly pleasant, and Rosie was full of endearments and caresses and we made love hotly enough and continued to do so.

"Presently Rosie told me she was with child again. Life is an odd thing, Cousin Eleanor. Before Tessie's birth I was so proud and happy I could think and talk of nothing else, while Rosie was cross and pettish; now I did not greatly care about another child, Rosie having killed that joy in me. But Rosie now seemed truly happy. She took far more trouble over the preparations for this birth than for her first child, and sat about the house sewing and singing quietly to herself and smiling—not that she was much hand at sewing, but it was pleasant to see her trying so earnestly. She showed me more affection—I mean wanting me to stay always beside her and the like—than she had ever done before, and I, poor fool! began to think that after all we should be really happy together. Rosie had been very young when we married, I reflected; perhaps too young and thoughtless to be a mother; now she was a little older she would be wiser and all would be well.

"And so we come to that night of May when all my life was blighted. It was Tuesday, Annotsfield market day. Rosie was only a few weeks off her time, as far as I knew; she seemed heavy and tired and downhearted, I thought, when I left her that morning. Old Dennett at the mill had sent up word to say he was very poorly—he had been ailing for some time and had taken a turn for the worse—and begged me to ride round by the mill in Iredale where Dan was working and ask him to come to see his father before it was too late. So I rode off in good time to put in this errand on my way to Annotsfield. Dan wasn't for coming but I persuaded him—however, that's by the way. But it made me late getting into Annotsfield, and with one thing and another, having plenty of business to do and buying some things Rosie wanted for the child and so on, I was late getting away, so that it was quite dark, with the moon in and out of clouds, by the time I turned out of Iredale. As I came up the brow, riding briskly, anxious to get home, I saw light streaming out of Upper Hey. It was such a broad shaft that I thought the door must be standing open and sure enough as I drew near I heard children's voices and hurrying steps, Jacob running into the house from the door where he'd been watching and calling out: 'Here he is, Mother! Here's Uncle Charles!'

"I drew up by the door and Lucy came out shading her eyes from the light behind her so as to see me and calling my name.

" 'Is there anything wrong? Is there something wrong with Rosie?' I asked quickly.

" 'Oh, Charles! Rosie's had her baby,' cried Lucy. She went on all in a flutter, telling how word had come up from Wool Royd soon after I left that morning, that Rosie had tripped over a stool or stepped off a stool or something and her pains had begun. There was no time to send for the doctor so Lucy had fetched the midwife from Booth village, who had been very loth to come because she had another case she was expecting very soon, and sure enough in the afternoon the other woman needed her so she had to leave Rosie, but the child was safely born by that time and Rosie seemed well, so Lucy stayed with her and had only just come back because after all she must put her own children to bed and Adah was with Rosie—and so on and so on till I was fairly dancing with impatience to be off. At length I couldn't stand Lucy's babble any longer, but rode off in the middle of a sentence. Lucy ran a few steps after me.

"'Charles, Charles!' she called. 'It's a boy—you have a son.'

"This made me all the more eager, as you can imagine, and I had a sudden gush of feeling for Rosie and for my two children, and even for myself as an upstanding young man of twenty-three with a prospering business and a lovely wife and family; I quite squared my shoulders and threw up my head as I thought of my responsibilities and how finely I meant to meet them. I was riding as fast as was safe considering the steepness and roughness of the lane down to the mill—perhaps even a little faster—and the mare made a good deal of clatter among the rough stones, so what with this noise, and the moon being behind me, anyone down in the mill yard could both see and hear that someone was coming. I was about half-way down the lane when I heard a terrible cry—a cry that made my blood run cold.

"It was Rosie's voice. I struck my mare violently with my heels—I don't wear spurs, I hate the cruel things—and she sprang forward snorting and rushed through the water-splash and up the bank. Then she stopped dead, almost throwing me. Rosie's voice seemed to have come from the yard and I looked round anxiously and shouted her name. But there was no-one there; it lay empty in the moonlight. I dismounted and stood a moment quite silent, listening, and in that silence I heard a queer faint little cry on my other hand, from the direction of the mill pond. I turned my mare aside out of the way and looked—there were ripples in the water, and something white, a long white streak it looked, lay on the surface near the bank. I ran to the side and the moon coming out just then I saw to my horror it was a tiny child, it looked like a doll with its hands just faintly moving, it wore a long robe or shawl or something of silk and lace and this had spread out on the water, d'you see, and kept it afloat. I knelt and tried to get hold of this robe but it was just beyond my reach, so I struck out into the pond—the water's about eight feet deep at the near end—I'm not much hand at swimming but I've splashed about as most boys do in the reservoirs in the hills.

I got the child in one arm and climbed out on the bank, splashing and slipping and dripping and a bit mazed and terribly troubled about Rosie, and there were Dan Dennett and his sister Martha confronting me on the path. I say 'confronting' because that's how they looked; Martha glaring at me accusingly and Dan with his face white and his eyes starting out of his head, staring at me as if I were a ghost or something. Dan and Martha were both at the mill, you see, on account of their father's illness. Martha fairly snatched the child from under my arm—it was Dick, of course, cousin, as you've guessed.

"'Where's your wife, Charles? Where's James?' Dan said hoarsely.

"'Nay, that's what I want to know,' I said in a dazed stupid way. 'I heard Rosie cry out a minute ago. I'd best get up to the house—you bring the baby, Martha.'

"I started off towards the lane, but Dan began 'Nay' and stretched out one arm to prevent me, and Martha suddenly screamed:

"'It's no use trying to get out of it that way, Charles Moreys!'

"'What do you mean?' said I, bewildered.

"'I saw your Rosie in James's arms on the path by the pond,' panted Martha. 'From the window of my father's bedroom.'

"Can you imagine what I felt then, cousin? I hope not. I shouted madly and ran about the yard crying 'Rosie! Rosie!' for first I thought I would go up to the house, they must be there, and then I thought they must have slipped out of the yard at the other side and crossed by the bridge. Then Dan Dennett seized me by the arm.

"'Don't you see, Charles?' he said sternly. 'They're in t'pond. They were on t'path, and noise of your coming startled 'em—I heard clatter mysen—and they fell in t'pond.'

"I jumped into the pond and thrashed about and shouted frantically but could find nothing and presently Dan Dennett, calling and exhorting me, pulled me up the bank. By this time the noise of the shouts and the splashing had roused all Booth and the houses round, and there were ten or a dozen people standing in the yard. Adah was there too; I seized her arm and shouted at her, where was Rosie, where was my wife, was she in the house? Adah shook her head. At this Tom Greaves turned to Lucy—they were both there now, I don't know how or when they came—Tom turned to her and asked her in a quavering tone:

" 'Lucy, where is James?'

"Lucy threw her apron over her head and burst into tears. The crowd murmured pityingly, but Dan Dennett pulled down her apron and took her hands roughly away from her face and told her she must speak the truth, so she stammered it out. It seemed James had left Upper Hey immediately she returned to it after spending the day at Rosie's bedside.

" 'We must drain t'pond,' said Dan Dennett.

" 'Aye! There's nothing else for it,' said Tom.

" 'Charles, you go and change your clothes. Lucy, do you take that child to Upper Hey and care for it,' said Dan Dennett sternly—he seemed to have taken charge of the proceedings and all obeyed his orders.

"I stumbled up the lane and went into Wool Royd and ran up the stairs to our room with the rose-pink curtains. The door stood wide open; the lamp was burning; the room was empty except for little Tessie, who slept peacefully in her cot in the corner. The bedclothes were pulled over to one side of our empty bed and lay sprawled over the floor, as if they had been thrown off hurriedly. My heart sank. Till then I had not really believed in the awful things which seemed to be happening; surely it was all nonsense, incredible nonsense, a mere nightmare which could not be true. But the empty bed, the sprawled bedclothes, convinced me otherwise. Hardly knowing what I was doing, panting and exclaiming and stumbling about the room, I tore off my soaked clothes and drew on dry shirt and breeches. But as I turned to take up a coat, I heard a shout from the mill yard and hope rose again in my heart and I dropped the coat and ran off at full tilt out of the house and down the lane.

"You've never seen a mill pond drained for cleaning, I expect. We do it every two or three years usually, but I own I had neglected it since Father's death, being busy getting married and so on. You see, the bottom gets silted up with sludge, mud and leaves and weeds, to the depth of a couple of feet or more, if you leave it overlong. When we drain it we usually put a skip—one of those big baskets on wheels we move the wool in—turned sideways, at the shuttle—that's the narrow place where the water runs out—to catch the fish. There's trout in the pond; my father would keep a couple for Wool Royd and let the men share out the rest, so that they enjoyed cleaning the pond because they got a good supper that night. Well, Dan Dennett had fixed up a skip as usual and had brought out some lamps from the mill and lighted a brazier as well, and the moon kept coming in and out from behind the clouds and the water was pouring out of the pond and every now and then the light, red or silver, would catch one of the fish which was leaping and struggling in the skip and the men would give a shout—whether because they saw it was a fish or because they thought it was something else, I didn't know. When they saw me they nudged each other and fell silent. I stood by the shuttle and watched the water drain away. I can't tell you how I felt—except that I was in pain from head to foot—all of me seemed to be seared with agony.

"At last the water was all gone; the skip was full of silvery fish, flopping and twisting, and the thick black mud gleamed in the moonlight. And then we all gave a cry of horror. For there—Oh God, how can I tell it?—there lay the two bodies, partly covered in the slime. There was James's shoulder protruding and Rosie's white elbow—the bodies were intertwined. I was so struck I couldn't say a word, but just stood there dumbly, swaying. Adah at my side made enough clamour for two, wringing her hands and wailing out laments in her own gipsy language. The men had quite a job getting the bodies out, for the slime was slippery and seemed to suck them into it. They had to fetch ropes and ladders and Dan Dennett went down into the bottom of the pond and put the ropes round James and Rosie—they were both quite dead.

"At last their bodies lay in the yard, side by side. Martha wiped the mud off their faces with the corner of her gown. Tom Greaves went off to fetch the constable. I still stood there, stupidly gazing down at Rosie, unable to say a word. She was still very pretty—in her nightgown with a crimson cloak tangled round her shoulders. Then Dan Dennett came up and put his arm through mine and turned me to him and offered me a brimming tankard and said: 'Drink this, Charles.' I took it from his hand and drank, and he urged me to drink again and so I drained near a pint of brandy without intending it. Then the tankard dropped from my hand and I pitched forward on my face to the ground and knew no more."

CHAPTER X

CHARLES MOREYS covered his eyes with his hands and was silent. Only his panting breath sounded against the roar of the gale.

I found myself kneeling at his side, my arm about his shoulders.

"Oh, my poor, poor cousin," I began: "Believe me——"

"For God's sake, Eleanor," said Charles Moreys roughly, "cease this silly formality of calling me cousin. After all I have told you tonight, formality is out of place between us."

"Charles, then," said I—though with some timidity. "It was a terrible, terrible tragedy, Charles. Poor Charles! Poor Rosie! But how had it happened? What was Rosie doing by the pond?"

"You ask that?" said Charles Moreys angrily. "Have you no sense, Eleanor? Have you not listened to what I told you? My brother and my wife had been lovers of course— their intrigue began the year before while I was away wool-buying—Dick was no eight-months child as Lucy would have me believe, but their full-time child—they were running away from my dreaded vengeance—my noisy return startled them and they tripped and fell into the pond."

I sat back on my heels, considering, then said calmly: "I don't believe a word of it, cousin."

"How dare you speak to me like that?" cried Charles Moreys, raising his head and glaring at me furiously. "Do you suppose I would lie on such a matter?"

"No, no! But it's all so strange. If they were guilty, why should James and Rosie wait till their child was born? Why not escape earlier? Why drag a woman only a few hours past childbirth out of her bed? No—there is some other explanation. Besides—Dick is your son."

"No!"

"But the locket round his neck, Charles?" I persisted.

"What locket?"

"The locket with the portraits of you and Rosie."

"I gave that to her on our wedding day," said Charles Moreys sombrely.

"It was round Dick's neck when he was taken from the pond. Would your wife have put it on the child if he were not your son?"

"Who says it was on Dick's neck in the pond?"

"Dick told me so."

"That is just an invented tale," said Charles impatiently. "He could hardly remember it himself, could he?"

"Did you not see it round the baby's neck when you rescued him from the pond?"

"Good God! Do you suppose I was in a state of mind to notice such a trifle as a locket?" cried Charles.

"But would not the doctor know whether Dick was in fact an eight or a nine months' child?" said I hesitantly. "It seems to me I have heard——"

"The doctor never saw him."

"The midwife, then?"

"Midwives will say anything to soothe a doubting husband," said Charles angrily. "It is their trade."

"All the same, I should like Dr. Bradshaw to see her and hear what she has to say."

"My God, I will not have all that mud raked up again!" cried Charles. "Can you not see what agony it is to me? In any case," he added with a bitter laugh, "the woman's long since dead."

I sighed.

"What happened to poor Dick after his mother's death?"

"Lucy took him and brought him up, for a while. After all, he was her husband's."

"No, Charles, no. Yet if James and Rosie were innocent, why was Dick there in the pond at all?"

"Ah, my dear," said Charles Moreys sadly: "I fear it is beyond even your wit to devise a reason. Besides, they were not innocent; they were guilty. Adah admitted it."

"Adah!"

"Aye. When I came to myself next day, Dan Dennett and Tom Greaves and Martha and Adah and the constable were all in Wool Royd talking about the affair—along with every other soul in Moreydale and Iredale and Annotsfield, I suppose—nineteen to the dozen. I had to make depositions and attend inquests—but it seemed that while I lay there drunk they had mostly fathomed the matter. Adah had long suspected the intimacy between James and Rosie. I taxed her with her disloyalty in not telling me, and she wept and said she had hoped it would end—she was not sure of it—or rather, she had wished not to be sure of it—she thought it would make me unhappier to know than not to know—she did not wish to deprive Rosie of the chance of returning to right conduct—and so on. So really the date of Dick's birthday is of little consequence. Their attempted flight is the proof of their guilt."

"But Charles, their attempted flight is by no means proved. In fact, you do not really know anything about James and Rosie for certain."

"Don't you see that that is what maddens me, child?" cried Charles. "I don't know. I shall never know." He struck the arms of his chair with his clenched fists, repeating: "I shall never know. Never!"

"It is strange and very sad, Charles," said I, "that you and my father both should suffer this torment of doubting."

"Aye," said Charles, turning his haggard face to me, "it is strange. We are not lucky folk, we Moreys. If one were superstitious, one would say there was a curse on us."

"So there is, and no superstition in the matter," said I. "A wrong was done by your father to James and his mother, and nothing here will go well until that old wrong is righted."

"I agree with you, my dear," said Charles Moreys. "And after my death it will be righted. Tessie and Dick will share

162

the Moreys properties between them, and Dick is James's son. But you must pardon me if I do not view that prospect with enthusiasm."

"Could you not give Wool Royd up now to Joah and Jacob?" I persisted earnestly.

"So that we could all go bankrupt together? Under the skilful management of Joah and Jacob, I assure you the mill would be closed within a twelvemonth. The neighbourhood would not thank me either—the mill is a great convenience for the clothiers hereabouts. No! I must just go on as I am doing now, and earn the living for all of them. The whole lot hang on my shoulders; Lees and Greaves and Dennetts and old Mr. Hervey and all, their livelihoods depend on me."

"Oh, Charles!" said I, weeping.

"Why should you cry over it, Eleanor?"

"It is such a cheerless prospect for you."

"Cheerless enough."

"It is because you are so strong and able, Charles; the weak always cast their burdens on the strong shoulders."

"Why, as to that, I can carry Wool Royd well enough. It is my household—I won't call it a home—which depresses me. A daughter who cares for me only when I bring her gifts—Tessie is very like her mother—a son who is no son, a couple of idle dissolute nephews—they are no great comfort."

"Jacob is not idle and dissolute," I protested.

"No. He's just a silly wool-gathering lad who's turned against his best friend," said Charles Moreys, frowning.

"How does it happen they all live with you?"

Charles sighed and began heavily to tell me what followed on the drowning tragedy. Dan's action in making him drunk, heavily censured in the neighbourhood as indecent, lacking respect for the dead and altogether improper, was in fact a blessing—"that is, if to keep me alive in such circumstances was a blessing," said Charles sardonically. Sodden and stupefied by the great quantity of brandy he had taken, Charles felt the talk and the actions of Wool Royd flow by him in a heavy mist; by the time he was fully alive again to his situation, the first awful hours were over.

The deaths of James and Rosie were officially pronounced, after much long argument, accidental; the bodies were buried in the Marthwaite churchyard down in Iredale; the wronged husband was alive and had to resume ordinary living. He locked the bedroom he had shared with Rosie, for to look on it was agony. He investigated his brother's affairs on Lucy's behalf. Not one penny of the money left to James by his father three years before remained. James had debts all over the district and even Upper Hey was mortgaged. Charles settled the debts, repaid the mortgage, and put Tom Greaves and his wife and child to live at Upper Hey with Lucy, Tom to carry on the clothier's business there, the profits to be shared between Tom and Lucy.

"I thought it would be good for both of them. I suppose it was then," said Charles, sighing, "while they were playing together as children, that Jacob and Mary Greaves took a fancy to each other. Lucy kept Dick, as I told you, and I lived at Wool Royd with Adah and Tessie. But after a year or two, you see, when the scandal and talk had died down a bit, Dan Dennett naturally enough wanted to marry his old love, Lucy. By that time old Dennett was dead and I'd got Dan back to be miller for us, so he could keep Lucy in comfort, and she was very willing."

"I don't imagine Lucy and Martha were very comfortable together, sharing a household," said I.

"You're right, my dear. But in any case, Dan was all the world to Lucy. The difficulty was the two boys, Joah and Jacob. Dan wouldn't take them. Nor, of course, Dick either. Dan said he wanted no children of James Lee's getting, in or out of wedlock, by his fireside."

"So you took them."

"I took them. What else could I do? A child or two made no difference to me—nothing makes much difference to me since Rosie's death—and I was fond of Jacob. I took them both as my apprentices. But they've run rather wild, you see. Whether because of Joah's roughness, or because as he grew up he turned seducer like his father—or," concluded Charles Moreys bitterly, "because I am so ill looked on—I don't know, but I cannot keep any servants here but Adah.

The house, as you saw, grew continually more neglected and uncomfortable."

"You should have married again, Charles."

"What, and have children, with Dick to play half-brother to them? I think not, Eleanor. We have had enough half-brothers in this family."

"Oh, Charles!" said I sadly. "You are the kindest, the best, the most generous of men, and all your troubles have come upon you because of your generosity."

"It is an agreeable change for me to be flattered, my dear," said Charles Moreys, smiling at me very kindly. "For everyone else of my acquaintance seems to consider me the source of all their troubles. I am thought a cuckold, a false brother, a brutal husband, an unkind uncle, a harsh master, a drunkard and even a murderer, and I believe Joah's sins are put down to me as well—they must be mine since they come from Wool Royd. Your kindness and help have been a great pleasure to me, a real balm on my wounds. I thank you most sincerely."

I was still kneeling beside him. It is astonishing what a strong emotion can be caused by the person of one you love, when that person is seen very close at hand for the first time. One longs to touch, though softly, to caress and comfort—especially when the man is in such distress as my cousin Charles was at that time. I did not venture to touch his fair head, his broad shoulders, though I longed to do so with all my heart; but I could not resist laying my fingers very gently on his hand. The moment I had done so I was horrified by my forwardness and lack of modesty, and drew my fingers quickly away. But Charles Moreys laughed very kindly, and took my hand in his and turned it over and very gently kissed the palm.

"Your hand and your heart are both as soft as—no, I will not say silk or satin or any such foolish fancy," said Charles Moreys, laughing again. "I will say as soft as a carding of wool—but believe me, Cousin Eleanor, nothing is softer or more cosy to the touch."

This pleased me very much, because it seemed such a real and true comparison, and one, too, very near to Charles Moreys' heart. He cared too much for his trade to draw any false artificial compliments from it. So I smiled with happiness, and did not withdraw my hand from his, or rise, though perhaps I should have done so.

"Who is that?" cried Charles Moreys suddenly, releasing my hand. "There is a face at the window!"

He started up and, pausing only to lift me to my feet, ran from the room. I heard the sound of the opening door and the sound of quick light footsteps on the paved yard, then he called loudly: "Eleanor!" I hurried after him.

"We have sat so long, discussing my woes, we have outlasted the storm," he said, pointing upwards.

Indeed the rain had ceased and the wind was dying. High up in the sky sailed a round, clear, silver moon and one bright star shone between dark scudding clouds. A last subdued gust of wind sighed round the corner of the house and rustled my dress as we stood there, then the air was still.

"Did you find anyone at the window?"

"No—I must have been mistaken. The night is peaceful now, Cousin Eleanor," said Charles Moreys in a kind tone, drawing my arm through his own. "Let us walk up and down a little and forget our cares."

"I wish life could be as peaceful for you as the night," said I, following his step. The light from the lamp within the dining-room cast a broad yellow shaft across the courtyard, warm and homely, in pleasing contrast to the cold white light of the moon.

"Ah, well!" said Charles Moreys, sighing. "We must do our best. I shall take your advice, Eleanor, and send both Tessie and Dick away to school, marry Jacob to his Mary—I shall have to provide them with an income, I suppose, but that is not impossible—and struggle on here alone with Joah."

"You will break Dick's heart if you send him away."

"Why, in heaven's name?"

"The child adores you."

Charles gave an exclamation of disgust. "Then the sooner he goes away the better," said he. "As for you, my dear, you must go away too."

"Go away?" I repeated faintly.

"Yes. As soon as it can be arranged."

This harsh judgment, after so much kindness and confidence as had passed between my cousin and myself that evening, quite stunned me. I stood still and bowed my head. After a moment my grief drove me into speech, and I murmured stupidly enough:

"Why—where must I go?"

"Have you any notion, any plan for yourself?"

"None."

"You shall not go till we can arrange something agreeable for you. You shall not want resources, you shall not find yourself in any difficulties," said Charles Moreys in a soothing tone. "You are a member of the Moreys family and I shall of course provide properly for you."

In a blaze of anger I snatched my arm from his and raised my head. "If you imagine I shall accept money from you, Charles Moreys, you are infinitely mistaken," I said.

"That is like you, Eleanor," said Charles in his kindest tone; "but I shall not allow it."

"*You* not allow it! You have no authority over me. Tell me why you send me away. It is not fair to send me away without telling me the reason. Your father did so to my father, but I shall not allow you to do so to me."

"What a spirit you have, Eleanor!" said Charles in mock admiration. "Your eyes are blazing with anger against your unfortunate cousin."

"What have I done to displease you?" said I, striving not to weep.

"Nothing."

"Why do you dislike me?"

"You silly child," said Charles Moreys impatiently: "Don't you see, I am sending you away because you please me too much, I like you too well? If you were to stay here I might love you."

"Oh, cousin!" said I faintly.

"And that would not be the right thing for you, my dear. So you must leave me."

There are times when modesty is a cowardice and a betrayal. Charles had opened his heart to me; it would be ungenerous to conceal my own.

"Why would it not be right, Charles?" said I, raising my

eyes to his and speaking in a steady tone. "I love you with all my heart; I would give the last drop of my blood to serve you."

Charles Moreys exclaimed.

"My dearest child, my darling little Eleanor!" he said fondly, passing his arm about my waist and turning me towards the door. "This is all a mistake. You cannot love a man like me. You must not. My life is irreparably broken. I am hopelessly ruined and embittered—a broken man, discredited, dishonoured and suspected."

"You are bruised and wounded, Charles," said I; "you have been terribly injured. But you are neither broken nor dishonoured."

"You are cold, you are shivering, child, let us go in," said Charles.

"No. Let us speak our minds to each other. I am not a child, I am a woman."

"You are fifteen years younger than I am," said Charles, laughing—his laughter however had not a happy ring in it.

"Charles, for God's sake be serious for once. I wish to stay with you, if you wish it. Tell me the truth, do you wish it or do you not?"

"Listen, Eleanor," said Charles, still laughing. "This is all a mad notion of yours—a foolish fancy. When did you begin to have this fancy about me, eh, you foolish cousin?"

"The first moment I saw you."

Charles exclaimed again and fell silent. Then he said softly: "And I about you, in the same moment."

He took my face between his hands and bending towards me from his great height, very gently kissed me. It was a moment of happiness so exquisite as to be almost torture.

"But what is the use—nothing can come of it," said Charles bitterly, releasing me. "You must go away and leave me, and I shall slip back into all my old wretchedness. I am hedged about with misery and mystery and have no right to drag any woman into it."

"We can find a way out of it together."

"How?"

"I will comfort you, Charles—I will console you."

"You think we should marry, do you?" said he sardonically.

"Why not?" said I, gathering all my courage.

"And Dick and Tessie? And Joah and Jacob?"

"Nothing will ever convince me that Dick is not your son."

"You are maddeningly persistent on that subject, Eleanor," said Charles in an angry tone, handing me somewhat roughly through the doorway. "We must go in now, or you will be put down as another of my misdemeanours. Light your candle and be off with you to bed."

I was vexed and I did not scruple to show it, for I was determined that the completest sincerity should always obtain between myself and Charles Moreys. I therefore turned my back on him and stooped over the candlesticks which were placed each night by the lamp on the hall table.

"I am thinking of having the mill lit by gas next autumn," said Charles, who was lounging on the dining-room table and watching me through the open doorway.

"If I am to leave Wool Royd that cannot concern me."

"You are vexed with me, Eleanor."

I said nothing, but my hand trembled so that the candle wick would not catch alight.

"Here—take this," said Charles suddenly, and he threw to me my reticule, which he had found beside him on the table.

Taken unawares, I dropped the candle and did not catch the reticule.

"You do not behave with proper dignity, Cousin Charles," said I, trembling between grief and vexation.

"I am everything that is bad, wicked and abominable," said Charles, coming to me and picking up my reticule and lighting my candle. "And that is why you must never leave me."

He took me in his arms, and this time his kiss was not gentle.

CHAPTER XI

I ESCAPED from him at length and ran upstairs. The weight of the reticule in my hand reminded me that I carried the key of Dick's room in it, and I was ashamed to have forgotten the poor child for so long a period. I opened his door softly and went in to look at him. He was fast asleep. I held the candle near his pillow and could not but smile, though ruefully, at the sweet and delicate lines of his small face, which to me appeared a singularly exact replica of Charles Moreys'. I drew the coverlet gently over his injured shoulder and kissed his forehead.

It was then I remembered that when, a few moments ago, I had seen Charles perched on the dining-room table, Dick's pitcher of milk which I had placed on it before was not standing there. I thought of the face Charles had seen at the window, and it occurred to me to wonder where Joah was; I had not seen him since Charles threw him from the house that afternoon. Had he really gone to Annotsfield, as Charles had ordered? Uneasy and disturbed, I locked Dick's door again when I left his room and took the key away with me. As Charles had said, we were indeed still surrounded by misery and mystery. But surely the two of us together could battle our way out of it.

BOOK FOUR: ADAH

CHAPTER I

To you, Edward and Catharine, who know all the Moreys story and its cause, it may well seem strange, stupid, even laughably foolish, that I did not at once perceive its secret, which to you glares out of every utterance, every incident. But believe me, while an action is still in progress, still incomplete, certainty as to its logic and significance is incomplete as well. At times in a lurid flash one sees it all clear and resolves upon decisive action; then in the next few days the persons concerned behave so naturally, their actions seem so commonplace, that one cannot credit one's previous suspicions and indeed forgets them in the customary routine of ordinary life.

Again: to you, Edward and Catharine, it cannot seem that the question of the marriage of Charles Moreys and myself was ever in doubt. But to me during the next few weeks nothing was less certain. There were times when my position in Wool Royd, sitting waiting as it seemed for Charles Moreys to make up his mind whether or no to lift his finger and beckon to me, appeared intolerably humiliating. There were many moments when I doubted his affection for me, when I suspected that his plea I should stay with him was made only to save me from pain, that the quixotic generosity which had betrayed him with his brother was once again about to saddle him with an undeserved and unwanted burden. At such times—they were usually in the afternoon, when Charles had been several hours gone from the house and the children were proving difficult—at such times my heart felt as if it were being twisted between cruel fingers and I longed to make Charles an angry scene, scold him hysterically, even beat at him with my fists. At other times my pity for his wrongs was so fierce, my love for him so strong, that my whole soul seemed to go out to him and whatever he did was right and noble in my eyes. These times came usually in the evenings, when he was at home.

After the storm the weather settled and suddenly spring was with us. It came so much later than in the south that I had begun to believe that the seasons did not mean the same in Yorkshire as in London, but now May was here, suddenly everything in Moreydale took on beauty. The trees across the beck unfurled fresh young leaves; the cuckoo sounded; the sloping fields became a rich pattern of red and yellow and white amid the green—sorrel and clover, buttercup and hemlock amongst the tall, waving grass. The gnarled hawthorn at the turn into the lane was covered in pink blossom with a most intoxicating scent, the lilacs and the flags beside the mill pond bloomed white and purple. The larks sang, the lapwings—birds new to me which I never tired of watching—cut swift curves through the evening air; some delicious little robins appeared hopping about the yard from a nest the secret of which Dick had cherished. (I should not have known them for robins myself, for they showed no red about their breast but wore brown feathers tipped with yellow; but both Dick and Charles knew them well.) As soon as Dick was strong enough, I took the children out of doors as much as possible, and sometimes in the evening, when Charles was in a good mood, he joined us. As we strolled through the fields or along the moor paths, the hills green in the sunshine, the children running ahead and playing amicably together, Charles talking about the birds and the becks and helping me carefully over the stiles, I was most blissfully happy. Then when we returned to Wool Royd and, supper over, the children went to bed, Charles would call me down to sit with him, and while I sewed he talked to me of affairs in the mill, or we looked over letters from schools for Tessie together. Though he did not kiss me again or speak one word of love or marriage, I felt that our lives were united forever, we should never part.

Then next day Charles's mood would apparently change and he became cross and sardonic, very sarcastic with the children, cold and repressive with me. Something was wrong with the steam engine at the mill, about which Jacob had the temerity to disagree with his uncle. Sometimes Charles encouraged the lad to express his views, and they conducted a conversation which, though unintelligible to the rest of us, evidently gave them pleasure; but sometimes Charles snubbed poor Jacob unmercifully, asking him if he thought he knew better than Watt, and the like. (Who this Watt might be, I did not then know, but I could see that Jacob thought very highly of him.) If however Tessie joined in the talk on her father's side, as she sometimes did in a syco-phantic way to curry favour, Charles turned on her and rent her, telling her she was a silly ignorant little girl and should hold her tongue when her betters talked, and so on.

But I am running on too fast; let me return to the first day after I heard Charles's story.

I woke early that morning, to find the sun pouring through the window at an oblique angle, filling one corner of my room with gold, while the rest lay in shadow. It struck me that this was now symbolic of Charles's life and mine: our love made a rich sunshine in our hearts, however dark, gloomy and obscure the world around us might be. I felt so joyously excited, I so longed to see my dear Charles, I wished so keenly for my life, now so full of promise, to begin again after the dullness of sleep and move on into its glowing pattern, that I could not endure to remain in bed any longer; and it was with much relief and happiness that, hearing the distant clatter of milk-pails, I bethought me of fetching some fresh milk for Dick. I dressed quickly and slipped downstairs. In the kitchen Adah was mumbling and grumbling over the hearth as she lighted the fire. Hitherto I had been careful never to trespass in any way upon Adah's domain without politely asking her permission, but now, feeling in my foolish happiness that I was Charles Moreys' affianced bride, I took a large white jug from its hook in the cupboard without a word of request, merely throwing her a light-hearted good morning. At the clink of china Adah started and raised her bent form; then opening her black eyes wide she stared at me and at the jug with such intensity that I coloured and felt uneasy. But the sunshine in the yard made me happy again, and I tripped along to the cowshed and had the man fill my jug—he seemed more good-tempered and affable this morning, as if he were acquainted with my happy secret; indeed the very cows, their brown-

and-white sides heaving gently, seemed to turn milder eyes upon me, as if they knew their master loved me.

Imagine my joy when, as I returned along the yard picking my way among the pools left by last night's rain, I met Charles himself, on his way down to the mill before breakfast. I blush to say this, but such was my youthful egoism and conceit at that moment, that I rather expected a little sweet praise and flattery for my kindness in fetching milk for poor Dick; indeed I had a pretty deprecating smile all ready for it. Instead of that I met an explosion of wrath. Why did I demean myself performing such tasks, which nobody had asked or ever would ask of me? Why did I think myself better qualified to attend to milk than persons who had dealt with it all their lives? Considering the state of the milk he had found at Dick's bedside last night, the less I had to do with it the better! Perhaps my interference had something to do with Dick's frequent illness! This last was more than I could bear; I stepped back—and I daresay my eyes blazed, to use his word, with resentment—and prepared to deny it hotly. But as I gazed angrily at Charles, I saw him so pale, so perplexed, so tormented and haggard, that my heart melted again towards him and I said nothing, but simply bowed my head in submission.

"I do not mean to be harsh," said Charles, touched as he always was by any sign of sadness. "But leave it to Adah for the future."

"I will do just as you say," I replied gravely.

I called him neither *Charles* nor *cousin*; he was not in a mood for the first and God knows I did not wish to thrust an unwanted intimacy upon him, yet I could not bring myself to sacrifice all I had won last night by addressing him formally. If he chose to take it so, too, my remark meant much—indeed it meant my whole life; if not, it was only Dick's drink that was in question. He perceived the implication clearly enough, however, for he exclaimed and gave me a look of mingled distress and affection; but he said no more and hurried away down the lane, and I continued on my way to the Wool Royd porch very much cast down. Indeed I felt a strong inclination to weep with hurt and disappointment. But I told myself that we had many difficulties ahead of us through which we must fight our way, and this reminder on their threshold was probably very salutary.

Quite shorn of my former pride, I went upstairs very soberly and visited Dick. The child had had a good night and looked a better colour than he sometimes did, but his shoulder was paining him and he was a little fretful. It was strange how different Dick, and presently Tessie, looked to me now that I knew their mother's story; for a moment I felt a strange fierce jealousy of Rosie, hot and very bitter, rise in my mouth, and for just that moment I knew how all stepmothers are said to feel, for I could easily have spoken sharply and woundingly to the child. But then Dick's sweet, pale, unhappy little face and tousled golden hair, and his blue eyes which were so like Charles's eyes looking at me so beseechingly, melted my heart again and I sat down and cuddled him up to me and smoothed his hair and dried his tears and told him some silly tale about my fear of cows to make him laugh, and all was well between us. The locket hung round his neck as usual, and I said to him in a careless tone:

"How do you know the locket was round your neck when you were found in the mill pond, Dick?"

"Aunt Lucy told me—Mrs. Dennett," said Dick.

I promised myself gladly the pleasure of telling that fact to Charles—or stay: I would ask Mrs. Dennett first, so as to be certain. While I thought this, Dick had opened the locket, and I looked down again at those two young pictured faces. I suffered much in that moment. It was a strange irony, I thought, that I, who most naturally would detest Charles Moreys' first wife and rejoice in her infidelity, was set with all my force to prove her innocent. I looked at this strange fact and looked at it again, but it remained a fact; I believed that Dick was Charles's son, that Rosie had not sinned, and that the only way to save Charles's happiness was to convince him of it. After a moment of struggle with myself, I took up this burden strongly and gladly. As soon as I had done so, I hated Rosie no more but felt only a deep pity for her. Poor Rosie! Poor, young, frightened Rosie!

"I will be true to you, Rosie," I said mutely. "Do not fear; I will care for your children."

I gave Dick a drink of milk and put what was left away carefully in a cupboard, and tried to think how I could contrive to get him milk fresh from the cow, until he was well enough to fetch it for himself. Jacob, I thought, might be employed on the errand, for I neither dared nor wished to disobey any command of Charles Moreys.

My next duty was to speak with Tessie. So much had happened since her attack on Dick and myself the day before, I could scarcely recall the details of her behaviour. But when the bell sounded for breakfast and we found ourselves alone together in the dining-room, Charles and Jacob having gone to the mill as usual, I saw that Tessie remembered it all very well. She was terribly afraid; her face was almost olive in its pallor, her eyes stared like a hare's, she trembled.

"Now, Tessie," I began in what I hoped was a mild but firm voice, when we were seated at table. (I could not help a rueful smile at my plight, that I, who as an only child had had nothing to do with children, should now have to struggle with these ill-brought-up and difficult young scamps; nevertheless I accepted the task.) "Now, Tessie, I am sure you are very sorry for what happened yesterday." I paused expectantly; Tessie muttered something indistinguishable. "So let us make a fresh beginning with this fresh day, and speak no more of yesterday." Tessie again muttered, somewhat more hopefully. "But of course I expect you should mend your behaviour to Dick, Tessie," said I in a warning tone.

"It is true what I said about Dick," objected Tessie, tossing her head.

"That remains to be seen—I do not myself believe it for a moment," said I. "But in any case, Tessie, you and Dick have the same mother, and therefore are brother and sister. You should be kind to each other and love each other."

"I don't love Dick," said Tessie at once.

"You will certainly make *him* hate *you*," said I with emphasis, for I was vexed.

Tessie appeared somewhat disconcerted by this notion, which seemed never to have occurred to her before. Her flimsy little butterfly nature could not endure hostility.

"What do you think I should do, Adah?" said she, turning to the old woman, who was bringing to the table a dish of eggs.

"Do as the pretty lady tells you, for the time, my gorgeous," said Adah soothingly.

I did not much like either Tessie's appeal to Adah against me, or Adah's phrase *for the time*, but the results for the moment were good; Tessie's face cleared, she ate her breakfast with relish and was docile in the schoolroom that morning, even continuing to struggle with her sums—poor Tessie, her arithmetic was ever a tearful tangle!—while I was absent during Dr. Bradshaw's visit.

The physician was pleased with Dick's progress. The child being so delicate, as he said to me after his examination, he had feared the consequences of the shock and fright, almost more than the actual physical injury.

"Why is he so delicate, Dr. Bradshaw?" said I boldly.

"I seem to remember hearing that he was not a full-time child," said Dr. Bradshaw; "and then his immersion in a pond within a few hours of his birth was very shocking. Still, he should have recovered from all that early history by now. I am not entirely satisfied, I must say, with his general state of health."

As far as it went, this was on Rosie's side, but it did not go very far.

"It was your father who told you? About Dick's birth, I mean?" I murmured.

"Oh, it was general hearsay. Do not press Dick over his studies—give him fresh air and good food—I will call again the day after tomorrow," concluded the doctor, and took himself away quickly to his gig, which he had left in the mill yard.

As the day wore slowly on my heart began to ache with yearning for the evening, when I should, I hoped, see my love; but when the evening came at last, my hope was disappointed. True, Charles came in to supper, but he was silent and preoccupied at table and did not ask me either to accompany him when he visited Dick or to sit with him downstairs afterwards. This was a blow to my pride as well as to my love, and I was truly relieved when presently, as

Jacob and Tessie and I sat upstairs in the schoolroom, we heard the front door knocker sound and Adah slowly usher a visitor into the dining-room. Charles, I thought, had perhaps expected this visitor. Jacob recognised the voice, and said gloomily that it was Mr. Tom Greaves from Upper Hey. I suggested that perhaps some discussions were on foot concerning Jacob and Mary, but Jacob said even more gloomily that he did not think so.

You may imagine that after such an experience I rose next morning in a very different mood from my happy expectations of the previous day. During a wakeful night I had rebuked myself roundly for my childish and immodest hopes of love-making on Charles Moreys' part; mere pride, I told myself, forbade that I should again behave in such a lovesick and feeble fashion. A woman's refuge when her heart is sore is usually in the work of her house, and I was no exception; looking around for a task my eye lighted upon the drawing-room in Wool Royd—a large handsome apartment on the right of the hall which I had never seen used—and I determined to set it in order that day.

In a vigorous, bustling, hasty manner very unlike my usual calm I overrode Adah's grumbled objections and Tessie's constant distaste for work; I brooked no denial and had Tessie polishing the furniture out in the courtyard in the sunshine, Adah scrubbing the floor, myself washing china and beating the dust out of books, very early in the morning and kept us all hard at it all day. Occasionally Dick's pale little face would appear at the window above, as he gazed down at us in wistful yearning. Presently (perhaps because Dick made thus a continual audience for her, which she always liked) Tessie caught the contagion of my desire to have the room finished before supper time; she ran about bright-eyed and willing, tossing her curls and seeking to be praised for her hard work, in a manner which seemed to me, now that I knew her mother's story, very sweet and touching. Poor Tessie! She could be turned this way or that, almost at will; with Joah away, as he was at present, she became a very different person. Jacob coming in at midday for a meal gazed at us with that sickened and downhearted expression which men reserve for women's household cleaning activities, but Charles had ridden off to Annotsfield on some errand or other and did not return till the evening.

By the time he came in, the room was all restored and quite glittering with cleanliness; though the sun was bright the wind was cool, so I had bidden Adah light a fire, and the flames reflected in the furniture and the china in a very pleasant cheerful fashion. It was a handsome apartment, as I said, with green silk curtains and chair-seats, a small table inlaid with a chess board, some old medical books, finely bound—the property of Charles's surgeon grandfather, I supposed—on a neat shelf which just fitted them, together with agreeable china and carved chessmen and other such curios in cabinets. Tessie and I, very much brushed and washed, seated ourselves in genteel poses on a sofa by the fire as we heard Charles and Jacob approaching. Jacob seemed to have given his uncle some account of our activities, for without waiting to be summoned Charles came to the drawing-room door and threw it open and looked in curiously, wrinkling his nose as if in expectation of buckets of water and mops. The change in his expression as he saw his fine room looking bright and tasteful and lived in, as it should, was very pleasing to me, though I took care to keep my eyes down demurely and not look up at him. He was in a good humour at supper and teased Tessie and myself and Adah about our work, asking if our arms ached, offering us second helpings to keep up our strength, and so on. He did not ask me to go with him when he visited Dick, but clearly he had spoken kindly to him, for the child was radiant when I went up later to settle him for the night.

When Charles came down from Dick's room, without speaking he went straight to a great armed chair by the hearth and seated himself in it and I saw he had been used to sit there always in the old days, with Rosie on the other side of the hearth in a matching chair. This gave me a pang, but such pangs must be the lot of the woman who loved Charles Moreys now; I accepted them, and did not shrink from them, I was prepared to endure them for his sake.

I went up to Dick when Tessie went to bed—Jacob as usual had withdrawn to the schoolroom and was writing some copies I had set him—intending to go to my room after, for I did not intend to offer my company to Charles Moreys unless it was asked for. But as I came out from Dick's room I heard Charles calling me.

"Eleanor!"

The sound of my name, in his impatient, impetuous tones, was very sweet to me; I looked over the balustrade and there he was in the hall, one foot on the step as if meaning to fetch me, frowning a little but smiling too.

"Come down; I have much to say to you," commanded Charles.

I took some sewing in my hand and went down very gladly.

When he had seated me beside the hearth he began telling me, very eagerly, all his financial affairs. He had been to Annotsfield to see his attorney, Mr. Battye, and made sure that all his earnings at the mill, all the rents of his land, were his income and that he could do as he liked with them; if he chose to save from them, he could bequeath those savings at his will. Only the mill and the land themselves were in trust for his children. The significance of all this, namely that Charles could provide for Joah and Jacob, and if he were to marry again he could provide for his wife, by what he earned and saved and by that alone, was clear to me, for from long struggling with my father's business I am not inexperienced in such matters; but if it was clear it was also highly embarrassing, since no proposal of marriage had been made between us and thus I had no standing in the affair and no right to express an opinion. I listened therefore with grave attention but said nothing; I saw why Charles was so anxious that Joah and Jacob should become capable of earning for themselves, and I saw again, with increased clarity, how greatly it would be to Joah's advantage for Dick to perish, presuming Joah succeeding in marrying Tessie; for then the whole of the Moreys estate would fall into his hands, instead of the half. I saw also, with a sudden chill, how greatly it would be to Joah's disadvantage for Charles to marry again and have more children. For a moment I wished heartily that the Moreys had no wealth at all, since then none of these difficulties would obtain; but then I reflected that Charles would not be happy in a minor sphere in life, he was used to having the power to be generous, to command. I sighed.

"You find these affairs tedious?" said Charles at once in a vexed tone.

I shook my head.

"Disheartening, then?"

"No. But, Charles, Tessie and Dick *must* be kept away from Joah."

"Have I not promised it?" said Charles impatiently. He threw himself back in his chair and exclaimed: "Ah no! It is all too difficult, too great a burden—I cannot ask anyone to share it with me."

"Charles," I began, raising my head.

But at this moment Adah entered, bearing, I was sorry to see, a glass and a bottle of wine, which she put down on a table at Charles's elbow. I was not, therefore, able to continue my speech of reassurance, and indeed I hardly knew how to frame it without appearing either too reluctant or too bold. But perhaps the tone of my voice and the look in my eyes conveyed what I felt, for Charles's expression softened and though he told me to be off to bed and leave him to his troubles, his voice was kind and he smiled at me with that warmth and sweetness which was his peculiar personal possession.

So the days went on, uneasy, uncertain, sometimes happy, sometimes agonisingly painful to me. I know that once as I climbed the stairs after Charles had sharply dismissed me, I said to myself: "When I look back on this time, I shall wonder how I endured it." And this came true; looking back at it now, I savour its anguish again and wonder. I made no hopeful plans; I simply struggled on from hour to hour, knowing only that I must and would continue to love—to love Charles, to love Dick and Tessie, to feel a milder but quite genuine love for Jacob—and to serve them as and when I could, to the utmost of my ability.

A DAY came at last when we took a real step towards happiness, though it was painful enough at the time.

Catching Charles when he was in a cheerful mood, I had urged upon him the need for church attendance for the children. He scowled and jeered a little but did not like to refuse me, and gave orders that Jacob should drive us down to Marthwaite Church next Sunday in the gig. Dick, always docile, was pleased with the notion; Tessie I conquered, God forgive me! by promising that she should wear her new bonnet—so great was Tessie's love of finery, I sometimes wondered how far Rosie's marriage with Charles had been brought about by her reluctance to surrender the feathered hat.

So when the Sunday came we three set off cheerfully. Jacob, however, was gloomy at being kept away from Scape Scar Chapel and Mary Greaves. He mourned and lamented almost all the way to Marthwaite—a distance of some three miles—until even the children grew tired of his gloom and Tessie exclaimed impatiently that Mary might like him all the better if he were not tied so tight to her apron-string. This was such a new notion to good honest Jacob that he opened his soft brown eyes as wide as saucers and fell silent, pondering the matter, as we could see, for the next mile, then solemnly shaking his head. At this Dick, always soft-hearted, was moved to say:

"Perhaps you'll see a girl in Marthwaite you'll like better than Mary, Jacob."

"Never!" exclaimed Jacob earnestly.

Mary Greaves does not know the rare worth of such a faithful, simple, honest love, thought I; not without some heartache.

It was so long since any Moreys had attended church that none of the children knew which was the Wool Royd pew, and Jacob edged hesitantly up the aisle, bending to read the painted names, while all the congregation gazed at us disapprovingly. However, Dick found the pew at last on the opposite side, and we hastened in, leaving Jacob ahead of us somewhat stranded so that Dick bounded up and down above the pew door calling "Hist!" to him, to the infinite amusement of the congregation.

To my surprise Tessie took a fancy to church. Whether her simple silly nature, poor child, was impressed by the orderly ceremony, or whether (as Dick said) she enjoyed the admiring gaze of several young men who appeared to appreciate her new bonnet, I do not know; I am always willing to give Tessie the benefit of the doubt (poor Tessie!), but admiration was the breath of life to her, and she had not hitherto had many opportunities of receiving it. Some of the lads in the church, though they appeared a trifle uncouth to my London taste, were personable enough and seemed respectable, and I was not sorry for her to see young men other than Joah and feel that they admired her. Tessie was in truth a very beautiful girl and knew by instinct all those coquettish actions which attract men to women. (Alas, I myself know none of them.)

Unfortunately—or perhaps I should say fortunately, considering the consequences—this little success went to Tessie's head. Not content with chattering all the way home about her young admirers (while Jacob grew even gloomier at the thought of the opportunities Mary was enjoying at chapel in his absence) she carried her excitement to the dinner table, and regaled Charles with an account of her conquests. Her simpering delight in her own prowess was really touching because so innocent and young, but I did not expect Charles to see the matter in that light, and sure enough his brow grew black and he told her sharply not to be a little fool. Tessie pouted and tossed her curls, and, in order to regain the general approval which she felt she had lost under her father's rebuke, looked around to see if Dick had committed any misdemeanours to which she might direct attention. Adah had brought in a pitcher of milk and set it beside Dick, but as often happened he had left it untouched.

"Dick hasn't drunk his milk," announced Tessie virtuously.

As no-one took any notice of this she repeated it several times, while Dick in alarm gazed at her imploringly.

"Come, Dick, drink up your milk," said Charles at length

in the vexed (and as I now understood wounded) tone he usually employed to the child.

"I don't like it unless it's fresh from the cow," wailed Dick, beginning to cry.

"Upon my soul!" exploded Charles. "You have a fastidious taste, sir! And do you expect Eleanor to wait on you, then? Is that why I find her carrying milk about the yard like a dairymaid? Drink it up at once and let us have no more of such nonsense."

"Why don't you like it unless it is fresh from the cow, Dick?" I said, laying my hand on his to give him courage.

I own I was truly frightened at my temerity in putting the question, for I trembled at the thought of what his answer might be. But since Joah was absent, I thought the moment a good one to probe this matter to the core, and so I ventured.

"Adah puts drows in it," sobbed Dick, clinging piteously to my hand.

We were all so astonished by this reply that there was a moment's silence, then everyone exclaimed at once.

"Drows? Drows? What kind of language is that to be used at this table?" cried Charles angrily, his fair face crimsoning.

"What does the word mean?" I enquired faintly.

"It is a gipsy word meaning poison."

"Poison!"

Dick put his head down on my arm and howled, terrified.

"Poison or drug or strong medicine or brimstone or something of that kind," said Charles impatiently. "Where has he got hold of this ridiculous notion? You fondle him too much, Eleanor."

But all the incidents about Dick's food and drink clustered together strongly in my mind to support his accusation, not least that on the very first day of my arrival, when Dick changed his plate of porridge for Tessie's and Tessie was sick afterwards.

"Let us at least ask Adah what she has to say to this," said I steadily.

"Surely, Eleanor, you are not so foolish," began Charles, fuming.

184

I did not change my look or tone as I said quietly: "You will oblige me by asking Adah, Charles."

Unable to refuse me, Charles shouted "Adah!" in a fury.

Adah came hobbling in. She had taken of late to covering her filthy petticoats with a clean apron when she served our meals, but her snaky locks still hung about her neck in a most unkempt and unpleasing fashion, and her face and hands looked all the more sallow by contrast with the white linen.

"Some more gravy, master?" she said in her most respectful and soothing tones.

"Adah, do you ever put any drug into Master Dick's milk?" demanded Charles, point-blank.

"Yes, master," said Adah.

"You do?" said Charles aghast.

"Surely. I put in the medicine the doctor gentleman ordered when poor Master Dick's cough was so bad."

"But that was three years ago!"

"He would not take his medicine and the doctor told me to put it in his drink," said Adah in a tone of martyred virtue.

"No wonder the child is sickly and has no appetite," fumed Charles. "Listen, Adah. Nothing whatever is to be put into Dick's food or drink without the express orders of myself or Miss Moreys."

"I served in this house before you were born, Master Charles!" screamed Adah suddenly. She advanced close to the table, grasped it in her dark claw-like hands and thrust her face into her master's, her black eyes gleaming.

"I have never denied it, Adah," said Charles carelessly.

"And must I after all these years obey this chit?" screamed Adah again, gesticulating towards me.

"Yes, you must."

"Why? Why?"

"She is a daughter of this house; Walter Moreys' daughter, a grand-daughter of my grandfather," said Charles.

"A curse on Walter Moreys, a curse on him, I put my curse on him, I put my curse on his daughter!" raved Adah, raising her clenched fists and shaking them at me in savage imprecation.

"What have you against Walter Moreys?" said I. Pride gave me courage, for I was cut to the heart by Charles's speech. Surely if he ever meant to announce our marriage, he would have done so then, when stating the grounds of my authority over Adah. Thus, though my voice was quiet, I spoke with all the fierce anger provoked by humiliation. Adah lowered her hands and looked at me balefully.

"Walter Moreys was too fond of his brother's wife," she said with a sneer. "It is a custom in the Moreys family."

Charles exclaimed.

"That is a base lie," I said. "My father never had such a thought in his head."

"It's why John Moreys threw him out of Wool Royd."

"Then John Moreys was most pitiably mistaken."

"Walter Moreys should have minded his own business!" cried Adah, her eyes sparkling with rage. "Why should he interfere and spoil everything? Why should you, Walter Moreys' daughter?"

"This is intolerable," Charles interrupted coldly. "And very unfit for the ears of the children. Leave the room, Adah. Eleanor, take that howling brat upstairs."

I rose to obey and led Dick out. Tessie flew after us, her courage unequal to remaining with her father. The last glimpse I had of the room was of Adah tossing her head in triumph as she hobbled out, and Jacob sighing heavily and taking up his knife and fork in dogged determination, while Charles, his face white and haggard, poured himself a glass of wine.

Dick was hysterical and had to be put to bed and Tessie was almost as bad, and I own that when I had soothed them and settled them I threw myself face down on my own bed and wept my heart out; for the moment, the affairs of the house of Moreys seemed altogether too much for me. Exhausted by the expenditure of so much emotion, I fell asleep, to be woken by Charles's voice saying in a quiet friendly tone:

"Eleanor! Eleanor!"

This was so sweet to my ears that, believing it part of a dream, I tried at first not to wake; but starting up suddenly, found that the hours had moved on and Charles was knocking quietly and courteously at my door. I hastily smoothed my hair and went out to him, when he begged me to come down and make some tea—Adah had gone out, he said. I was astonished at this, for as I have said Adah never left the house or had hours off duty like other servants; but it seemed Jacob had caught sight of her crossing the bridge, clad in a black silk mantle Charles had given her by which she set great store. I wondered if she had left Wool Royd for ever, but Charles said impatiently no, she had such vagaries occasionally. I gathered my strength and went down into the kitchen and made tea. Charles and Tessie and presently Dick, too, came down and stood around watching me admiringly but quite ignorant how to help unless I instructed them; Jacob, however, was useful in making up the fire. When we sat down at last I noticed that all of us, even Charles, looked pale and subdued and rather red about the eyelids; but Dick, who had omitted to brush his hair so that it stood up all round his head in a very endearing fashion, had a watery smile, too, and a great air of relief—as well he might, poor child, since he had shed at last a burden he had carried for years.

"Where did you learn that word *drows*, Dick?" said Charles to him after a while.

"I've heard Adah say it about her brews on the fire," mumbled Dick, holding his head down, frightened as always when his father spoke to him.

Charles sighed. "Why did you not tell me—why did you not tell Eleanor?" he asked in an exasperated tone.

Dick hesitated and swung his foot, afraid to say that he had been afraid. "I was going to tell Eleanor," he got out at length.

Charles sighed again.

After tea, as it was a sunny pleasant evening, I proposed to take the children for a walk to soothe their nerves. Charles accompanied us, Jacob remaining at home sunk in gloom.

As soon as we had reached the open moors and the children had run ahead, I turned to Charles.

"What do you make of all this, Charles?" I asked him anxiously.

His face, which had become the more serene the further we left Wool Royd behind, clouded again: "Make of what?" he said in a weary impatient tone.

"Of Adah and my father, and of Adah and Dick."

"As to your father," said Charles, speaking slowly and evidently choosing his words with care: "I think you have your question answered, Eleanor. Your question as to why my father dismissed Walter Moreys from Wool Royd, I mean. The reason is now clear."

"But you do not believe my father was too fond of his brother's wife!"

"No, no—his letter to me begging for information as to the reason for his dismissal proves that no such notion ever entered his head. But I believe *my father thought so,* and that was enough."

"My father was young—only sixteen years of age."

"No doubt he was a fine upstanding young fellow, and had his own charm," said Charles sardonically. "You see that Adah believed the story to be true."

"Yes! And she was wrong! And she believed that *your* brother was too fond of *your* wife, Charles! Perhaps she was wrong there too!"

Charles looked considerably startled. "Well, it might be so," he said grudgingly at last. "But it is useless to dwell on it—we shall never know."

"But what of the drugs Adah put in Dick's food and drink?" said I, and I poured out all that happened, large and small, concerning this matter since I came to Wool Royd.

"For God's sake, Eleanor!" Charles interrupted me. "Show some sense! What is the meaning in all this? Adah is, I agree, a silly old woman, an ignorant servant to whom all directions must be explicit and plain if she is to understand them. She was told to give the mixture——"

"Who told her?"

"Dr. Bradshaw, I suppose. She was told to give the mixture, not told to stop giving it, so she continued to give it. She probably believes that she has done Dick great service, tended him faithfully through the years."

"On the other hand," said I, "it might be that someone

wishes for Dick's death and has taken this slow natural-seeming mode of accomplishing it. The drugs have the advantage, too, of keeping Dick back, making him a peevish sickly child whom you do not love and do not therefore pay much attention to."

"Come, Eleanor, this is foolishness, this is unworthy of you," said Charles impatiently. "I look to you for sense and intelligence, not for such silly tales. For God's sake do not become infected with the mystery of Wool Royd. Who would wish Dick's death?"

"Joah."

"In God's name, why?"

"He will marry Tessie and take all Wool Royd. And your savings, Charles—you will most certainly not leave them to Dick, will you? For you think he is not your son."

"According to you he will be dead before he can inherit anything."

"I do not think he will die too soon," said I, "for then, with that thorn gone from your side, you might marry and have other children. That would not suit Joah. It is a devilish scheme."

"It would be devilish if it were true, certainly. But look, my dear," said Charles (in that maddeningly soothing tone men employ to women whom they think unreasonably excited): "I have told you before: Joah has not the brain of a fly—he could not possibly conceive all this elaborate conspiracy. How could he deceive Adah about the drug? You can hardly imagine Adah is in collusion with him!"

"I do not know," said I thoughtfully.

Charles laughed. "Your brain is over-heated, Eleanor," said he comfortably. "Adah has served me and mine faithfully for nearly half a century. I owe her much. What should I have done without her these last twelve years? No other domestics would remain with me. All this pother over a cough medicine!"

"But *what* cough medicine?" said I. "Do you suggest that a bottle from the apothecary has lasted three years?"

"It is probably some noted gipsy brew," began Charles.

"There I agree with you."

"From what you say, it is a wonder Dick is still alive at all."

189

"Indeed that is so. But the child takes his own precautions. He eats only when he is served from the common family dish, and drinks milk only when it is just come from the cow."

"I believe you are right on one point—the child truly *believes* he is being poisoned. We must humour him a little on that for a time."

"Am I allowed then to fetch him fresh milk in the mornings?"

"You are a very obstinate and exasperating young woman, Cousin Eleanor."

"I am a Moreys, Cousin Charles," said I.

We both laughed, and Charles tucked my hand beneath his arm, and so we walked on happily together. There is a verse about basking in the sunshine of a smile, and Charles Moreys' smiles were always sunshine to me, however my heart might ache at his apparent indifference and delay. I rejoiced, too, most truly that some of the shadow over Dick at least was dissipated. Yet all the time it nagged at me that Adah said James and Rosie were lovers, Adah said falsely Walter Moreys my father had loved his brother's wife Caroline. There was some significance, some point in this I was sure, but as yet it escaped me.

When we returned to Wool Royd, we found Jacob in the yard moodily throwing stones at a bottle he had set up on the wall. It was a dismal occupation for a hearty young man on a pleasant Sunday evening, and I felt truly sorry for him, knowing only too well the pangs of unsuccessful love myself at that time.

"Are you not going to Upper Hey this evening?" I said to him as we passed.

Jacob shook his head. "I am not invited," he said.

"Cheer up, man!" said Charles. "Show some spirit! Put on that fine new waistcoat of yours and go over and show yourself."

"I should not be welcome," said Jacob gloomily.

"Nonsense," said his uncle, laughing.

"It is not nonsense!" cried Jacob, all his griefs suddenly bursting forth from his full heart. "After that scene at dinner-time today—there are always scenes at Wool Royd—

Adah could be heard screaming a mile away—I shall never win Mary while I live at Wool Royd."

"Perhaps you'd like to go elsewhere, eh?" said Charles.

He spoke roughly because (as I knew) he was hurt, but Jacob did not understand this and went on muttering in an aggrieved and resentful fashion.

"But where could you go, Jacob?" said I, not in an oratorical rebuking style but as if I really wished to know, being desirous always of playing the mediator.

Jacob sniffed and shifted from foot to foot. "I should like to go to Birmingham to Boulton & Watt," he blurted.

This was Greek, as they say, to me—indeed I knew more of the Greek alphabet than of these names—but to my surprise Charles seemed pleased. His face cleared.

"Why, that's a very sensible notion, lad!" he said heartily. "If you're really interested in engines and such. And besides," he added with a touch of his usual sardonic humour: "happen it'd help Mary Greaves to make up her mind."

At the first of these remarks Jacob brightened considerably, at the second he laughed, looked down and scuffed his foot in the dust, embarrassed but not altogether displeased. Uncle and nephew promptly fell into an animated conversation about the new steam engine which it seemed Charles had ordered from Messrs. Boulton & Watt in Birmingham. Since the summer seemed likely to prove a dry one, it was important to secure this engine quickly to supplement the beck's water-power, but many letters and plans had already passed between Messrs. Boulton & Watt and Wool Royd, without complete satisfaction to either. In a moment it was agreed that Jacob should set off for Birmingham the very next morning, and discussions of measurements and powers followed. I left them to it and went into the house, well satisfied.

Adah had returned and, mild and obsequious, served us an admirable supper. Dick shrank from her as she approached him to lay dishes on the table, but she showed no awareness of this; tonight her yellow wrinkled lids were lowered over her gleaming eyes discreetly. Charles was very kind and pleasant with her, to make up for his harshness at dinner-time, for his soft heart always pained him if he inflicted pain on others. Jacob and Tessie were in high feather—Jacob excited by the prospect of Birmingham, Tessie because a message had come from one of the families she had met at church that morning, inviting her to a party. Dick, speaking knowledgeably about the young robins and receiving a kind answer from his father, plucked up his courage and began to eat with appetite. For my part, I was well pleased to see those within my care—for so I regarded all at Wool Royd— friendly and cheerful together. So the meal passed off well.

CHAPTER III

ON the morrow Jacob set off for Birmingham, and Joah returned to Wool Royd.

This exchange, as you may imagine, was far from agreeable to me; indeed I was sharply chagrined when Joah appeared at the supper table; I felt a shudder of repulsion as I saw again his heavy body, coarse features and tangled black hair. It seemed he had been staying with old Mr. Hervey, Rosie's father (who apparently still lived in Annotsfield), and had ridden out to Moreydale that day to beg his uncle to allow him to return home. I judged that Charles had given him a very severe scolding before permitting him to do so, for Joah appeared subdued and almost nervous; he kept his eyes on his plate, addressed himself to nobody but his uncle, and showed as good table manners as probably lay in his power. Charles for his part looked cross and harassed and Dick regarded Joah fearfully and dared not speak; only Tessie was lively, chatting eagerly about the forthcoming Marthwaite party. She seemed to have forgotten she had ever been interested in Joah, and though I usually deplored her fickle habit of mind, in this case I could not but be glad of it.

"Eleanor," Charles interrupted her: "Mr. Hervey has sent word by Joah that it is overlong since he saw his grand-children. You had better take Dick and Tessie into Annots-field to see him tomorrow."

"Oh no, Father!" wailed Tessie, all her animation stricken from her face.

"Shall I drive them, Uncle?" offered Joah in an obsequious tone.

"No. I'll send the carter. You can stay at Wool Royd and do some work."

"I don't want to go. Let Dick go," said Tessie crossly.

"You can do some shopping afterwards," offered her father sardonically.

The struggle between the wish to shop and the wish not to visit her grandfather showed so clearly in Tessie's face that it was saddening as an example of the levity of her nature; Charles watching her gave a hard laugh which grated on my ears. Dick seemed to share his sister's despondency, so that I wondered very much what manner of man Rosie's father could be, thus to unite them in dislike of him.

It was less dislike than dread, I found the next day as we entered the neat house in the quiet back street where Mr. Hervey lodged. As we approached we heard the tinkle of a piano.

"Perhaps he'll have a pupil," Dick whispered hopefully to Tessie.

As I motioned to him to open the gate into the small flagged area for us, however, the notes ceased. The children's faces fell as I thought ludicrously, but when the thin, silent landlady had ushered us into Mr. Hervey's presence, I understood their discomfort. Mr. Hervey was a small but dignified old man, extremely pale and clean, who still wore the wig and knee-breeches of the preceding century; cold, stiff, formal, with thin lips and set features of a handsome cast, it was easy to guess that he disapproved severely of the Moreys' careless manners and did not hesitate to make them aware of it with that frigid sarcasm which wounds children most. He looked them over keenly now and, as children will, they drooped before his gaze and showed themselves to least advantage. I had the satisfaction of knowing that they were clean and properly dressed, however, and he made no adverse comment on their appearance, but having placed a very slight kiss on the brow of each, waved them to seats on stiff uncomfortable chairs. At this point he reproved Tessie for the unseemly disposition of her feet and knees, so that the child blushed in embarrassment. After one glance of chill hostility in my direction he averted his eyes and left me ungreeted. Perhaps he expected that I should seat myself and thus give him an opportunity to despise my manners, but I had been brought up in London after all and I remained politely standing. He now turned to me; since I did not speak he addressed his grand-daughter.

"Theresa, be so good as to make me known to this young lady."

At this Tessie gaped speechless, but Dick came to the rescue.

"This is Miss Eleanor Moreys, Father's cousin. She's come to live with us at Wool Royd."

"Ah yes! I have heard of you from Joah Lee. Pray be seated, Miss Moreys."

With a bow and a flourish of his fine white hands, he indicated a chair.

Something in his gestures and his mode of speech struck a remembered note.

"Are you not from France, sir? Are you not an emigré?" I enquired. "My father knew Miss Burney and General d'Arblay." Showing myself to poor advantage, like the children, beneath his discomforting stare, I blurted: "My father once sold a book to the great Dr. Johnson!"

A cold smile appeared on Mr. Hervey's thin lips.

"Pray do not imagine that I am an aristocrat, a nobleman of great estate fleeing from the guillotine," said he drily. "I came to England before the Revolution—I married an English wife. It is true that I have not found myself able to return to my country since 1789, and shall remain in exile as long as the Corsican usurper occupies the throne. But I am no General d'Arblay nor have I had any transactions with the great Cham; I am a mere music-master; nay, I also teach dancing. Theresa—Richard," he continued, turning upon the children, who had been listening to this speech with interest, but now blenched, "why have you given up your music and dancing lessons?"

The children turned crimson and wriggled in their chairs, and I guessed that Tessie had begged her father to let them cease the dreaded lessons and that Charles, with his usual careless kindness, had granted this indulgence.

"Is it you, Miss Moreys, who has ordered the discontinuance of their music lessons?"

I replied: "No, sir," in as colourless a tone as I could find, seeing no reason to incriminate poor Charles.

Perhaps my discretion pleased him, for he let the subject drop and spoke to Dick about his dislocated shoulder and the children's recent studies. Meanwhile I glanced quietly round. M. Hervet, as I must now call him, for his name was properly thus spelled, occupied two rooms, with folding doors, now open, arranged between; a piano stood in the front, we sat in the rear. I wondered rather that the old man should be able to afford such an agreeable ground-floor establishment, and suspected (rightly) that Charles's generosity alone made it possible. Were these the same apartments in which Rosie had lived with her father? Had this round table at my elbow supported the feathered hat? It was a painful reflection.

"So, Miss Moreys," said M. Hervet, turning to me: "I hear you undertake the education of my grandchildren?"

His tone was perhaps slightly less inimical than before, but I was now on my guard and replied coolly:

"For the present, sir."

"Richard and Theresa, you may play with the *bibelots*," commanded M. Hervet, with a dismissing wave of the hand.

The children flew joyously to a glass-fronted cabinet in the front room, whence they extracted some small china animals, quaintly carved ivory chessmen and the like. On their knees on the floor, squabbling mildly over these pretty toys, they seemed happy and well occupied, and a slight smile curved M. Hervet's thin lips.

"Now, Miss Moreys, let us have a little talk together."

"Very willingly," said I politely but untruthfully, I fear.

"It seems you have won my son-in-law's confidence and are now placed in charge of his household. May I therefore enquire what your plans are for my grandchildren?"

"I believe it to be necessary for Theresa's welfare," said I, adopting the formal tone which he had chosen, "to keep her away from her half-cousin Joah—at any rate for a time, until she has more experience on which to base a judgment of him."

M. Hervet bowed his head. "I agree," he said. "Joah—what an uncouth name!"

"I proposed to Theresa's father, and I believe he will agree, to send her for a time to some extremely well-conducted boarding establishment for young ladies—not too far away, however," I added hastily, feeling a pang of sympathy for poor exiled Tessie.

"I might be able to help you there," said M. Hervet. "I visit all the best establishments of that kind hereabouts to superintend the music-teaching. I will write a list of the most suitable for my son-in-law."

"I am sure Mr. Moreys will be greatly obliged," said I. "As for Richard, his health must first be re-established."

"And that again seems, perhaps, to require separation from Joah?"

"Yes!" I exclaimed with emphasis, delighted to find this unexpected understanding.

"Why cannot that young man be sent away to work at some distance? The other brother, Jacob, though loutish, is harmless, but Joah is irreclaimable. I have tried the experiment and I know."

"Charles Moreys feels himself responsible for the care of his half-brother's children."

"It is stupid, it is really stupid," said M. Hervet impatiently. "Over and over again Charles sacrifices his chance of happiness to his foolish quixotism, is it not true?"

"It is true," said I. "But I do not feel that it is foolish."

"I urged him many times to rid himself of that disreputable half-brother James. Had he done so, my daughter would be alive today."

"Charles is incapable of injustice, especially when it would further his own interest," said I.

"Ah, you love him," said M. Hervet in a designedly careless tone.

At this I could not prevent a hot colour rising to my cheek and brow.

"It is not very *convenable* for you to remain at Wool Royd in the circumstances; do you not feel that yourself?" went on

196

the old man. "Unless indeed there is some question of marriage between you. Ah, I see there is. May I congratulate you, then?"

"When Mr. Charles Moreys announces such a marriage, congratulations will be in place."

M. Hervet looked at me shrewdly.

"Ah, you have a doubt," he said. "But I think you are mistaken; you need not doubt. Charles would not have sent you here otherwise. He is a man of honour; he thinks doubtless I have a right to see the woman he proposes to put in my daughter's place."

I sat silent, holding my head up by an effort of will, but suffering much.

"I suppose, then, that Charles has confided the story of his previous marriage to you?"

"Yes, he has."

"May I ask, then," continued M. Hervet in his cold sarcastic tones, "what opinion you have formed about my daughter?"

"I believe that she was innocent and I am sure that Richard is Charles's son," said I.

"Indeed! Indeed!" said M. Hervet. "That was hardly to be expected from one in your position, Miss Moreys."

"You do not know me and have no right to make such a judgment," said I firmly. "I speak what I believe to be the truth."

There was a pause. Then M. Hervet rose stiffly to his feet and made me an elaborate old-fashioned bow. "I thank you on my daughter's behalf, Miss Moreys," he said.

I was touched by this and bowed my head in reply.

"You are no doubt aware," continued M. Hervet, seating himself with formal grace again, "that there is no evidence to the contrary of what you have said. My daughter disliked James Lee. She had been well brought up and her feelings were in control, but she disliked coarseness, and James was coarse. Any story of long-continued intrigue between them is all a chimera invented by that hot-headed simpleton of a Charles and his credulous neighbours."

"There is Adah's testimony," I objected, though with reluctance.

"Ah! Adah! She is a strange personage. Her evidence was given from spite. My daughter disliked her very much and wished Charles to dismiss her, but he would not."

"It surprises me to hear that, for Adah lamented your daughter's death very keenly," said I, remembering Charles's account of how, when the bodies were drawn from the dam, Adah had stood at his side wringing her hands and wailing.

"That is nonsense, that is impossible," said M. Hervet impatiently. "I tell you they detested each other. Adah is a two-faced personage. My advice to you is to beware of her, and get rid of her if you can."

I sighed. "Charles will not dismiss her without a cause."

"If I can aid you in that matter, I will do so," said M. Hervet.

"How do you explain the drowning tragedy, then, M. Hervet?" I asked him earnestly.

He shrugged. "How do I know?" he said. "There are a dozen possible explanations. All I know is that Charles chose the wrong one. And now," he went on, raising his voice so that the children could hear him, "it is time for you to go. I have a pupil who comes."

"May I set the hourglass?" asked Dick, running up to the table where this object stood but not venturing to take it in his hand.

"We do not mark the hour till the pupil is come, my dear," M. Hervet rebuked him. His tone was kind, however, and he laid his hand for a moment on the child's bright head.

Tessie and Dick suffered his farewell salute with a politeness born of relief, and flew for the door. The ceremony of my leave-taking took much longer for the old dancing-master bowed me out in an outmoded but very courtly fashion, bending over my hand as if he were indeed the aristocrat he disclaimed himself to be.

Once the little gate had closed behind them, Tessie and Dick skipped along the street, shouting with glee. I was disconcerted by their bad manners and called them back rebukingly, but they ran about me laughing and I had not the heart to be severe with them, for indeed I felt the same relief myself. I looked back in deprecation, however, at M. Hervet; but to my surprise he seemed pleased, and actually came down the little path towards us. I paused to hear what he had to say, expecting a message for Charles.

"I see they are happy with you," he said.

I was much pleased, and smiled. But at once his face changed to the look of chilly contempt it had worn when we first entered his rooms.

"You are late, Miss," he said coldly to the unhappy pupil who approached the gate.

Poor Rosie! Surely after such a frosty father, Charles's fond warmth of heart must have seemed like heaven to her! But perhaps she had been so nipped, so chilled in her young feelings that it took time before she dare credit that she would not be scolded if she spoke as she wished. Courage, I felt, was not a quality one could reasonably expect from Rose Hervet. Poor Rosie! My jealousy sank; I wished only to take her in my arms and comfort her. Do not fear, Rosie, I repeated; I will be true to you; I will care for your children.

CHAPTER IV

I HAD hoped to see Charles alone for a moment that night, to speak to him about M. Hervet and about Dick's locket, if nothing else. But at supper he was frowning and moody, and when Tessie began an account of our visit to her grandfather, he cut her off abruptly, saying that he had seen M. Hervet himself since we left and knew all that had transpired. After supper he went down to the mill; the steam engine was misbehaving itself again and work was much delayed—the whole mill was full of wool waiting attention, said Joah to Tessie as he followed his uncle, even the counting-house. No doubt this was very trying for Charles, but I should have been glad of an opportunity to sympathise and regretted that he did not give it to me. Next morning, too, he was not to be seen; while Dick was tired after yesterday's excursion and Adah chose that morning for one of her periodic cleanings of Rosie's locked room, so that my heart was altogether low. (The sight of the pink hangings, the remembrance of how Charles ran up to the room on the fatal night and found it empty of his wife, gave me great pain; I understood well why Charles could not bear to see it and kept it closed.)

Tessie, however, was in high spirits, as it was the day of the Marthwaite party, which she was to attend in company with Mr. and Mrs. Greaves and Mary. By ten o'clock in the morning she had all her finery laid out on her bed, and kept making excuses to leave her lessons and run in to admire it yet once again. Silly though this was, there was something pretty and playful in her eagerness and I could not find it in my heart to scold her; and even Dick began to smile and brisk up and take an interest in the party, from Tessie's continued lively chatter. Dick had indeed a sweet, kindly, merry disposition, like his father; he liked to see people happy, and listened now to Tessie's high-flown fancies about what she would do at the party, with his blue eyes wide and his childish mouth gaping in pleased astonishment. Tessie, who adored an audience, found this very agreeable, and—partly I think, too, from their fellow-feeling at M. Hervet's yesterday—they became quite friendly together.

"Would you like to see my dress now, Dick? Would you? Say you would!" cried Tessie.

"Yes, I would," said Dick obediently, glancing at me, however, to see how I received this.

I saw no harm in it, and took him by the hand and led him into Tessie's room, Tessie dancing on ahead in gleeful enjoyment. There was nothing very grand about the dress, for it was the same muslin I had made for her to wear at the Upper Hey party, but it had been freshly washed and ironed and looked very white and clean and smooth, and the two children gazed at it in great admiration. Then I felt Dick's hand tremble a little in mine, and suddenly he blurted:

"If you like, Tessie, I'll lend you my locket to wear at the party."

"Locket?" said Tessie, frowning in perplexity. "What locket?"

"Only to lend, mind," said Dick. "You must give it me back afterwards."

This remark, showing how much he prized the trinket, made Tessie more eager in the matter.

"What locket? Show it me!" she cried imperiously.

Dick put his hand inside his shirt and drew out the locket. It was certainly a handsome piece of jewellery, much finer than I had thought when I saw it before by candlelight; gold, with a front of black enamel, on which were initials entwined in diamonds. *C* and *R* I made them out to be, as the diamonds sparkled in the sunshine.

"Oh, Dick!" cried Tessie in an ecstasy, "will you really lend it to me?"

"Yes" began Dick; "only you must give it back——"

The rest of his sentence was smothered in an embrace as Tessie threw her arms round him and kissed him.

My feelings as I saw this were strangely mingled. Tessie's action was at bottom mercenary, yet it was very pretty and I could see how, in her mother, such a glow of gratitude might entice a man like Charles, whose generous nature delighted in open-handed giving. For all my good resolutions this thought was something of a pain to me. On the other hand, all my best self rejoiced to see Tessie and Dick united. If my own love was doomed to failure, my own heart to sorrow, I told myself, at least my sojourn in Wool Royd had served the happiness of these children. I strung the locket on a piece of rose-coloured ribbon to match those on Tessie's dress, and with many exhortations to her to be very careful of the jewel for it was valuable and her father would be angry if she lost it, I tied it round her throat, where it certainly enhanced her charming kittenish beauty.

Both children were so wildly excited by this episode that I sent them to lie down in bed in the afternoon, Dick because he needed the rest, Tessie to be fresh for the evening. I myself sat sewing alone in my room, and if a hot tear or two crept down my cheek, I do not even now blame myself for them. My situation was so ambiguous, so wounding and disappointing, that it might have perplexed and distressed a much older and more experienced woman—after all, I was not yet twenty at that time. So dreary seemed the day, so sad my heart, that I was thankful when it was time at last to dress Tessie for the party. But scarcely was this process completed—indeed I was just tying on the locket—when Adah came panting up the stairs to announce Mrs. Greaves.

I was surprised and dismayed; I had thought the arrangement was that I should take Tessie to Upper Hey and deliver her to Mrs. Greaves' care, not that she should be called for at home, and I feared some mistake had been made as to time, which had inconvenienced the Greaves family. This I deprecated, as much for Jacob's sake as for Tessie's. I went downstairs hurriedly, therefore, and was pleased to see that Adah had shown Mrs. Greaves into the newly furbished drawing-room. There she sat in purple satin, a feathered bonnet nodding on her head, in which garb her somewhat coarse features would have looked out of place had not her firm erect carriage given her a certain homely dignity. She seemed less sure of herself this afternoon, I thought, than when I had seen her before, for she fidgeted the lap of her satin dress with her fingers, making a disagreeable scraping sound. This arose because her hands were roughened by honest work; I respected the work and so tried to disregard the sound; her habit of sucking at her teeth I found less justified and more disagreeable.

"Tessie will be down in a moment," I began. "I had thought I was to bring her to you—I am truly sorry if some mistake has incommoded you."

"Nay—I come early o' purpose to see you, Miss Eleanor," said Mrs. Greaves.

Her Yorkshire tone and phrase, so much more marked than at Upper Hey, surprised me. Clearly she was ill at ease, and fell back into the speech of her less prosperous childhood, as people do unknowingly at such times. I waited for her to unfold her purpose, in smiling reserve.

"My Tom tells me that you and Charles Moreys are to wed," she said.

You may judge whether I was astonished. The hot blood rushed to my cheeks and for the moment I was incapable of utterance.

"Charles told him the other night. He wants us at Upper Hey to take Tessie for a week or two after, and Lucy to take Dick, so you and he can have a time alone."

I was still perfectly amazed and could not utter—indeed if

I had been able to speak I should not have known what to say.

"Listen, love," said Mrs. Greaves earnestly, bending forward and laying one of her large rough hands on my knee. "Listen. You mustn't do it. You mustn't wed him."

"Why not?" said I faintly.

Before answering, Mrs. Greaves looked furtively round the room, as if fearful someone might hear what she had to say. Then she bent forward still more, so that even in the anguish of the moment I could not but fear for her purple seams, and whispered:

"He's a murderer, love, that's why."

"No," said I.

"Aye, but he is!" persisted Mrs. Greaves. "I don't say but what he had reason, mind. But it's a fact. He drowned his brother and his wife in his own mill pond."

The gusto with which she said this, her hot breath fanning my face, her foolish nodding feathers, her implication that it was a worse crime to drown somebody in one's own pond than elsewhere, roused me to a passion of disgust which helped me to reply. Not that I ever doubted Charles, but a false accusation sometimes stuns.

"What makes you credit such a preposterous story?"

"I saw it with my own eyes," whispered Mrs. Greaves, nodding her head.

"What exactly did you see, Mrs. Greaves?" I asked eagerly.

"I was sitting at my dying father's bedside," she went on with the same portentous gusto which had vexed me so before; "he was miller at Wool Royd then, you know. I was sitting there, and our Dan was standing at the foot of the bed so's Father could see him—he'd asked to see him, you understand. Suddenly we heard such a cry! Such an awful screech it was, Miss Eleanor, I can hear it still!"

"Yes—Charles Moreys heard that cry as he rode down the lane," I said.

Mrs. Greaves slowly shook her head.

"Nay, love," she said. "It's only likely you'd want to think so, but that's not the way it was. I heard this screech and I turned sharp round and looked out of the window, and there I saw Rosie Moreys with James Lee's arms around her on the path by the mill pond. Then someone came up behind and pushed her, and she fell in. Leastways, she was falling in, you understand, when I jumped up and ran for the door, shouting out to Dan about Rosie and James and the pond. We were a bit delayed like, you see, because my father got a fright from the cry and me jumping up, and he started and fell sideways and of course couldn't pull himself up, so I had to go back, and Dan too, to raise him again and prop him with the bolster. And by the time we'd got down the stairs and out of the house and across the mill yard to the pond, there was Charles Moreys standing alone on the path, soaked to the skin, dripping pools of water all around him, with the new-born babe in his arms and such a look on his face! I never want to see such a look on any man's face again. Dan asked him where James and Rosie were, and he made out he didn't know and was for going off up to the house, but I stopped him and told him I'd seen them on the bank, and Dan told him they must be in the water, and he jumped in and threshed around but of course he didn't get them out, and then we drained the pond and there they were, dead as doornails."

It was indeed a damning story, and if I had not heard Charles's account previously, heaven knows what I might not have believed. But Charles had confided in me and I knew what to say.

"But your brother—Mr. Dan Dennett—heard the clatter of horses' hoofs *after* the cry. He thought that the noise of Charles's approaching gallop startled the lovers and they fell into the pond."

"Aye—that's what Dan says he heard, and he sticks to it. But I saw what I saw and I stick to that. I *saw* a dark figure push Rosie into the pond."

"Did you recognise the figure as Charles Moreys?" I asked with scorn.

"Nay! The night was half moon and half cloud and there were deep shadows and I didn't see his head or face. But I saw what I saw—I saw someone push Rosie in. Who else could it have been but Charles Moreys? He caught them at it and he struck his wife down. I don't say he hadn't cause to do it, but he's a murderer all the same."

"I should have expected a man in that situation to strike his brother first."

"Aye, so should I, I daresay. But he didn't, he pushed his wife. And while Dan and me were busy with Father, I suppose Charles struggled with James Lee and thrust him in t'pond as well. He were strong enough, Miss Eleanor: he's strong enough for anything, is Charles Moreys. But I didn't see that, you understand. I know nowt about that. For all I know, Rosie might have dragged James Lee down wi' her, like. But I saw Charles Moreys push Rosie, and nobody'll ever get me to say owt else."

"You saw *somebody* push Rosie."

"Who else could it have been? I don't say Charles hadn't cause, mind. I don't say I don't feel for him. But he murdered his wife as sure as I'm sitting here—and I don't want my Mary to marry into a murderer's family, you see, Miss Eleanor. And you're so young and nesh—I thought it my duty to come and warn you. You mustn't wed him, love."

"I shall marry Charles Moreys if he wishes it, Mrs. Greaves."

"Oh, he wishes it all right. He told my Tom so. He's settling up all his affairs now so as to see how he can do for a new wife."

"Did you tell your story at the inquest, Mrs. Greaves?"

She hesitated, then said: "Well, no. With Dan being so positive the other way, and me not seeing Charles's face, you see, it didn't seem worth while."

"That was wrong," said I proudly. "You should have told it so that Charles could have denied it before the world."

"But suppose he couldn't deny it, you see?"

I allowed all my scornful disbelief to show in my face.

"You don't believe me, do you, love?"

"I don't believe Charles Moreys murdered his wife."

Mrs. Greaves hesitated again, then she covered my hand with her own and spoke in a tone much more heartfelt and less portentous than before. "All his conduct since goes to prove it, Miss Eleanor."

"How can you say that?" I exclaimed, greatly surprised.

"My Tom's the kindest man in the world, and the best husband—I've loved him ever since he were a lad," said Mrs. Greaves. "But he isn't clever. His best friend couldn't call him clever. Then why did Charles Moreys put him in charge of Upper Hey, and lend him money, and all that? Why does he let Tom get behind in his wool accounts without a word? That's not Charles Moreys' way with his other debtors, Miss Eleanor, I can tell you. No; he sends them a curt letter enough, asking for the money and saying he can't bear such an old balance any longer. I don't say anything about him making Dan miller, for Dan's a good miller and a sharp clear-headed chap for all he doesn't talk much; but why should he favour my Tom so? Tom's such a simple well-meaning man, Miss Eleanor, he doesn't see that it's a bribe to me to hold my tongue. But I see it, and it makes my bread taste bitter in my mouth, for I feel it's Charles Moreys' bread, a murderer's bread."

"You continue to eat it, however, Mrs. Greaves!" cried I in a sudden rage, for it was intolerable to me to have Charles's generosity thus doubted and blackened. "But you need not trouble yourself; you can enjoy your worldly goods in future without any pangs of conscience; you can cease to hate Charles Moreys. Charles helps your husband because your husband once save his life."

"Saved his life!" repeated Mrs. Greaves, in her turn astonished.

"Yes, yes—on the crane," said I impatiently. "His brother left Charles dangling in mid-air. Don't you remember? Your husband ran up to the top of the mill and let the hook down."

Mrs. Greaves stared. "But was Charles Moreys really in danger? Of course I remember—he gave my Tom a golden guinea. But I didn't know it was serious, like."

"In another minute he would have fallen to his death on the stones."

"Charles told you that?"

"Yes, yes. Three weeks ago."

Mrs. Greaves sat back in her chair, decidedly disconcerted. The purple dress and feathered bonnet looked even more unsuitable than before now that they framed a doubtful and troubled face.

"I never thought of that," she said.

We sat in silence, though not in peace, for a few moments; I was on fire with indignation on Charles's behalf, while Mrs. Greaves had to consider the possibility that for some dozen years she had been in a terrible mistake. At length she sighed.

"I saw him push her, Miss Eleanor," she said. "Poor Rosie! Not that I ever cared for her—she were a vain silly piece and Tessie's just the same. But we've all on us a right to our own lives, Miss Eleanor. Poor Rosie! She belled out with fear as she saw him coming, and then he pushed her in."

"You saw someone push her."

"Who else could it have been?"

At this moment the door behind me opened, and Dick, looking pale and alarmed, peeped in.

"Tessie wants to know if something's gone wrong about the party," he mouthed at me.

"No, nothing," said I. "Tell Tessie to come down now, and do you carry her cloak."

"She's in the hall now," said Dick in his ordinary tones, much relieved.

I glanced at Mrs. Greaves, who rose and tried to reassume her ordinary self-satisfied expression. We went out of the room together. Tessie stood there without her cloak and bonnet, longing as usual to display herself. Mrs. Greaves' sharp eye passed over her approvingly, and lingered on the jewel at her throat.

"You know the locket?" I said.

"I know it—the trinket cost enough—her mother was fond of showing it," she replied in a dry tone.

"It was round Dick's neck when he was taken from the pond, was it not?"

"Yes. Well, Tessie," said Mrs. Greaves in an artificially cheerful manner, clearly disapproving of all talk of the pond affair before the children, "you and I must go.

Good-bye, Miss Eleanor. I wish you well," she added after a moment's pause, "but you're on the wrong track, love, you are indeed."

Adah, who had come up now, put the crimson cloak round Tessie's shoulders and I tied her bonnet strings while Mrs. Greaves drew her mantle more closely over her purple gown. The two were about to set off for their party when quick steps came along the yard and Charles appeared.

"I haven't seen Tessie cross the beck," he said crossly. "Has she not gone yet? She'll be late." At this point his glance fell on Mrs. Greaves. He stared at her, amazed, then he began to laugh. Leaning against the doorpost with his head on one side and his blue eyes sparkling, he addressed her in a teasing tone. "Well, Martha! To what do we owe the honour of this visit, eh?"

A heavy colour rose in Mrs. Greaves' face but she looked him squarely in the eye, for which I respected her.

"It's years since you've condescended to enter my house, Martha. But now you've broken your rule, perhaps I may hope you'll come and dance at my wedding?"

"And when is that happy event to take place, Charles Moreys?"

"In a week or so—I have the licence in my pocket."

Mrs. Greaves gave me a severe glance.

"Well, you'll go your own way I suppose, the pair of you. But don't come whining to me about it afterwards, Miss Eleanor."

"I promise you that," said I, very quiet and cold.

"Well, we shall see what we shall see," said Mrs. Greaves, tightening her lips. "Come, Tessie."

With her head in the air she marched out of the house.

It had been in my mind to attack Charles roundly, to reproach him for allowing me to discover his intentions towards me only from others, to tell him how wretched I had been, thinking he had forgotten or regretted his words of love. But when I saw him laughing boyishly, with the same gleeful grin on his face as brightened Dick's, as they both stood watching Martha Greaves' departure down the yard (which indeed being full of injured dignity was some-what pompous and waddling), and when I reflected on my poor Charles's wretched history, the load of misery and suspicion he carried on his shoulders, the malice with which that mercenary woman poisoned the very air he breathed because she took his bounty against her conscience—when I thought of this I could not find it in my heart to scold him. Instead, I shook my head at him indeed and said: "Charles! Charles!" but in a pleasant laughing tone, as if everything was right between us and he had never caused me a moment's uneasiness. My reward was that he turned to me eagerly.

"What day will you fix for the wedding, Eleanor?" he said. "Let it be soon—I am tired of this waiting, this feeling I must not say a word of love to you because you are under my roof and in my care."

I was filled with shame because I had never thought of this simple and honourable explanation of his conduct.

"Next Thursday?" went on Charles. "Or better still, Wednesday? Tuesday is market day, but Tuesday if you will."

"Whichever you wish."

"Nay, it is your privilege to choose. But let it be Wednesday, then," said my dear Charles with an air of great satisfaction. He took my hand, and might perhaps not have kept his vow of self-denial in the matter of love passages, if Adah, who all this while had stood in the background, had not now stepped forward and addressed him.

"Master, I'm loth to take you from your pleasure," she said in her blandest tones; "but a messenger came from Mr. Hervet for you a little while ago, a lad, one of his pupils."

Charles's face clouded, as it always did when anything which concerned Rosie was mentioned.

"Why didn't he come to the mill? I didn't see him cross the bridge," he said.

"He came the top road, this side the valley and in at our back door, and then went on his way," said Adah indifferently. "Mr. Hervet's ill—the visit yesterday was too much for him. He is palsied all down one side and fears he is in a bad way and wishes to see you immediately."

"Good God! What next?" said Charles. "Am I never to

209

have a moment's respite from my troubles? However—I must think of the old man. I must ride to Annotsfield at once, I suppose."

"Stay and eat something first," I entreated.

But Charles would not. He was ashamed that he had exclaimed at the first hearing of the news upon his own troubles rather than poor old Mr. Hervet's, and wished to atone for this by immediate compliance with his father-in-law's wishes. Having sent Dick off to order his mare to be saddled, he stayed only to change his mill coat for the blue one he wore to market, then rode away at once. At the water-splash he turned in the saddle to wave his hat to us, which I found very sweet and agreeable.

"Is it true, Eleanor? Are you really going to marry Father?" said Dick as we stood together on the doorstep, watching.

I said: "Yes," in a moment of great happiness.

"And never go away from Wool Royd?"

"Never."

Dick threw his arms round my waist and reached up his face and kissed me.

"You are a brave woman, Miss Eleanor," murmured Adah behind me admiringly.

"I am Walter Moreys' daughter," said I.

"All will not like the match, but I wish you well and hope your words come true," continued Adah.

"Thank you, Adah," said I in a friendly tone, for she could not really wish for a mistress above her in the house after so many years without, so I thought her words kind in the circumstances.

"Aye—I hope your words come true," repeated Adah. She gave one of her harsh cackles and slipped away into the kitchen.

I bethought myself then to wonder what poor Tessie was thinking of all this, in the gig with Tom and Martha Greaves and Mary. She was never very quick in understanding what others said, unless it concerned dress or her own pleasure; she must have heard her father's announcement of our marriage and was perhaps feeling now much afraid and bewildered. I was vexed with myself for not thinking of her at the time and uttering some soothing reassurances to her. But I comforted myself; she would forget the matter at the party, and I would put all right when she returned, or tomorrow morning. Now that I was secure in Charles's love, I felt full of hope and confidence.

CHAPTER V

WHEN it came supper-time and I found I had to preside at a table where only Joah and Dick were present, my spirits received a slight check, for without the support of Charles's authority, and with Jacob and Tessie absent, I felt singularly lonely and bereft. But I rallied and told myself that I was to be Charles's wife and nobody at Wool Royd would dare, knowing that, to cross or harm me. So I spoke pleasantly to Joah about the family in Iredale who had invited Tessie to their party; did he know them, who were they and so on. He replied in a most smooth and affable manner, saying that Mr. Stancliffe was a justice of the peace in Iredale and describing his large house recently built and the various members of his family, among which I was pleased for Tessie's sake to hear there were some sons. In Joah's view these sons were sticks, but he expressed this opinion with more moderation than might have been expected. Indeed he spoke in quite an interesting and sensible style, so that I was not surprised to see little Dick gaze at him wide-eyed, nor to hear the child exclaim suddenly:

"I never heard you talk so nicely before, Joah."

Joah's dark cheek flushed and he gave an embarrassed guffaw.

"There are two roads to every place, and the wise man chooses the pleasant one," he said.

I did not quite perceive the bearing of this remark, but supposed that he had decided to gain his uncle's approval by showing Dick and myself goodwill.

The dish Adah offered to us was stew of some kind, and I served us all from the big dish, feeling obscurely glad for

Dick's sake, even yet, that we were not to have separately prepared portions. Yet the meat was savoury and Adah had taken pains to put on her white apron and serve the meal with the proper silver and china, and as I looked round the room and saw it clean and fresh and orderly, and Dick no longer a cowed neglected brat but an endearing well-looking child, and even Joah learning as it seemed good manners, and thought of Tessie happy at her party, Jacob displaying his arithmetic in Birmingham and my dear Charles laughing at the door, I felt reassured and could not help preening myself a little on the change my presence had wrought at Wool Royd. Fool that I was! For pride goeth before destruction, as the writer of Proverbs says.

True, a slight unease pricked me again when Adah, smiling, brought in his silver mug filled with milk, for Dick. He, too, seemed to regard it fearfully, and looking at me with a puckered brow murmured with something of his old whine:

"I don't want it, Eleanor."

"Take it upstairs and drink it in bed," said I with assumed cheerfulness, intending that he should not drink it till I had tasted it myself.

Dick's face brightened and he agreed.

He was dropping with sleep, poor child, after the various excitements of the day, so as soon as supper was finished I sent him straight to bed. Wishing Joah a pleasant good-night, to which he replied with an attempt at a bow, very boorish but still politely intended, as I thought, I retired to my own room, and began turning over my small stock of dresses and linen, considering how I could best attire myself for my wedding so as not to disgrace my husband. My blue crape might, I thought, do very well, but perhaps Charles would prefer me to have a new robe made—I could not decide whether I thought this from true consideration for Charles or because I myself hankered after it, and so was unable to judge what would be my right course of action. From these and other sweet secret ponderings I wrenched myself to go to say good-night to Dick and put out his candle, as was my habit.

He was almost asleep, his blue eyes blinking drowsily; the

milk stood untouched on the table by his side. Somehow this indication that he shared my unease doubled it; my hand shook as I made haste to pour the liquid away into the ewer on the washstand. The splash seemed as loud as a cataract, and suddenly I became very conscious of the quiet of the house. There was no sound of voices, no step on the stairs; the mill, too, was quiet, from lack of steam not running late as it sometimes did. In spite of myself I listened, and as I listened there came a kind of stealthy creak and rustle on the landing outside. My heart jumped. But there are always such noises in old houses, I told myself; Charles will laugh at me when I tell him my fears in the morning. But perhaps he will not return tonight, perhaps he will be obliged to stay a day or two in Annotsfield. At this thought such a wave of longing for Charles and his protection came over me that the tears pressed behind my eyes, my throat choked and my lips trembled.

"I will lock Dick's door, and my own too," I said indulgently to comfort myself, and turned to place the key in the lock outside before blowing out the candle.

The key was not on the inner side of the door. Wondering idly when I had last used it outside, I pulled the door gently towards me, so as not to wake the sleeping child. The key was not in either side of the keyhole.

For a moment my heart stood still with fear. But then anger rose up in me, hot and strong; after all, as I had said to Charles, I, too, was a Moreys; I would not allow myself to be so easily defeated. I will stay in Dick's room with him, I thought, quick and firm; Joah shall not harm him; I will wedge the door with a chair; if Charles has not returned by the time Tessie comes, I will ask Martha Greaves to stay the night with us. The creak I had heard was now repeated; very quietly, I leaned forward and looked out along the landing. It was a night of moon and cloud, so that beams of silver light came and went fitfully through the casements; in this light, uncertain in duration but clear while it was there, I saw, quite distinctly and without any possibility of mistake, Joah standing at my bedroom door.

Then indeed the chill of horror coursed through my veins, for I understood his blundering sentence at the supper table about taking the pleasanter way. There were two ways to prevent me from diminishing his inheritance by marrying his uncle: murder and seduction. He meant to take the second, to him pleasanter, way, and had taken all the keys from the doors so that I should have no refuge from him.

"I will ring the big bell," I thought quickly: "I will summon help—the bell will bring Dan Dennett if I ring it loud enough."

I waited only till Joah had turned the handle of my door and entered my room, then ran, quickly and softly, down the stairs and stretched up my hand for the bell rope.

But the rope of the bell had been tossed up over the rod, so that it was out of my reach.

For a moment I paused, and thought of fetching a chair or buffet to stand on so as to reach the rope. Then I heard an outburst of loud angry oaths from Joah, who had discovered my room to be empty, and a rush of clumsy movement towards the stairhead. I opened the door and flew from the house.

But Dick, Dick! I have left him there with Joah, I thought in agony as I ran—still, he is asleep and the mug of milk is emptied, Joah will think he has drunk the drows —God grant he is thus deceived at any rate, I thought, panting. I had not yet turned out of the yard when I heard an angry cry, and in a moment heavy footsteps rang behind me. It was a relief to know that it was myself and not Dick he meant harm to. All my mind now was but a single thought: to reach the miller's house, to reach Dan Dennett. I ran as swiftly as I could—and being slight and small, I have always had some speed in motion—but tonight movement seemed as it does in a nightmare, my feet were heavy, my muscles would not stir. I strained towards the house but it came no nearer. One side of the lane was moonlight, one was shadow; I kept along the dark side so as not to be seen by Joah, for he seemed close behind; I could hear the loose stones jarring as his heavy foot fell on them. Now at last I reached the foot of the lane, where the paths divided. The nearer way to the miller's house lay mercilessly white, every line of bush and grass and stone bathed in a broad shaft of moonlight. As I crossed the lane and set foot in this white shaft and my shadow came out beside me, a triumphant shout came from Joah; in terror I swerved back into the darkness and ran on.

It was at this moment that I realised, with a thrill of almost superstitious horror: *This is what Rosie did*. Rosie fled from the house in fear, her child in her arms, for she was a mother; Rosie ran towards the miller's house for help, Charles being absent; Rosie shrank from the moonlight which would reveal her to her pursuer; Rosie ran along this path I was now traversing, for this path skirted the mill pond. Rosie struggled against James Lee as I should soon struggle against James's son Joah; Rosie lost her life in the process.

At this point in my thoughts, while I still ran on, panting, crouching in the shadow of the bushes, I gave up, deliberately and willingly, all thought of saving my life, for the sake of saving Charles's happiness.

"Let it be all as it was with Rosie," I said to myself. "If they find my body in the pond, at least they will know that Charles did not drown me, since he's in Annotsfield."

Joah crossed the shaft of moonlight and ran down into the mill yard by the other side of the pond. Fool that I was, I felt a real disappointment, for this, I thought, was not as it had been with Rosie.

Then it came to me that perhaps, after I was drowned, my body would not be found until the next time the pond was cleaned—if Joah managed matters skilfully, I should just disappear. By the time my body was found, Charles's absence in Annotsfield would have been forgotten, would have become difficult for him to prove; another burden of suspicion would be loaded on his shoulders. I stooped and hooked the stuff of my dress on a bramble and tore at it viciously till a patch of muslin hung from the thorns, and Joah heard this sound of rending and with a chuckle of triumph swerved and ran round the farther end of the pond towards me.

It is one thing to decide to accept death willingly for the sake of those you love, another to stand and take it passively when it approaches. As Joah drew near, all my love of life, my longing to see Charles once more, rose up in my heart and I turned instinctively to flee away from him. In this way I faced up towards Wool Royd. A gleam of white caught my eye as I swung. And then I knew what had happened to poor Rosie; I knew the secret which had blighted Charles's happiness, I knew whose hand had deprived Rosie of her life. For there in my path, her apron glimmering in the moonlight, stood Adah, no longer a bowed subservient crone, but towering erect, her dark face handsome as a devil's, her black eyes sparkling with triumphant rage. She called out to Joah in her gipsy gibberish, telling him I suppose that she was there to help him—and he answered her *in the same tongue.* I looked from one to the other; their faces in the moonlight were alike, their speech the same. I knew then that Adah was John Moreys' mistress and James Lee's mother; it was her wrongs which had poisoned the house of Moreys for fifty years. Everything fell into place; from the story of my father, whom she had caused John Moreys to chase away because his chance phrase about her and her master going *both* to Annotsfield as if together had made her believe he guessed her secret, to the drows for Dick and the false message which had taken Charles away tonight to Annotsfield so that she might prevent his marriage. It was her son James for whom Adah had wept, that night at the pond, not Rosie; to give her son, and after his death her eldest grandson, the wealth of Wool Royd had been her single aim. Perhaps it was Dick, the new-born son, the heir to Wool Royd, whose life Adah and James had threatened that night long ago, rather than Rosie's; perhaps Rosie had died nobly, defending her child. We shall never know, I thought, as all these matters came clear and orderly in my mind in a single lightning flash; but one thing I know: I am not Rosie; I am not a woman weak in body from child-birth, cowed in mind by a cold harsh upbringing; I am strong, I am spirited; my quiet manner conceals a passionate nature; I love Charles Moreys; I am a Moreys myself after all. If I am to drown, I thought, Adah shall drown with me; I will take this evil spirit of Wool Royd down with me into the grave. I ran towards Adah. And as she sprang down upon me with a wild laugh of triumph I screamed aloud, and screamed again, and threw my arms tight about her waist and would not be dislodged, though she beat at my head and tore at my arms and my face with her long nails. Joah came up behind and seized me by the waist and tried to pull me off, for he could not thrust me into the pond without endangering his grandmother. But all my sorrow for my father, my love for Charles, my passion for protection for poor little Dick, lent me strength; I locked my fingers behind Adah's back and clung to her and screamed. Adah called out in her gipsy tongue again and Joah struck me heavily and I fell to my knees; I felt my strength going but I did not unlock my hands; I will take this load off Charles at least, I thought; Adah shall not trouble him again.

So we three struggled there on the bank. There could be but one end to a struggle between a young girl and a heavy full-grown man assisted by a tough lean crone, and if they had got their hands to my throat, the end would have come sooner and been in time for them. But I suppose they hesitated between trying to stifle my screams and trying to heave me off, and doubtless they were afraid the fingermarks might show if they tried to choke me, in the case my body were found quickly. At any rate the end did not come soon enough for them; for Dan Dennett hearing my continued screams came running from his house across the yard and seeing these two raining blows on me, raised his fist and struck Joah aside. He struck hard, putting into the blow I suppose all the hatred he felt for Joah's father, who had robbed him of Lucy, and Joah caught off balance staggered and reeled and fell off the path to the stream many feet below. Then Dan seized my arm and Adah's and jerked us apart.

I have noticed in story-books that after such moments of crisis and danger are over, a blank is always put, and when next one meets the heroine, she is sitting at ease in a quiet parlour, wearing a becoming bandage, with the man she loves gazing at her very tenderly and closing the story with a kiss. But in real life no blanks can be put, the chapter can never be broken off; the moments which follow crises have to be lived through, and they are very terrible. I am not one of those women who are lucky enough to cut short pain and distress by fainting, I remain always very conscious and aware. So now I was aware of my disordered hair and torn dress and bleeding face, and raised a trembling hand to remedy them; I found I could not stand and sank to the ground, and was painfully aware of the brambles and nettles which surrounded me. I clearly saw Dick come running down the lane in his nightshirt, pale and terrified but all the same coming to my assistance, brave little boy! I called out to him to beware of stones and thorns because he was barefoot, but knew my words were not intelligible. I gasped out to Dan Dennett: "Adah is James Lee's mother —Joah's grandmother—they tried to murder me because I am to marry Charles," and thought how lunatic it sounded. I saw Lucy come running along the pond path towards me, and stop, and gaze downwards, with her eyes and mouth very wide open and somehow distorted. I lost sight of her for a moment then, because other men came running into the yard, both from the bridge and down the lane which passed Wool Royd, and I noted that some carried sticks and others pitchforks. Then I heard Lucy say in a soft frightened tone:

"You've killed him, Dan love."

"Nay!" said Dan Dennett, startled. "I didn't hit hard enough for that, surely."

He dropped my wrist and Adah's and went down the bank and Adah plunged after him. I, too, went down, placing my feet sideways on the steep bank as Dick had taught me, but Lucy was afraid and stretched out her hand towards me piteously, so that I had to go back to help her. She trembled so much that I had to support her and it was not easy, so we were long in descending and by the time we reached the bottom not only Dan Dennett and Adah but Dick and a couple of neighbours were standing there looking down at Joah, who lay on his back in the stream, with the water washing his black hair against his cheek and his mouth slackly open.

I had certainly no love for Joah, but I could not bear to see any living thing lying thus, uncared for and in danger of drowning, so I asked somewhat sharply if he could not be raised at once.

"Nay, there's no hurry, Miss Eleanor," said one of the

men, who proved to be the Wool Royd cowman: "he's dead, you see."

At this Dick crouched down beside Joah, and putting one hand beneath his head, raised it gently, then let it fall again. It rolled to one side in a most strange and sickening manner, and Dick said:

"His neck's broken."

"Poor boy! My poor son! Poor Joah!" said Lucy, trembling.

"Happen he's saved a worse end, Lucy," said her husband very soberly, putting his arm round her.

But Adah fell on her knees in the stream beside Joah's body and gave a fierce wild cry, and raised her hands to heaven and cried out in some of her gipsy language, and tore at her hair so that it fell in a great dark cloud about her, and bowed herself over Joah and kissed his lips and stroked his face and put his black hair back from his forehead, and wailed again and wrung her hands, till it was piteous to see her.

"Why does she take on so?" said the cowman, puzzled.

I said: "She is his grandmother."

A kind of sigh rose from all the people present—by this time there was a row of men standing on the path above our heads.

"Did you ever know that, Lucy?" said Dan, turning to his wife sternly.

"Never! Never!" wept Lucy.

"Tha mun get out o't'road now, mother," said the cowman in a kind tone to Adah. "We mun lift him out o't'water, tha knows."

Adah stood up, but when Dan and the cowman had raised the body between them she seized Joah's hand and would not surrender it, though the passage up the stream to the level of the bank, and along the path to the mill yard, was difficult. When they reached the yard they laid the body down, for it was heavy, and awaited the arrival of the constable. Lucy stood beside her son, weeping quietly and fidgeting with her handkerchief, but Adah knelt down and threw herself over her grandson's body, covering him with her long dark hair. Her posture of grief was so noble and so tragic that, in spite of all her sins, I felt deep pity for her. After all, she had been deeply wronged. I knelt down beside her and put back the hair from her face and touched her hand and said:

"Adah, you still have a grandson left; you have Jacob."

"Jacob has not the spirit of our race," wailed Adah. "He is a gorgio, not a romany. Joah was a true romany, my son's true son. His blood beat when mine was near."

She looked at me as if she did not know me, without hate or fear, then bent over Joah again, adjusting his dress and hair in a very piteous fashion.

In the midst of all this tragedy a ludicrous note was struck, as it seemed to me, by the arrival of the Greaves' gig, containing Martha and Tom, Mary and Tessie. Somehow the appearance of this trim well-painted vehicle, drawn by a neat brown cob which had an air of surprise at finding itself amidst all this crowd and excitement, struck me as comic; I began to laugh and could not stop myself. (The narrow red line painted round the body of the gig, and Martha Greaves' purple satin, seemed particularly funny.) I still retained sense to place myself in front of Joah's body so that Tessie should not see it, but I suppose my appearance, bleeding and dishevelled, must have frightened the child, for she began to weep, and in this Dick joined her, scrambling suddenly up into the back of the gig and putting his arms round her in a brotherly fashion which pleased me. (At least, I thought to myself wearily, we shall have no more trouble there; now that Adah's identity is established, her hostility to Dick proves she has no cause to think him her grandson. All that story was a lie, to discredit Charles's son in his eyes.) Everyone talked at once, telling Tom and Martha what had happened, and then Martha climbed down from the gig and came to me with her harsh features working, and she put her hands on my shoulders and looked into my eyes and said:

"It seems I was wrong and you were right, love."

Suddenly I was so tired that I could no longer stand. I staggered and leaned against Martha, and she helped me up into the gig and told Dick to stay in the gig with Tessie, and Tom turned the smart brown horse and drove us all

When it came to my turn to be questioned, I had to forgo all thoughts of modesty and tell how I saw Joah enter my room, how he had previously made an attempt upon my virtue, how the bell-rope had been tossed up out of reach, how I had run from the house and been caught between Joah and Adah, and how between them they had almost thrown me into the pond and would have done so had not Dan Dennett arrived. The coroner, naturally enough, did not understand why Joah had changed his plan from seduction to murder, or why I had been so sure of it, and looked dubious when I explained that he meant to prevent me from becoming his uncle's wife. Indeed, without mentioning Joah's intentions towards Tessie, which I wished to avoid, there seemed little sense in it. But here Mr. Battye, Charles's lawyer from Annotsfield, an old wizened little man but very shrewd and able, was of great help; he was not allowed to give direct testimony, as it was judged irrelevant, but by interpolating explanations, popping up and down continually, he contrived to convey to the court the terms of John Moreys' will and the interest Joah had in keeping Charles single, very clearly and well. Dan Dennett told how he had seen Adah and Joah raining blows upon me so that he thought I should be killed, how he had struck Joah on the shoulder sideways to free me, how he had heard Adah acknowledge Joah as her grandson, and so on. Neither Dan nor I had clearly seen Joah's fall, but Lucy had seen him stagger and lose his footing, and in a low tearful murmur told of this.

Adah was now summoned; she came in between two court officers, in a curious gait both stumbling and stamping, and folding her arms stood erect glaring round at us all from very bright scornful eyes. Her hair, so wonderfully black and long, had not been dressed, and streamed over her back and breast, so that she looked fearfully wild. I own I shuddered and turned sick when I saw her, and Charles put his arm round me protectively. The coroner asked her many questions, but she would answer none, and when he threatened to commit her for contempt of court, she was silent to that too. As I say, I think she was already quite out of her mind, but she still looked so handsome and full of fire that no one thought it. The coroner sighed and tried again:

"You were with the deceased, Joah Lee, and Eleanor Moreys, on the bank of the pond?"

At Joah's name Adah threw up her hands to heaven in a great wailing cry.

"Why had you gone to the pond? Why did you follow Eleanor Moreys? What were you doing on the bank of the pond?" persisted the coroner, trying all ways to get an answer to his question.

Adah's bright mad eyes roved towards us. I was sitting next to Charles, as I have indicated, and suddenly she seemed to take this in, and she cried out in a fury:

"I drowned your other wife and her brat, Charles Moreys, and I'll drown this one too!"

While all present gasped with horror and even the coroner turned pale, Adah went off into harsh screaming cackles of laughter, throwing herself back and forth, and pointing at Charles with both her forefingers (which were brown and gnarled) in a very horrible way. The coroner in a weak voice ordered her to be removed, and told the jury to consider their verdict.

I could tell from his directions that he thought this verdict should be *justifiable homicide* against Dan Dennett, and I felt greatly distressed, for it was not Dan's blow which had killed Joah, but Joah's fall, and that Dan should have to suffer the formality of a trial for having saved my life, would be a great wrong, I thought, and a great grief to me. But I need not have troubled, for after a few minutes' absence the jury came in all beaming and pronounced it *accidental death*. The coroner reared and bristled at this, and doubtless it was wrong from a legal point of view, but right enough, everybody thought, in true justice, equity as they call it. We were fortunate in having as foreman of the jury a man not easily browbeaten or put down, that obstinate red-headed clothier whose wool James Lee had once lost and Charles had gathered, Mr. Oldroyd of Syke Mill in Iredale. Charles had Tom Greaves give him and the other jurors a refreshment after the inquest at the Pack Horse inn in Booth, he himself being busy with making the funeral arrangements.

All these matters fell upon Charles, partly because Jacob was, after all, still only a young man and inexperienced, but mainly because poor Jacob was in such a state, he was incapable of any action. Jacob was affectionate by nature and had truly loved his brother; to find him so suddenly dead was bad enough, but to find him set down as an intending ravisher or murderer or both, was horrible. Jacob, always a kind, good, well-meaning lad, felt himself disgraced and dishonoured, quite cast away from decent folk. Then, too, he seemed quite overwhelmed to find himself Adah's grandson. Whether it was that he disliked her personally, or that his pride was hurt because she was a gipsy and a servant, I could not quite tell, but seeing his misery and humiliation, I perceived why John Moreys had kept the identity of his illegitimate son's mother a secret, which I had not altogether understood before. (And indeed for many years such illuminations of the Moreys' former story from time to time occurred. It is so in general; as life goes on we meet experiences which teach us to understand earlier happenings—often too late to be of any use.) In his distress Jacob turned to his mother, which was natural and proper; Lucy and Dan took him home with them to the miller's house, and Lucy's timid but warm love, poured out upon him unstintingly now that she found him ready to receive it, was his great comfort. She nursed his head on her breast all afternoon, and coaxed him to eat as if he were a child.

Adah for her part took not the slightest notice of Jacob, but watched all day again beside Joah's body. In the evening when, in Charles's presence, the coffin was brought and Joah was placed in it, Adah lent her assistance, but as soon as the coffin lid was laid on, she gave one of her wild mourning screeches, and tossing her arms, ran out of the house to the moor and stayed away.

Next day the funeral took place. Charles, so Lucy told me later, spoke very kindly to Jacob but a little sternly, saying that there might be folk watching, and he must control himself and act like a man. Poor Jacob, gazing forlornly up at his uncle, promised to do his best and kept this promise pretty well; pale and red-eyed and with his lips trembling, he held up his head and by clenching his fingers together contrived not to weep.

As Charles had foretold, there were many spectators; it was very clear that their interest in Joah was not friendly and they even shouted menacingly at Jacob; at this Charles drew Jacob's arm through his own and stared them down. (So Dan Dennett told me; no women attended so I was not myself present.) As they came out of the church after the service and went into the graveyard, Adah was seen roaming about on the hillside just above, and at that awful moment when dust is thrown upon the coffin, Jacob suddenly gave a start and a cry, finding her unexpectedly at his elbow as he stood at the graveside. For the last time she raised her dreadful wail, and tore her hair and beat upon her breast; then moved away, stalking through the crowd, which drew back in horror from her.

As she reached the lych gate, two men stepped forward and read a warrant and took her into custody.

Then her strength gave, and she could not walk. This, I think, was the truth, but the law officers, having seen her a moment before proud and upright, did not believe it and thought she was wilful and would not. They held her by the elbows and urged her forward, but she fell to her knees; then losing their temper they dragged her by the armpits. This cruelty was intolerable to my dear Charles; dropping Jacob's arm he left the lad staring vacantly and pushed through the crowd, and using his great strength picked up Adah in his arms and carried her to the coach which the constable had waiting. The law officers got in beside her and the coach drove away, and Jacob, who had followed Charles, threw himself on his uncle's neck and sobbed like a child.

CHAPTER VII

You may imagine that after all these tragic and wretched events, when Charles came to Upper Hey to see me that night he looked infinitely weary, pale and haggard. He told me all that had happened at the funeral, Martha Greaves sitting with us all the time as though she thought we ought not to be left alone together, which vexed me. At the close of his account, after a pause, Charles said in a meaning tone:

"It is Wednesday tomorrow, Eleanor—the day you selected for our wedding."

"But surely you are not thinking of marriage!" cried Martha. "You must wait awhile—it would not be decent at present."

"Do you wish to postpone our marriage, Eleanor?" said Charles drily.

It was one of those moments which readily bring misunderstanding between a man and a woman. The woman tends to fear that the man must wish what he suggests, and from modesty she shrinks from forcing herself upon him; yet if she appears to agree with the suggestion, naturally the man is hurt and takes her at her word. But I had long since determined that there should be nothing but truth between myself and Charles Moreys. Now the truth was that, during all these troubles, I longed with all my heart to stand as a helpmeet at Charles's side. Accordingly, though I own it cost me something to be so bold in Martha's presence, I shook my head and said: "No," quietly but quite firmly.

Martha looked down her nose and pursed her mouth, but Charles brightened and laughed and said:

"That is well, because I have arranged the wedding with the Vicar for ten o'clock tomorrow morning."

BOOK FIVE: THE HOUSE OF MOREYS

CHAPTER I

HERE again, if this were a story-book or a fairy tale, I should close it by saying that I married Charles Moreys and we lived happily ever after. This is entirely true; for we married, we were blessed with two beautiful fair children (a son and a daughter), we enjoyed great prosperity and our love for each other continually increased. But real life is not as simple as a fairy tale; we had our difficulties, and there are things that remain to be told.

CHAPTER II

BUT first let me tell how Charles and I were married.

Although Charles had chosen an early hour for our wedding so that it might be quiet, Marthwaite Church was crowded; indeed so many wished to be present that they could not all get into the church, but thronged the grave-yard outside and even lined the roadway. This, as it appeared from their smiles and hat-doffing, was out of compliment to Charles, to show the sympathy of the neighbourhood for his long and undeserved sufferings. For his sake I was pleased to see all these friendly faces about us, though for myself I own I trembled very much and had some difficulty in keeping back my tears, as on Tom Greaves' arm I passed up the aisle between all those gaping curious faces. I would have preferred Dan Dennett to give me away, but he was too shy and reserved a man to play this part; besides, Joah was his stepson, after all.

Charles looked terribly haggard as I approached and I understood what he was feeling and felt with him; he was remembering his first wedding and its hopes and disappoint-ments and final tragedy. However, as soon as he saw me looking timid and overfaced, the natural kindness of his disposition overpowered his own trouble and he smiled at me with all that warmth and sweetness in his look which I loved so well. I began my vows in a faint and halting tone, but I could see that this troubled him, so I gathered my strength and held up my head and made myself speak firmly, though of course in a quiet tone such as becomes a woman on such occasions. Charles himself spoke up very manfully, and I must say it was infinitely sweet to me to hear him take the beautiful vow to cherish me *till death us do part*. The touch of his fingers on mine as he put on the ring was warm and comforting. So we were married and went into the vestry and signed our names, and Charles then kissed me very tenderly.

When I came down the aisle afterwards, on his arm, the church bells rang, and as we walked down the path to the gate, where a chaise waited, somebody began a huzza, and suddenly all the crowd were cheering and clapping. Charles, handing me very carefully into the chaise, was obliged to pause with one foot on the step, and with his hat in his hand (his fair head glowing in the sunshine) thank them on behalf of himself and his wife for their kind expressions of approval.

"Friends, I take this very kindly on your part," he began. "It is good——" (Here his feelings overcame him.) "You must forgive me," he got out after a moment, "if I say no more."

They cheered again and someone called out: "Bravo, Charles!"

When at last my husband sat beside me in the chaise, taking my hand and kissing the palm and laughing, he pretended that these demonstrations were on my account.

"You are a heroine, Eleanor my dear," said he. "You have solved the mystery and brought sunshine to the house of Moreys."

But that of course was only his joke; the applause and affection were meant for him, and who deserved them more?

You, Edward, who have not yet married, will marvel perhaps that I think it worth while to record these details; but you, dearest Catharine, know by experience that a woman's wedding day is a very great day in her life and she often fondly recalls it.

In view of our circumstances at the time, Joah's grave

barely filled in, Adah in prison, and so on, we held no large festivities such as would ordinarily have been proper; but we gave a small family wedding breakfast at Upper Hey, and at the Red Lion inn in Marthwaite (where Charles sometimes held his Pay Day) there was free entertainment for all who chose to seek it. I thought this might prove unnecessarily costly, especially when I saw the large concourse round the church, but said nothing on the subject, not wishing to presume on my new position as Charles's wife, to interfere in his financial affairs. When the account came up from the Red Lion a week or two later, however, though he rolled his eyes in a joking way he had, he paid it pretty cheerfully.

I had feared that Tessie would be unhappy on the wedding day, seeing another woman as it were supplant her in her father's affections; for Dick I was not troubled. But as so often happens in life, which always has some unexpected turn with which to surprise and confound one, just the reverse actually happened. Tessie was in her element amid the crowds and the huzzas, and laughed and talked and bridled and enjoyed the compliments she received on her looks and dress, while Dick moped about in corners. But perhaps he was not really moping, only over-excited by the recent events and their happy termination. He was always a child of great sensibility. I stroked his head and comforted him a little, but catching a sharp glance from Charles desisted. I saw at once that to reconcile these two and coax Charles into feeling what a man should towards his son, was to be one of the great tasks of my married life. I will tell you presently how, and how far, I was successful.

After our healths had been drunk and one or two kind speeches made, Charles and I quietly left the house and walked together, arm in arm, down the lane and across the beck and up to Wool Royd. It was a lovely, clear, sunny evening, and I could not help thinking, with a happy smile, of that cold black night, five months ago, when Jacob drove me first to that unknown and barbarous-seeming destination, Wool Royd. How much had happened since then! How happy I was now compared with my state in February, in spite of all our troubles!

Appropriately enough, as we crossed the bridge there was poor Jacob leaning slackly against the parapet, evidently waiting for us to approach. (He and Lucy had not attended our wedding, as was only proper since they were in mourning for Joah.) Jacob straightened himself up as we drew near and in a low tearful voice muttered:

"I wish you both all happiness."

We were both much moved. Charles put his arm about the poor boy's shoulders and hugged him and I, not venturing, however, to touch him, for he could not but blame me in some part for his brother's death, thanked him warmly for his goodwill and told him how much I valued it. To see his pleasant foolish face cast in such dejected lines was very sad to me, and as Charles and I moved on I vowed to do all I could to restore the poor lad's happiness. This was a vow soon put very severely to the test, but I am thankful to say that with my dear husband's aid I was able to keep it.

So Charles and I passed on to our home and began our married life together.

You, Edward and Catharine, know your father's kind, generous and merry (if somewhat wilful) temper so well, you do not need to be told of it; our married happiness, too, has been a familiar spectacle to you. But I love to dwell upon it and to narrate its course as it grew deeper and stronger and surmounted all the obstacles which the history of the house of Moreys put in its way.

Our embraces were most beautiful and happy; and to lie in my husband's arms and feel his strong heart-beats against my own was to me always a most exquisite pleasure. But many a man—as I have often noticed in my dealings with other married couples—passionate enough and jealous enough in his love towards his wife, is surly and careless in his dealings with her in their everyday life. Never was it so with my Charles. His protective care was ever about me; I nestled into it like a kitten into strong loving hands.

He was always ready to understand and share my household cares; it was he, for example, who found the excellent William and Dolly, whom you have known so well. William was a young Annotsfield soldier when I first knew him, discharged from the Army on account of a bullet in his leg which made him limp and prevented him from getting good employment; Charles, impetuous and generous as ever, seeing him as a porter in the Cloth Hall struggling to carry heavy pieces, swept him and his wife into our kitchen at Wool Royd as butler and cook, which posts they have filled all these years to admiration. From the circumstances of their engagement they were devoted to Charles, and in this devotion they included Charles's wife and family, so that our association has always been most pleasant. But it was not only in such large matters that Charles assisted me; in those small details which make or mar everyday life, he always sprang to my aid. Did I need to open a stiff window, reach a high shelf, carry some weight, about the house, Charles's hand always reached over my shoulder to do it for me. The first week of our marriage he had a carpenter from Marthwaite come to measure me for a footstool, so that I could sit comfortably and sew in one of the great drawing-room chairs. The man, I thought, was somewhat amused by Charles's insistence upon meticulous measurements, so that I blushed; when he had gone Charles, taking me on his knee, teased me about my high colour, pretending to warm his hands by my cheek and so on.

"You are too good to me, Charles," said I.

"Listen, my dear," said Charles, drawing my head down upon his shoulder: "I am a warm-hearted, affectionate man by nature, though some folk doubt it."

"Who ever doubted it?" said I, indignant.

"Martha Greaves," said Charles with a grimace. "Well, as I say, I am a warm-hearted chap; I love to help and protect, and the weaker and gentler folk are, the more I like to help 'em. For a dozen years I've had nobody to cherish. I'm bound to make a right pet of you, so don't you try to cross me in it, Eleanor; just kiss me instead."

You may imagine what happiness it was to welcome such a husband each evening to the home. At the sound of his step and his cheerful whistle, I put all griefs from my heart, and ran to meet him, glowing with happiness. Charles being so tall and strong and I so small and slight, he could lift me from my feet with perfect ease; and it became his habit to do so every evening on his return from the mill, enfolding me in his arms. This moment a thousand times outweighed for me all the difficulties of the day.

For there were of course, as I have said, difficulties and troubles. No life, however happy, is entirely free from pain, and though we had found the right thread which led to the heart of the skein, the destinies of the various members of the house of Moreys were too intricately entangled to be made straight without some care and struggle.

CHAPTER III

AFTER a time of great joy and excitement, it is difficult to return to the quiet habits of everyday life. When the day came for Tessie and Dick to return to Wool Royd, Charles was short-tempered, and I confess that I privately sighed. However, I made their rooms very clean, and laid a bunch of flowers on their beds, and had Dolly bake a very handsome pie for supper, and ran to meet them with open arms and a welcoming smile, for I wished them to be happy and not feel that I was a harsh stepmother. As it turned out, I need not have been anxious; for they were so thankful to be home again and away from the severe discipline of Martha Greaves that they threw themselves upon me like young puppies, leaping and kissing and frisking, and ran all over the house, laughing, and at supper time talked incessantly about Martha's stiffness and how much pleasanter Wool Royd was than Upper Hey, so that Charles's cross look left his face and he laughed with them. I tried mildly to check them and pointed out that Mrs. Greaves had been very kind in entertaining them.

"True—very true," said Charles with a mock-solemn look. "It is kind of her, too, to make home seem so agreeable."

At this they all fell to giggling again, and it was very pleasant to me to see them thus merry together, and a great relief to find the children's homecoming pass over so smoothly.

Our first trouble, therefore—thought it is a shame to call it a trouble, especially in view of what resulted—was a visit from old M. Hervet. Charles had sent Tom Greaves down to Annotsfield to tell him all that had happened, but naturally Rosie's father wished to hear his daughter's vindication from Charles's own lips; and he kept sending messages which grew increasingly peevish, asking Charles to visit him. Charles was very reluctant to go.

"Then write a letter to the old man," said I.

"I'm no great hand at letters, Eleanor," said Charles, rolling his eyes, and when I remembered the letter he had written to my father, I could not but agree with him.

At length M. Hervet sent a formal letter, saying that he proposed to pay his respects to Mrs. Charles Moreys at Wool Royd on Monday next. Charles was for putting him off, but though I shrank from the visit as much as he did—perhaps more, for a reason which I will mention presently—I knew that it would not be right to postpone the old man's satisfaction any longer. Accordingly I urged Charles to send Jacob down with the gig to fetch M. Hervet on the day named.

"Jacob! As like as not he'll upset the old man in the beck," said Charles in a vexed tone.

For he had begun to lose patience with Jacob, who seemed still unable to rouse himself from his grief and bewilderment. After he had spent a week or two sitting about at the Dennetts' house with slack muscles and bowed head all day, Charles spoke to him sharply and told him he must rouse up and come back to work, if he wanted ever to win his Mary. At Mary's name Jacob sighed deeply and shook his head. Of course he obeyed his uncle and turned up at the mill every morning, but he was useless there, standing about idle and dreamy so that he was in everyone's way, and forgetting or what was worse confusing messages. I thought myself he would have done better to return to Wool Royd, where Dick and Tessie would make cheerful young company for him, not to mention that under Lucy's loving but rather feckless care his appearance and manners were deteriorating. But Lucy was his mother, after all, and if the Dennetts chose to keep him with them and he chose to stay there, nothing could be said. I thought a drive down to the bustling streets of Annotsfield might help to rouse the poor lad, and said so.

"Happen you're right," said Charles. "We'll try it, anyway."

On the day arranged, Jacob set off early, so as to bring M. Hervet to Wool Royd in time for dinner. Charles was so gloomy, and Dick and Tessie so subdued, that William and Dolly were quite concerned and asked me if they had done anything to vex us. I reassured them and tried to put on a cheerful lively air, but in truth my heart was heavy too, for I feared M. Hervet might wish to see any new arrangements we might have made at Wool Royd, or ask about his daughter's belongings. There were no new arrangements worth the showing and his daughter's belongings were not to be seen, for the locked room, the room which had been occupied by Charles and Rosie, was still locked. This was privately a grief to me. I felt that as long as the room remained locked, part of Charles's heart was locked in the past, and neither I nor a happy new life could fully enter it. The room Charles and I occupied, too, was small and sunless, so for every reason I wished the room were opened. But—though it may not always have appeared so in this narrative—I am a proud woman, and I scorned to mention the locked room to Charles. I did not relish either the notion of M. Hervet's cool smile if he should discover that Rosie's memory was still powerful with Charles, or Charles's vexation to have this discovered; but I could not speak of the room to Charles unless he spoke to me of it first. So my mood was not sunny as I stood in the Wool Royd doorway and welcomed M. Hervet to his son-in-law's house.

M. Hervet was not, however, the man to admire a sunny temper and possibly my cool formality suited him better than a warmer greeting, for he was as affable with me as the limits of his habitual ceremony allowed. Dolly had cooked us an admirable dinner and William, who was accustomed to wait on Generals, served it very correctly and well. It was mostly wasted, for the children were too frightened, Charles too gloomy and myself too anxious, to eat, while M. Hervet picked mincingly at his food as an old man will; but I could see that our table had made a good impression on him and was pleased. Presently I took the children away and left Charles and his guest to enjoy their wine together. They sat long, and from the pallor of Charles's face and the sweat on his forehead when at last he brought M. Hervet into the drawing-room, I could see they had been delving into the whole Moreys history. Then it was my turn, while Charles thankfully went away to the mill and the children to the schoolroom; and I had to describe all my adventures with Adah and Joah. It was not easy to do this in terms sufficiently composed to suit M. Hervet, and once or twice I was vexed to see a look of distaste cross his thin supercilious face.

"And what proceedings will be taken against Adah Lee?" he enquired when I had ended.

"I do not know, sir," said I—for indeed this matter was a dark place of anxiety in my thoughts.

"Charles must harden his heart and have a case brought against her."

"Charles is not very apt to harden his heart."

"Then you must harden it for him. It is your duty."

"I shall try to perform my duty as a wife," said I, very coldly.

M. Hervet gave me a shrewd glance and dropped the subject. Then he began to skirmish, as I had guessed he would, about the subject of his daughter's personal belongings. I told him plainly they would be divided between Dick and Tessie, and to forestall any further enquiry added that when the division had been made and the house rearranged, I should be happy to welcome him again and show all these matters to him. My cheek burned as I said this and my choice of expressions was not as easy as I wished; he gave his cold smile and bowed his head in reply without speaking, so that I felt humiliated. Luckily just then William brought in tea and the children followed. This was an agreeable diversion, for Dick did well with handling cups and Tessie for once sat up straight in her chair instead of lolling. But after the tea had been taken away a long, long hour of tedium and constriction followed. The children huddled themselves on either side of me on the sofa and nestled up to me so that I was obliged to put my arms round them, though I was far from wishing to hurt

M. Hervet's feelings by appearing to take possession of his daughter's offspring. Tessie grew drowsy and had to be nudged from time to time to keep her awake; Dick, who was always more nervously aware than his sister, fixed his eyes on his grandfather in a look of watchful alarm which must have been disconcerting, if anything could disconcert M. Hervet. At last, at long, long last, Charles came in to say that Jacob and the gig were waiting.

We three looked up at him in eager relief. Charles turned pale and the sweat started again on his forehead.

I kept my smile fixed on my face but I was cut to the heart, for I guessed what he was thinking. *These are Rosie's children, this is Rosie's father; if all had gone well, if my life had not been ruined by the consequences of my father's sin, it would be Rosie herself sitting amongst them.* "Oh, Charles, Charles!" I thought in agony.

"Dick, Tessie—get your hats," commanded Charles. "You can ride down as far as the Ire Bridge in the gig with Jacob and your grandfather, and walk home together."

Dick and Tessie hesitated, doubtful, as I saw, whether the pleasure of the ride outweighed the prospect of another half-hour with M. Hervet. Charles knew this well enough and laughed, but would take no denial.

"Be off now," he said, pulling Dick up from the sofa. "You can ride together in the back of the gig. No walk, no supper."

Cheered by the thought of sitting apart from their grandfather the children shot from the room, tossing their arms and laughing. Soon, to my very great relief, the gig drove off, the old man swathed in cloaks beside Jacob, the children pushing each other playfully in the rear. I returned to the drawing-room very soberly. Charles followed me.

"You saw that I was upset, distressed, when I came in just now?" he said.

"Yes, I saw it. But I understand, Charles," I went on hurriedly, turning to him. "They are Rosie's children and Rosie's father—naturally you wished you saw Rosie with them. I understand perfectly."

"No, my dear Eleanor," said Charles, drawing me to him and kissing me. "You do not understand at all. It is true that

I thought: these are Rosie's children, poor Rosie should be with them. For a moment I imagined it was so. And my heart sank like a stone. I felt a terrible loneliness. If Rosie had lived and she were my wife instead of you, I should be a miserable man. Is it wrong to feel like that? Happen it is. But I can't help it."

This was happiness indeed. But not wishing to appear to clutch it too greedily, I buried my face in his shoulder and said nothing.

"Listen, love," said Charles in his kind loving tones. "Come upstairs with me and let us look into the locked room. It is stupid to keep it locked; it is bad for us, it is bad for the children. Whether I can ever compose myself to sleep in it, I do not know; but I must try, I think."

"If not, we can put Tessie into it," said I quickly.

Charles frowned. "It is too big and handsome a room for that little minx," he said.

"Tell me, Charles," said I when we stood together in the locked room. "Do you wish it to remain the same, or shall I try to change it?"

"Change it," said Charles briefly. "There is plenty of stuff about the house and in the store-room."

In spite of himself he looked ill at ease, so I said no more but led him away downstairs to the supper table.

Accordingly next day William and Dolly and I set to work with a will and took every piece of furniture out of the locked room. The handsome rose-coloured bed-hangings and curtains I put in Tessie's room, and divided the furniture between Dick and Tessie. At this Tessie, who had been rather sulky and pouting hitherto, became happy and excited and helpful, and she and Dick ran about the house with flushed faces, carrying buffets and chairs and bolsters in their arms and laughing at each other over the top. The press and the chest of drawers were full of the most exquisite dresses and underlinen, with laces and ribbons and gloves and small dainty shoes enough to stock a shop, all in good condition and scented with lavender. Remembering M. Hervet's circumstances I knew that Charles must have lavished all these upon his pretty Rosie. But I need not feel jealousy of her now, only pity; poor Rosie! Her life had been short, difficult and tragic; altogether too hard for her butterfly disposition; one could not grudge her a few brief enjoyments of luxury. I told Tessie that all these clothes were hers and we would have them made modish for her; whereupon her eyes widened in ecstasy and she ran away to her own room and was seen no more for the next hour, when, going in to take a pink cushion, I found her trying on a white silk dress before the glass, the floor about her strewn with garments—she had emptied every drawer in her impatient vanity. Some words of reproof rose to my lips and I was about to utter them when my eye was caught by a little packet of yellowed paper, a very tiny square, much folded, with some spidery writing, which lay on the floor where Tessie's ransacking of the dressing-chest had cast it. I picked it up and read in a childish staggering hand: *C's air.* What can this be, I thought? Something Rosie treasured? I unfolded the paper very carefully so as not to tear it, and there lay a curl from my Charles's head; its texture and soft gold were now too familiar to my hands and eyes for me to mistake it. I uttered no word of reproof to Tessie but kissed her instead, and folded the paper and took it away and put it in a little drawer in Charles's dressing-table.

By the evening the locked room was transformed. In the storeroom above the cowshed there was much furniture, old of course but some of it very graceful in my opinion. The hangings of the bed were now a soft pale blue, with a quilt of the same rather faded but beautiful brocade and window-curtains to match; and there was even a pale blue cushion of the same fabric, which I put in an armed chair by the window. The bedside carpets were also blue in colour. The ewer and basin were of fine blue-and-white foreign-gilt china, and there were some pretty china figures, cherubs, for chimney ornaments. There was a tall swing glass to match the elegant chairs, and a painted buffet with a design of blue and white and gold flowers. When we had polished and washed all this and arranged everything neatly and set the window open to let the summer sun in, it struck me that these happy coincidences of colour and shape were not accidental; the pieces had all formed part of a bedroom once before, a room which might have been called the Blue

Chamber. Remembering the fair complexion and blue eyes of Charles's mother Caroline in the portrait in the dining-room, I surmised that this had been her furniture, bought for her on her marriage, and it pleased me to think that my father had perhaps seen and handled it.

All this rearrangement had taken longer than I thought, and I had only just begun to tidy my appearance, and Dolly to prepare the supper, when Charles came back from market. I could not bear that he should enter the house without a greeting, so I hastily threw on a bedgown and ran to the stairhead and called him to come up and see the results of my day's efforts. He smiled and ran up the stairs cheerfully, · but I could see that he was really uneasy and put on this pleased air for my benefit, so I resolved at once not to demand any expressions of satisfaction from him and to be ready to give up the plan of moving into this room without any reluctance, if he desired it.

"What do you think of it, Charles?" said I in a calm unexacting manner as he came in. "We can move in here or not, just as you wish."

"It is very peaceful," said Charles, glancing about him. "What have you done with the other furniture?"

I told him, then put into his hands the little yellowed packet.

"Ah, poor Rosie!" he exclaimed, turning over the lock of hair. "Poor child! I remember when she cut this."

"She loved you, Charles," said I softly.

"Happen she did—as much as she was able," said Charles. "Poor child! Her life was wretched."

He sighed, and refolded the packet; then laid it back in the drawer from which I had taken it.

"Yes, it is peaceful here," said Charles, and just as he was, still wearing his riding-boots and with his whip under his arm, he threw himself down on the bed and laid his head back on the bolster.

Repressing the remark which every housewife desires to utter on seeing riding-boots deposited on a brocade quilt, I moved about the room quietly, straightening the china figures and so on, waiting for Charles to declare his decision. But he did not speak, and when I turned back to the bed

I saw that his eyes were closed and he was breathing deeply. He had fallen asleep. As I looked down at him lying there, with the deep lines in his forehead belying the youth proclaimed by his long golden lashes, it seemed to me that this was the first truly care-free sleep he had enjoyed since Rosie's death twelve years ago. I tiptoed from the room and ran down to tell Dolly she need not hurry with supper.

When I returned, with the usual perversity of events Charles had woken, and was busy transferring his shaving tackle, his best shirts, whips, hats and other such treasures to our new Blue Chamber. He had already discovered, too, that one of the cherubs had a tip off his wing and some of the handles of the furniture were broken. Next morning he sent up a carpenter to repair these, and he was always very solicitous in care for the room, and presently bought an agreeable painting in a gilt frame, a seascape with blue waves, to hang above the mantelpiece. As long as we remained in Wool Royd, as you remember, it was always our room, and we were very happy there.

CHAPTER IV

It was two days after our removal into our new room, when I was feeling secure in Charles's love and our future happiness, that the blow fell. As soon as Charles entered the house that night I knew that something was wrong. He did not smile, he did not whistle, and though he caught me up in his arms as usual, he did not hug me with joy and pleasure, but rather as though he wished to protect me from some threatening evil.

"What is the matter, love?" said I immediately.

"Oh, Eleanor!" said Charles in a tone of despair. "I should never have married you."

"It is too late to say that now, my dear," said I in a playful tone—for indeed I had already some reason to think I was with child, and had communicated this to him the night previously, when he had shown great delight in it.

"Don't tease, Eleanor," said Charles sadly. "The trouble is too serious."

"You are tired, love," said I, "or you would not see it in so gloomy a light. Surely there is no trouble we cannot overcome together."

He sighed and looked so wretched that I was alarmed, and drew him into the drawing-room and made him sit in his armed chair and fetched some wine for him. He barely sipped it, then put the glass down and said in a low voice:

"It is Adah."

My heart sank.

"There will be a case against her and we must give evidence?"

"No. She is mad. Doctors and magistrates have examined her and they say she is mad and therefore she cannot be indicted. She is *non compos mentis*, a lunatic, and cannot be arraigned on a capital charge, that is how they put it. A law officer has been with me this afternoon to tell me."

"But, Charles," said I, puzzled, "we do not *wish* Adah to be arraigned, do we? She has had many wrongs, and I should not like to think of her being transported.

"Then what shall we do with her?" said Charles. "Send her to some Bedlam or other? Have her locked up and chained?"

"Oh, Charles!" said I. He did not add: "Or shall we bring her to the care of her friends, at Wool Royd?" But I knew his meaning, and for the moment I felt I could hardly bear it. To have Adah again at Wool Royd? That dark shadow again over the house? There was Dick to think of, after all, and perhaps my own children. On the other hand, if Adah had had her rights from John Moreys, she would have been the mistress of Wool Royd. "Oh, Charles!" I said again, and I knelt down beside him and laid my head on his knee, for this was my life's bitterest moment.

Charles stroked my hair, fondling me.

"She is no kin of ours, she is Jacob's grandmother," he said. "Jacob and Mary could marry and take her into their house."

"We cannot do that, Charles," said I, weeping. "We cannot spoil their young life together."

"You are younger than Jacob, Eleanor," said Charles; "and a bare few months older than Mary."

"Still," said I, lifting my head, my face all tear-streaked, "we cannot do it, husband."

"No, we cannot do it."

"We must have her here, at Wool Royd."

Charles sighed. "Aye—I see nothing else for it. I should never have married you, Eleanor!" he exclaimed in agony. "You must leave me—you must go away! I have no right to demand this sacrifice; I can't bear to make you so wretched."

"It is the children who worry me, Charles, the children! How shall we keep her so that she is not a blight on their happiness? Where shall we put her? The room she used to have, on the ground floor beyond the kitchen, is given up to William and Dolly."

"There is the store-room above the cowshed, and the little closet next to it. We can put her there, with a woman from the village to look after her, and a barred door to cut it off from the rest of the house."

"Yes," said I, weeping.

"No, we won't do it!" cried Charles suddenly. "We won't have her at Wool Royd!"

"Yes, we must."

"Eleanor, there is only you in all the world who would accept this duty so nobly."

"It is for you I grieve, Charles!" cried I, throwing myself into his arms. "It is so unjust, so unfair to you! Are you never to have any happiness? Is your expiation of your father's sin never to be ended?"

We clung to each other and wept together.

"Have you told Jacob, Charles?" said I at length, when my fit of sobbing had died down.

"No. I thought it best to make our own decision first."

"I fear he will take it badly. And Dick? He will be heartbroken! He has been a different child without Joah and Adah!"

"Dick and Tessie must go away to school."

"For these few weeks we have all been so happy," said I, weeping again.

"We will not receive her," began Charles again.

We repeated our arguments over and over; but what was

the use? Adah was a murderess, in intent if not in fact—we should never be entirely certain of her hand in the death of Rosie. But she was also a poor old woman, wronged, crazed and destitute through the ill conduct of Charles's father; we could not throw her on the dungheap and go our way rejoicing.

Next day Charles sent carpenters and masons to the house, and within a week the two rooms were cleared and cleaned, and bars put to the windows, and an entrance with a strong door made from our Wool Royd landing. "We are exchanging one locked room for another," I thought bitterly, as I went about the business of finding mattress and bolster and blankets, curtains and table and lamp, for Adah's comfort. When the rooms were finished, they looked clean and neat and even pretty, and the elderly woman from Booth village whom Martha Greaves had found for me as an attendant for Adah seemed much pleased. She was a kind old thing, but she did not stay long; indeed we had a succession of old beldames for this purpose; they were always being summoned away to daughters' confinements or grandchildren's illnesses, and naturally obeyed these family calls without caring for our convenience, so that Dolly and I were often left, in spite of all Charles's efforts, to wait upon Adah ourselves.

My fear that Jacob would take the matter ill was only too well justified. When it was all arranged and the date of Adah's coming settled—Charles was paying for her maintenance meanwhile, in York—Charles kept Jacob in the mill till the men had gone, then took him into the counting-house and told him. Poor Jacob broke down at once; crying out: "No, no! Not here, Uncle Charles! Not here!" he burst into tears and ran out of the mill to the Dennetts' house and sobbed on his mother's shoulder. An hour later he came up to Wool Royd looking pale and wild, and told Charles he could not remain here, within sight and sound of his grandmother; he wished to return to Birmingham to Messrs. Boulton and Watt's factory, immediately. He also wished to marry Mary Greaves at once and take her with him.

Charles was furious—chiefly, I think, on my account. He

and I had been sitting in the drawing-room when Jacob came; Jacob asked to speak privately to his uncle and the two men went across to the dining-parlour together. To my great distress and alarm I heard their voices continually rising in anger; at last I could bear it no longer but laid down my sewing and went out into the hall. Just then Jacob rushed out of the dining-room, with tears on his cheeks and his pleasant open face all pulled awry; Charles followed him, quite scarlet from rage and shouting. Jacob flew from the house, banging the door after him, and I tried to soothe Charles's temper, at first with little success.

"All falls on you—why should Jacob leave his grand-mother for you to tend? And then the cowardly cry-baby thinks he is fit to take a wife," stormed Charles.

This battle raged for several days, and at first it seemed likely to go ill for Jacob, for you may well imagine that Mrs. Greaves was not anxious to see Mary married to Adah's grandson and Joah's brother. She was, therefore, eager to pack Jacob off to Birmingham out of Mary's way, and as Lucy and I were equally eager for his departure, though not for Martha's reason, Charles found himself outnumbered, and after much grumbling, gave way. But that Jacob should take a wife with him seemed to Charles outrageous.

"He's not fit to care for a wife. He's barely able to care for himself. Mary's a nice, good girl and he shouldn't wish to drag her down. I'm still paying money to Birmingham for him to learn the trade, and he thinks he can support a wife!"

"Mary will be a support to him, perhaps," said I—rather too earnestly, I fear. "That happens sometimes to a husband with a good wife."

"Does it indeed?" said Charles with a spark in his eye. "It had better not be so in this house, Eleanor!"

He went off and slammed the door behind him.

At this moment, with Adah coming on the morrow, Dick and Tessie snappish and resentful because I would not satisfy their curiosity about the purpose of the barred room, and now Charles vexed with me, I own I should like to have sought the relief of tears. But tears—and I address this particularly to you, my dearest Catharine—tears in a woman have a very different effect before and after marriage. Before, they are an invitation to the man who loves her, to soothe and caress and offer his protection, to promise her a more agreeable life under his care. After, they are a reminder to the man of his responsibility for his wife's happiness. If he is hard and selfish, they are a vexing reminder; if like your father he is tender and generous, they are a troubling reminder; in either case they give him pain. I had already learned this by Charles's severe distress when I wept about Adah, so now I struggled to master my tears. I was glad I had done so when William suddenly opened the drawing-room door and announced:

"Miss Mary Greaves."

Mary had brushed her brown hair very thoroughly and all her dress was neat and clean, but she had not put on any finery to visit me, for which I thought well of her. When I had greeted her and seated her on the sofa, sitting very erect with her hands tightly clenched and her brown eyes wide she burst forth at once:

"Mrs. Moreys, I have come to ask you to help me and Jacob."

"My dear, I am trying to help you," said I, not without a little vexation when I thought of my recent efforts. "But could you not be patient for a while, and let Jacob go to Birmingham alone?"

"I dare not let him go alone, Mrs. Moreys," said Mary. "In the state he is in, if he goes alone he will take to drink and bad company."

This is not a child, a silly girl, I thought; she is a woman fighting for her man; she has sense and spirit; I respect her. "He might even take a wrong turn and become like Joah," added Mary in a low tone.

"You are right," I said. "But in that case Jacob must stay on in Moreydale till you can be married, and Adah comes here tomorrow."

Mary shuddered. "It will kill Jacob if he sees her!" she cried.

"There is no need for him to see her; he need not come to this house," said I, rather coldly.

"He will know she is here—he will hear her cries," objected Mary.

She is her mother's daughter after all, I thought; she does not care to what she condemns others, so long as she saves the one she loves. Would I have done the same for Charles? I wondered.

"Then what can we do?" I said. "It is not possible for you to be married before tomorrow morning, Mary. Even if Mr. Moreys withdrew his opposition—and I must remind you, disagreeable as it is, Mary dear, that Jacob is dependent on him at present for his livelihood—your father and mother would never agree. It would look as if—it would be bad for your reputation, Mary."

"As if I cared for my reputation compared with Jacob!"

"But your mother would never agree."

"Then I shall run away with Jacob without getting married."

"Come, Mary," said I. "You are talking nonsense."

Mary set her mouth and looked obstinate.

"We could get married in Birmingham," she said.

"Mary, you know quite well it is wicked to go away with a man unmarried."

"Not with Jacob it wouldn't be," said Mary. "It would be more wicked to let him go to Birmingham alone. Surely you understand that, Mrs. Moreys?"

The picture of Charles as he used to sit drinking alone rose before my eyes, and I felt a strong sympathy for Mary. Had I been in her place, I believe I should have acted as she did—but then, Charles would never have shirked his duty and thrown me into such a difficulty.

"It is unmanly of Jacob to put you in such a position," I exclaimed.

"But it's been so terrible for him, Mrs. Moreys."

"He has only to wait three weeks for the banns to be put up and a proper wedding arranged."

"You will persuade Mr. Moreys to agree to a wedding then?" cried Mary, her brown eyes sparkling.

I sighed. "I will try," I said.

"Then why can't Jacob go and wait in Annotsfield with that old man, the one that Joah stayed with?" said Mary.

"M. Hervet? That is a very sensible suggestion," I was

beginning, when William ushered Mrs. Greaves in upon us.

Between hurry, the summer sunshine and vexation, Martha, though not in her best purple this time, was hot and panting. She attacked Mary roundly for coming to Wool Royd without her knowledge, and as good as told me to mind my own business. I felt some sympathy for her, for if Tessie had gone thus to Upper Hey to seek Martha's advice I should have been vexed; much more then for a real daughter.

"It is partly my business," I answered her mildly; "since Jacob is now my nephew."

"Charles Moreys disapproves of the marriage and you know it."

"No—he simply wishes Jacob and Mary to wait a little while."

At this Mary broke in, repeating that she would not let Jacob go to Birmingham alone, and we all argued our own views of the matter with much determination, our voices, I am afraid, growing shriller and angrier as we proceeded.

"Jacob Lee is a good-for-nothing ne'er-do-well," shouted Martha Greaves at length, "and neither Tom nor I are minded to let him have our daughter."

"I shall never marry anyone but Jacob," cried Mary.

"Jacob is a good, kind lad, and they love each other."

"You can't live on love," snapped Martha.

At this brutally candid statement of her view of life, which admitted no considerations save those of worldly prosperity, my temper suddenly left me.

"You have blighted the life of one innocent man for years by your unjust suspicions," I cried angrily. "Do not be guilty also of ruining his nephew!"

Martha stared at me in amazement. Then suddenly her hot red face twisted and tears spurted from her eyes. With a sound between a wail and a groan she started to her feet and hurried from the room and from the house; we saw her pass the open windows, trotting in a fever down the yard; she was sobbing raucously.

"Go after her quickly, Mary," I urged. "Take her part against me, and comfort her."

Mary, still agape at this extraordinary behaviour from her

mother, whom she had never before seen disconcerted, obeyed me in a daze.

I sighed and felt ashamed of my temper; yet after all what I had said was true and I was not ashamed of that.

A moment later Charles came in. I was surprised to see him, not thinking it was yet time for him to return from the mill; but the afternoon had passed while we three women had disputed.

"What the devil have you been saying to Martha Greaves, love?" he enquired with a laugh. "You seem to have sent her away with a flea in her ear. I met her in the lane fairly bellowing."

Holding my head down in some embarrassment, I told him all that had happened.

"Well, my dear," said Charles in a very kind tone, when I had finished, "I suppose I had better go write a note to M. Hervet. Or stay—I can take Jacob down to him tomorrow, on my way to York to fetch Adah."

Thus it was all settled, and next day Charles took Jacob with him down to Annotsfield.

It was about eight o'clock at night when I heard the wheels of the chaise Charles had hired in York come rolling down the hill to the beck and then creak and thump slowly up the rough lane to Wool Royd. (We had sent Tessie and Dick to Upper Hey for the evening, so that they should be out during Adah's arrival.) I own I was heartsick and daunted as I came down to the door to meet Adah. It was a lovely summer evening, very still and warm, with a clear pale blue sky, quite cloudless; the trees and the hills lay calm and contented in the evening light; everything seemed serene except myself. If only Adah were not coming, I thought rebelliously; if only I were meeting Charles as usual, how happy I should be! Only these few weeks of happiness, and then this great cloud on our life, this trial! My heart was so heavy that it was with great difficulty I forced myself to stand erect and smile; only my concern for Charles enabled me to put a quiet face on my trouble.

The chaise drew up by the front door, and Charles descended.

At the first sight of his face my heart lifted. I knew his

expressions so well, I saw at once that the trouble was not to be as great as we had dreaded. Without speaking to me Charles turned to the chaise, and with much care and difficulty he and the coachman lifted out the other passenger.

But this was surely not Adah, I exclaimed to myself, astonished. Instead of a fierce wild gipsy, proud, sly and dangerous, I saw only a poor decrepit imbecile old woman. Her hair had grizzled and had been cut short in prison—so that she could not hang herself with it, I learned later—and fell about her face in smooth grey strands; her body had thinned, her bosom fallen. She could not stand, but clung pathetically to Charles and the coachman, her wrists quivering and her pulse jumping with the effort. Having taught myself always to remember, as I have said before, that if Adah had her rights she would be mistress of Wool Royd, I had decided before what would be a proper greeting for her, and I now stepped forward and said in a voice I strove to make friendly:

"Welcome home to Wool Royd, Adah."

She smiled at me and nodded pleasantly. But her mouth hung slackly open, her eyes were vacant of expression.

"She understands nothing, love," said Charles quietly. "Go ahead and open the doors—I shall have to carry her."

He took her up in his arms and carried her up the stairs and into the room prepared for her, and the village woman and I undressed her and put her into bed; and there she lay, quiet and mild, pleased with everything and understanding nothing, for the thirteen years which her life lasted.

When I came dowstairs again, Charles had taken the coachman down to the mill to put away the chaise for the night and stable the horses, and Dick and Tessie were running up the lane to Wool Royd. They had heard the chaise pass and were eager to know the identity of our visitor. With what unspeakable thankfulness I greeted them, you may imagine.

"Adah has come back to us—she will live in the room above the cowshed," I told them cheerfully.

Tessie scowled, Dick turned pale and shrank.

"She is ill and quite changed, and I want you to come and say goodnight to her."

"*I* shan't come. I don't want to," said Tessie, tossing her head.

"Very well, Tessie. Go up to bed, then. But, Dick," I said, taking his hand, "I want you to be brave and come and see her."

Poor Dick gave me a wretched, imploring look and his hand trembled in mine, but just then Charles came in, bringing the coachman for some supper; feeling Charles's eyes upon him Dick gave a great sigh and allowed me to draw him out of the room, for he would make any effort rather than display cowardice before his father.

I led him upstairs and past the barred doorway—which stood open; there was never any need to close it—and into Adah's little chamber. Adah lay in bed with her eyes closed; she looked a frail, exhausted, pitiful little person. Hearing our steps, I suppose, she opened her eyes and looked at Dick and myself, but without recognition.

"Why, poor old thing!" exclaimed Dick pityingly.

Very fortunately, Charles had followed us upstairs and heard this. He was pleased, and stroked Dick's head, which of course gave Dick great pleasure.

Soon we were all in bed, and the house lay hushed and quiet. Charles, who was tired after his journey, fell asleep quickly, after we had spoken together of the strange mercy of Adah's condition. But I lay awake long—not in restlessness, however, but in deep peace and thankfulness.

Jacob and Mary married about a month afterwards. Thanks to the taste, and doubtless to the stinging sarcasms, of M. Hervet, to whom Charles had supplied money to furnish out Jacob, the boy appeared in very handsome trim at his wedding. His glossy black hair had been cut and arranged and he was dressed with a sober richness, so that everyone said what a good-looking young man he had grown into. He seemed to have recovered his spirits and smiled without cessation throughout the ceremony. Mary's dress I did not care for, and Charles felt the same; it was a trifle too elaborate for her simple comeliness to carry; but her large brown eyes, beaming with hope and happiness, were beautiful. The wedding breakfast at Upper Hey was very lavish, and both Charles and Dan Dennett drank, I am sorry to say, rather more healths than were good for them. Charles carried it off well, but Dan Dennett reeled so, he could not walk home, and Charles had more or less to carry him. They stood giggling together at the Dennetts' door so long—for I think both were not sorry at heart to see Jacob's departure—that I lost patience with them and walked up to Wool Royd, and I was undressed and lying in bed when Charles at last came home.

"Do not scowl at me like that from those large grey eyes, Eleanor," said he, laughing. "I am properly drunk and I know it, but a wedding is a privileged occasion. You shall not often have to complain of this in me."

He sat on the bed and asked if he were forgiven with such agreeable endearments and caresses that after shaking my head at him and uttering his name once or twice in a reproving tone, I began to laugh and let it pass, and when he bade me kiss him, as his habit was, I complied with my usual ardour. I mention this because it was in fact the last time I ever saw him the worse for liquor.

To return to Jacob's wedding: as the young couple drove off Martha Greaves threw herself into my arms and wept on my shoulder. I comforted her as best I could, for I was truly sorry for her to lose her daughter, though in my heart I grieved more for Lucy Dennett, who for Jacob's good let her son go without a murmur. The marriage, however, as you know, turned out an extremely happy one, though childless, and Mrs. Greaves several times visited their home in Birmingham.

Jacob proved to have a curious kind of knack with these new steam engines, and with Mary's sound sense to keep him on the right road, he flourished exceedingly. Presently he began to call himself *Jack* instead of Jacob; Mary always wrote of him so in her letters, and the Greaves took it up also. Charles scoffed at this and was apt to say "Jack?" in a wondering perplexed voice when this name was mentioned, but he humoured Jacob in the matter to some extent, addressing letters to him as *J. Lee*, which would do for either name, and so on. He also sent continually very handsome presents of cloth for both Jacob and Mary, and carpets for their various houses, not to mention much money in their early years and when Jacob first began his own factory. But I do not think Charles ever quite forgave Jacob for his behaviour in the matter of Adah. In some curious way, too, the fact that Adah now was nothing to be afraid of, nothing to run away from, made his contempt for Jacob deeper. However, this did not grieve Charles as it had done in the days before our marriage, because he had other matters, more agreeable, to think of.

CHAPTER V

ONE of the great cares and joys of my married life was Dick.

After the discovery of Adah's identity and her words at the inquest, Charles fully admitted Dick to be his son, but he was not at first truly fond of him, except at rare moments. He now noticed everything Dick said or did and from anxiety about his character and upbringing was apt to be a little sharp, a little critical to the child, which made Dick suffer, for he continued to love his father dearly. On the other hand, if anyone said anything *about* Dick to Charles he was apt to be touchy, so that I had to go carefully between them. But to see Dick grow into a tall smiling lad, quite merry and natural in his ways—though always rather too easily cast down—was a continuing pleasure to me, and soon after my marriage this pleasure began.

To use a Yorkshire expression, now that Dick was no longer "pined," that is to say, half-starved: now that he had plenty of wholesome food set before him and could eat it heartily, and was not cramped in mind by the fear of Joah, he soon gained strength and began to put on height and weight. It was not two months after Dick gained a step-mother, as I often reflected with pride, when I saw that his hand was now large enough to clasp his silver christening mug without difficulty, so that his grubby little forefinger no longer appeared crooked over the top. From this time forward his appetite grew and grew till it became a joke in the family; indeed Tessie teased him cruelly about it till Charles was vexed and thundered at her. (When Charles thundered, everyone at Wool Royd trembled, just as in the old days, but such occasions grew rare and I own I took them without alarm; I was never afraid of your father after I married him.) What we did not understand sufficiently at first was that Dick himself was growing as much as his appetite. Charles indeed remarked from time to time with some annoyance that Dick's coats and breeches seemed always to be too short, displaying his (still thin) wrists and ankles; he called the boy to him and tugged at them, but without avail. We did not perceive the reason until one day Dr. Bradshaw, visiting Adah, who had a cold, congratulated us on the improvement in Dick's health, and added to Charles:

"How the boy shoots up! He'll be as tall as you, I daresay, Mr. Moreys, when he's fully grown."

Charles's look of astonished wonder, and I must say of not unmixed pleasure, was amusing to see.

This incident gave him an excuse for beginning upon me again about Dick's going to school, which was a favourite theme with him at this time. Tessie—about whose affairs I will speak later—went to school in the autumn after our marriage, and Charles wished to send Dick then also, but I resisted him. Charles grumbled but let me have my way, and we sent the boy down to the Vicar of Marthwaite every day instead, for lessons. I was determined to keep Dick at home for another year; partly to re-establish his health completely, for I thought him not yet fit for the rough-and-tumble of school, but partly from a notion, perhaps foolish, which I secretly held. I was with child, and I had made up my mind that the disagreeable Moreys tradition of strife between half-brothers should be broken, and Dick should love his new brother (or sister). This was much more likely to happen, I thought, if Dick were at home when the child was born and took an interest in him from the beginning, than if he arrived from school after a couple of months' absence and found the child a general favourite, firmly established in Dick's home.

I thought I had judged wrongly in this when my confinement came, for my labour was long and difficult, so that I could hardly rejoice at first in the birth of my darling little son, and I had to stay in bed much longer than is usual. During this time Charles was frantic with anxiety and I think found Dick's presence a nuisance, while Dick, poor lad, was wretched enough and sat about in corners, moping and pale. But, thank God, I was right after all. When at last I grew better and was able to sit up and felt my spirit return, one day I got Lucy to help me—for Lucy, I found, was excellent with children and invalids, very sweet and kind in caring for their comforts, if a little slovenly about their behaviour and appearance—and I dressed you, my darling Edward, in your best robe of fine cambric and lace, to show you off to your father when he should come home. You were always a most beautiful babe, with plenty of fair hair and very blue eyes, and a fair, easily-flushed skin, like your father's. Lucy and I were admiring you as you lay in the crook of my arm, and talking baby language to you, and Lucy was admiring the fine workmanship of your robe, when suddenly I thought with a pang: This is what poor Rosie did to Dick, the night she was drowned.

"Where is Dick, Lucy?" I asked. "Tell him I want to see him."

Dick, who had been in the kitchen talking to William, came in rather sheepishly, smiling in an embarrassed way and falling over the furniture, as young boys do.

"You have not met your brother formally yet," said I, laughing. "Come here, Dick, and make his acquaintance."

Dick, as if confronted with some peculiar new kind of frog or insect, gave you, Edward, a suspicious sideways glance. By the greatest good fortune you chose that moment to move your hands slightly and utter a small coo, whereupon an odd smile, perplexed, astonished but delighted, slowly stole over Dick's face. (His hair was on end and his shirt-collar dirty, as usual; oh dear, thought I, it is time I was up and about again, the house is going to sixes and sevens.)

"Am I allowed to touch him?" asked poor Dick, whose life hitherto, as I reflected sadly, had been made up mostly of prohibitions.

"Certainly," said I.

Dick put out one finger and very softly stroked the back

of Edward's hand. Edward cooed again and moved his fingers and toes, and from that moment Dick and Edward were fast friends and have always remained so. Dick beamed all over his face and sat down on the bed and, taking Edward's hand in his, listened with the greatest interest to all Lucy's praises of the infant—Lucy admiring Edward's ears (which were certainly very neat) and pushing up his sleeves to show his firm round little arms and turning up his robe to display his delicious toes, and so on, while I smiled with pride and at the same time tried to smooth down Dick's tousled locks, for Charles hated any kind of personal disorder.

I tell this incident, partly because it is the foundation of the strong brotherly feeling which has always existed between Dick and you, Edward, but partly also because it had (or so I like to think) another importance in Dick's life. That evening as Charles and Dick sat at supper downstairs, alone together, what must Dick do but say suddenly:

"Father, have you seen Baby Edward's toes?"

"What's the matter with his toes?" cried Charles, springing up in a panic.

"Nothing," said Dick, astonished.

"Then what the devil do you mean by giving me a fright like that?" stormed Charles. (My darling husband's language was always somewhat intemperate.)

"I didn't think he'd have all his toes so soon after being born," explained Dick. "I thought he'd be more like a tadpole."

Charles, muttering and grumbling, sat down to the table again, but after a moment threw down his knife and fork and came rushing upstairs to me, where to my amazement he insisted on examining Edward's feet. Finding them to be perfect and indeed singularly well made, he held them in his hands in a very loving manner, and meeting my astonished gaze began to laugh and tell me about the fright Dick had given him.

"And you will have given him one," said I, smiling. "Go down to him love, or he will think you are angry."

When Charles re-entered the dining-room Dick turned to him the woebegone face and frightened look which

Charles particularly disliked to see in his son, but feeling happy and relieved about his beautiful little Ned (as Charles always called Edward) he reflected that the boy's mistake was natural enough, and fell into a harangue to him such as I suppose must always take place at some time between a father and a son, ending up—and this is my point—by telling him that the human frame was very wonderful, as, if he looked at his great-grandfather's books which were on the shelf in the drawing-room, he would see. To Dick his father's words were always law, so he went immediately to the old surgeon's books (which had come to Caroline Moreys after her father's death) and began to turn them over. From that time onward Dick, who in the evening always sat in a corner with a book, gave up his torn, dirty, childish books and pored over these medical volumes—they had fearful pictures which he would not show me, so that I was sometimes troubled about the matter, but his face looked so serene and serious when he was busy with them that I concluded there could be nothing wrong.

At the beginning of the next half-year, Charles got his way and sent Dick to school in Annotsfield; the boy stayed there all week but came home on Saturday until Sunday night. I am afraid poor Dick was very unhappy at school at first. He was just the kind of boy to find school life difficult, being dreamy in mind, very sensitive in his feelings and not very strong in his body, having moreover suffered a bullying persecution from Joah all his life which had almost broken his courage. For the first few months, when he came home he looked pale and dazed and miserable and always bore some bruises, so that I was wretched about him, and one Sunday night when he was just setting off to walk back to school he threw his arms round me and cried very pitifully:

"Oh, Eleanor!" (For so he was allowed to call me, though Charles did not much relish it.) "If only I could stay at home with you and Father and Ned!"

I flew off to Charles and implored him to let Dick stay at home this once, but he would not hear of it. So then I begged him at least to write to the headmaster and make a protest about the bullying of the boy. But Charles was adamant.

"No, my dear, no!" said he. "What is the use, Eleanor? The boy must learn to defend himself—there are far worse things in grown-up life than at school, and he must learn to hold his own."

So poor Dick had to set off, pale and sniffing, though a little cheered by a half-guinea which I slipped into his hand.

"You spoil him, Eleanor," said Charles.

"I cannot bear to see anyone unhappy," said I, almost weeping myself.

I felt quite cross and vexed with my husband and ready to quarrel with him, but Charles refused to be provoked.

"I have benefited too much from your soft heart to complain of it, Eleanor," said he.

"But Charles, that poor child! Alone and friendless amid a set of heartless bullies!"

Charles laughed. "He will find his feet," he said.

Sure enough, a few weeks later Dick came home with a shocking black eye, looking very smug. He was hardly inside the house before he began to pour out breathlessly to his father a long confused story about some big lad who had been twisting the ears (I shuddered) of a small boy, who might, said Dick, easily have been Ned.

"So I hit him," said Dick with great satisfaction. "And then we had a fight."

"Did you win?" enquired Charles, who seemed highly pleased.

"Well, we were stopped before we finished," said Dick. "I don't think I won exactly. But I wasn't beat."

I was shocked, for I hate the thought of all fighting and hurting, but Charles laughed and took Dick out for a walk so that he might hear the history of every blow, and they were a good deal more friendly together after this occurrence.

For some weeks I watched Dick apprehensively lest he should show signs of becoming brutal. This did not happen; he remained kind and gentle in nature and had few fights, and I came later to understand that it was only when some smaller child was bullied that his anger rose. His own wretched childhood under Joah's oppression made him passionately sympathetic towards their feelings and this passion grew and grew till suddenly he forgot all fear and hit the oppressor with all his strength. But it was while I watched him thus carefully that I saw something I had missed before: namely that Dick went often in and out of Adah's room. Remembering that for years Adah had diminished Dick's health by a slow poisoning and meant eventually to take his life, such visits seemed unnatural and I was troubled by them. One day, hearing his voice in her room, I went in. He was sitting on her bed, holding one of her thin brown wrists in his hand. Adah, whom we kept very clean and nice in a pink bedgown, was gazing at him from her bright vacant eyes with a look which in a sane person might have been called smiling fondness, and they were laughing together. I felt partially reassured, but some of my uneasiness still remained, and as Dick and I left the room together, I said doubtfully:

"You would not hurt Adah, would you, Dick?"

"Of course not!" said Dick, flushing angrily.

"Why do you go so often to see her, dear?" said I.

Dick scowled, quite in his father's fashion, and broke away from me.

We had an arrangement now with Dr. Bradshaw that he came to see Adah once a month without being sent for, and the next time he came I told him privately my worry about Dick. He listened thoughtfully. It was Dick's summer holidays and he was down at the mill with Charles. Dr. Bradshaw said he would make the excuse of wanting to examine the lad to see if he had caught a fever which was prevalent in Annotsfield, to draw him aside and have a talk with him.

From the nursery window (which was once Joah's and Jacob's room) I saw Dr. Bradshaw come out of the mill with Dick, and watched the two pace slowly round and round the mill pond. Although I had now long forgotten the attack on my life by the mill pond, just as I now rarely thought of Joah's dead body in the nursery, at moments of alarm and anxiety these images were apt to recur and darken my mind, and I felt a growing uneasiness lest some wretched twist in Dick's character might be in process of revelation in that place, so fatal to the house of Moreys.

When Dr. Bradshaw beckoned a man from the yard and he went into the mill, obviously to fetch Charles, I could bear it no longer; picking up Edward, who was rather vexed at being snatched from his playthings, I hurried out of the house and down the lane towards the mill pond. Just as I reached it I saw Charles, with a look of delight, take Dick's head between his hands and kiss him on the forehead. I was overjoyed but astonished and hurried towards them.

To you, Edward and Catharine, your brother Dick has always been so essentially a medical man that you probably cannot imagine a time when his vocation was not recognised. But this was the first time we had heard of it. Dr. Bradshaw told us that Dick was much perplexed because on the one hand he longed to be a doctor—he visited Adah because she was an invalid, a patient, and loved to take her pulse and listen to her heart-beats—and on the other he felt that he ought to go into the mill with his father. But Charles was profoundly moved to learn that his son wished to fulfil an ambition he himself, as he had told me, had held as a lad; he would have loved to follow his grandfather's profession, and was delighted that Dick should, so to speak, do it for him. He therefore gave his consent immediately and most cordially to the project. From that moment, indeed, Charles loved Dick as a father should love his son, and Dick was no longer afraid of him in the old way.

You know the various steps by which Dick became a qualified physician and surgeon; the apprenticeship with Dr. Bradshaw, the years in Edinburgh, the hospital in London and later in Heidelberg. He is now one of the most valued doctors in the whole West Riding, especially as regards children's ailments; I myself never hesitated to consult him about my own children, and he seems likely to be equally familiar in Catharine's nursery. He is singularly able to win children's confidence; with some little gift or understanding word or gentle caress he soothes their fears, so that they submit willingly to his examination even when it is painful. He has the same gift of soothing and cheering, too, with very old people. From the time when he settled in Annotsfield as Dr. Bradshaw's partner he always attended Adah. It gave Charles and myself very great pleasure, I must say, to see him ride up to our door on his smart cob, descend, remove his gloves, take Adah's pulse and enquire after her ailments with serious, skilled concern, then write out some learned-looking prescription. He is prosperous today, even wealthy, having taken over Dr. Bradshaw's practice when he retired; he has two fine carriage horses and an elegant brougham and a solid house in Church Street.

The only matter, indeed, in which Dick has not fulfilled every hope which his father and I have had for him is that of marriage. He has never married, and will not I think now do so. It seems as if you and he have been turned from early matrimony, Edward, by your father's first experience; but that is a mistake, my dear boys; nothing is so conducive to a good life as marriage with the right person. I should like to see you both in possession of the happiness I enjoyed for so many years with your dear father. I have lately thought, Edward, that you are becoming interested in Sir John Stancliffe's youngest daughter—a very sweet, charming young creature she is too; but Dick, though always very gentle and courteous with women, never seems to show a preference, which is a pity. However, he is so wrapped up in his doctor's work, he perhaps has no time for marriage.

CHAPTER VI

Now I must return to speak of Tessie.

As I said before, Tessie went to school, a very superior and expensive school on the Leeds road in Annotsfield, in the autumn after the marriage of Charles and myself. How we ever got her there I do not know, for she varied from day to day and hour to hour, indeed a dozen times in every hour, as to whether she was willing to go or not. At length Charles put down his foot and thundered at her, saying that she must go without any more ado, he would have no more nonsense about it. In this scolding he called her *Theresa*, as he usually did when vexed with her. (The name was Rosie's choice, I gathered; I believe it was her mother's.) Tessie fell silent and seemed to brood, and after a moment enquired:

"What will they call me at school, Father?"

"They will call you Miss Moreys chiefly," I struck in.

Tessie's bright eyes opened wide and she gazed at me in astonishment, and then from me to Charles to see if he thought what I said true. Finding no disclaimer from him, she turned to me again and perceived I was not joking. She said no more, dropping her eyes so that her long dark lashes veiled them, but a half smile crept over her face and it is my belief that this promised ceremonious address, which tickled her vanity, had more to do with her acceptance of the notion of going to school than all her father's commands and my representations of the accomplishments she would acquire there, though the outfit of dress which had to be bought for her was also a great help, in persuasion. Tessie indeed was so fond of dress that she was even willing to accompany me when I bought clothes for myself—now that I was Charles's wife, I fully accepted the necessity of doing him all the credit I could in my appearance. (It is true that Tessie's eyes would wander and she would begin to yawn long before the dressmaker had finished my fitting.)

The week before her departure proved a stormy one. At that time I was some months gone with child and in a rather sickly and nervous state of health; Charles was concerned about me and not disposed to forgive Tessie easily for any trouble she caused me. I was anxious, for Charles's sake, that we should have no wild tearful scenes of farewell at the school when I left Tessie there, and at the same time I felt truly sorry for Tessie, so spoiled and unused to discipline, when she should be plunged thus suddenly into the narrow conventional world of a young ladies' boarding-school. You can imagine therefore how I dreaded the actual day of her departure. Charles urged me to stay at home and let him take her, but that I did not think it kind to do, so Tessie and I set off in the gig in the morning with a man from the mill driving us and Tessie's luggage behind. The excitement of donning her new clothes and flourishing her new reticule kept up Tessie's spirits until we turned into the lane, when the poor silly child burst into a roar of tears, and howled all the way across the mill yard and through the village of Booth, so that people came out to watch us pass and I felt like an ogre. But when we turned into Iredale she became more cheerful, and was merry and talkative and turning her head eagerly from side to side and tossing her dark curls, when we entered Annotsfield.

The Miss Hansons' house was large and well ordered, and they themselves were silver-haired gentlewomen, truly well mannered and highly equipped with learning—M. Hervet had guided us well in our choice of school. Their drawing-room was full of tasteful furniture and china and they wore sober but handsome silk dresses, so that Tessie was impressed. There were several of their pupils there with relatives, fathers as well as mothers, elder and younger sisters and even one or two brothers, to all of whom we were introduced, so that it was quite a social occasion. Tessie, being subdued, behaved quietly and looked very pretty and I saw, with relief, that she had made a good impression. The dreaded moment of farewell came at last and I turned to her to kiss and hug her and assure her we would write to her often, but just as I took her in my arms and began: "Goodbye, dear Tessie," she exclaimed:

"Oh, there's Miss Aspinall's mother! I must say goodbye to her!" and ran away to a large lady on the other side of the room.

I must admit I felt disconcerted, not to say humiliated, but the elder Miss Hanson, a very discreet and dignified woman, came up to me and quietly urged me to slip away then, while Tessie's attention was engaged elsewhere. I could see that she understood my situation and meant kindly by both myself and Tessie, so I took her at her word and left, and had myself driven immediately home to Wool Royd.

When Charles came home from the mill that night, as soon as he had kissed me he said in a resigned tone:

"Well, where is she?"

"Tessie?"

"Who else?"

"She is at school," I faltered, perplexed.

"Nay! Has she really stayed there? Have you learned to harden your heart? I made sure you'd bring her home," said Charles, laughing in great relief. "I thought she would cry, and your heart would melt and you would cry, and you'd bring her back to Wool Royd."

"Really, Charles!" said I, blushing—for in truth I had feared myself that it might happen so.

"She'll come back tonight somehow," said Dick with a great air of wisdom, though he had not at that time, as you remember, had any experience of school himself.

"I reckon she will—we'd better leave a storm lantern lighted," said Charles.

Twice that evening he thought he heard wheels, and went out to see if it were Tessie returning. Then he and Dick fell into a discussion of how long it would take Tessie to walk from beyond Annotsfield to Wool Royd, supposing she ran away from school but could find no vehicle to bring her. Dick was sure Tessie was too lazy to walk, and Charles began to have visions of the child perishing by the roadside and to wonder whether he should ride down to Annotsfield in search of her. I was a little piqued by all this and said nothing, but at last told them Tessie had not cried at parting. Charles was astonished.

"And you, Eleanor? Were you also dry-eyed?"

"We had no real parting!" I cried in some vexation, and told him about Miss Aspinall's mother. Charles's face changed.

"And had Miss Aspinall a brother too?" he asked.

"Why, yes, I believe so," said I, puzzled.

"Why did you not tell us that before," said Charles, settling down in his chair and opening out the *Leeds Intelligencer*. "Tessie will be happy if her fellow-pupils have brothers. Go and put out the lantern, Dick, it will not be required."

Dick, giggling, obeyed.

I am afraid that Charles thus rightly characterised Tessie's schooldays. There are only three other things which should be said about them. The first is that the Miss Hansons soon perceived Tessie's incapacity for book-lessons, and sensibly tempering the wind to the shorn lamb, put her in the lowest class and gave her only the simplest tasks to do. Even these she was not well capable of; she could never be relied upon to do the simplest sum accurately, and her letters were shockingly ill-written and misspelled, though vivid in their headlong way. But she acquired a good surface of manners, and she always looked so pretty, and was so foolish and childish and so incapable of any sustained malice though avid enough in her own immediate interest, and then, too, I am afraid I must say, she was so well known to have a wealthy father, that she became quite a favourite and was asked to many parties and became the subject of many flirtations. The young men, however, always seemed to draw back just at the moment when they should have become serious, as if they found Tessie's silliness outweighed even her wealth and beauty when they came to think of marriage. Tessie shed some tears of vexation over these sudden retreats of her admirers and could not endure Dick or her father to tease her about them, but her heart was never concerned and she never for a moment perceived their real reason.

The next point was this: it was while Tessie was at school, and owing to her vanity, that we began to call our house *Laverock Hall*. Tessie sent letters to us at that address; at first they went astray but afterwards people grew used to the new mode. Then one Saturday when Tessie was at home, in the holidays, she invited some of her school friends (and their brothers, of course) to dinner and we made considerable preparations for their entertainment, but they were late; the hours rolled on, the dinner was ruined, but they did not come. At last Tessie in a furious burst of tears roundly accused Charles and myself of disgracing her! She had told her guests to come to Laverock Hall, nobody in the neighbourhood would know where it was, her guests would wander all night on the moors, but she would prefer that to being known to live at a place named Wool Royd. I have never raised my hand to a child but I own I longed to slap her then. Charles, however, said in a surprisingly mild tone:

"Well, Dick and I had better go and and look for them."

An hour later he returned with the guests, whom he had found down by the Stancliffes' great house near the Ire Bridge in Iredale. Poor Tessie was hard put to it to receive her guests with becoming dignity, but Charles exerted himself to win them, flattering the lads and flirting with the girls till they all adored him. Dolly and I did our best with the dinner and we made no apologies, so all passed off well.

Then one of the misses, more malicious than the rest—or perhaps her chosen beau had been paying too much attention to pretty Tessie—just before leaving turned the conversation round again to their late arrival, explaining (in very loud tones) that nobody seemed to have heard of Laverock Hall. Charles took this up promptly, and getting out an old map which was a copy I believe of that attached to the title-deeds, showed the name in print for all to see, under pretence of indicating the house's situation.

When the guests had all gone save one lad who was talking to Tessie in the yard, I said to Charles:

"It seems to me we must now call this house Laverock Hall."

"Aye!" said Charles, laughing ruefully. "Well, it is the old name, after all. Will it trouble you, Eleanor?"

"Not at all," said I primly. "It will be convenient that the house should have a name separate from the mill."

We looked at each other and suddenly laughed, for in truth we were not averse from the change, and when Tessie came in looking rather afraid and hangdog, Charles said kindly:

"Well, Tessie, it seems we now live at Laverock Hall."

Charles and Dick and I laughed; Tessie coloured and tossed her curls, but said condescendingly:

"I think you have all improved since I went to school, don't you, Father?"

The last thing I have to tell about Tessie's schooldays is less pleasant. It is simply this: never at any time then, or indeed in later days, did she show the slightest interest in my children. During her schooldays there was only you, Edward, and when I was vexed with her and trying to subdue my vexation I sometimes strove to believe that if there were a girl-baby Tessie would feel more kindly; but afterwards when Catharine was there, it proved not so. Tessie seemed always to regard you children as mere tiresome pieces of furniture. She brushed against you carelessly, sometimes even knocking you down, so that you cried, as the best of children will when hurt or frightened. She could not pick up a child safely—as for carrying one, I would never allow it—while feeding or dressing a baby was quite beyond her and she thought it tedious and disgusting. I could not credit her indifference at first, it seemed to me so unnatural in a girl, and I repeatedly tried, by asking her to help me to bath and dress Edward and so on, to rouse her maternal instincts. But it was useless and even dangerous, and I had to exercise great self-control to place Edward even for a moment in her careless unfeeling hands. At last one day I came back into the room where I had left Edward with Tessie for a moment while going to prepare his bath, to find Tessie gone and Dick carefully nursing Edward. I exclaimed and sprang forward in alarm, but Edward lying in Dick's lap was kicking and cooing contentedly. As I bent to pick up my baby, Dick whispered in my ear:

"Don't leave him alone again with Tessie, Eleanor."

I looked at him in astonishment.

"Tessie would be sorry, perhaps, if Edward had an accident, but it's too late then to be sorry," said Dick. "She'd gone away and left him on the sofa—he might easily have rolled off."

I said nothing, but most scrupulously followed the boy's advice thereafter. I cannot deny that this incident somewhat changed my feeling for Tessie.

By the time Tessie was seventeen her beauty had blossomed and she was a most lovely girl, but—in spite of all the Miss Hansons' efforts—irretrievably vain and silly. She was extravagant, too, so that I dreaded to take her near the shops in Annotsfield, especially as this year, 1812, was a bad year for trade, owing to the continuing war with Napoleon Buonaparte, which prevented our ships from taking our cloth to continental harbours, so that it could not be sold abroad. Bankruptcies abounded in the West Riding, the poorer people suffered the miseries of lack of employment, and even Charles, who so loved to be generous, had warned me to be careful in my housekeeping. As I was again with child, I saw how necessary this was, since children inevitably increase a family's expenses. However, Tessie was to leave Miss Hansons' at the end of this half-year, so her school fees would be saved to Charles—unless, as was too likely, she contrived to spend them in dress and entertainment.

Indeed we considered removing her earlier, for the

country was in a very disturbed state that year. Some of the out-of-work men had banded themselves together against the new machines which were being introduced into the cloth manufacture; they came round to lonely houses at night with masked faces and demanded money and weapons, and drilled secretly and sent threatening letters and attacked mills and the like, calling themselves (why I do not know) Luddites. This alarmed me very much, for though Charles was sorry for the out-of-work men, I knew his proud temper would not endure tame submission to any Luddites; if they came to Wool Royd or Laverock Hall they would get a fierce reception and in the affray Charles might be hurt. Charles assured me that it was not scribblers and fullers such as he who used the new machines, but those who dressed the cloth after it had been sold to the merchants; but I thought he said this only to reassure, and did not altogether believe him. On the other hand, several cloth manufacturers of the district, including Mr. Oldroyd of Iredale, had asked for soldiers to protect their machines against the Luddites, and these soldiers were billeted in Marthwaite and Annotsfield and were often brawling and drunken about the streets, so that it was hardly safe for a decent woman to go out of doors. Altogether, therefore, we felt uneasy till we could get Dick and Tessie safe at home under our own care. But I was expecting my second child in a couple of weeks, and knowing Tessie's views about infants, we thought it best to leave her at school till my confinement was over.

This was how it came about that on the evening of Tuesday April 28th, 1812, poor Charles, who was in Annotsfield as usual, it being market day, was greeted as he entered the George for a drink before riding home, with three pieces of bad news. The first was that Mr. Oldroyd had been shot by the Luddites on his way home from market; the second, that Charles's wife had been brought to bed prematurely and was like to die; and the third, that his daughter had run off with an Ensign of hussars who had been guarding one of the manufacturers' mills outside Annotsfield.

With regard to Mr. Oldroyd and Tessie, the news was true, but with regard to myself, only very partially so. I was putting Edward to bed upstairs that evening and Lucy was watching me, when I heard outside a voice calling loudly:

"He's been shot dead!"

I thought Charles was meant, and before Lucy had time to run down and bring back from William the fact that the murdered man was Mr. Oldroyd, the shock had thrown me into premature labour. My little Catharine hurried into the world as she hurries into everything, and if it had not been for Lucy I might have fared ill. As it was, with Lucy's help no great harm was done save a feeling of great exhaustion on my part, and by the time Charles (who arrived at a gallop) reached Laverock, he found he had a lively little daughter and I was able to exchange smiles with him.

"It is a pity, Eleanor," said he in something of his old sardonic tone, as he bent to kiss me, "that you don't know more of the cloth trade. Then you would know that the Luddites have nothing against *me*—*I* do not use cropping frames."

"There was no particular advantage to be gained, Charles," I managed to say, though I was a trifle breathless, "in postponing our daughter's birthday for a fortnight."

Charles laughed and went off to look for Tessie and Ensign Lacey.

He found them in York, where the poor silly children had contrived to get married, and brought them back to Moreydale with him. The Ensign was in grave danger of being cashiered for being absent from his duty just at the moment when, owing to poor Mr. Oldroyd's murder, the soldiers were particularly needed, and Charles had to beg him off from his colonel. This Colonel Hunter, a man not much older than Charles himself, Charles found stiff and formal, but very honourable and decent, and they took a liking to each other. But Charles never liked Ensign Lacey, for he was not one to suffer fools gladly, and the poor lad certainly was something of a fool, the only son of a widow who had spoiled him. For my part I did not think too badly of the Ensign. Certainly he wore his thin dark hair brushed forward in a style said to be very modish which did not really become his pale face and receding chin, though he himself attached great importance to it, using scented pomades and the like, which Charles found quite intolerable. But he was a well-bred young man, with polite manners and a kind heart when you could reach his heart through his affectations, and he certainly adored Tessie, though I will not say he was indifferent to her fortune, of which Tessie had given him an exaggerated account. He talked a great deal in a high voice, lisping when he remembered to do so and using a great many military expressions which we did not understand; when Dick once or twice asked him the meaning of them, he seemed a good deal taken aback and his explanations were confused, as if he did not understand them very well himself. It was his hussar's uniform, I think, which had attracted Tessie to him; all those buttons and frogged braids, and that elegant little coat hanging from one shoulder, called a dolman.

It would not be fair, however, if I did not record that the marriage was on the whole a happy one. The soldier's way of life at that time was very agreeable to Tessie; living in lodgings in garrison towns, with no settled home and no responsibilities, suited her exactly, as did the being fêted as the wife of a hero. Moreover, her husband had the same tastes as herself; they both loved dressing and dining and dancing and wining, not so much for the actual thing as for the display it made.

But it was just there, of course, that the trouble lay; their weaknesses were the same and so when they were together their silliness was doubled. They were always in debt—the sudden arrivals of Tessie in a hired coach, the franked letters, the visits from Ensign Lacey or some of his brother officers who went stamping about Charles's counting-house swearing military oaths and drinking brandy, to which we were continually subjected, always ended in inroads on Charles's pocket. So much was this the case that on seeing his father open one of Tessie's letters, a year or so after her marriage, and begin to frown, Dick enquired sardonically:

"How much is it this time, Father?"

It was just about this time that Dick decided to become a doctor, and our joy in this was a very happy counterbalance to the worry Tessie caused us.

No woman was ever more peevish than Tessie when she found she was with child. She wrote me a letter in her big sprawling hand, asking outright what she should do "to stop it." I replied inviting her to come to Laverock for her confinement. This she declined, for Laverock Hall was too far out of the world for her present taste, and the child, a son (whom she was careful to call Charles), was born in Southampton. When he was a few months old, however, in the summer of 1814, we suddenly had a letter from the Ensign, requesting permission to bring his wife and son to stay at Laverock for a time, as the air of the town where they were stationed at the moment was not suiting the child. I thought the Ensign displayed, beneath his formal sentences, a very honest care for his son, and so did Dick, but Charles frowned as he read the letter.

"It is all very well, Eleanor," he said. "But now peace is signed, Lacey's regiment may well be reduced or disbanded. I will not have them coming here to live on us."

"But the child?" I said.

"Oh, he must come, of course," said Charles. "But take care, Eleanor, or Tessie will leave him with you always."

To some extent this came true. The Laceys came and brought their child and left him with us.

Poor Baby Lacey! When the Ensign put him into my arms—for Tessie never at any time showed any interest in him—I was so shocked I did not know what to say. A dark wan little thing with a sweet sad look, he was so small, so ill fed, so ill clad, so—I must say it—dirty, that his appearance struck me with horror. However, in the three years we had him with us we changed that appearance greatly; we fed him up with new milk and gave him the benefit of fresh air and a wholesome way of living and turned him into quite a rosy child at last. Dick was never fond of him, but tended him carefully. Charles made no response when teased or congratulated upon becoming a grandfather and I do not think he loved the child, but he was extremely kind to him, being I think sorry for him. As to his father's career, there were a great many alarms and excursions about his regiment's future, when suddenly all that was put an end to by the return of Napoleon from Elba and the resumption of the war. Lieutenant Lacey (as he was by this time) went over to the Low Countries with his regiment, and was presently killed at the battle of Waterloo.

Poor Tessie, who was in Brussels, was left quite adrift and in the dumps. As soon as we saw poor Lacey's name in the gazette, we wrote to tell her to return to Laverock, and presently Charles went to London to fetch her.

He returned looking stern and troubled. It seemed Tessie had already married another officer in the same regiment, a Captain Givern. Charles had seen this man in London and he had had the effrontery to demand money, almost with menaces, from him. But Charles was not the man to come to on such an errand; his spirit was quite as fierce as any Captain's.

"Listen, Eleanor," he said. "And you, Dick. That man is a gambler and a bully. Neither of you are ever to send money to him or to Tessie without my express permission."

While I grieved that poor Tessie should after all fall into the hands of a man like Joah, Charles was troubled by the thought of such a man inheriting a quarter of Wool Royd.

"He must be kept out of the mill at all costs, Eleanor," he said. "Sell some property and give him the money, but don't let him inside the mill or he will ruin you."

It grieved me to hear him speak as if he should soon die and I should survive him. However, next moment he was speaking of a plan he had for starting a factory down in Annotsfield, for Edward's benefit, so I presumed he had no intention of dying for the present.

The next we heard of Tessie was a letter from Colonel Hunter saying that Givern had been killed in a gambling brawl, and the next was a letter from the same Colonel Hunter, requesting Charles's permission to marry Tessie.

"She will be a General's wife soon, at this rate," said Dick —Dick never had any good words for Tessie.

But Charles and I were greatly relieved that Tessie should come into the care of a good honourable man like Colonel Hunter, older than Tessie and therefore perhaps able to exercise authority over her.

All this time little Charles Lacey was living with us at

Laverock. We were willing to keep him for as long as was necessary, and Tessie would have left him with us for ever. But her new husband the Colonel took a more serious and responsible view, and came with Tessie to Laverock to fetch him. Dick was away in Edinburgh at his medical studies, so that Tessie had no pointed remarks from him to prick her vanity, and with some assistance from Dolly and myself, she played the part of good wife and loving mother, in her husband's presence, very prettily. Although I was a little uneasy when I saw her glowing beauty beside the grey hairs and serious countenance of the Colonel, I thought that she seemed to have some real respect for him and that the marriage might not turn out too badly. Charles sighed when I privately expressed this view.

"Aye, happen. If she stays with him," he said.

I own it was an immeasurable relief to us when the regiment was ordered out to India and Tessie and her husband and child sailed away from England. I chided myself often for this heartlessness on my part, but to know that she was thousands of miles from us was a true joy to me, for many reasons.

CHAPTER VII

HERE again, if this were a story-book, I should arrange the three deaths of which I have now to speak in a convenient order, putting M. Hervet's after Tessie's and Adah's, so as to settle every detail clearly. But it did not happen like that; whether fortunately or otherwise, I cannot tell.

M. Hervet fell ill at the time of the battle of Waterloo. Although he hated Buonaparte as a usurper, he could not endure to see his beloved France defeated, and when Annotsfield was rejoicing over the Allies' final victory, with bonfires and flags and ringing of bells, his poor old heart grew overcharged with contrary emotions, and he suffered some kind of seizure. He lingered for three years—so that he knew of Tessie's marriage to Colonel Hunter, of which he heartily approved—but as an invalid. Charles offered to bring him to Laverock to live but he would not, preferring to remain in his lodgings with his pianoforte and his *bibelots*. I visited him very regularly, sitting with him when his housekeeper went out, for he could not be left alone, and giving him always the latest news of Dick and Tessie. To this he always listened intently and then in his thin old voice asked many questions, which as regards Tessie it was not easy to answer, for she never wrote at any length herself and the Colonel dwelt more on military affairs than on domestic matters. The Hunters had no children and little Charles Lacey remained a delicate child; that much at least was certain.

By degrees M. Hervet resigned himself to allowing me to perform for him those intimate services necessary for one in sickbed, but he always received these in a rather petulant and grudging manner, so that I was surprised one day when, as he laid his head back on the bolster I had shaken, he observed in his most precise and formal manner:

"I hope, madame, that when you shall be old, you will have someone as kind as you are to serve you."

"You are too good, M. Hervet," I replied with the same formality, a little confused by the intricacy of the compliment.

"If there were something in which I could serve you, I would do it gladly," continued the old man.

I hastened to say that his restoration to health was the best pleasure he could give me. But he was not listening; he looked at me sideways from his pale eyes and seemed to be considering, I thought, whether to say something further. There was a pause. Old folk do not like to be hurried, so I did not speak but waited quietly, and he lay very still for a long moment. Suddenly he raised his hand from the quilt and opened his lips as if to speak; but then he seemed to change his mind; he let his hand fall and closed his eyes.

"But there is nothing," he said.

He died a few days later without recurring to the subject, and though later I regretted this silence, at the time I was not sorry.

Adah's death did not take place till some five years later —it was after Dick had become Dr. Bradshaw's partner. She had been growing very frail for some time; her body was as light and small as a child's and it seemed as if she caught cold if one so much as opened door or window. I have mentioned before how the women we employed to tend her sometimes left us abruptly in the lurch, and this was one of those occasions, when Dolly and I looked after her ourselves. It was Sunday afternoon; Edward and Catharine were out on the moor, Dolly and William were still busy clearing the dishes after our Sunday dinner. Dick, as was usual with him on Sundays, had dined with us and was strolling outside the house with his father. I heard Adah coughing very painfully, and went up to her room to give her the soothing medicine Dick had prescribed. I raised her on my arm and offered the medicine; she drank, then raised her eyes to look at me. I started back so abruptly that I spilled the medicine. For her eyes were not the vacant eyes of the mild, foolish, chuckling patient we had tended all these years, but the gleaming, angry, hating, knowing eyes of the old Adah. I put down the glass and made haste to leave the room; Adah's sardonic glance followed me and a thin ghost of her former harsh cackle sounded. I ran downstairs and called from the front door to Dick, who came in quickly.

"Adah is herself again, Dick," I told him. "It is horrible."

"Ah," said Dick in what Catharine calls his doctor's voice, and he ran upstairs. I followed him.

He went into Adah's room and crossed to the foot of the bed and leaned on it, turning on Adah a serious medical scrutiny. Adah gazed back at him, and again that faint whisper of her old sardonic laugh came from her thin blue lips.

"I'm poisoning you, my little gentleman," she said, nodding her head at Dick; "but slowly, so that nobody will know. Joah wants me to hurry, but I know my own drow best."

It seemed such a strange and sinister mixture of past and present, that she should know Dick now but think of him as a child, that I shuddered.

"Don't let it trouble you, Eleanor," said Dick in a low voice. "The end is near. Go now—there are things that I should do. I will call you at the last."

I went downstairs to Charles, who was now sitting in the drawing-room, trying his new spectacles on a pamphlet Dick had brought him.

"Adah is dying," I said. "Oh, Charles, she is her old self and it is horrible."

"We had better go up to her, we ought to be with her," said Charles, rising.

"Dick sent me away—he will call me when it is time."

"Oh," said Charles in a peculiar tone. "Well, we must obey the doctor, I suppose."

A few minutes later Dick came in.

He said gravely: "Adah is dead."

"Oh, Dick! You ought to have called me—I ought to have been with her at the end," I reproached him.

Dick said nothing. His father glanced at him shrewdly.

"You wanted Eleanor out of the way lest Adah should let out some secrets on her deathbed," he said. "Did she say anything about Tessie?"

Dick coloured and made no reply.

"What did she say? Come on, man," said Charles impatiently as Dick still hesitated. "Don't be afraid. I can guess what she said. I've guessed it for years. It's only this wide-eyed innocent, your stepmother, who is ignorant of it —or likes to pretend she's ignorant, for my sake."

At this I looked down in embarrassment, for indeed the latter was true; since Tessie grew up and her true nature revealed itself ever more fully, I had often had to prevent myself from indulging in surmises about her parentage, for fear Charles should read them in my mind.

Dick glanced from Charles to myself.

"You each guess and hope the other does not," he said.

"Leave us alone—we can manage ourselves. Tell us what Adah said. How did she put it?" Charles pressed him. "Did she say outright Tessie was her son's child?"

"She exclaimed in triumph that in spite of Joah's death, her grandchild would inherit half Wool Royd."

"Half! She forgets Edward and Catharine—or rather, she has never known them. Well, I suppose Tessie will have to have a quarter," said Charles. "We cannot begin disinheriting Tessie at this stage. Poor Tessie! She is your half-sister after all, Dick, and my niece."

"Yes. But, Father, I dislike to think that her son bears your name when he has no right to it," said Dick.

"There is an easy remedy to that, Richard," said Charles, laughing. "Marry; get a son of your own and call him Charles; then he will be a second Charles Moreys."

Dick smiled rather stiffly—for to Charles's amusement he had grown a trifle prudish since becoming a full doctor—and said nothing.

When he had gone to give the necessary notice of death, I said to Charles:

"What made you guess about Tessie, Charles?"

"Oh, a thousand things," said Charles, rustling the pamphlet impatiently.

It was then that I regretted M. Hervet's silence, for I felt sure he had known the truth of Rosie's secret.

"But, Charles," I continued, puzzled, "how could Adah scheme to marry Joah to Tessie if they——"

I stopped, unable to utter the terrible words *had the same father*. But Charles understood.

"Perhaps gipsies do not view these things as we do," he said. "Or perhaps, once Joah had got Tessie's inheritance by marrying her, Tessie's life would not have gone on for ever. What do you think?"

I shuddered and was silent. But presently I went and sat on the arm of my husband's chair, and putting my arm about his shoulders said:

"You told me yourself that Rosie disliked Tessie but was glad to bear Dick. Tessie need not have been Rosie's fault, Charles."

"If it will give you pleasure, Eleanor, I will believe so," said Charles cheerfully. "But frankly I do not now care one way or the other."

CHAPTER VIII

It was very noticeable to me, and a little sad though I understood it, that Charles felt much more kindly towards Tessie now that he was sure she was not his daughter.

We had been troubled lately by Colonel Hunter's letters, which seemed a trifle sad in tone. The Colonel was far too much of a gentleman to complain of his wife, but still the turn of his sentences, and small facts which slipped through his words—such as that little Charles Lacey needed a play-mate, *seeing he is so much alone*—made us uneasy lest Tessie should be neglecting her duties. When a scrawled note came from Tessie commanding me to send her a new ball dress (every particular of which was most meticulously described) and the letter from Colonel Hunter enclosing the note spoke of being *so much older than my dear Theresa,* I sighed, Dick groaned and Charles said sardonically:

"Tessie's up to her tricks again. I think I shall write to her myself," he added, a spark lighting his eye.

"Do, Father," urged Dick. "You're the only one she ever took notice of."

Accordingly that evening Charles made a great to-do about this letter, clearing a space for himself on the dining-room table, putting on his spectacles, having Edward sharpen a pen for him and the like. He bade us all leave him alone, and of course we obeyed, but I lingered behind the rest and coming back to him murmured in his ear:

"It would break Tessie's heart if she thought——"

"She has no heart, my dear," said Charles.

"Well, it would ruin her completely if she believed——"

"Have no fear," said Charles. "I will be very fatherly."

And indeed he wrote her a most excellent letter, in content if not in grammar, telling her how fortunate she was in her husband, what a wretched life of widowhood she might have had without him, how she could show her gratitude to him, and so on, together with a blunt refusal about the ball dress which he retracted in the last paragraph. All this was inter-spersed with amusing stories about Dick, Edward, Catharine, Laverock and Wool Royd, calculated to recall sweet memories to Tessie and touch, if anything could, her heart. He signed this lengthy but lively epistle *your loving father* and read it aloud to me with great pride.

We never knew whether this letter reached her or not, for a few months later we had a brief heartbroken letter from Colonel Hunter, saying that Tessie and little Charles Lacey had both been killed by some raiding Afghans. Somehow the letter struck us all as odd; the finding of the murdered bodies was very clear, full indeed of horrible detail, but how Tessie and her boy came to be exposed to such danger remained obscure.

"What was Tessie doing near Afghans?" objected Dick.

He repeated this so often that Charles's patience snapped, and he said crossly:

"What does it matter? She was committing some imprudence—running away from her husband or riding where he had forbidden her to go, or some nonsense of that kind. Some piece of selfish silliness, you may be sure, has cost Tessie her life at last."

I was much distressed. It was terrible to think of poor Tessie's lovely body mutilated; more terrible still to imagine the awful moments of fear which were the last of her life. Poor Tessie was never very brave. I grieved to think that I had failed in my duty to her, and wondered much what I could have done differently to make her into a better and happier woman. There had been moments when I loved Tessie very well, and would have loved her better still if she would have allowed me.

But Charles, though he shook his head and sighed and said: "Poor little Tessie!" from time to time, seemed to think that all was for the best.

"She had three husbands and three wedding outfits and she died before her beauty left her. She could hardly wish for more," he said.

Poor Tessie!

CHAPTER IX

So NOW I am free to tell of the long, glowing happiness of my married life. Many years of perfect happiness Charles and I spent together, especially (I must confess) after the dark side of the Moreys family were gone and I was surrounded only by those I loved: Charles, Edward, Catharine and Richard.

Of course we had our cares. You, Edward—so intelligent, so handsome, so quietly resolute, with occasional flashes of fire when they were necessary—you have never caused us any anxiety, only pride and admiration. But our darling naughty Catharine was a different matter. Her delicate ethereal beauty, her sparkling azure eyes, her tossing hair (so fair and fine, like spun silk) made her look a little angel as a child when she was in repose—but then she was very rarely in repose, always in wild tomboy action. For climbing trees, galloping fierce horses, falling into streams, ascending precipices, separating fighting dogs, swinging on the crane hook and defying any person she saw ill-treating a child or animal, there was never your equal, dearest Catharine! These escapades caused us great alarm at first, but gradually we came to learn that Edward, without any fuss or excitement, always quietly rescued you, and brought you home, soaked and tattered perhaps but laughing and undamaged. How many times of an evening, you two asleep upstairs after a wild day on the moors, there would come a knock on the Laverock door, and in a moment William would announce in a peculiar tone: "A man from the village, sir"—or from Iredale or Marthwaite or even somewhere further afield. "I've put him in the dining-room." Charles would dash down his newspaper and take off his spectacles and give me a grimace which meant: "Catharine again!" and go off buttoning up his coat and assuming a stately expression. Sure enough, the man, some respectable farmer or clothier, would begin in vexed tones:

"I thought I ought to tell you, Mester Moreys—I saw your Cathie this afternoon"—on top of Scape Scar Crag, or in the middle of the River Ire, or in a field with a bull, or slapping the face of some village lad who had kicked a dog or otherwise displeased her.

Charles developed a special behaviour for these interviews. He listened gravely, and at the conclusion of the complaints thanked the man with great dignity and sincerity and promised to scold his little daughter in a suitable manner.

"I will speak to her severely—I will not mince my words, I promise you."

At this the man's face would change as a look of regret came over, clouding it. "Nay!" he would say: "Nay! I don't know as there's any call to sort Miss Catharine. She weren't doing no harm. It were only for her own sake, like, I come and tell you."

Charles now allowed his own expression to soften. "She *is* a little wild," he would admit regretfully.

"Well, childer!" would say the man, shaking his head over all children. "Childer, tha knows, Mester Moreys! Still, they're worth it."

Charles now gave him a glass of ale and they parted excellent friends with no more said of Cathie's misdemeanours.

For everyone loved the little Catharine and she was indeed a most lovable child: the truest, sweetest, warmest heart, the most loyal in her affections. If we had been grieved with her for some wild doing, she listened restlessly to our mild scoldings, shifting from one delicate foot to another and flying off the moment we had done without any expressions of regret, so that Charles and I sighed sometimes and shook our heads over her. But then she would skip into the kitchen and rapidly bake a batch of curd tarts such as her father loved —her pastry was wonderfully light, so that the tarts rose into golden fluffy towers; or she would lay a nosegay beside each of our plates; or I would come down in the morning to find all the plants watered, the lamps filled, the drawing-room ornaments dusted—these were her ways of showing that she loved us. (I hope you have not forgotten your ways of baking, Catharine, just because you have married a man of title.) With you, Edward, Catharine has always been at her best; most quiet, most responsible; you do not need to talk, you understand each other.

Dick and Catharine together always remind me of a large Newfoundland dog with a little terrier skipping and barking round it, the large dog following the small one's quick movements with slow, bewildered, but not unfriendly eyes. (Dick's build is rather plump and massive; by the time he was twenty he was very little shorter and distinctly heavier than his father.) Indeed in Cathie's very young days I was beginning to be unhappy about their relationship, for Cathie's tongue, like her father's, can be sharp, and she teased Dick about his dark coat and solemn doctor's ways, and liked to tousle up his hair with a quick gesture as she passed, which grieved poor Dick, who had trouble enough keeping his hair down without Cathie ruffling it. I could have cured this in a moment by telling her of Dick's sad early days, but I wished her to feel, not pity but respect for her brother, so I left it for awhile, and when Tessie came with Colonel Hunter to fetch away little Charles Lacey, of course Tessie cured it.

For both of you, Edward and Catharine, you being then eight and six years old respectively, took a hearty dislike to Tessie, I am afraid. Edward saw through her very soon, disliking her affectation of considering Laverock very provincial and remote, and noting how she always felt faint if there were any work to be done about the house, Cathie came to hold the same opinion more slowly, but with even greater force. It was my private task at that time to try to persuade Tessie on Dick's behalf to return the locket he had lent her (which she had never surrendered in spite of repeated requests); this Tessie, though I told her how much he valued it, how their mother had put it round his neck and so on, always refused to do.

"It's the only good piece of jewellery I have," she said, and "What does a man want with a locket?" and: "I'm the eldest after all," and: "Dick is always so selfish," with other such peevish objections, which ended always in hints that Dick or her father should give her some other jewellery to replace the locket, which she would then give up. This Dick could not and Charles (because she had had so much from him already) would not, do.

Cathie standing beside my knee while these arguments went on—for I had to take my opportunity while the men were out, not wishing to put Tessie in a bad light before her husband—Cathie, as I say, hearing all this, fixed her eyes on Tessie in amazement and wonder, never having heard utterances of this kind before. At last one day when Tessie was as usual bemoaning her inability to return the locket because of her lack of jewels suitable to her position, Cathie impulsively stretched out her little wrist, on which was a tiny gold bracelet Charles had bought for her, and exclaimed: "You can have this, Tessie." Even Tessie, I think, felt a trifle ashamed at this; she crimsoned and pushed the child's arm away and told her sharply not to be a silly little girl.

This affair threw Catharine entirely on Dick's side; she said no more at the time, but when I set her to hemming handkerchiefs for a Christmas present for her father, she said of her own accord: "Two for Father, one for Ned and one for Dick," and when Dick came home from Edinburgh, she threw her arms round his neck with a loving warmth which astonished but delighted him. As she grew older, of course, she came to respect Dick's skill in healing, admiring him when he set her kitten's broken leg or dosed Catharine herself after a surfeit of green gooseberries. She still sometimes impatiently cries out on him to stand up for himself, not to be so good, and so on, but she is deeply fond of him, though perhaps in rather a protective manner except when somebody is ill. As for you, Edward, Dick and you have always been true friends, as I have told; from your early childhood when you walked down the lane for the first time holding his hand, to the day last week when you with your quiet smile gave him some excellent advice about investing his savings, you have understood each other's qualities and respected them.

Well! Like every mother, I could tell about my children for ever, but I must now explain how it was the house of Moreys came to move down into Annotsfield.

This was something of a trouble to me at first. We were happy at Wool Royd, Laverock I should say; the air was good for the children; moreover, I did not know how little Catharine's pranks would be received in Annotsfield. But after Tessie's death, when Edward was rising thirteen, Charles, who had long been talking about building a cloth factory in Annotsfield, suddenly decided and bought the land for it. I could see that his restless and determined temper would no longer be satisfied with Wool Royd, which was now in such perfect order that there were no fresh improvements to be made there, so I acquiesced, though rather reluctantly, in the change.

"You don't understand, Eleanor," said Charles, who was pacing up and down our bedroom (the Blue Chamber) at Laverock, while I lay in bed watching him. "This is not only for myself. It is for Ned. He will never settle at Wool Royd."

"Why not?" I exclaimed, alarmed.

"It is too small for him, too obscure, too remote. He must have a larger place to give his talents range."

"You have very great faith in Edward's talents," said I, a little troubled.

"Aye, that I have. And so have you," said Charles. "Don't pretend to me, Eleanor; you know you adore your son."

"What shall you do with Wool Royd and Laverock?"

"Keep them and put Dan Dennett in charge. He can come and live here. Jacob may visit his mother more often if she lives at Laverock Hall," concluded Charles sardonically.

While the factory was building Jacob came to Annotsfield to take measurements and give advice about the boiler, engine house, shafting and so on. He brought Mary with him and they stayed with us at Laverock. They had recently visited London, for Jacob's advice was much in demand, and Jacob (or Jack, as Mary asked us to call him) began telling tales of the wonders of London in a somewhat pompous and exaggerated style. Charles grew restive under this and at last exclaimed crossly:

"You forget, Jacob, your aunt was born and bred in London."

Poor Jacob looked very much taken aback and hardly said a word for the rest of the evening, while Mary, I could see, was vexed, for the Lees were prosperous now and accustomed to receiving deference, Jacob's talent in his trade being really very considerable. I tried to smooth the matter over but not with complete success, so that it was a relief to me—and a pleasure too, for I always had a soft spot in my heart for Jacob, as the person who brought me to Wool Royd—when next day at the dinner table you, Edward, and Charles and Jacob, who had spent the day in the new factory, all talked together in a most animated fashion about the steam engines, though in language we women could not understand. You have always paid tribute to Jacob's talents, Edward, and have brought him much business, while he for his part keeps the new Ley Mills equipped with all the latest devices. I cannot help saying, however, that I wish Jacob had never entered Ley Mills, though that is said without any bitterness towards Jacob.

Well, so we moved into Ley Mills and Ley House and spent

many years of perfect happiness there. I say "perfect"—of course we had minor troubles. Sometimes Charles woke up in a gloomy mood and would murmur to me, laying his cheek against mine, that he blamed himself for the ill fates of his brother James and of Joah. He should have acted differently to them, he thought, though how, he could not discover. I too felt guilty about Joah, for it is not right to dislike people just because they are not handsome, and I had made no effort to help Joah. So Charles and I sorrowed over the house of Moreys together. But when I thought he had grieved long enough, I knew the way to cure him; I began to blame myself aloud for having failed in my duty to Tessie. This always brought Charles out of his gloom with a bound.

"Nonsense! You did everything in the world for Tessie!" he would cry, raising himself in the bed to look down sternly at me.

Then I said: "And so did you for James and Joah, and for everybody else with or without claims upon you," and I drew his head down to me and kissed him till he grew cheerful.

Again, Charles was sometimes worried by periods of bad trade, sometimes on the other hand by his abundant prosperity.

"I am not sure that it is right for the wealth of the country to get into such *lumps*," he said to me once. "It should be scattered amongst more hands.

When I repeated this to you, Edward, you frowned a little and seemed to consider, and then said slowly:

"Still, it is right to make better cloth and sell more of it, and I do not see how else it is to be managed."

We certainly grew very grand and wealthy, so that we sometimes laughed over it together, but we were very glad to see the house of Moreys rising in importance, and Edward and Catharine flourishing in their new setting as if they had always belonged there. I have not yet, and never shall, get over the idea of my little Catharine's marrying a peer, but nothing would suit Lord Intake else, and certainly he is a most good and earnest and charming young man, and Charles liked him.

As for you, Edward, your eminence quite alarms me. My darling Charles was always just a little too wilful and restless to attain a high rank in public affairs. He sometimes grumbled a little about this to me, saying that men sucked his brains for advice and his pocket for help, and then went and voted for someone else. But afterwards, when he saw Mayors and Sheriffs and so on in their scarlet cloaks, walking solemnly along with pursed lips and serious faces, he always laughed and told me he was thankful not to be one of them. But now that Ley Mills has grown so very large and important that people come from distant places (even from abroad) to see it, and you are a member of the first Annotsfield Town Council although so young, Edward, and already noted for your sound sense and excellent speeches, I can see that eminence in public affairs will come to the house of Moreys through you, and I am glad that your father saw the fair beginning of your career and was proud of it.

I must write this last page very quickly because I know I shall weep over it, and then Dick will gently scold me for looking pale, and prescribe carriage exercise.

It was the year when the new young queen, Victoria, came to the throne that the great extension of Ley Mills was made and the new steam engine and shafting installed. Your father, my darling husband, was standing with Jacob in the long shed, discussing some technical matter, while you, Edward, were fortunately at a little distance, having gone to ask some question of a foreman. Suddenly a piece of the shafting overhead, on which Jacob's workmen were busy, escaped from their hands (or from its holding brackets, I do not know) and began to fall at one end towards your father and Jacob. If Charles had leaped aside at once, he would have saved himself; if Jacob had not moved, the shafting would have struck Jacob. But it was never Charles's way to think first of himself, and true to his own nature, he turned and pushed Jacob violently aside, out of danger; and so the shafting caught him.

They brought him over to the house on a piece of planking belonging to the new construction. Jacob wept without restraint, for in truth in spite of certain surface estrangements he always loved his uncle dearly. You, Edward, were pale and cold and spoke very quietly; perhaps only I, who had given you your power of reserve, knew how much you suffered. Dick and Catharine were sent for and came hastily; Catharine, looking very lovely, trembled in silence, and you, Edward, put your arm about her to comfort her. We had sent for another doctor but he was out on his rounds, so it was Dick who felt his father's pulse and then looked across at me expressively. Charles caught the look and I saw in his eyes that he knew he was dying; he was never one to pretend to himself or shirk what was painful. He turned his head—still very fair, only a trifle faded from its youthful golden—and looked at me, and his pale lips moved as if trying to speak. To utter words was beyond him, but I knew he meant to say the command he had so often light-heartedly given me: "Kiss me, Eleanor."

I bent and kissed him on the lips, and so that great heart, Charles Moreys, died in my arms. But he died a happy man, surrounded by love, under a clear sky of respect and honour; by saving the life of Adah's grandson at the expense of his own he had paid his father's last debt, there was no longer any cloud over the house of Moreys.

Note by Sir Edward Moreys, Bt., M.P
November 19th, 1894

To MY son Charles: The foregoing manuscript, written by your grandmother, has always been very carefully preserved and I hope you will pass it down to your eldest son in good condition. (Perhaps it might be well to have it rebound.) Not only is her account of the early history of our family highly interesting as a story, but it gives a contemporary picture, unintentional and therefore authentic, of life in a textile scribbling mill in the old days—Wool Royd was the first such mill to be erected in the Annotsfield district.

My father, a man of tremendous personality whom every-one loved, a hero of old time, generous, frank, bold and extremely handsome, emerges powerfully in the story, but my mother's character is less clearly defined. She has not done herself justice and I wish to put this right.

There were three mysteries in the Moreys' affairs when my

mother became acquainted with them, all concerned with half-brothers and all springing from John Moreys' sin with Adah Lee the gipsy; the first concerning the dismissal of Walter Moreys by his brother, the second in the next generation concerning James Lee and his brother's wife Rose Hervet, and the third in the third generation concerning Dick and Tessie. Charles Moreys knew only the second mystery; my mother knew the first and third. By putting them all together, all the mysteries were solved.

But this only became possible because my mother won the trust of all concerned except the Moreys' enemy, Adah, so that all confided in her. My mother could hardly proclaim for herself the force and warmth of her character by which she achieved this: the all-embracing compassionate love, the firm integrity, the dauntless courage and the power of reasoning, which lifted her so far above the average person of her day, whether man or woman. (She had a very sweet sense of fun, too, with which she agreeably dissolved my father's thunders.) As her son I wish to proclaim these qualities now with admiring gratitude, and put on record the fact that without her the mysteries would have remained for ever unsolved, the shadow uncleared from the house of Moreys.

Made and printed in Great Britain
for the Companion Book Club (Odhams Press Ltd.)
by Odhams (Watford) Limited
Watford, Herts
S.754.ZSA